A Fall Into Light

A NOVEL

WS PARRY

Published by

Impermanence Studio

First Copyright 2015. All rights reserved.

First paperback edition, 2015
(published under the title *The Passion of Patience*)

Second paperback edition, 2016

Third paperback edition, 2018

ISBN-13: 978-0692052129

This is a work of fiction. While, as in all fiction, the literary perception and insights are based on experience, all names, characters, places, and incidents are either products of the author's imagination or are used fictitiously. Other than the historical figures referenced herein, no reference to any real person is intended or should be interpreted.

DEDICATION

To Olivia, Zoe and Eleanor, thank you for your patience
as I navigate my way through this crazy world.

To Priscilla, you are the inspiration for everything
in my life. You are my heart, my soul, my voice.

ACKNOWLEDGMENTS

This is a fictional story. But like all fictional stories it borrows from real places and events. I want to thank all of those from the Mystic area for helping to bring this fictional story to life. I dedicate this novel to all of you, without which, this story could not have been told.

CHAPTER 1

Mystic, Connecticut

The area now occupied by the downtown village of Mystic Connecticut, inhabited for centuries by the Pequot Indians, and first settled by European settlers in the 1600s, was originally named Portersville by the settlers, which is what you will see on maps from that time. Somewhere in the 1700's Portersville was renamed Mystic. We know this because the maps that appeared after that were drawn with the name Mystic over the area that had been formerly drawn as Portersville.

No one knows for sure who came up with the name Portersville or why our forefathers changed it to Mystic, but everyone who grows up here eventually learns and then passes to the next generation a very corny joke about how the town acquired the name Mystic. Though now considered somewhat politically incorrect, it seems to have amused the townsfolk here for generations, and it goes something like this: When the first Englishman arrived in the Mystic area, he came across a local Indian man standing knee-deep in mud about twenty feet from the bank of a river. The Englishman asked the Indian the name of the river and the Indian replied by pointing down at his feet, saying "Me stuck! Me stuck!" I told you it was corny.

Despite that bit of silliness that has been passed from generation to generation, Mystic has a long and storied history, more so than one would think for such a small town in America. Many of those stories have been captured, documented and shared by not just the writers that have lived and visited here over the centuries, but also by the artists and musicians.

The most important and defining part of Mystic's long and storied history revolves around its relationship with the sea. This long heritage with the sea is not only what defines Mystic but it is what has defined its residents, their culture, professions and passions for the last several hundred years and maybe longer.

Recorded history of the Mystic area starts with the Pequot Indians who dominated this small section of New England for a few hundred years before they were nearly wiped out by the English in the 1600's. These Indians derived their food and livelihood from the rushing waters now known as Fishers Island Sound, which sits between Long Island in New York and the eastern end of the Connecticut coastline near the border with Rhode Island. The longboats that the Pequot built from large felled trees were often taken all the way across Long Island Sound to trade with other Indians tribes, often using wampum, made from shells found along the shores of Long Island Sound, as currency. Paddling a hollowed-out tree trunk across Long Island Sound is quite a brave feat considering no one would dare take a boat across Long Island Sound nowadays unless it was large enough to withstand the three to five foot standing waves that the rapid currents can cause as Long Island Sound drains out to the Atlantic Ocean in its twice daily ebbing tide.

Once the English settled in Mystic they established it as a great seafaring port. The highly protected tidal basin now known as the Mystic River provided deep water passage for nearly a mile up the river away from the Sound. This allowed a few shipyards to be built in the protected shallows of the river north of the now famous bascule Mystic drawbridge that crosses the Mystic River and connects West Mystic and East Mystic.

During the 1800s, entrepreneurs like Charles Mallory and the Greenman brothers turned Mystic into one of the great shipyards of New England where hundreds of clipper, whaling and other ships were built and sent out to travel the world. Many returned with the whale oil that kept the lights burning throughout New England prior to the electrification of the towns along the Connecticut Coast and inland.

During the late 1800s, the steamships that Cornelius Vanderbilt ran from New York City to Boston actually terminated in the Mystic area. From there a train would take passengers on to Boston. So until the train lines were finally completed up the New England coast, getting from New York to Boston in the fastest way possible, a rather popular route in the 1880s, meant taking a Vanderbilt steamship from New York to Mystic and then continuing on a train to Boston. This brought a great influx of folks to the area who had to kill time during the stopover, and the shore towns responded with lots of bars and other places where the steamship passengers could party as they waited for the train, or vice-versa if going south. So at that time the Mystic area began to gain a reputation as a bit of a party town with both New Yorkers and Bostonians.

At one point around the turn of the century, a hotel casino was built on Mystic Island, a very small island at the mouth of the Mystic River where it dumps into Fishers Island Sound. Vanderbilt began running a ferry from New York City right to Mystic Island to deliver gamblers for an evening or two of fun.

While through a strange set of circumstances explained a bit later, gambling has returned to the Mystic area, shipbuilding never really stopped. From the nuclear submarines that are built in the Thames River, the larger river west of the Mystic River, to the Mystic Seaport museum that rebuilds antique whaling and fishing ships in the same location that Charles Mallory built his ships in the 1800s, to the backyard boat projects by locals who, with the best of intentions, occasionally get them to the point where they can launch them into the water. As such, Mystic remains a Mecca of boats and boat owners. If someone ever bothered to count, it likely has more boats per capita than any town in the northeast. Its population of 4,200 supports over fifteen shipyards and marinas that hold and support thousands of boats.

If you live in Mystic you own a boat, usually two or three, and sometimes more. In Los Angeles they brag about their cars, in Mystic you brag about your boat collection. If John has two boats, Sam has to have three. And what you do on the water is also very important. It seems everyone is divided into one of two camps. You either are a fisherman or a sailor. If you are from the working class or your wealth is new, you most likely get up every morning thinking about fishing. You probably have a motor boat that is completely tricked out with fishing gadgets: fish finders, rod holders, fish tanks, scaling boards, etc. If you are of average means your vessel is between 18' and 24' which means you can go out into Fishers Island Sound to fish, but any further out to sea and you risk capsizing in the heavy seas. In the inland waters you look for the striped bass or blue fish that troll the inland waters chasing the smaller fish.

If you happen to be in a better financial situation, you have a motor boat over 25' which means you can go out to sea, past Montauk Point at the tip of Long Island, where you lose sight of land, and can fish for bigger catch such as tuna and shark.

My husband Bill, who I married twenty years ago, is a fisherman. While most men fish as a hobby, like my father and many folks from the Mystic area, Bill has made it his profession. Bill owns one of the commercial fishing boats that run from the commercial fishing docks in Stonington. Bill's life revolves around going to sea, which means so does mine. Being a commercial fisherman is one of the toughest professions there is. Movies like *The Perfect Storm*, and television shows like *The Deadliest Catch* capture the danger there is in commercial fishing. While Bill has never lost any of his crew, there is a memorial at the commercial fishing dock in tribute to the local lives lost at sea in pursuit of the profession.

Despite the excitement and danger, commercial fishing is not a lucrative profession. It requires a tremendous amount of capital to purchase and keep a commercial fishing vessel afloat. As fishing stocks have been depleted over the years, the government has placed quotas on the amount of fish that can be taken from the sea, which means once Bill and his fellow fisherman have reached their quota, they are done for the season. As you can surmise from that, Bill and I are working class folk.

The other camp, often referred to by the fishermen as "ragheads", are the sailors. If your wealth has been around for a few generations, you spend your days thinking about the next time you can get out on your sailboat, or the next regatta you will be racing in with your college buddies.

It takes a strange disposition to be a sailor. Those with motor boats cannot fathom why someone trying to get from Point A to Point B would choose to do it at 6 knots (about 8 miles an hour) when a motor boat can go over 20 knots. But that's the thing about sailors and sailing, for sailors the pleasure is not in the destination, it's in the journey. If it takes 8 hours instead of 1 to get from Mystic to Newport, that's not a bad thing.

The feeling of driving a 50' sailboat that weighs over ten tons at 5 knots with nothing but a slight breeze across the water is a feeling that will sustain a sailor for their entire lives. While fishermen get off on the challenge of outwitting Mother Nature, to catch that fish despite its billions years of evolutionary-taught escapism, sailors get off on the challenge of co-existing with Mother Nature, using the wind and tides to overcome natural inertia. Understanding how the sun heating the land at the break of day draws onshore breezes that will carry you through the morning, and how the changing tides may bring wind shifts that will carry you through mid-day, and then knowing that the wind may die at sundown as the land cools back down, only to pick back up again a few hours later, that's what gets a sailor excited.

To fish or to sail, it is a debate that has been raging since humankind learned to exist on the sea.

There is actually a third camp that people fall into when it comes to the sea, but that camp is scoffed at by both the fishermen and sailors in town. An expression that you hear often in Mystic, heard from both the fisherman and the sailors, one of the few things they can agree on by the way, is: "I'd rather be on the water than in it." Those who would rather be "in" the water are the third camp: the beachgoers.

Coastal New Englanders whose families have fished or sailed for generations look at beachgoers as invaders. They are not usually from the coastline, they come from inland or the big cities, and for those that live along the coastline, beachgoers do just that: they invade. They start showing up in late June and for the next eight weeks through Labor Day, with over-stuffed cars filled with over-stuffed bodies, clog the roads, clog the bars, and if it wasn't for the general good-natured disposition of coastal New Englanders who seem to put up with anything that comes their way with humor and humility, beachgoers might even be a nuisance.

The good news for residents of the Mystic area is that the favorite beaches of the beachgoers are in Rhode Island about ten miles east of Mystic. Misquamicut Beach, Charleston Beach, and Scarborough Beach on Narragansett Bay are the beaches that attract the inland beach goers. At some point, politicians with some civic planning foresight built multi-lane roads and highways that funnel beachgoers right from the main Interstate to those beaches, bypassing the local Mystic roads.

The Western-most beach in Rhode Island, on Napatree Point in Watch Hill, is a dividing line in many ways, dividing not just natural geography, as Rhode Island shore beaches give way to the rocky coastline of Connecticut, but it is a cultural divide also as it divides the two distinct cultures of those who would rather be on the water from those who would rather be in it.

Though they will never admit it, even fishermen and sailors occasionally do go to the beach, and when those "on-water" folks from Mystic do that, the beach on Napatree Point is where they go. Napatree has the benefit of having virtually no public parking available for beachgoers, the only way to really get there conveniently is by boat. So those "on-water" folks take their little runabout motor boats over to the inland side of Napatree Point and then walk the 100 yards over to the ocean side to the beach, walking through one of a few paths that have been carefully cut through the dunes to protect the beach grass that holds the sand in place.

Since in all practicality it requires a boat to get there, the inland folks hardly ever venture to Napatree. Which means it has remained a bit of a secret for the locals from the area. They get to experience the beach and all it has to offer: waves, sun, and surf, without having to experience the beachgoers and all they have to offer, which we will leave to the imagination.

CHAPTER 2

Patience

Despite Mystic's centuries-old fame for its seamen, sailors and ships, of course the story that put Mystic on the cultural map recently is the story captured on film about a pizza parlor and a few girls that came of age that worked there. It has been twenty years since the film crews that invaded this small town to capture that story left Mystic. That was an exciting time for my high school friends who were part of the story. At first we were all surprised that anyone could be so interested in the lives of a couple of blue collar Portuguese girls from Connecticut who happened to work in a pizza parlor, but throw in one handsome rich guy and a steamy affair, and I guess the story tugged a few heart strings.

After the cameras stopped rolling my friends were minor celebrities for a few months with newspaper articles and a few TV interviews, but eventually the media blitz moved onto the next story and things got back to normal. Since then, like most quiet sleepy New England towns like Mystic over the past few hundred years, things have pretty much stayed the same: quiet and sleepy.

In small New England towns, as the years and generations slip by, the same stories seem to repeat themselves generation after generation. Births, teenage crushes, marriage, kids, affairs, a reshuffling of a few relationships, old age, and death. This pattern seems to repeat itself with every successive generation, and ours has been no different. Most of the stories that have been captured and told about Mystic Connecticut, including the one put to film, all have some combination of those essential elements and the story I am going to tell is no different.

I should probably introduce myself, my name is Catherine DiCastro, Cat for short, and like the girls in the last story, I am the daughter of Portuguese parents, and like most Portuguese in the Mystic area, I come from a family of fishermen. As immigrants came to this country in the 1800s, each nationality seemed to settle into a different part of the country. The Swedes and other Nordic immigrants mostly went to Minnesota. The Irish went to Boston and New York. Italians settled around New York and New Jersey and up the coastline into Connecticut. As for the Portuguese, we centered on Rhode Island and the towns just over the border into Connecticut.

It should not surprise anyone that Portuguese make their living on the water. The Portuguese have spent most of their existence on the water. Being on the Atlantic Ocean side of the Iberian peninsula, with Spain closing the door to any thoughts of eastern expansion, the Portuguese had to look to the seas for expansion, and expand they did. Starting in the 1400s, the Portuguese empire grew to become the first truly global empire in history spanning almost every continent, from Europe to Africa to Asia. Some of the greatest seafaring explorers were Portuguese, including Ferdinand Magellan, the first to circumnavigate the globe. The first European to round the southern tip of Africa was Portuguese, as was the first European to discover Japan. As you can tell I am a proud Portuguese.

The story about Mystic that was made famous in film was about a pizza parlor and a group of my high school friends who worked there. This story starts about twenty years after the last story ended and is the story of another group of friends from the same high school class.

While there is a good locally owned pizza parlor in every town along the Connecticut shore, most likely because the first pizza was made nearby in New Haven, the restaurants that really set the New England coastal towns apart from the rest of the country are their lobster and clam shacks. And this story starts out in a clam shack that has become a bit of a legend in Mystic called the Black Duck, or simply "the Duck".

The Duck has an interesting history itself. The last owner of the Duck had been given the restaurant from the previous owner, who had received it from the owner before him. As it turns out, I was next in line. I had been working here for the last 25 years helping run it, so it was logical transition. I guess that is another long standing tradition here in Mystic. Work the counters at the Duck for twenty five years and you get to own the place lock stock and barrel as a reward. No purchase price, no contracts, you just get handed the keys and one day you go from being an employee to being the employer. In that way no one really owns the Duck. You are the caretaker of it for twenty to thirty years and then hand the keys to the next loyal person.

Not much has changed with the place over all those owners, for instance we still have the same tables and chairs. There have simply been too many great messages carved into the tables over the many years to replace them and wipe out all that town history. First crushes? Carved into the tables. Teenage rivalries? Carved into the tables. We did update the menus a few years back with some healthier options. I guess some New England traditions have to change. But New England is funny that way. In LA if something has been around for three years it is outdated and no one wants it. In New England it has to be around for at least thirty years before anyone thinks it's worth investing any time to get to know.

Between the income that I earn from the Duck and Bill's income as a commercial fisherman, we are barely getting by. My best friend Amy Mason and her husband Charles get by quite well. True to form, while we are fishermen, the Masons are sailors.

Just like the teenagers who stop by every day to hang out, the Duck is still the hang out place for my group of friends just as it was for us when we were teenagers. Amy and Charles come by once a week with their three beautiful teenage daughters to eat dinner. My two teenage boys help behind the counter after school and on weekends when they aren't playing in some baseball or football game.

Despite the great divide in wealth between us, Amy is my best friend. Despite the fact that the Masons are one of the wealthiest families in New England and have been for years, Amy and Charles are great people, mostly you would never know they have the money they do, unless of course you happened to get invited to their house, or happen to see them out in their sailboat. That is another long-standing tradition in Mystic Connecticut. If you have money, you don't let on. For years, Charles father, Charles Sr., drove a Volkswagen Beetle. He could have afforded a Rolls Royce or two or three. But that's not how we do things in Mystic. This is not LA.

Amy, Charles and I grew up together. Although Amy was not from one of the wealthy families in town, she was the most beautiful girl in Stonington High School, the local high school we attended, and even though Charles was a few years older and went off to boarding school at Choate, as is the tradition for the Mason family, he was well aware of Amy, as was every other teenage male within five years and a thirty mile radius. After he came back from college to work for Mason Industries, the family business, Amy and Charles reconnected, they fell in love and were married in one of the most amazing fairytale weddings Mystic has ever seen, one that most could only fantasize about.

As is the tradition, they were married in St. Marks, the local Episcopal church, and held their reception at the Masons Island Yacht Club, the private club started by Charles' great-grandfather and a few other wealthy gents back at the turn of the century.

Yes, not only do the Masons have a lot of money, they have an island named after them. It's actually an interesting albeit tragic story of how the Masons acquired the island and it goes back over 300 years.

In the 1600's the Pequot Indians were one of dozens of Indian tribes that dotted the southern coast of New England, sharing the land and ocean and trading with each other. When the English came across the Atlantic in the 1600's, starting in Boston, they slowly migrated farther and farther south into what are now Rhode Island and Connecticut. While most Indian tribes learned to coexist with the newcomers, the Pequot were not so accommodating. They were warriors, and as such from time to time would push back on the expansion of the Englishmen into their lands.

After a few incidents where Englishmen were actually killed by the Pequot, it became clear that something had to be done about the Pequot Indians. So Captain John Mason, a relatively young man in the English military was sent over to America by King George with the orders to do something about the violent Indians making trouble for English settlers in Southern New England. After attempting to negotiate with them to no avail, a plan was hatched to finally deal with problem once and for all.

15

The Pequot were "long house" Indians, which meant that their style of village had a series of long houses that were shared by multiple families. The entire village was surrounded by a primitive stockade fence made up of tightly connected cedar trees buried deep into the ground and that stood up above ground over twelve feet to form an impenetrable barrier. As was tradition, the Pequot village had only one entrance that was also the only exit. The village looked somewhat like the army stockade forts built in the Western United States in the 1800s to protect the cavalry from the western Indians, and probably where the cavalry got the idea.

Captain Mason arranged a pact with the Indian tribe to the west of the Pequot, the Mohegans, who were descendants of the Pequot, and who over the years had their own violent conflicts with the Pequot to their east. Captain Mason led a group of English soldiers accompanied by a band of Mohegans, and surrounded the Pequot Indian village one night once everyone was in for the night. The archers began to shoot flaming arrows into the village and set it ablaze. To escape the intense heat, the Pequot indians tried to flee through the only exit, but as each one came out they were shot dead by the Englishmen: men, woman, and children. It was a bloody and horrible massacre of over 600 Pequot Indians and the tragic story is still told today to successive generations of those who live in Southern Connecticut.

This act would have completely wiped out the Pequot tribe except for a hunting party that was at their northern encampment that night. Upon learning of the fate of their families, the remaining Pequot indians "surrendered" to the English and were provided with a small tribal reservation about fifteen miles north of Mystic where they barely existed for the next three hundred years.

You actually most likely know of the Pequot Tribe and may not even realize it. After the massacre, the surviving Pequot divided into two tribes, the Mashantucket and the Paucatuck. In the 1980s, Skip Heywood, the grandson of the last remaining full blooded Mashantucket Indian woman, started a bingo parlor in a mobile home on the few acres of land that was all that was left of the Mashantucket Pequot reservation. With some cunning and assistance by a Connecticut Governor with 300 years of collective English guilt for what happened to the Pequot all those years ago,

Skip parlayed that bingo parlor into a casino. You might have heard of that casino, Foxwoods, which is now the largest casino in the world, and the Pequot are now the employer of over 10,000 of the descendants of the English settlers that nearly wiped them out. The story of the rise and fall and rise of the Mashantucket Pequot Indians of Mystic Connecticut is part of the storied history of the area, and is an incredible story of karmic survival, but one for another day.

For his "bravery" Capt. John Mason was granted hundreds of acres of land along the Connecticut shore, and that grant included an island about 1.5 miles long and ¾ mile across that stands about 100 yards from the mainland at its closest point. While the mainland portion of Captain Mason's land grant was slowly sold off over the next few hundred years and eventually became the eastern side of the town of Mystic, the island, which was eventually named Masons Island, was kept in the family. It was only in the late nineteenth century that the Mason heirs began to sell building lots on the island as well, mostly to wealthy families from New York looking for a summer residence, that Masons Island started becoming more than solely a Mason family compound.

As more building lots were sold off over the years and more homes were built, the Masons retained a large plot of land in the middle of the island for the family estate that had been built on the island at the turn of the century and has been for the last few generations the family home for the current patriarch of the Mason family. Until recently, that was Charles' father, Charles Mason, Sr. Two years ago, Emma Mason, Charles Sr 's wife, passed away and Charles Sr. suffered a stroke, which required him to move into the Mystic Manor Rehabilitation Hospital, the Charles Mason wing of the hospital to be exact, since Mystic Manor hospital is one of the long standing businesses of Mason Industries.

With Emma gone, and Charles Sr in Mystic Manor, it became time for Amy and Charles Jr. to take their place in line, and they moved into the family estate on Masons Island. With his father in poor health, Charles also took over daily operations of the family company.

While Mystic is a town with hundreds of years of stories to tell, this particular story involves a few of my childhood friends that did not make it into the last Mystic story made famous in film. Besides Amy and Charles, this story includes Henry Moore. Henry was Charles Jr.'s best friend as we were growing up and as such, for the most part, Henry grew up in the Mason home. Henry's father was a professor at Connecticut College in nearby New London and his mother was a local artist. Needless to say, living on a professor's and artist's incomes, the Moore's were not a wealthy family but they were brilliant and avid intellectuals and lived in a small winterized summer cottage on Masons Island near the Masons. Like Charles and Henry, Henry's father and Charles Sr were also very good friends. Henry was like another son to Charles Sr. and was also Charles Sr. favorite sailing partner on the family sailboat, the Pequot, the name of which was subtly controversial based on the history of how the Masons ended up settling in Mystic all those centuries ago.

Tragically, while Henry was away in his sophomore year of college his parents were killed in a horrible automobile accident as they were coming home one evening from dinner in Mystic. A local electrician, driving home drunk that night from the local dive bar, went through the red light where Masons Island Road intersects with the Boston Post Road, colliding with Henry's parents and neither of Henry's parents survived. The entire town was devastated, especially Charles Sr and Emma, who had lost their closest friends. The Mason family basically adopted Henry at that point, and Charles Sr., as one of Henry's father's closest friends, made sure that Henry had the means to finish his college education, something that Henry has never forgotten.

The other important person to this story is Patience Passion. How would one describe Patience Passion? Patience is two years younger than me. After Amy finished high school, Patience was the next beautiful girl to work her way through our high school. But in addition to being beautiful, Patience was an enigma, a complete free spirit. She was always the first one of the girls her age to do anything. Skinny dip? Age 8. Smoke pot? Age 10. Have sex? Age 13. If it was to be done, Patience would always do it first. That of course brought scorn from everyone, not only the other girls her age, but also the parents who made it their business to keep an eye on what was going on with the teenagers. But much to their chagrin, Patience did not care. All the boys loved her, from those her age to the boys like Henry and Charles who were three to four years older, and all the girls were jealous. And when teenage girls get jealous, they get mean. My daddy used to tell me when I came home crying from being tortured at school by the alpha females, that the most vicious creature on the face of the earth is a 14 year old girl.

In our little social world at that time, most of that meanness was directed at Patience. But in the most graceful and cool way, Patience never cared. She never cared what anyone thought of her or her quirkiness, she was operating on a completely different plane that only she could understand. Except for Henry. Henry always understood Patience. Of all our friends, despite being a few years apart Henry and Patience were closer than any of us. But it was a bond of deep friendship. He adored her and she him, but not in any sexual way, it was more of an older brother and a younger sister. They mostly protected each other. When Patience got into trouble, Henry was always there to save her, defend her, punch out the lights of whatever boy that tried to take advantage of her, tell the mean girls to kiss his ass, you get the picture.

Patience is the daughter of Lois Passion. After Patience, Lois Passion is the most amazing woman I have ever met. For the last forty years, Lois has been the Mason family's gardener, caring for all of the numerous estate gardens that surrounded the Mason estate. But these were no ordinary gardens. Charles Sr. and his father before him, were avid gardeners, taking a scientific approach to gardening. Mason Industries started as an herbal drug company, and it was these gardens that produced the plants where the research was done that allowed the Masons to create the company that is now one of the larger privately owned companies in the Northeast. Between Charles Sr and his father, the two of them have over forty new species of plants credited to them. But with their company growing quickly into other areas of medical products, Charles Sr needed a full time person to care for the gardens, someone who shared his passion and knowledge of the healing capabilities of herbs. That person was Lois Passion, and for many years Lois and Charles Sr. were partners in this project to discover new herbal remedies and maintain the gardens.

For this Lois has been provided with a cottage to live in on the Mason estate. This is where Patience was raised and where they both still live today. Growing up, Lois was thought of as a bit of an eccentric. As the Mason's gardener and an active participant, some might say the instigator, of much of the herbal remedy research done there with herbs, she would concoct remedies for all kinds of illnesses from herbs grown on the estate. But to us kids Lois was basically a 1960s hippy, and as kids, we all adored her. Compared to my strict Catholic parents, Lois Passion was the coolest lady you would ever meet. She was who we all went to when we got in trouble, either with our parents or a boyfriend. She would sit you down with a cup of tea that she made herself from the garden and always have the most odd but truthful way to look at every situation. She did not think like any of the other parents but she always made you see the truth in the situation you were facing. You could be absolutely truthful with her, you could tell her exactly your part in the crisis, and you knew that Lois would never betray the secret. But somehow, if a confession to your parents was needed, Lois always knew how to get you to do it, despite the consequences.

True to form with Lois, no one knows who Patience's father is. It has always been assumed that Lois, who rumors say got around a bit when she was younger as part of the 60s generation, got pregnant from some affair she had with someone along the way, and Patience was the result. I like to think she got pregnant on purpose. She wanted a child but was way too free-spirited to accept the possessiveness of the typical man in the early 1960s.

Maybe that helps to explain how Patience became Patience. She basically inherited her mother's free-spirit and quirkiness and then expanded on it as Lois and Patience researched Eastern spirituality and other alternative ideas that did not hold any interest for the rest of us. But while Lois had a cool spirituality to her, Patience was spiritually gifted. And I do not mean a traditional Christian or Catholic spirituality. Patience had a way about her that could cut right through the layers of bull that most of us operate in and know what you were thinking, probably long before you knew yourself. But she was always positive, she would lift you up when you were down. It was another reason that the alpha females despised her.

While I greatly admired Patience, it was a secret admiration. I was a teenager and like most teenagers I wanted to climb the social hierarchy of high school. The way that high school social status among females goes, the meaner you are, the higher your social status. It would have been social suicide for a girl to be friends with Patience Passion. So despite admiring her spirit, once in high school I had to admire her from afar. It is something that I am deeply ashamed of to this day. Patience was an amazing soul, an old soul, someone who had the maturity of a sixty year old when she was ten. The rest of us were just stupid petty teenagers in comparison.

Amy was the only person to whom I could confess my admiration of Patience. She felt the same way. But despite being gorgeous, Amy's working class family background kept her from being in the alpha female group, so we both played along with the game. Make fun of Patience, get invited to the cool parties. Of course we always knew better than to criticize Patience in front of Henry or Charles. Henry was her protector and Charles was like a brother since Patience grew up on the Mason estate with Charles.

When Charles and Henry graduated from high school, as was expected they both went off to Yale for their undergraduate education. All Mason boys went to Yale after Choate, and Henry went along with Charles. Two years later Amy and I graduated and Amy went off to University of Connecticut, a more affordable place to go to college. College was not in my cards. I was from a blue collar Portuguese family, and that was my destiny, to stay blue collar. I just kept working at the Duck, the same restaurant that I had worked at since I was fifteen. It paid the bills. It paid for my first apartment. It kept me in town near my parents.

When Henry's parents were killed in his sophomore year at Yale, Henry really had nowhere to come back to in Mystic. His parents' house was sold after their death to pay off their debts. He could not live with the Masons, an occasional house guest as a teenager was one thing but living there as a young man was another. So he basically just stayed at college in New Haven year round. When he went off to Harvard for his PhD, he then stayed in his apartment in Boston. Funds were short and without a place to stay, returning to Mystic in between semesters at school for the summer was not in the cards for him. He would occasionally come back for a weekend or two during the summer and over Christmas, but never for more than a day or two.

Since I was not hanging out with Patience after high school, I had burned that bridge by my behavior in high school, over the years we rarely spoke other than to say hello as we passed in town. So I am not sure exactly what happened to the relationship between Henry and Patience once Henry left Mystic for college. At some point I think they just drifted apart just as Henry drifted apart from all of us after high school.

When Henry was at Harvard getting his PhD he met Ellen Chandler, a steel-eyed, raven-haired beauty from Los Angeles. In every way that Henry was, Ellen was not. He was patient and gentle, she was aggressive and controlling. He was compassionate, she was quick-tempered. He was broke, she was a Chandler, one of the more prominent and wealthy families in Los Angeles. We'll never understand what they saw in each other, but they met at Harvard and started dating and got engaged shortly before they both graduated in the same year, he with his PhD in English and she from Harvard Medical School.

After graduation they moved to Los Angeles. That's where Chandlers live. They married in a big Chandler wedding in LA and basically that was the beginning of the end of our close friendship with Henry Moore. He kept in touch with Charles from time to time, so we would all get updates on how his life was going, but none of us had talked to Henry for over twenty years. Despite Henry's absence, I had always thought that the deep relationship that Henry and Patience had growing up would never simply go away, the friendship they shared back then was a lifelong bond and would always remain very strong and deep, despite the absence.

Henry's abandonment of Mystic was emotional for all of us, but we all knew it was Ellen and the Chandlers behind it, so we were more sad than angry. Charles, who was the only one invited to their wedding, and had stayed in touch with Henry enough to know the story, had always told us that Ellen was basically a complete bitch. Like many people from very wealthy families, she is one of those people that needs to completely control everything in their lives. Marriages are supposed to be of equals. In that respect Charles suspected they did not actually have a marriage because it was not a marriage of equals. She dominated every aspect of the relationship.

The Chandler family, like most wealthy dynastic families, requires absolute loyalty. When marrying into those families, whatever life you had before you joined the family is left behind. Previous friends are tolerated yet patronized since it is expected that you will run with a new crowd now. Family is allowed as long as they keep their distance. And most importantly, while you are allowed to marry into the family, you must understand that you are never really part of the family. You are constantly reminded of your second class citizenship, and to quote a recent reality TV show, you are constantly though subtly reminded of the fact that you could get voted off the island at any moment. And when you get voted off, you can expect to be shut out so thoroughly that you will be less than you were before you arrived. Their lawyers will make sure of it.

With Chandler summer houses in California and vacations in Europe, there was also no time for Henry to come to Mystic to visit even if he had a place to stay. Basically Henry just got completely absorbed into the whirlwind of a wealthy family. Along the way, as they talked more and more sporadically, Charles began to see a slow change in Henry. It is not that he was getting wrapped up in the Chandler way and becoming arrogant with a hefty dose of LA fake, it was that he was being drained of his spirit. Somewhere along the way Henry just stopped being Henry.

After his PhD and move to Los Angeles, Henry got a job teaching at UCLA. He has been there ever since, rising through the ranks to full professorship a few years ago, and had recently become the Chair of the Chandler School for English Studies. He basically had cloaked himself in everything Chandler, at home and at work, and Charles was convinced it was killing him.

Upon graduation from Harvard Medical School, Ellen's residency in Los Angeles led her into neuroscience. Over the past 20 years, Ellen has become one of the country's foremost experts on rehabilitation from traumatic brain injury, especially from stroke. This is a specialty that is performed in a hospital setting not in private practice and over the years Ellen has risen through the ranks to become assistant Chief of Neuroscience at Cedar Sinai in Los Angeles.

Henry and Ellen never had children. Ellen was career oriented and in my opinion, likely too selfish for that. The story that Charles painted

23

was not a pretty one. Charles was convinced that Henry was in an extremely caustic and domineering relationship with a very wealthy woman and he was being held there in chains by a financially bleak future if he attempted to leave. Henry had managed to put himself in a position where his entire life, career and future depended on his being loyal to the Chandlers. Of course Ellen knew this full well, she knew how trapped he was and of course she loved it, she enjoyed the power it gave her and she took full advantage of it.

CHAPTER 3

The Call that Changed a Town Forever

One day a call came to Ellen Chandler that started in motion an unstoppable chain of events that changed all of our lives forever.

Mystic is a small town but it is a tourist town. With the Mystic Seaport, the largest museum in the country dedicated to wooden shipbuilding and the sea, the Mystic Marinelife Aquarium, the nearby beaches, the Mystic Arts Festival and a whole bunch of other events, we get a lot of tourists. That's great for me since it's probably what keeps the Duck in business.

Besides those tourist traps, the only other significant establishment in Mystic is the Mystic Manor Rehabilitation Hospital. Despite being in the small town of Mystic, Mystic Manor is actually one of the leading rehabilitation hospitals in the country specializing in patients with brain trauma, mostly stroke victims. The Masons and Mason Industries, which had expended into other areas of medicine over the years, look at Mystic Manor as a wonderful research facility. And that is where the phone call to Ellen came from.

Mystic Manor was looking for a new Chief of the Medical Staff. And Ellen got the call. No one knows for sure what prompted the call to Ellen. She clearly was extremely well qualified, but so were hundreds of others in the United States. Some suspect that it was Charles Sr.'s doing.

His health was failing and he deeply missed Henry. He also knew from his son that Ellen was qualified for the position. The thought is that this was Charles Sr.'s way to get Henry back to Mystic so he could see him before he died. Whatever the reason, the call to Ellen came and it came directly from Charles Sr. himself. Charles Mason Sr. one of the most respected retired executives in the medical industry, offered Ellen Chandler the position to run his hospital, the hospital his family founded and the hospital that he himself was now a patient of and relying on.

But what was most stunning to everyone, especially Henry, was that she accepted. A Chandler not living in Los Angeles is like a British Monarch not living in England. Maybe Charles Sr. caught her in a weak moment. Maybe Charles Sr., as one of the more respected executives in the neuroscience industry, still had it in him to be persuasive despite his slow speech from his stroke. I like to think the truth is that there were powers beyond anyone's understanding at play. The universe needed Henry Moore to return to Mystic and this was the only way it was going to happen.

As the offer and acceptance came in the late spring, it was decided that Henry would finish out the semester teaching at UCLA and then Henry and Ellen would move to Mystic and Henry would take a well-deserved sabbatical to write the book he had been trying to write for the last few years. So the plans were made, Ellen and Henry would move to Mystic in June.

That week, the day before the normal day that Charles Jr. and Amy have their weekly dinner at the Duck, he asked Amy to round up all of their childhood friends to come to dinner at the Duck because he had an announcement to make, it was good news. So the old gang got together for dinner that night, all wondering what Charles was talking about. Sometime after the meals were served the conversation that would change so many lives began.

I spoke first. "So Charlie, you got us all here, what the hell is going on? You're kind of freaking us out here."

Melissa was next, "I think I know. Amy's pregnant!"

"Bite your tongue" Amy blurted out. "If he wants another kid, he's gonna have to do it with wifey number two. I am never going through labor again." Everyone screamed with laughter.

"So you're not pregnant?" Melissa pressed.

"No, I am not pregnant, people!" Amy replied adamantly and looking somewhat indignant.

"Damn!" Melissa replied.

"Ha! I knew it! Pay up, pay up!" my husband Bill interjected. "I knew that wasn't it. Each one of you owes me twenty bucks and I want it right now, I can't trust any of yous. Woo-hoo big payday today! Big paaaaay-daaaaay."

Bill can be obnoxious and as his wife I can tell him so, "Alright, alright, you're so damn smart, now calm down there cowboy." Turning to Amy I asked, "then if that's not it, what can be so big that you need to bring us all together to tell us?" I asked.

Charles started, "drum roll please" and as Charles was tapping his fingers on the table as if he was playing a drum, confessed, "Henry Moore is moving back to Mystic."

There was dead silence. I have known this group of people for forty years and I have never seen them speechless in my entire life. But it happened. No one said anything, stunned silence drifted through the room. A couple of jaws actually dropped.

Finally Bill broke the stunned silence in his ever so eloquent fisherman language, "Are you shittin' me?"

All I could do was keep repeating the phrase, "Oh, my God! Oh, my God! Oh my God!" like a robotic Valley Girl doll whose voice recorder is skipping.

And then I had to ask the obvious question, knowing all the things that Charles has said about Henry's marriage and about Ellen, "with or without the bitch?"

Amy responded quickly while others were laughing at my characterization of Ellen, "wow, way to bring out those claws before you have even met the bitch! I am sorry, did I say bitch too?"

Ever the diplomat, Charles interjected quickly before the criticism of Ellen got out of hand and someone said something they would truly regret, "yes Ellen is coming to Mystic with Henry, or more like, Henry is coming to Mystic with Ellen. My father persuaded Ellen to take the job at Mystic Manor that Dr. Jones is retiring from next month. Dad called her directly and offered her the job, and she accepted, it was almost like she knew the call was coming. But then again dad can be rather persuasive when he needs to be, even at 81, and even with the whole stroke thing.

"They will be here in one month and it looks like they are moving into the Sullivan house on School House Rd. I'll be picking them up at the airport and bringing them back to Mystic on June 15th. So, I was thinking, I think we should throw a big welcome home party, and I think we should do it here, is that okay?"

I replied. "Of course, of course! Do you think I'd actually let you have a welcome home party for Henry Moore at the pizza place around the corner? Really Charles?"

"Sorry, but the Duck is your place now so I had to ask to be polite"

"Of course, of course. I wouldn't have it any other way."

After a few more minutes of stunned silence, the conversation started again.

Amy, who had been mostly quiet the whole time, asked one of the questions that we all were thinking, "I wonder if Patience knows?"

I responded, "what is the deal with them anyway? Does anyone know if they have even spoken in the last twenty years? I mean, the way that Henry sort of abandoned her, abandoned us all, she has a right to be pretty pissed off. Honestly, I am a little pissed off myself. I think I may punch him in the chest right before I give him a big hug. Or maybe I'll hug him first and then punch him in the chest."

"Now hold on there little lady." Charles responded in his best John Wayne impression, "there's not going to be anything of the sort." Returned to his normal voice, "what Henry needs is a huge bunch of hometown Mystic lovin'. I think he's actually really depressed."

That was Bill's opening, "Well he's been living in a prison for the last twenty years, that'll do it to ya, I oughta know".

I gave Bill a death stare, "What the hell does that mean? God you can be such an asshole!" I said as I punched Bill in the arm real hard.

Bill winced, "See what I mean? I exist in a prison of violence." At that everyone broke out into hysterical laughter.

"I'll show you some violence," I said as I tackled Bill and we went down on the floor pretending to wrestle, but after thirty seconds starting kissing.

"Okay, here it comes. You two are hilarious. You fight and screw, fight and screw. Can you just have a normal relationship? Does it always have to be at the extremes?" Amy asked with fake frustration.

I replied "You're just jealous that we can keep having sex even though we are fighting!"

"You bet I am. Charles, what's with that?" Amy asked turning to Charles.

"I'm not touching this conversation with a 10 foot pole." Charles joked.

"You wish you had a 10 foot pole," Bill jumped in a way only a fisherman can.

At that everyone broke out into hysterical laughing squeals as Bill and I got up from the floor with our arms around each other.

I winked at him, "Love you sweetie."

"Love you too," Bill replied.

"But you're still an asshole!" I couldn't let him off the hook that easily.

"Thank you dear, I try very hard because I know how much you like it." Bill blurted back.

Getting back on topic I asked, "So who is going to help me throw this party?" Everyone's hands went up. "Okay, let me think about what we can do and I'll text you tomorrow with some ideas."

"Sounds like a plan." Amy responded. And with that everyone went back to finishing their dinners and the conversation went back to normal Mystic things. Every few minutes for the rest of the night someone would say "Wow, I can't believe he's really coming back."

For the next four weeks we went about our normal lives while we arranged for a pretty simple get together at the Duck. The plan was for Charles to pick Henry and Ellen up at the airport at around 5 pm and bring them straight to the Duck. We would have a bunch of the old friends there to surprise them. Deep down we were all looking forward to seeing Henry. But just as much as that, we were really looking forward to meeting the infamous Ellen after hearing so much about her over the years. Was she really as much of a bitch as Charles made her out to be? Maybe she was a really nice person. Being from Los Angeles, I assumed she was perfect looking. Perfect face, boobs, and perfect figure. She was obviously incredibly smart. Harvard Medical School. Neuroscientist. She would not have been offered Dr. Jones job otherwise.

The more I thought about her, the more I didn't like her. The more I thought about her, the more I didn't like me.

When I was in high school I had dreams of going to college with the others. I was smart. Very smart. I graduated as the class valedictorian, and probably could have gotten into an Ivy League college like Charles and Henry. I was a great writer too, Henry always told me I could write better than he. But despite whether I could have or not, college was not in the cards for me. If my family had a tradition of going to college, they would never have asked me to stay home and work to help pay the bills. They would have let me go and figured it out somehow. But no one in my family had ever gone to college. Well actually that's not quite true, my cousin Fernando went to college after high school a few years before I graduated from high school. He lasted all of about six weeks before he showed up one day at home. No one ever asked any questions. He simply resumed his role in my aunt & uncle's family as a bread winner, just like he had done in high school working on my uncle's fishing boat.

Life comes at you fast when you graduate from high school. You are forced to make incredibly important and life changing decisions, right when you are really the least equipped intellectually and emotionally to do so. I made a series of decisions. Keep working at the restaurant. Marry Bill at twenty years old. Have kids. Each of those decisions was an indication of the path I would be walking on throughout my life. All of those decisions combined placed me clearly on a path that there was no getting off of. The woods were dense on either side of my path, like a New England forest filled with briars and spider webs. Veering off of my path would have been like heading off one of the hiking trails that are cut through a dense New England forest, it would have been incredibly terrifying to see my way through, and while likely not fatal, it would have been downright painful.

CHAPTER 4

The Reunion

The day finally arrived for Henry and Ellen's arrival in town. We decorated the Duck and put a sign on the door: "Closed for Private Function". I hate turning away business, but this was a once in a lifetime event. We were all set for their arrival. As 6:00 approached a whole bunch of the old gang were there and we hid in the back room. With every car that came down the street someone would yell out "Shhhhhhh." Finally we could hear a car pull up and Charles voice as he got out of his car. As they walked up the steps we stopped talking, the door opened, Charles, Henry and Ellen walked in and we all yelled "surprise!"

Henry and Ellen were startled, just as they were supposed to be. After a minute had passed to let them get used to the scene, Amy went up to Henry and gave him a big hug, "It is soooo good to see you, you do not know how much I have missed you."

"Thanks Amy, I have missed you too," Henry replied.

I was next. As I walked up to him, I said "I promised everyone I was going to do this" and when I got near enough I punched him right in the chest just as I said I was going to. "You deserve that for staying away so long," and then gave him a huge Portuguese hug.

"Damn, you still got your right jab." Henry replied. "And yes I deserve to be punched a few times, so have at it," and he held out his arms as if to give me permission to punch him.

"Nope, I'm good. All it took was one punch." And I gave him

another big hug.

It was Bill's turn, "I wish I was so lucky, she never stops with one punch with me." He blurted out, as he walked over to give Henry a big manly bear hug, "so great to see you dude! It's been way too long."

"Bill. You old son of a bitch, you have not changed at all. Charlie tells me you are working on the water. You have to tell me all about it. I remember we used to dream about starting a lobster business when we were kids."

"Well my dumbass husband actually did it, while you smart guys went to college and got real jobs." I interjected and everyone laughed.

One by one, while everyone came up and gave Henry a big hug, Ellen stood near the door being completely ignored. In a best case scenario, Henry would have introduced everyone to Ellen as they greeted him, but it was clear he was a bit overwhelmed with the reception. After everyone had gotten to say hello, Henry said, "Wow! You guys are all too much. This is just awesome." And after another 30 seconds Henry finally came to his senses and realized he had not introduced Ellen to anyone. "Damn, where are my manners. Everyone, I would like you all to meet my beautiful and brilliant wife, Dr. Ellen Chandler. Ellen, this is everyone," as he gestured to the crowd.

Ellen, who had stood there patiently, finally spoke, "I am really overwhelmed by the reception in this cute little clam shack. Henry has told me so much about you all, and now I know why he has wanted to come back to visit for so long. "

All of a sudden I realized my fears were true. Not only was Ellen Chandler beautiful, with perfect perky boobs, perfectly clear alabaster skin and a smokin' hot LA body, she also spoke with such practiced perfection. I was even more self-conscious than before. I did not like the "cute little clam shack" remark, but I was going to let that one go, it was cute after all.

After the small talk, Henry started to tell the story of how it ended up that he and Ellen were in a position to move to Mystic. He talked about his life since leaving Mystic, his job at UCLA, he described what it was like being a college professor like his dad. He even talked about the few years after his parent's car accident and why he could not come visit as often as he wanted.

After about two hours of more catching up, a few in the crowd started heading home and it was down to twelve of our closest friends including, Bill and I, Charles and Amy, and Henry and Ellen. By then we had quite a number of beers so we were getting loose and laughing quite a bit. We started reminiscing about our childhood and the stories began to come out.

Charles relayed the first one, the most classic story of all from our childhood, Henry's 18th birthday story, which is now complete lore in Mystic history, so much so that it even has a song written about it.

Charles began: "Henry I have to tell Ellen your 18th birthday story."

Henry blushed, "Oh, no, here it goes. Honey I want you to remember that we all did stupid things when we were teenagers."

"And you are no exception, yes I know dear." Ellen replied. "I can't wait for this one"

Charles continued, "Henry and I and a few other friends had gone out drinking for Henry's birthday and got completely plastered. Our friend Bob was driving, I was in the front seat, a few other friends were in the back seat with Henry who was in the passenger side back seat.

"Ellen you'll see tomorrow when we drive around Masons Island in the daylight, but on Masons Island we have speed bumps to keep the cars from going too fast on the island. It has become a habit for us to attempt to drive around the speed bumps by steering the car far enough to the right that the right side wheels of the car miss the bump, but this means driving really close to the side of the road.

"Another feature of Masons Island is that the mailboxes are only allowed along the main road. For side streets, the residents of each street have built a mailbox rack where you have a number of mailboxes, one for each house on the side street, nailed about six inches apart on top of a flat board. There are a few mailbox racks that happen to be right next to one of the speed bumps.

"On the way home from drinking, Henry was really not feeling well and leaned his head out the passenger rear window to throw up. Unfortunately he did that just as Bob decided to drive around a speed bump, which happened to be one of the speed bumps on the island with a row of mailboxes next to it."

"Don't tell me'" Ellen said as her eye rolled back in her head.

"Yep I think you're starting to see where this is going. Henry's head, which was sticking out the window, hit the first mailbox at what was probably 25 miles an hour, and then went down the line of every mailbox just like Wile E. Coyote in a Warner Brothers Roadrunner cartoon."

"Oh, no! That's horrible! But completely hilarious." Ellen said as she put her head in her hands in mock pain. "Were you hurt dear? Now we know the reason for Henry's odd behavior!"

"That's what we all said for a few years after that." I interjected.

Amy jumped in, "It actually could have killed him, but we all assume that because he was so drunk, his head just bounced. The worst part is what these drunken idiots did next. Once everyone realized what had happened, they did the only thing a group of drunken 18 year olds could do: the absolute wrong thing. They took him home, snuck him upstairs while his parents were sleeping, put him to bed, and fled the scene as fast as they could."

"You make it sound like we were idiots." Charles said.

"You were!" Amy and I yelled out in unison.

"We were all idiots," Henry responded.

"You needed to go to the hospital." Ellen said like the physician she was. "You probably had a concussion."

"I probably did because I have no memory of any part of the mailbox incident, which is probably for the best. All I know is that I woke up the next morning with the screamingist headache and my pillow covered in blood. When I went to the bathroom to see what happened, the whole left side of my face was swollen, red and cut up. I called Charles to ask what the hell had happened and he told me the story. I basically hid in my room for two days waiting for the swelling to go down."

A few more stories of Henry's childhood were shared with Ellen, who seemed to take them all in stride. It was getting late when Henry asked a question that changed the tone of the conversation. "Hey as we were driving through town I saw a white Subaru wagon parked in front of the Army Navy store that had "The Passion of Patience" painted on the driver-side door, is that Patience's car?"

Amy responded, "Yes that is Patience's car."

"So tell me, how is she doing? And what kind of business is the Passion of Patience?"

"Was Patience one of your high school girlfriends?" Ellen asked Henry with a slight grin on her face.

Knowing that was going to be a complicated answer for Henry, I stepped in to answer Ellen's question, "no Henry and Patience never actually dated, they were just good friends." I then turned to answer Henry's question, "you know Henry, it's really strange, but even though I live in the same town, and God knows it's not a big town, I don't get to talk to Patience very much other than to say hello in the supermarket or where ever we may run into each other. She became one of the first yoga teachers in the area like twenty years ago, and she's pretty well known around here for that, at some point everyone has been to one of her classes, but it's weird because lately she has somewhat disappeared, she no longer teaches any of the yoga classes that any of my friends go to. But the Passion of Patience is the name of her Yoga business."

Amy jumped in, "Well I see her more often because she still lives with her mom in the cottage on the island, and we occasionally talk, but she definitely keeps to herself. She teaches classes for my mom and her friends at the Y. They are totally into it. They even think she's a spiritual healer. My mom's constantly coming back from Patience's classes and calling me to tell me about energy flow and other Eastern mysterious stuff she learned that day. My mom of all people, a life-long Catholic, talking about her Chi and Karma, it's just hilarious."

I stepped in, "I think Patience also does something at Mystic Manor, right Charlie?"

Charles answered, "Yep, she's had a regular Yoga class at the hospital for years now. She works with the patients with mobility problems, mostly elderly folks who have had a stroke. The class is quite popular; the patients seem to think it really helps them. Dr. Jones is somewhat skeptical, but his feeling is that if the patients think they are benefiting from it, what's the harm? She has worked with my dad ever since his stroke and he can't say enough about what she does for him."

Ellen spoke up, "well, we'll have to see about that. I plan to introduce some of the therapy techniques we developed and used at Cedar

Sinai once I take over from Dr. Jones. I know Yoga can be a good thing for improving mobility, but I would want someone who has been trained in the method we use. Yoga can be counterproductive in therapy if an untrained teacher is pushing people into poses not appropriate for their condition." The way Ellen said that struck me as a little harsh, maybe we were starting to see the real Ellen come out.

Bill, who was pretty drunk by then, and had been uncharacteristically quiet for the past hour or so, finally jumped into the conversation. In only a way that Bill, in his best drunken blue collar fisherman Southern New England accent could, slurred out, "Well I think I know why the old men at the Manor like Patience."

"Oh here we go," I said.

"She's probably flirting with the old geezers."

"Jesus Christ Bill, you are such an ass," I chastised him. But he didn't stop there, "Well we all know what she was like as a teenager. I mean, she was my first."

I gave Bill a look that would stop a charging rhino, "What the fuck? You told me you were a virgin when we got married!"

"What the hell was I supposed to tell you when you asked me a question like that?" Bill continued, "that I had had sex with a bunch of girls in high school?"

I was dumbfounded, "Oh my God, you son of a bitch!"

And then he continued, "Oh come on now, anyone else want to admit the truth, that Patience was their first?"

Two more hands were reluctantly raised from other guys in the room. I don't know what came over me, but I was so pissed off at Bill at that moment for lying to me about being a virgin when we got married, I admitted to something I had never admitted to anyone in my entire life, not even Amy. I raised my hand.

Everyone started staring at me for a few seconds before understanding what I meant by raising my hand. Amy jumped up from her chair, "are you shitting me?" Bill, who took a few more seconds to understand what was going on, finally figured it out and shot me a look of absolute disbelief.

I had to explain, "What? We were in our teens. We were down at

Secret Beach, we were talking about boys and sex and such and the next thing you know we started kissing. Before long we were in the water with all of our clothes off, and we were exploring each other's bodies. It really was kind of innocent and beautiful."

"Oh my God! My wife's a lesbian!" Bill moaned.

I shot back, "I am not a lesbian you dumb-ass, I had an encounter with a girl when I was a teenager. That doesn't make me a lesbian. We have children together, and my God, you get sex almost every night! Not that I enjoy it every night mind you!" Everyone laughed at that.

During the entire discussion about Patience, Henry was getting more and more agitated. At some point he had gotten up and was pacing the room.

Ellen, who had been mostly quiet as she listened to us talk about Patience, jumped in for the rescue in her doctor expertise, "Actually Bill, I wouldn't worry, same sex liaisons are pretty normal for teenagers as they begin to explore their bodies and their sexuality. I doubt your wife is a lesbian. Patience does sound like quite a spirited girl though."

Bill blurted out, "she wasn't just spirited, she..." Before Bill could finish, Henry lost it. He lunged at Bill with his finger pointing at him, and with pretty intense anger, and said, "Okay that is enough. I get sick to my stomach when I think about the way you guys took advantage of her. It's not something you ought to be bragging about since it probably qualified as statutory rape. She's right," he said pointing at me and said these last words slowly and deliberately to Bill, "you are an asshole."

With that Henry walked out the front door and onto the front steps. As I got up to go after him, I gave Bill a long "I could kill you" stare and tried to say something but nothing would come out of my mouth, instead I just growled at him.

I met Henry outside and apologized profusely. "Look you know Bill is a dumb ass, he always has been. He shoots his mouth off, especially when he's drunk, he didn't mean anything by it. You know he liked Patience as much as anyone did, he was just trying to be funny."

"Yeah I know, I am so sorry, but you know how I felt about her when we were young, I guess I didn't realize how much of those feelings are still in me."

"Man, apparently so. Come back inside, please?" I asked.

With that Henry and I went back into the main dining room, and Bill spoke up, "Dude, I'm so sorry, I forgot how you felt about Patience when we were growing up. You're right, I am an asshole, my bad, I should never have started this whole conversation. Are we good? I really am glad to see you back here."

"Yeah we're good Bill. I am the one who should be sorry. You throw this beautiful party for Ellen and I, and I go off and start yelling like a madman trying to defend the honor of a girl that I have not even spoken to in over twenty years."

At that Charles spoke up, "you know Henry you were not alone in trying to protect Patience back then. When each of the Mason boys turned twelve, we each got what we called 'the talk'. Dad would sit us down and give us the birds and bees lecture. Of course by twelve we had a pretty good idea about it all, but it was important to him to have the talk, so we listened. He would start off by telling us that we were approaching manhood, that we would start to take an interest in girls, and soon would start to date and find ourselves in situations where sex might be possible. He told us of the responsibility in being a Mason, that the whole town watched us more closely than others. He wanted to make sure that we would not embarrass the family with scandals.

"And then he would end the lecture with a talk about Patience. Because she lived in the cottage on the estate, she was often seen walking around the grounds with Lois. He'd say 'So young man I expect that soon you will start to be interested in girls, but you must promise me, Patience is off limits. She lives on this property as an invited guest. If I ever find out that you have made any advances on Patience, in any way, the hammer will come down hard. Once you graduate from high school, you will be on your own. No college funds will be provided and no job in the Mason Industries will be offered. Are we clear young man?"

After a few moments of silence Amy spoke up, "Wow Charles, you never told me that story. That's just so bizarre."

"No actually it makes sense" I chimed in. "Patience was a gorgeous young girl and she was living on the estate. If you boys were going to be exploring your sexuality, it would make sense that Patience would be the natural target of all those raging hormones."

"Yes she was a gorgeous young girl," uttered Henry barely above his breath.

"Cheers to that!" Bill yelled as he got up from his chair and raised his beer mug as he tried to break the tension in the room and recover from his earlier remark. "To Patience," and everyone held whatever glass happened to be near them, and all yelled "To Patience."

For most of the discussion about Patience, Ellen had been listening quietly but intently. When Henry reacted with such anger to Bill's remark, it surprised Ellen and clearly bothered her immensely. Obviously there was something between Henry and Patience that was more than just a friendship. His friends say they had not dated, so it was not an old girlfriend crush. She made a mental note that this was something she was going to need to keep an eye on if Henry was going to live in the same town with Patience Passion.

Shortly after the tension died down, Ellen announced she was getting tired and needed to go to sleep. Charles and Amy had insisted that Henry and Ellen stay in the main house on the estate since there were plenty of bedrooms. After some hugs and small talk in the parking lot, Charles, Amy, Henry and Ellen all got into Charles' BMW and drove off as did the rest of our friends leaving Bill and I to clean up the plates and glasses.

Upon arriving at the main house Charles pulled into the circular driveway that leads to the front door. They all got out and Charles and Henry grabbed the luggage from the trunk and carried the suitcases upstairs to the guest bedroom. Amy and Ellen followed and they all made their way up to the bedroom upstairs. Along the way, Amy gave Ellen the quick tour of the necessities of the old house, the location of the bathroom, how to jiggle the handle of the old toilet, let the hot water run for a minute, and other small talk. After putting the suitcases in the room, and while Amy was giving Henry and Ellen the run down on the house, Charles excused himself to go put the car in the garage, which he had left in the driveway. When Charles got into the car he noticed that Henry and Ellen had left a backpack in the back seat. He put the car into the garage, grabbed the backpack and headed back upstairs to give it to Henry.

Meanwhile upstairs, Amy said goodnight and excused herself to her bedroom, and Ellen and Henry went into their bedroom and closed the door just as Charles was coming back up the stairs to give them the backpack.

As he got to the top of the stairs Charles heard a very heated discussion going on in Henry and Ellen's room.

When Henry had closed the bedroom door after their goodbyes with Amy and turned around to ask Ellen about the night, she pounced. "You worthless piece of shit! How dare you treat me that way in front of people I don't even know? Have you lost your mind?"

"Whoa, what the hell are you talking about?" Henry responded.

"You know damn well what I am talking about. First you let me stand there for five minutes when we first arrived and did not introduce me. You were so engrossed in 'your friends,' you didn't notice I was standing in the corner looking like an idiot? And then you completely embarrass me in front of all these people I have never met by swooning over this Patience person. Patience this and Patience that. She sounds like a little slut."

"She wasn't even there, how is it possible that I could swoon over her? And are you telling me you are jealous of a woman I have not seen nor talked to in over twenty years? Really Ellen?"

"You are such an infantile asshole. I'm not jealous, I am a Chandler, we don't get jealous of nobodies. What I am, is furious that you would make such an ass of yourself defending the little tramp right in front of me? Do you know who I am?"

"Here we go again. You're a Chandler, I know, I've heard the speech a million times. 'Treat me with the respect I deserve.' Will you be calling daddy next to threaten me with something? 'Cause we all know that's where it goes next."

With that Ellen lost it. "Get the fuck out of this room. Now! I don't even want to look at you until you apologize to me! And not one of your measly half-assed apologies," Ellen screamed as she grabbed a pillow and a blanket from the bed and threw it at Henry. "And your little girlfriend is toast. The moment I take charge of that hospital you can bet your little dick that she's a gonner. Spiritual healer my ass. She's a snake charmer making sick people believe they are getting better. Christ you are such as idiot." With that she opened the door, pushed him through it, and slammed it behind him.

Once out in the hallway, Henry found Charles sitting on the floor about fifteen feet down the hallway. It was clear he had heard the entire conversation. They looked at each other for about thirty seconds without saying a word. Charles got up onto his feet and shook his head from side to side in disbelief. Henry gave a sigh and they started walking down the stairs to the living room without saying a word. Henry threw the pillow and blanket on a living room couch and finally spoke, "let's go for a walk in the garden."

"You got it man." Charles replied and they walked out the French doors that led to the garden in the backyard.

Once they had walked about one hundred yards away from the house, Charles started. "Dude, I am speechless. I hope to God she's not always like that, but something tells me she is."

"Unfortunately, that's kind of the way it's been for the last ten years or so." Henry responded.

"That's just friggin scary, why, uh, how, do you put up with that? Amy would never think of talking to me that way, nor would I ever talk to her that way?"

"It's a long story." Henry clearly didn't want to talk about it.

"Well let's hear it, I got all night." Charles responded, trying to be the best friend to Henry that he wanted to become again.

"It would take a lot longer than one night." Henry was still reluctant to talk about it.

"Well we've got all summer. But let's start with the Readers Digest version." Charles was insistent.

"Charlie it's actually not that complicated of a story, I mean, I bet even Mr. C student in English at Yale could write that script," Henry said, chiding Charles for his not-so-quite stellar performance when they went to Yale together. "Poor orphan boy meets rich girl. They think they fall in love, but its for all the wrong reasons. Poor orphan boy is lost in the world and needs a home. Rich girl is incredibly controlling and in need of a victim to control. Rich girl has tremendous success in her career, completely ignoring the fact that her family's money opened every door for her that she could want.

"Meanwhile poor boy doesn't have that kind of career success. Those doors don't open when you marry in, you've got to be blood. She begins to resent his lack of success. He is constantly reminded that he's a nobody, and without her and her family he would remain a nobody."

"I hate to say it but I think your wife is a total bitch."

"Wow Charlie, thank you so much for that incredible insight. You're a real psychic."

"One more question then, why the hell didn't you get out years ago? You have no kids to fight over."

"I couldn't. They wouldn't let me. You come from a wealthy family, you get this shit. When you marry into a dynasty, you are a sycophant, a second-class citizen. And what's worse, it's not like they say that to you once and forget it. There are daily reminders, the sideways glances, the cutting you off mid-sentence like what you have to say is never important, like rich people are the only ones who can think through a problem correctly.

"When your spirit is just about sapped and you start thinking about getting out, they somehow know it and leave you obvious hints of what they will do if you try and end the marriage; you know you will be cut off as fast as Queen Mary's head on the chopping block. Jobs disappear, friend stop returning your calls, you lose all access. What's worse, you lose all access to the entire social scene that you gave up everything else for. You become a pariah; at best you get to hang out with all the other rich drunks at the dive bars who've disgraced their family enough to get pushed out, but not so much to be completely cut off." Henry stopped.

Charles jumped in, "I get it man. I guess it could have been easy for the Masons to become that type of family. For some reason we have avoided that fate. I guess it's the ole New England swamp Yankee in us."

"Your family is special, Charlie, you know that and I know that. Your father is one of the most kind and caring people I have ever known and your mother was a saint. I guess part of me thought that all rich people were that way. That was a massive misjudgment on my part."

Henry continued, "Once they endowed the Chair of English Studies at UCLA, and I was nominated to fill it, that was it, there was no going away. I was locked in forever. They owned me lock stock and barrel. My personal life, my friends, and now my entire professional life was tied to being a Chandler. At the beginning you just turn off a part of your personality to accommodate the new reality. But at some point many years later, you realize that you have been slowly turning off parts of your personality more and more until you just don't even recognize yourself anymore." Henry paused for a few moments to think, and then continued, "Charlie, basically you realize you've been living in a world of slow and subtle omission."

Wanting to change the subject from himself, Henry asked, "Hey so tell me about your dad. I know he had the stroke and has been in Mystic Manor for the last year or so. Is he getting back on his feet? He must be doing somewhat okay, because I'll tell you, the only time I have ever seen Ellen Chandler be that respectful to another human being in my life was the night she got that call from him to offer her the job. She actually called him sir."

"Yeah, my dad always had a way of communicating that made you sit up and listen, no matter who you are. He's actually doing much better. He has regained most of the movement in his left leg. His arm is still very weak. His words have mostly come back, but his ability to talk quickly and fluently is still not there. He has to fight for almost every word. The great communicator now commands respect with his death stare more than his words."

"The death stare, I had forgotten about that. It would send shivers down your spine. There was nothing worse than getting the death stare from Charles Mason. You knew your goose was cooked." Henry actually shivered as he spoke. "Do you remember the time he almost caught you and Betsy McCoy about to have sex in the back seat of the antique Model A that your family kept in the garage for all those years?" Henry asked Charles.

"Remember? It'll be seared into my brain forever. He opened the garage door when Betsy and I were both lying down on the back seat with my pants down around my ankles and my hand up her shirt. We both heard the garage door open and shot up like squirrels. I was able to get my pants back up and jump into the front seat before his eyes adjusted to the dark, or so I hoped. When he got over to the car it looked like a scene from Driving Miss Daisy. I was up in the driver's seat with my hands on the steering wheel, Betsy was in the back seat pretending to file her nails, saying, "Now driver, remember to drive slowly over the bumps, I don't want to mess up my hairdo."

"Dad, a bit surprised, looked at me in the front seat and then looked at Betsy in the back seat and said, "Okay kids, chauffeur time is over. Time to go outside and play. As I got out of the car in front of him, both our eyes were drawn down to my fly, which I had somehow managed to forget to zip up in the rush of getting dressed, and my white tighty-whiteys were sticking out through the zipper."

"Death stare?" Henry chimed in.

"Good lord. Death stare times ten. I gulped, turned ashen white, and I knew he knew, so I did what any thirteen year old would do, I ran. Betsy running after me and yelling, "Charles what's the hurry!" all the way to the pond."

As Henry and Charles were talking and walking, they had finally reached the statue garden. It's where Henry and Charlie always used to go to talk about serious stuff when they were kids. They stopped talking for a few minutes and just stared at the life-size statues. Henry finally spoke, "So it is true that the statue of the naked Indian chief was modeled after your grandfather? Rumor is he stood naked for a few days so the sculptor could get every part correct. And as far as I can tell he got every part correct."

"No one knows for sure, but it is probably true," replied Charles, "gramps had a bit of a wild streak in him and he seemed to like to be naked. We recently found a photograph from the 1950s of a Halloween party where everyone is dressed up in costume. If you look closely you will see that there is a man in the photo completely painted from head to toe in gold, with not a stitch of clothing on. That was gramps."

"Oh my God, that is hilarious. It's amazing he could get away with that in the 1950s."

"Well being a Mason has some advantages."

"Well man, if one of those advantages is being half as well endowed as the man who modeled for that statue, Amy is a very lucky woman."

"Well not half, maybe three quarters." Charles responded as they both broke out into hysterical laughter.

"Damn it is so good to be home again. I have not laughed like that in..." pausing, "I can't even remember the last time I laughed like that."

"It's okay man. You're home. You're among friends. Everyone here loves you as much as the day you left. You are part of the Mystic lore man." With that Charles started singing a song they had both sung many times, Henry joining in after the first two words, "and his head hit the mailbox!" Again more laughter.

When the laughter subsided, they could hear some rustling of leaves, someone was coming up one of the paths from the gardener's cottage. As the person got closer Henry could see it was an older woman, and finally saw it was Lois. As she approached them, Lois spoke, "Well he finally made it. Damned it Henry Moore, it certainly took you long enough."

Not quite knowing how to respond to that, he said "Why yes ma'am, it certainly did. I'm sorry about that."

"First don't you dare call me ma'am, it was always Lois and will always be Lois. Come over here and let me look at you." Henry stood up and walked to Lois. She grasped his upper arms in her hands and took a good hold, closed her eyes, and took a deep breath.

After a minute or so, she continued, "Second, do you know what it took for me to get you here?"

"Well whatever you did, it worked, and once again I am reminded why I was completely in love with you throughout my teenage years."

"I was one hot momma wasn't I?"

"The hottest, and you are still one hot woman." And with that, all three of them broke out into laughter.

Lois continued, "Henry Moore you've not been following your Noble Path. You've been walking on someone else's path and when you do that you lose yourself and everything you value. You need to get out of the darkness young man, stop stumbling your way through life and get back onto your own path, the one that keeps unfolding itself in front of you every day despite you not taking it." Lois paused and then continued, "come by the cottage tomorrow and have some tea, will you?" And with that, as mysteriously as she had walked into the statue garden, Lois Passion walked right out.

Charlie and Henry looked at each other the same way they looked at each other thirty years ago when Lois would say something like that, dumbfounded. You never knew if you should laugh, or be scared as hell.

Henry muttered, "what the hell was she talking about? Walking on paths? My path? Noble Path? Someone else's path?" Though he pretended he had no idea what Lois was talking about, it was pretty clear to him what Lois meant. Charlie shot him a look and nodded. It was clear he understood also. Henry and Charles both smiled.

"Maybe its time to go to bed." Charles said.

"It's been one hell of a long day." Henry responded as they started walking back to the house.

"Tomorrow I was planning on giving you and Ellen a tour of Masons Island and Mystic. Do you think after tonight you'll both be up for that?" Charles asked.

"Sure. She'll act like nothing happened. That's what Chandlers do. Their public persona is perfectly quaffed. All the dysfunction in those families happens behind closed doors."

"Alright, now I can't have you sleeping on the couch. The kids will see you in the morning and wonder what you are doing. So you'll have to sleep in the old guest room," Charles was referring to a small bedroom off the hallway that led to the garage. It was the room that Henry slept in whenever he spent the night when they were kids.

"Just like old times." Henry responded.

"Just like old times, Henry Moore. Damn its good to have you here again."

CHAPTER 5

The Manor

The next day, just as Henry predicted, Ellen acted as if nothing had happened the night before. She did not know that Charles had heard most of their argument and Henry was not about to tell her. After breakfast, the four of them got back into Charles' BMW and Charles gave them the tour he had promised the night before.

They started with Masons Island. As Charles drove around the quiet winding streets of the small island, every street seemed to evoke a memory and Charles or Henry would relay a story starting "Hey do you remember...." and go on to describe some memory from their childhood. Amy or Ellen would blurt out an occasional "oh my God, you guys are so funny" or "that just sounds dangerous."

There was the place where they set up a bicycle jump using a gravel pile and a two by six board at the construction site of one of the houses built in the 1970s. There was the fishing dock they built on the ice pond that sits in the middle of the island, but they both got strep throat from accidentally ingesting the dirty pond water during its construction.

Of course they had to stop and pay homage to the row of mailboxes where Henry had his 18th birthday head bash, Henry and Charles taking turns to recreate the incident that will never be forgotten.

They made their way to the Yacht Club and walked the grounds with more stories of teenage conquest. There was the story of the bicycle that was hauled up to the top of the Yacht Club flag pole as a prank but then was accidentally let go and came crashing down, and the ensuing fight between Charles and Bruce, the owner of the bike. There were other stories of skinny dipping after hours with one girl or another or whole groups of teenagers.

Charles pointed out the Pequot at its mooring in the cove. Pequot was a 55' Hereshoff yawl that had been in the Mason family for a few generations. It was one of the most beautifully designed sailboats in the area. It was no longer raced in the local regattas since it could no longer hold its own racing against the newer generation of fiberglass racing boats. But Charles still took it out a few times a month for day sails and once a summer sailed to Newport or Martha's Vineyard for the traditional week long Mason family cruise.

After they completed the tour of Masons Island they headed off the island over the causeway that connected it to the mainland and continued into downtown Mystic. Charles and Henry continued the guided tour, reminiscing about kids they knew, "hey, wasn't that so and so's house?" as they passed some distinctive antique home that Mystic is famous for; or relaying more stupid teenage stunts, "do you remember when we got arrested for trespassing for building a play fort in the abandoned Mystic train station?" as they passed the now beautifully restored train station.

After they drove over the drawbridge to the west side of the river and into the main drag of downtown Mystic, once again they passed Patience's white Subaru parked along the main road. Whether Amy and Ellen saw it we'll never know, but if they did they were smart enough not to mention it. Henry noticed it but did not dare say a thing after last night's tirade. For some reason Charles, either on purpose, or without thinking, blurted out, "Hey there is Patience's car. Do you want to stop to see if she's in the Army Navy store? I am sure she would love to see you. I am not even sure if she knows you're here."

"While I appreciate that offer Charles, I am sure Ellen would like to finish the grand tour before we stop to walk downtown Mystic, maybe she'll still be there when we get back," Henry responded seriously but with a hint of sarcasm.

"Right, got it, much better idea," Charles responded with a heavy emphasis on the word "much". With that Amy shot him the look of "you are such an idiot", and Charles shot back the look of "oops, that was a close call."

After downtown Mystic, the last stop on the tour was to take Ellen to visit Mystic Manor. She had never actually visited the facilities before accepting the position. She accepted the position from what she knew of its reputation in working with brain injury patients, which was quite well-known and well-earned after a few highly publicized cases.

One in particular was the famous New York City wilding incident that became front page news for a few months in the mid 1980's. A female jogger in Central Park was allegedly attacked by a group of roving teenagers from Harlem, beating her nearly to death in the process. While it was later learned that none of the boys accused were actually involved in the horrific act, and they were eventually released, the victim was not so lucky. She was eventually sent to Mystic Manor for rehabilitation where she experienced a remarkable recovery from her very traumatic brain injuries.

Repeated news updates over the next few months by the local New York news outlets would report on the victim's progress of rehabilitation at Mystic Manor as all of New York seemed vested in her making a full recovery. A news van would drive out to Mystic every few weeks from New York to get the obligatory camera shot of the reporter speaking in front of the main building as she described the improvements in the victim. Eventually the victim returned home and the camera crews stopped coming, but the reputation of Mystic Manor was solidified in the media and with medical professionals all around the country, including Ellen.

The other more recent famous patient of Mystic Manor is essential to this story but it requires a bit more of the history of Mystic to understand the context.

During the Roaring Twenties, Mystic developed a reputation as an artist community when one locally famous artist from New York City built a summer cottage here. As his artist friends came to visit, some decided they wanted to move there too. Soon more artists were moving out of New York City looking to escape the horrendous living conditions in New York at that time and Mystic was becoming a thriving artist community. That group of artists eventually coalesced into the Mystic Arts Center which has become a thriving art gallery for the local community.

But despite the close brushes with art world fame over the years, Mystic has never had an artist quite as famous as Violetta Andropov.

Violetta was a very famous concert pianist. Originally from Russia, she had settled in Manhattan. When Violetta turned forty she had come to visit some friends in nearby Stonington Village, and fallen in love with the area, and decided to leave New York and settle in Mystic. She had now been living there for almost twenty years The fact that Mystic is only a two hour direct train ride on Amtrak to New York City and ninety minutes to Boston makes it a great place to live for those who have to travel to these two cities occasionally for work.

Traveling the world giving concerts for the two decades prior to moving to Mystic was financially rewarding for Violetta. It afforded her a very nice home in Mystic, one with a bigger piece of property than one would expect in an old fishing village. She existed quite nicely in Mystic, traveling to Julliard in New York as she needed for teaching and to the Boston airport to head off to parts unknown.

A year before Henry and Ellen's return to Mystic, Violetta suffered a serious stroke which affected the left side of her body. As a result, she lost the use of her left arm. Obviously this was a tragic result for a professional concert pianist. For about six months after her stroke, Violetta underwent rehabilitation at Mystic Manor. Because of Violetta's fame as a world famous concert pianist from New York City, and the nature of the tragedy that befell her, the New York news outlets were very interested in following her story. Once again, just like after the Wilding incident, every few weeks a New York news van would pull up and do a story on Violetta in front of the main building.

So it was with this knowledge of Mystic Manor's public reputation, in addition to the reputation within the medical community, combined with Charles Mason Sr.'s persuasive sales pitch on why Ellen should take the job that gave Ellen the comfort she needed to take the position at Mystic Manor sight unseen.

As Charles' BWM pulled into the driveway of Mystic Manor, Ellen got her first glimpse of the facilities. With redbrick buildings, some over seventy years old, and the traditional white columns that adorned the front of each building, it gave the hospital campus a collegiate look. The grounds were well cared for, bushes trimmed and large oak trees were limbed perfectly. Charles parked his car in one of the visitor parking spaces near the entrance and they all got out and walked through the main doors together.

Since this was a Sunday morning and an unofficial visit, there was no welcome committee for Ellen. Charles of course was a minor celebrity at Mystic Manor, so as they walked in the front door, the nurses at the nursing station at the entrance all greeted Charles and Amy warmly.

Sheri, the nurse-in-charge on Sundays, greeted them first, "Good morning Mr. Mason, to what do we owe this pleasure? Good morning Ms. Mason."

"Sheri please call me Amy, I hear Ms. Mason and I think of my mother-in-law." Amy replied with a smile.

"And what a great lady she was, God rest her soul." Sheri responded.

"Everyone, I would like to introduce you to Dr. Ellen Chandler." Charles said as he introduced Ellen to the nurses at the nurses' station. Ellen's arrival had been discussed for weeks, so the nurses all knew who Ellen was, the job she was about to take, and the fact that she was about to become their boss.

"It is so nice to meet you all. I have heard so much about the quality of care here, and we all know how much of that is because of the nursing staff. I can't wait to get to know you all better." Ellen said, trying to invoke compassionate emotion in her voice as she spoke to the lower level workers she will soon oversee.

Sheri continued to be the voice of the team of nurses, "We can't wait to get to know you either Dr Chandler. The hospital has been abuzz for a few weeks waiting for your arrival. I hear that you are going to start a week from Monday?"

"Yes Sheri, I plan on taking one week to move in and settle into our new house, and then start on Monday. Can't wait, so nice to meet you all." And with that the four of them moved on, Charles leading the way.

Charles Mason was practically raised in Mystic Manor, and knew everything about the place, every hallway, every closet, every secret door. Buildings built or upgraded during the Cold War terror of the 1950s and 1960s always included basements that could double as fallout shelters for when the eventual nuclear bomb was dropped.

The town to the west of Mystic, Groton, is the home of the US Navy's Nuclear Submarine Base, situated on the Thames River that divides the cities of Groton and New London. One mile down river is the Electric Boat plant, where, despite its name, General Dynamics builds nuclear submarines for the Navy. Practically directly across the river from the US Sub Base is the US Coast Guard Academy.

It does not take much imagination to realize that with such a high concentration of highly sensitive and nuclear-armed military facilities in the area, the Groton-New London area was on the top 10 list of Soviet nuclear targets if and when that nuclear war broke out.

While late night comedians joke about going to school in the 1960s and 1970s and having to endure monthly air-raid drills where kids were taught the horrors of nuclear radiation, and then told that to protect themselves they would have to get under the school desks where a ¾ inch piece of plywood was somehow going to protect them from a nuclear bomb, those in Mystic actually took this seriously. They all knew that they would be a target. Many of the fathers in town worked at the sub base or at Electric Boat, and being on the Top 10 list was the topic of more dinner conversations than they would like to remember.

So when Mystic Manor was eventually rebuilt and expanded, the architects built in a healthy supply of underground facilities that could act as fallout shelters. If that event ever happened, it was assumed that all patients would be moved to the basement and would have to live in the shelters for a while.

Coming up to the surface would not be possible for days due to nuclear fallout. Therefore all of the underground shelters were connected by passageways that led from building to building so people could move from shelter to shelter without having to go outside.

As the Cold War neared its end, the fallout shelters were eventually repurposed, the food stores were thrown away or sent off to homeless shelters, and the shelters were turned into storage facilities for the medical supplies and other things needed for the hospital. After some more time had passed, the passageways were eventually closed, the doors locked, the keys lost and slowly but surely they were forgotten. They were forgotten by everyone except for a couple of young teenage boys who never forgot about them. Boys who as teenagers would spend hours exploring the passageways that led from building to building, boys who set up forts and would play war games, each boy with their own passageway to call their own territory. One of those boys was Charles Mason and the other was his best friend Henry Moore.

As the tour wound its way around the hospital, a similar scene took place at every nurse station they came to. The lead nurse of that station would greet them. Niceties would be exchanged. Charles and Amy would be deferential and ask to be called by their first names. An introduction of Ellen would occur. Ellen appeared to be as kind as could be, and in many ways she could appear to be a very kind and generous person. The Chandlers of Los Angeles, despite suffering the inner turmoil and tension that plagued most very wealthy families, knew how to appear to be kind and generous people. They regularly donated funds to charitable causes, such as UCLA and Cedar Sinai Hospital. They won awards for their charity, more than one building in LA carries the Chandler name.

But as with most of the second or third generation of the super-rich, their generosity comes with a certain amount of detachment. There is no feeling of belonging to the lower classes that most Americans belong to. They swoop down into that community as they need, but the detachment is pervasive. Second and third generation wealthy truly believe that they were born into their wealth because they were supposed to be. They believe that their circumstance was destiny, it was pre-ordained. They will never admit this to anyone, to utter it to themselves is heresy, but second and third generation wealthy truly believe that their DNA is special, and it will only continue to breed special people.

Even when the money is all gone, and eventually most family fortunes are gone, that superior DNA is somehow still perpetuated and assumed. It is an amazing phenomenon actually, to think that one man, two or three generations ago, who started a company that through an equal combination of perseverance and luck managed to become worth a fortune, somehow the foundation of his success is a superior breed of DNA that is passed down to heirs for generations.

The insidiousness in this is that the other side of that belief is the equally strong, but equally silent belief that everyone else has inferior DNA.

While they believe that their circumstance was pre-ordained, they similarly believe that the lower and middle classes destiny was pre-ordained also. That is why old money people only associate with other old money people, and have such a difficult time associating with new money people. They look at new money people as having broken some aspect of natural law. "I am rich because I am supposed to be rich. You are not supposed to be rich. Your accumulation of wealth is against the law of nature, and it will correct itself and return you to your natural state."

In that Ellen was a typical third-generation wealthy American. Due to her profession, she dealt with the lower and middle class every day, and she was good at appearing to engage with them on their level. But it was an act. Deep down Ellen Chandler truly believed that she was of a different class of humankind, one with superior genes. But she was a good actress, and none of her staff would really ever know that. Henry on the other hand felt that every day. While she could put on a good act for her subordinates at work, spouses are another story. Spouses of second and third generation wealth, unless they also come from equally wealthy families, are reminded every day of their inferiority.

The last stop on the tour was to meet Dr. William Jones, the retiring Chief Physician of Mystic Manor. Dr. Jones, although in his early 70's, was a workaholic, so finding him at his desk on a Sunday was not unusual. Charles knocked on his office door, there was the obligatory cheery "doors open" and all four of them walked into Dr. Jones office.

Expecting a nurse or someone else, Dr. Jones was surprised to see Charles and Amy standing in his office, "To what do I owe this surprise?"

Charles, who called Dr. Jones by his first name, responded, "Bill I know you two have spoken on the phone a number of times, but I would like to officially introduce you to Dr. Ellen Chandler."

"Dr. Chandler. Well my replacement has finally arrived." He paused for a few seconds, and continued. "I guess I better pick up the pace on packing."

Charles, looking around the office at bookshelves filled with books, globes, knick-knacks, pictures on the walls, as it has for twenty years, half-jokingly said, "Um, Bill, have you even started yet?"

After some laughter, Dr. Jones replied, "I guess I better get started then."

Ellen, feeling a bit uncomfortable replied, "Bill I was hoping you would stay here for a few weeks until I get acclimated. It would be good for there to be some continuity as you hand over the reins to me."

"Nonsense, I would hate coming into a new job and have some old geezer who should have retired years ago looking over my shoulder. I'll have some of my grandkids come and pack it all up. So Ellen tell me, Charles tells me you have had great success repairing neural pathways through repetitive motion sensitivity training."

Ever the doctor, Bill Jones could not hold a conversation for two minutes without bringing his passion into the conversation. "Well yes Bill, Cedar Sinai realized great success through repetitive motion training. It appears that it's possible that part of motion memory is not stored in the cerebral cortex, but instead in the local muscle and nerve bundles. So despite cerebral damage, the motion memory still exists at the local level." And they were off. Quickly these two doctors, both leaders in their field, were talking about concepts that the rest of the group could not follow.

After a minute or two, they both realized that Charles, Amy and Henry were staring politely and Dr. Jones said, "well there will be plenty of time to discuss shop over the next few weeks, I'll agree to stay one month but no longer. You'll want me out of your hair by then and I don't want to feel like I am getting pushed out of my own hospital, I want to go out on my own terms."

"Great, then we have a deal?" Ellen responded, holding her hand out to shake hands.

"Yes doctor, we have a deal." Dr. Jones answered while shaking her hand.

"Okay then, I will see you bright and early next Monday morning," said Ellen, still shaking Dr. Jones hand.

"Well I am certainly glad that is settled." Charles butted into the conversation. "But I am starving, it is 1:30 and we have not eaten lunch yet. How about we all head back into town for some grub? I'm buying."

"Excellent idea!" said Henry, who had hardly uttered a word all morning, responded with intensity, "but I was hoping to say hello to your dad if that is possible before we go. Is he up for visitors?"

"He is probably taking his afternoon nap," replied Dr Jones. "He tires easily. I'd suggest you take a rain check and we will prepare him properly for visitors when you return another day."

Although Charles Sr. was an approachable man, and was sure to be happy to see Henry, his stature in the community meant certain protocols had to be followed. Surprise visits, even from family members, were not part of the protocol, so it was agreed that the proper reunion would be arranged in a few days.

"Shall we do lunch?" asked Charles again, obviously suffering from extreme hunger. The four of them walked back to Charles' car, and proceeded to head back into Mystic for some lunch at the Duck. As they walked in, we were just about done cleaning up after the normal Sunday brunch crowd. Their timing was perfect since there is always a lull between 2:00 and 5:00 on Sundays and that would give me time to talk to my friends.

As they walked in I yelled, "Hey there everyone! How was the tour? Can I get everyone drinks?"

Henry spoke first as he grabbed the back of one of the chairs at one of the tables near the windows and sat down, "It's funny, in some ways nothing has changed, but there are parts of town I don't even remember, or maybe just don't recognize."

"So Ellen what did you think of Mystic? Still excited to move here, or are you heading back to LA on the next plane?" I asked.

"You're so cute. I am good, very good. Masons Island is even nicer than Henry described. I love the way the streets roll and bend. It's so different than the LA beach communities where they line up huge beach houses in a row on small lots. Let's see, we went to Mystic Manor and I met Bill Jones. He is somewhat of a legend in my profession, so what an honor that was. Such a nice man for being such a visionary."

"So you're staying?" I replied, not wanting to let that go.

"Yes, I am staying. I start my job next Monday. Oh gosh Henry, that gives us only one week. I've got to call the movers to find out where they are. We have to unpack and get the house arranged. And then I have to find my bearings in town, I wouldn't even know how to find Mystic Manor at this point."

"Ellen I think you got this, if you can navigate Harvard Med School, you can navigate Mystic, Connecticut." I said trying to give her confidence.

"Well let's say that though I navigated myself through med school, I didn't really navigate myself around Cambridge very well. My sense of direction is not that well defined."

"Are we going to order some food?" Charles blurted out, not wanting to engage in small talk any more, "I am friggin' starving!"

"Okay, okay, Mr. 'got my knickers in a twist', will it be the usual? Or today will it be extra crabby?" I asked, making fun of his favorite meal, which for years has been home-made crab cakes with paprika, and his attitude at the moment.

"Very funny, I am only crabby because the service at this establishment is terrible. I'd like to talk to the owner please!" Charles responded in mock anger.

"You would, would you? Well the owner can be reached by walking right out that door there." I said pointing to the front door, "and don't let it hit you in the ass on the way out either!" I replied with mock attitude.

"Hey Sammy," I yelled at my cook in the back, "This preppy bag of wind here would like an order of crab cakes, extra crabby, with a heavy dose of entitlement."

"Okay boss, but the entitlement will cost extra," Sammy yelled from the kitchen.

"And can you make it a little lighter on the attitude" Charles yelled back to the kitchen.

"That's a no-can-do on the attitude," Sammy replied. "That's sprinkled into everything we do here."

"So we have experienced." Charles replied.

Henry looked at Amy and asked, "They can just go on like that all day long can't they?"

"Pretty much, the two of them have been flirting for years," Amy joked.

"Ouch!" Charles winced.

Again the group broke out in laughter but it was true, Charles and I could go on forever like that. We've known each other for so long, through all the good times and bad, that there was very little we couldn't kid each other about, and the topics that were off limits, I knew about.

After we ate the meals that were ordered, and we spent another hour reminiscing about our childhood, Charles and Amy drove Ellen and Henry back to their house. It had been a long weekend and Henry wanted to take an afternoon nap. While we were eating, Ellen had tracked down the moving truck with her cell phone, and it was to arrive in the morning and they would need to spend the next few days unpacking. Their cars were to arrive by truck the next day also so they would have their own transportation. That meant that for another day Henry and Ellen were relying on Charles or Amy for transportation and a room to sleep in, which of course they were completely fine with accommodating.

Henry and Ellen were renting the Sullivan-McCoy house. For some reason, houses on Masons Island get named after the family that occupied the house when you were a teenager. So while the "Smith House" might have only been occupied by the Smith family for five or six years, if it was the five years when you were a teenager, for the rest of your life you refer to it as the Smith house.

This makes for a confusing conversation when talking to Islanders of your parent's or children's generation. While you might refer to a house as the "Smith House" because that's who lived there when you were a teenager, your parents might refer to it as the "Jones House" because that's who lived there when they were growing up. Your children on the other hand might refer to it as the "Roberts House" because that's who lived there when they were teenagers.

Some houses on Masons Island stay in a family and get handed down from one generation to the next. When this is the case everyone can agree on what to call the house. It's the Smith House for you, your parents and your kids. On the other hand, some houses seem to get passed from family to family, and this is where all the confusion enters in.

The cottage that Henry and Ellen decided to rent on School House Rd. on Masons Island fell into the latter category. When Henry lived on the Island it was occupied by the Sullivans, so Charles and Henry referred to it as the Sullivan house. But the Sullivans were not there very long, the McCoys moved from a few blocks away after Henry had left for Los

Angeles and lived there right up until Henry and Ellen moved in. By then the McCoy's only daughter Betsy had moved away and when the McCoys finally passed away last year, Betsy decided to rent the house instead of sell it.

So throughout the process of finding a rental on the Island, both Henry and Charles had referred to the house as the Sullivan house, even though it had been owned by the McCoys for over twenty years, and Henry was renting it from Betsy McCoy. And yes, this is the same Betsy McCoy that Charles had almost got caught seducing in the back of the Model A by Charles Sr.

As one might guess, School House Rd is named that way because at one point there was a one-room school house on the road. That fact is actually its own Mystic story. Back in the late 1800s and early 1900s when one-room school houses were how we educated our children, the total population of Masons Island was less than ten, the Mason family had not sold off more than a few lots to others, nor had they built their current family estate, at that time Masons Island was mostly used as pastureland for grazing sheep. There were hardly enough residents to support a school.

Instead the one-room school house supported a wider area of families with children including mostly families that lived off-island. What's odd is that someone had the thought to place the local one-room school house, one that supported few Islanders but many mainlanders, on the island instead of on the mainland. Getting out to the island in the late 1800s and early 1900s was not an easy task. The early bridges that were built to connect Masons Island to the mainland at that time were not particularly safe, nor permanent. Every hurricane that came through Mystic up until the Hurricane of 1938 had completely destroyed any bridge or structure built to connect the island to the mainland.

So when the Masons Island one-room school house was still in operation, the school children from the mainland would have to walk across a somewhat unstable, wooden bridge to get there. Even in the middle of the winter when the temperatures in Mystic can get down to 0 deg and stay below freezing for days at a time. That is why it is a mystery to this day why it was decided to place the one-room school house on the Island and not the mainland.

The story of the Masons Island school house has an interesting ending. Charles great-grandfather happened to know someone down in Washington DC about the time a new museum was being built in the capital. Once no longer in use, Mr. Mason decided to give the school house building to the museum. So if you go visit the Smithsonian Museum of American History in Washington DC, and you see a one-room schoolhouse on display, that schoolhouse is the very same school house that was on Masons Island in Mystic Connecticut.

The current causeway to the Island was built after the hurricane of 1938 and before the hurricane of 1954. That time they decided to make it a more permanent structure. It was constructed of a base of granite rocks and paved with asphalt, with a twelve foot wide tunnel in the middle for small motorboats to pass underneath from one side of the causeway to the other.

Today, depending on how high the tide is at the time you want to go through the opening and depending on how tall your motorboat is, will determine if you can get underneath the Masons Island causeway. If you are lucky, you can skootch through. Otherwise you'll have to go all the way around the Island to get up the Mystic River, an obstacle that adds thirty minutes to the trip.

The current causeway survived the Hurricane of 1954 pretty much intact, and is still standing, although one of the young Islanders who tried to drive across the causeway in the middle of the 1954 Hurricane was not so lucky. He was actually swept right off the causeway with a poorly timed crossing, timed poorly because it was right when a large wave, driven by the hurricane force winds, came barreling up the Masons Island cove right as he was making his attempt to get home by crossing over to the Island and that wave lifted him and his car right off the causeway and into the drink.

He survived. He only reported this story to his children many years later when it was safe to do so, safe because it turns out that his father had fished the car out of the shallows a few days after the hurricane and sold it to one of his unsuspecting neighbors, and he had to wait until those neighbors had moved on before telling the story for fear they would get angry at the deceit that had taken place fifty years before.

While occasionally taking advantage of ones neighbors naivety was okay in Mystic, being ostentatious with one's wealth was not in vogue in Mystic, quite the opposite.

Many a wealthy family had moved to Mystic thinking they could spend and impress their way into the hearts of their new neighbors. One surefire way to get blackballed from joining the Masons Island Yacht Club was to attempt to impress your neighbors with your wealth in an ostentatious manner. Those were typically the families that came and went very quickly. And when they went, they always reported Masons Island to be a very closed and rigid culture. This was anything but the truth, many a family had moved onto the Island over the years and were wholly accepted into the community almost from the start.

Masons Island has never been a closed and rigid culture, it's simply that while it might take a fair amount of wealth to afford to buy a house on Masons Island, one's wealth is not what's going to get one accepted into the community. Understanding the unwritten rules of how to behave in a traditional New England community is what matters.

In that way non-New Englanders such as New Yorkers and Californians who come to Masons Island tend to move away rather quickly. When moving from somewhere where impressing the neighbors with wealth is what gets you invited to the local country club, moving to New England is like moving to a foreign country. It does not work, it actually has the opposite effect. And this is probably why small New England towns like Mystic have a general reputation of being unaccepting to outsiders. This is not true. If you ever move to a small New England town, keep this in mind. If you happen to be wealthy, your wealth is much better revealed in small doses over a period of a few years, not all at once in one big impressive and overwhelming, "Here I am neighbors, bask in my richness!".

Despite being from Los Angeles, Ellen Chandler had spent time in New England, and was an extremely intelligent and aware person. She learned and understood the rules at play in New England. So despite moving out of a very large Spanish style house in Malibu that was one of the Chandler family homes, and the house where Henry and Ellen lived for the past decade, Henry had convinced Ellen that they did not need to take on such a large home in Mystic. Mystic was not Los Angeles. Ellen agreed.

So Henry did a little research with Charles' help, and they settled on renting the Sullivan house from the McCoys. Once Henry and Ellen decided to rent the Sullivan-McCoy house, over the next few weeks Ellen and Henry had to plan out what pieces of furniture they would ship to Connecticut and what would go into storage in Los Angeles, keeping in mind that they were downsizing house size.

After all the planning, the movers finally showed up at their Malibu home and packed up their selected belongings which headed off on the cross-country trip. The day after Charles tour of Mystic, the moving van and car carrier arrived as planned at the Sullivan-McCoy house. The house was a cute three bedroom bungalow, one of the houses that Henry had really liked when he lived on the Island. With no children, three bedrooms were more than enough for the two of them. And despite being small, it was well kept and well-constructed with many built-ins and nooks, aspects that give charm to a house and make a house a home.

Once the moving van had arrived and the belongings moved into the house, Henry and Ellen took Monday through Friday to unpack their belongings from boxes and start their new life together in Mystic, Connecticut.

CHAPTER 6

Reintroductions

After spending the week unpacking and the weekend resting, the Monday that Ellen was to start in her new role finally had arrived. A few times over the weekend, Henry had driven Ellen around Mystic so she could get to know the town and get her bearings of the route to Mystic Manor.

When Ellen arrived for work at 8:00 am she pulled into the parking area dedicated for staff as Charles had instructed her to, only to find the very first parking space with a sign with her name on it: Dr. Ellen Chandler, Chief Physician. This made her happy. And unlike the Sunday before, this time there was a welcome committee. When Ellen walked through the main doors, she was completely caught off guard by a loud welcoming "Surprise" from dozens of staff members with signs and balloons. This made her even happier. For a woman known for her coldness, these two nice surprises actually brought Ellen Chandler to tears, a very rare occurrence. As she was being greeted and hugged by one nurse after another, with Dr Jones smiling and standing behind everyone, Ellen started to get her first sense of the culture of Mystic Manor, it was as much a family as a hospital, and it was a culture that was closely maintained and guarded by the Mason family.

After the greetings, Ellen was led to the office wing where she had first met Dr. Jones, and was shown her temporary office, the one right next to Dr. Jones' office. Once Dr. Jones was out in thirty days as agreed to by Ellen and Bill, Ellen was to take over his office.

Ellen's first week was busy simply getting to know the established protocols. Running a hospital is basically following a series of protocols that are created and managed based on government regulation, health and sanitary requirements, and other mandatory rules to keep the patients safe. Before Ellen could change things, she needed to know what the rules were to start. It was her goal to incorporate the medical procedures she had helped to perfect at Cedar Sinai that made that hospital one of the best in the world. But that would take time, and she first needed to establish and document the current rules so she could have a basis for comparison.

On their first tour of the hospital, Henry had asked to see Charles Sr. but was told it would have to be arranged due to his condition. During the previous week that visit had been arranged and it was set for Tuesday, Ellen's second day on the job.

On Tuesday morning, as Ellen was leaving for work, Henry mentioned that he would be over to see Mr. Mason that morning and he would stop by to see her at some point when he was there. Around 9:30 am Henry left home and arrived a few minutes later with about twenty minutes to spare before his scheduled appointment to see Charles Sr. As Henry was walking down a corridor to the wing of the hospital where Charles stayed, he turned a corner and passed one of the larger community rooms where he saw a number of older patients, some sitting in chairs, some sitting on the floor on yoga mats. He stopped for a second to take a look and as he scanned the room from left to right he was stopped dead in his tracks by a thunderbolt, at one end of the room stood Patience.

Henry felt faint. His knees felt like they were going to give way. A rush of emotion filled him that he had not felt in years. He felt like crying. He didn't move. He had not prepared himself for seeing Patience today. He wanted to see her but he did not want a surprise encounter, he needed time to prepare. After all, he had left with no notice, he never wrote or called to say goodbye. He had not called in twenty years to see how she was doing. He had no idea what Patience thought of him. She could hate him for what he did, and he would deserve every negative emotion she could muster, and he could not bear the thought of that outcome.

Patience had not seen Henry when he first noticed her. Not ready for an encounter, and still being in the hallway outside the door to the room, Henry moved to the side of the doorway where Patience could not see him if she looked his way. He was too paralyzed to move so he just watched the patients in the room.

It was clear that these patients were in physically rough shape. Traumatic brain injuries do horrible damage to the ability to move limbs the way that we all take for granted. Every lifting of an arm or leg requires tremendous concentration and effort. Patience was perfectly named. She worked with her students with the utmost love and patience as they struggled with every move she was demonstrating. But while the pain was obviously affecting most in the room, amazingly, all the students had a smile on their face.

After about five minutes of watching Patience work with the twenty or so patients in the room, Henry realized that he was staring so intently that some of the patients began to notice this handsome man staring at them and they began to stare back. The distraction of some of her students caught Patience's attention and her eyes were drawn to the doorway where a few of her students were focusing.

Once Henry noticed that the students were staring at him, he moved a bit to the left to bring Patience back into his field of vision and looked in her direction. At that moment, their eyes met. Patience had no idea that Henry was in town or the circumstances that brought him here. Henry Moore, who was her best friend as a child and teenager, who she loved more than anyone for all those years, the same Henry Moore who disappeared one day without saying goodbye and never came back or called or wrote, that Henry Moore was standing in the doorway of her class twenty years after disappearing from her life without warning.

To understand how Patience reacted next is to understand Patience. Patience smiled. Actually she beamed. A smile requires a few muscles around the mouth and face. A beam requires the use of one's entire body and complete aura. Her beam was noticeable to everyone in the room, including Henry. Henry, who for twenty years had been deeply anxious about what Patience would think of him, an anxiety that was partly the reason he just stayed away, saw Patience beaming, and she was beaming at the sight of him. At that, twenty years of deep fear and anxiety just vanished, just melted away immediately. That is why Patience Passion is spiritually gifted, she can melt away twenty years of fear and anxiety in another human being with a single smile. The best psychiatrists with the best drugs can't get those results.

Henry smiled back, he wasn't much of a beamer, but he was clearly very happy to see Patience. The sight of these two younger people smiling at each other got all the patients in the room to smile also. Henry then realized that he was going to be late for his appointment with Charles Sr., and it was clear that Patience was in the middle of a class, so he pointed to his watch and then pointed up, the universal hand signal for "I've got an appointment upstairs." And then he pointed to the floor, which meant "I'll be back." Patience smiled and nodded.

As Henry turned to continue walking to Charles Sr. suite, his eyes met Ellen's eyes, who was standing about ten feet away and obviously had at some point walked down the hallway and encountered Henry, who was watching Patience. As much as Henry felt a rush of warmth and love when he saw Patience, his blood instantly ran cold when he saw Ellen. As much as his face had been a beaming smile just seconds before, his face dropped and he went ashen white with a look of terror.

"Ellen, what a surprise, I am on my way to see Mr. Mason, will you join me on my walk?" Henry stuttered.

"I see you found Patience." Ellen's voice was deeply sarcastic and cold.

"Yes, and what a complete surprise it was. I was on my way to see Charles Sr. and I heard a familiar voice coming from this room. Anyway, it looks like she's busy leading a class, and I am late for my meeting with Charles Sr., I was about to head up his room, want to come along? It's been a long time since I was here and the Charles Mason wing of the building is completely new."

"You were here one week ago with Charles and I and you did a lot more just now than notice her, you smiled at her, no actually blushed at the sight of her."

"The whole scene caught me off guard, Ellen. Let's not forget, she was one of my best friends that I completely walked away from for the last twenty five years to be in a relationship with you. I don't think you can question my intentions. I have always felt guilty for blowing her off so thoroughly, so if I blushed it was likely out of guilt and shame, not anything else."

"Don't tell me what to think or not to think," Ellen said in a muffled voice that was barely audible but filled with intense anger. "I will question your intentions if and when I want. You should have been happy to end your relationship with all the other women in your life when we got engaged, it was the least you should have done. I have never expected much from you in our marriage, but that was the minimum."

"Can we not do this right here?" Henry pleaded.

"What? Are you afraid I might embarrass you in front of Patience?" Ellen asked with an emphasis on the word Patience that was now loud enough to be heard by those in the room.

"I am not doing this here. I am walking, follow me or not, but I am walking down this corridor." Henry said starting to get angry, and he walked off.

Ellen, who was not keen on being told what to do, or following anyone, especially Henry, did not budge. As Henry continued to walk away with his back to her, Ellen's stare made his hair stand on end. Even though he was looking the other way and could not see her cold stare, he knew from twenty years of being with Ellen what she was doing right now. The cold stare, the twisted smile, the thought that was never uttered but was so heavy in the air it did not need to be: "I will make you suffer for this one, you worthless piece of shit."

Henry could take the misery that would rain down on him when these episodes happened, and over twenty years they had happened hundreds of times. But Henry was not thinking of himself at that moment. At the sight of Patience, Henry had reverted into that teenage boy, that boy that protected a girl that he cared so deeply for. At that moment Henry knew that Ellen's method of making him pay for his little indiscretion was not to punish him, it was to punish Patience, and he made a vow at that moment that that would never happen.

As Henry got to the end of the hallway, he came upon a nurse's station and asked where Charles Sr. could be found. One of the nurses said she would take him there and escorted Henry right to Charles Sr.'s room.

Henry knocked and heard a somewhat familiar voice say, "Come in Henry, I've been waiting for you." Upon entering his room, and seeing

Charles Mason for the first time in over twenty years, Henry was slightly taken aback at the change in Charles Sr. Mr. Mason had always been a larger than average man, about 6' 2" and was well built, weighing about 200 lbs. What Henry saw was a man that who had aged quite a bit. He looked like he had lost a tremendous amount of height and weight. He saw a man whose vitality had once been so strong and vibrant but was now barely able to get up out of his chair to greet him.

"Henry, it is so good to see you young man, I have missed you greatly" Charles Sr. said as Henry approached him. "Sit down and tell me how you have been."

"It is great to see you again sir, and I apologize for staying away so long, that was not my plan, it just seemed to happen that way."

"No apologies are necessary with me Henry, it has always been your right to live your life the way you see fit, and it is no one else's business to try and change that. People think in their own self-interest, my boy, and if someone is trying to get you to change, it is usually their best interest they have in mind, not yours. There are very few noble people in this world."

"Thank you sir. Since we are being honest, the rumor is going around that you had some influence on Ellen getting the position here, and it might have had something to do with getting me back to Mystic."

Charles responded with a chuckle in his voice, "well there might have been some truth to that, but your wife is one of the best neuroscience physicians in the country I am told, she got the job because she deserved it."

"Yes she is, yes she is." Henry replied.

"Are you okay Henry? You're breathing pretty heavy and you look a little pale." Charles asked, noticing Henry's physical condition just after his run-in with Ellen.

"I am fine sir, I was running a little late so I ran a bit to get here, so I'm a little out of breath." Henry replied, not really telling Charles the truth. "The truth is I stumbled across Patience downstairs teaching a class. So I stopped to watch and I lost track of time."

"Ah, Patience, she will do that to you. She has certainly matured into quite a fine young lady, hasn't she? I am so proud of her. The folks here really like to have her come and lead them in those Yogi moves." Charles said, mispronouncing the word Yoga. "I don't quite understand it all, but it seems to help. Don't tell anyone, but she comes up here once a week to work with me, also. I get my own private lesson." Charles said almost whispering that last admission so no one could hear.

"Really sir. You, a yoga man? I never would have thought that", Henry said with a smile on his face and sarcasm is his voice.

"Well you know, you've got to keep up with the times Henry, or it just passes you by even faster. And I agree with the rest of them, I feel better and can move better after working with Patience than with my own doctors and physical therapists. I'm not sure why I am paying them all that money when a Yogi person is doing a better job."

They both laughed at Charles last comment.

"Have you been out on Pequot lately Charles? Some of my best memories are of us racing her around Fishers Island Sound. You know you taught me how to sail."

"Charlie tried to get me out on her last summer after my stroke but the doctors advised against it. I think they thought if I fell overboard, I wouldn't be able to keep my head above water while they were trying to rescue me," he said with a laugh, and then turning more melancholy, "little do they know that I would much rather go out like that than sit here in this condition for the rest of my life."

"Well sir, now that it looks like I'll be here for a few years, and you will get better, I promise that next summer you and I will take her out and race around Fishers like we did when I was a kid."

"That would be great Henry, let's look forward to that." After a few moments pause, Charles continued. "So Henry, Charlie tells me you are a full professor, just like your father, how proud he would be of you."

"Well you know it's a curse of sons to follow their fathers into their professions, and I am no different." Henry replied, as the both chuckled. "Honestly, the life of a college English professor is pretty charmed. You teach a few hours a day, read and grade some papers, and mostly you write your book because the grad students are doing most your work for you."

"I am sure it is much more difficult than that," Charles Sr. answered. "I remember your father would disappear from our poker games for a week or two at the end of every semester to read and grade all those damn papers. You couldn't pay me enough to do that."

"Well unfortunately they don't pay me very much at all, so it seems they got that backwards." Again they both laughed.

"So tell me about this wife of yours. Did we hire the right person for the job?" Charles asked, getting somewhat serious. "She must be pretty good if she kept you away from us all these years."

Henry was at a loss for words. After his altercation with Ellen a few minutes before, he was not really in an Ellen praising mood, but as the dutiful husband, he had no choice but to answer positively, even if it was a big lie.

Henry struggled as to find something positive to say and how to form the words that would not raise any suspicion. "Ellen Chandler is a brilliant woman." This was one of the few things that Henry could say about Ellen without crossing his fingers behind his back. And this was true, no matter what he thought of her, he could not deny her intelligence. She is one of the best scientists in a field that has become one of the hottest fields in medicine.

"Is that all you can come up with? She's brilliant? This woman is your wife." Charles seemed to be able to tell something was up.

"Well sir, your question was if you had hired the right person," Henry said with an emphasis on the "you", "you didn't ask if I had." Henry said with a smile. "And yes, I think you hired the right person. Ellen will bring some great new ideas to the hospital which I am sure will make a difference."

"So what's her weakness?" Charles pressed.

"Professionally?" Henry asked a bit puzzled.

"Yes Henry, professionally, I am not interested in her weaknesses in your personal affairs. I don't care if she beats you silly at home, as long as she keeps the doctors and nurses happy and productive in my hospital."

"Well sir I got to meet Dr. Jones last week, and he is such a warm and caring man, I am sure that it will take the staff some time to get used to Ellen's style."

"That's the Henry I remember," Charles said with a laugh. "You can turn any negative into a positive. So you're saying her bedside manner may need some improving."

"Well, yes, sir, professionally and personally," Henry said slowly and with a grin.

"Henry," Charles chastised Henry with a wink for getting too personal.

"Okay, so sticking to professionally, she's brilliant and her family situation never really taught her how to deal with, what should I call them, let's say the commoners. That's likely why she chose her specialty, it does not require as much interaction with patients as most other specialties. She could have become a plastic surgeon like most other doctors in LA."

"Speaking of the City of Angels, how have you enjoyed being there for so long? I can't imagine you could find a place more opposite than our little town here. It doesn't appear that you donned that Hollywood fake."

"If I did then I left it on the tarmac at LAX when I got on that plane, sir. LA is fine as long as you know what you're getting. You can't buy into the hype. If you go there looking for the hype, you'll love it. But if you are searching for normalcy, you'll get depressed, because it doesn't exist. All the stereotypes are 100% accurate. They are the shallowest people in the world. Even if they are not, LA just demands shallowness. Maybe it's the geography they sit on, at any moment it could all just slide into the sea, so there's no time for deep and meaningful conversations." He continued after a slight pause, "Charles, the thing I hate most about California and missed most about New England is the lack of humility. They must post signs at the border crossings that say 'Welcome to California, please leave your fruits, vegetables, and humility at the border.' I actually think they consider humility to be a personality disorder. At best it's considered a weakness, and at worst it's on par with leprosy. Use some self-deprecation or self-doubt in conversation and people will run from you like cockroaches off a sinking ship as if you just admitted to having Ebola."

"I am sure you found someone to commiserate with in twenty years." Charles responded after listening so intently.

"Actually my students have kept me sane. Enough of them are from other parts of the country, that their initial observations when they move there keep my memories of the east coast fresh so I can keep them alive."

Charles had some more questions, "And I'll assume being married to the Chandler family is a full time job. It's a shame how wealthy families can chew up and spit out in-laws dozens at a time." This was quite an admission coming from the patriarch of one of the wealthier families in New England.

Henry did not respond right away to that comment, instead his eyes drifted off and he went inward, and remained silent. After another pause he responded while looking out the window, "it certainly is an interesting dynamic. Loyalty and dedication is required. None is returned."

A few more moments of silence passed. "So where are you and Ellen living?" Charles asked.

"We have rented the old Sullivan house on School House Rd. from the McCoys." Henry responded using the same pat answer he has said time and time again over the past week.

"One of my favorites," Charles replied. "You know my grandfather actually designed and built that house. When the family first started selling lots on the Island to other families, at one point he decided he would try and sell completed homes, instead of just plots of land. That was his first and only one, I think he quickly realized that he was not a builder. It was serendipitous actually, because that was when he got the job selling herbal remedies, which eventually led to the formation of Mason Industries, and the rest is history as they say."

"Well that turned out well for the family," Henry chuckled as he responded. "And I had no idea your grandfather built that house. Charles Jr. must not even know that, or he would have said something."

"It's possible he doesn't." Charles Sr. responded. "Well Henry, I am getting a bit tired, it's time for the afternoon nap that I have earned with my years. Will you agree to come back again next week? I want to hear more about your job at UCLA. I thought about being a professor when I was young too, but family obligations took over and prevented that."

"I would be glad to." Henry had been waiting for the right moment to say something to Charles Sr. about being grateful for all that he was given, and he saw an opening. "Sir I am so grateful for all that you have done for me over my lifetime, I don't know how I can ever repay you."

"Don't you ever think that way Henry Moore. There is no debt to be repaid, nor were you some charity case. I am a businessman Henry, and you were an investment. I can't think of any better investment than in the education of a young mind. Walk an honorable path through life Henry, that's the only repayment necessary for this old man."

"That's a promise sir. I'll see you next week." And with that Henry shook Charles Sr. hand firmly and walked out.

That last statement struck Henry deeply. "Walk an honorable path" it reminded him of what Lois had said the week before about finding his own path. All this talk of paths, he did not know quite what to make of it, but when two of the people in the world that you most admire both tell you something, it gets your attention.

Henry headed back down to the room where Patience was teaching her class, it had been about thirty minutes since he left, and by the time he got there her class was just ending. He waited for all the students to leave and walked into the room where he found Patience picking up her things. She turned around and they stood and stared at each other from about ten feet away for over a minute without saying a word.

Henry finally broke the silence. "Patience Passion you are still the most beautiful person I have ever laid eyes on. I can't even begin to describe my feelings right now. I absolutely need to talk to you, but we, or should I say, I have a bit of a problem. My wife is Ellen Chandler, the new Chief Physician here, and she happened to walk by a half an hour ago when I was watching you teach your class. Let's just say that she is a pretty jealous person, so we need to go somewhere we can talk and I don't have to worry about being watched. Can you meet me outside in ten minutes down at the duck pond?"

"Of course Henry." Patience replied "Let me finish picking up my things. I'll take them to my car, and I'll meet you there." After a slight pause, she flashed that endearing Patience smile and continued, "It is so good to see you too."

Henry, reluctant to get even within five feet of Patience with Ellen lurking around, smiled, and turned and walked out. Half expecting to find Ellen around the corner again he looked in both directions but there was no sign of her. He quickly headed out the front door of the building and down the path to the duck pond. He chose that location purposely and with some advance thought, it was on the opposite side of the hospital from Ellen's office so not in view where Ellen might be watching from. When he arrived he sat down on one of the benches that line the pond and waited.

Henry was now quite emotional. He had been practicing the speech he was about to give for twenty years. First he would apologize for just leaving without saying goodbye. Then he would tell her how much he loved her when he was a teenager, how their friendship meant more to him than any other.

But the real truth is he had no idea what was going on in his head when he decided to move to Los Angeles without saying a word to her. After the death of his parents, he felt so unconnected to anything or anyone, so abandoned, so indebted, he was mostly numb, and in that condition he was not sure what he was feeling.

Henry had kept his eyes on the path to the Duck Pond for Patience and after a few moments he saw her coming down the path. This was the first time he had gotten a good look at her. After twenty years she had not changed a bit. Her blonde curly hair still fell lightly over her shoulders. Her greenish blue eyes still exuded the feeling that all is right with the world. While her frame appeared to be delicate, her walk revealed strength from years of daily exercise and what was likely a rigorous Yoga practice. That walk, it had not changed at all. Patience never seemed to fully touch the ground when she walked. She floated on the balls of her feet from one step to the next like she was walking on the moon, as if gravity could not seem to find her.

While all those things were simply radiant, nothing compared to her smile. Patience's smile was a language unto its own. She could have walked through her entire life and never uttered a single word. Her smile communicated an entire way of being, a religion, a spirituality. While the world's great religions require thousands of pages to lay out the rules and behaviors that are required of mankind to reach salvation, all laid out in psalms and prose in Bibles, Korans, or Gitas, all those words are rendered useless by the simple act of gazing upon the smile of Patience Passion. The Golden Rule is embodied in it. The world's greatest poets would have been that much greater if they just had the opportunity to gaze upon her glorious smile for a single second.

As Patience approached, Henry got up and walked toward her to meet her. As they neared, Henry opened his arms and Patience did too and as they met they gave each other a hug, a hug that was in the making for twenty years. Henry broke into tears. Tears gave way to sobs. After a few moments he spoke through his sobs, "I am so sorry. I am so ashamed. I left and never called." He gasped in between breaths broken by sobs.

"Henry. Henry. Look at me. Look into my eyes'" Patience lifted his chin up with her hand so his eyes would meet hers. "Henry, you never left me."

Henry looked at her with a puzzled look. She repeated herself, "you never left me," and she said these last few words slowly and with emphasis on each word, "because I never left you."

And with that Henry's sobs stopped. His twenty year preparation for this moment, the speeches, the practicing, the tears, the guilt, the excuses, all of it slipped into the ether. The wall that he had built around his heart melted. He once again realized why this person was the most special person he had ever met. He was in the arms of someone who was not operating by the same rules as the rest of the world. The powerful emotions that rule our moment to moment existence, the rage, anger, jealousy, guilt, fear, hatred and greed, it simply did not exist in the world for Patience. Patience's world was so fully developed and permanent that despite living in the material world that competed daily with the agendas of thousands of others, she never wavered.

Henry tried again, "You are still the most special person I have ever met. And I have met a lot of people over the past twenty years."

"I am sure you have, tell me about them Henry," Patience responded with a laugh. Henry laughed back and then they just smiled at each other. "I want to hear about all of them."

"That's going to take a while, we better sit." Henry joked and they walked to the bench and sat down.

"Patience, you have to realize that when my parents died, my world was completely shaken, turned upside down. I felt like I had lost everything. I questioned everything about my world and about myself. I lost my way, I lost my confidence."

"You didn't lose me Henry."

"But in a way I did. Not that you left me, but I lost myself and in the process I lost you. I wanted nothing but to go back to Mystic and spend the rest of my life with you, but my confidence was so shaken, I felt like the lowliest person on earth. You on the other hand were the most special person I knew. You deserved the most special life and the most special person to share it with. I no longer felt like I deserved you. If I had gone back to Mystic you would have sold yourself short to be with me and I could not let that happen. So the only way I knew how to save you from me was to go away, far away. I never called to say goodbye because I thought you would have talked me out of it."

"Oh Henry, that may be the perception you were having at that time, but it was not the truth. You sold yourself short and you sold me short in the process. I have never wanted anything to do with the lifestyle you thought I deserved. That was the material world speaking through you."

"As I said I was not thinking clearly." Henry responded.

"Well you probably were thinking clearly, but you were thinking through the eyes of a world that lives by a pretty screwed up set of rules. Imagine that. You would deny yourself your own happiness because you thought I deserved a different or better happiness, something different and better than what you thought you would be able to provide me. How screwed up is that? It was up to me to decide what was going to make me happy Henry Moore, not you."

"I screwed it all up, didn't I?" Henry whispered.

"Henry you didn't screw anything up. The past is as distant a memory as you allow it to be. This moment is the future and the past all rolled up into right now. So right now, at this moment, you and I are sitting here and we are together, and for me it feels like it was a few days ago when you left Mystic. Stop holding on to all of that Henry. It's done. It's over. You are here now. Be here now. Look at me. Be..... here....now!"

Henry smiled. Patience smiled back. He stopped seeing her for her physical beauty and began to enter a different world. It was the world that he existed in whenever he and Patience were together when they were teenagers. He realized that he had left that world long ago. He realized now that he did not even know he was existing in another world. Despite having left that world for twenty years, it all came rushing back, that feeling, that comfort, that dream-like state, he was back in it in a matter of moments.

"So tell me about those people you mentioned." Patience said getting back to their earlier conversation. "Start with this Ellen chick." Patience and Henry laughed.

"Ellen Chandler, wow, how do I describe her to someone who has never met her? She's from Los Angeles, she's a Chandler, of the LA Chandlers." Henry said that with his best Queen's English accent. "While her brother is basically a pampered useless trust-fund baby, Ellen is brilliant. She graduated near the top of her class at Harvard Med School and has excelled to the top of her field."

Patience responded to Henry's attempt at making that sound impressive, "While I bet that impresses someone, you know I don't care about that, what kind of person is she Henry? I know you Henry Moore, you are not superficial, you look deep. You are enchanted by someone's capacity to love, to be kind and fair. So she's your wife, you must be in love, how much of that love is the residue from how you entered the relationship twenty years ago, and how much of it is driven by who she really is today?" Patience asked very directly.

"Wow, bang, the Patience I knew and loved is still kicking. You still don't beat around the bush."

"And you are still the same Henry I know, the guy who loves to beat around the bush. Well answer the question, Mr. Moore."

"That's going to take a few minutes to think about." Henry paused for a minute or so while he thought about the answer. "I think you already have your answer. I said I loved you too much to saddle you with the Henry Moore that I thought I was at the time. You would have given me a level of love that I did not think I deserved. So I entered into a relationship with Ellen instead. I don't mean to say I didn't love her, but I guess she treated me how I felt."

"And how was that?" Patience asked the obvious question.

"Do I have to answer that?" Henry asked painfully. "I was a mess, I felt like a mess, she was not looking for an equal, Chandler's do not marry equals, in their minds they have no equals. But I am as smart as she is and so I could go toe-to-toe with her intellectually and she liked that," Henry paused for a second, thinking about the next line, and delivered it with a smile and laugh afterwards. "While she wanted someone she could control, she wanted it to be somewhat of a fair fight."

"And has it been a fair fight?"

"No. It has never been a fair fight. It was never going to be a fair fight. I don't think it is possible to have a fair fight when the deck is so stacked against you from the beginning," Henry paused again and looked at his watch. "Shit, I have to go. Ellen is going to wonder where I have been." With that Henry shot up from the bench.

"Okay Mr. Moore, you run off to the love of your life and I'll stay down here for a few minutes until the coast is clear."

"You are mocking me Patience."

"I'm sorry Henry that was not very nice, I can tell you are in pain. So this therapy session was on the house but next time I am going to have to charge you. Lowly Yoga instructors don't make much money you know."

"I am not buying the lowly Yoga instructor thing, somehow I think what you do with those people up on that hill is a lot more than just Yoga."

"Well that's part of my mystery and a good magician never reveals their tricks. You run off, don't want you to get in trouble."

"Okay, I am coming back to see Charles next week, what days do you teach here and I'll make a habit of coming on one of them."

"Same two days every week Henry, it's been the same two days for years, Tuesdays and Thursdays."

"Okay, I'll see you next week. I can't tell you how good it was to see you."

"Go, go!" Patience shooshed and with that Henry smiled at her and turned and walked briskly back up the hill to the main building.

CHAPTER 7

Ellen Assumes Control

Over the next four weeks Henry and Ellen established a new set of routines in their personal and professional lives as they settled into their new life in Mystic. The Sullivan-McCoy house had come together nicely, it was starting to feel like a lived-in home. The nooks and crannies that old-man Mason had built into all of the different rooms began to fill up with pictures and knick-knacks that Ellen and Henry had brought with them from LA..

For the most part Ellen was great about keeping the New England charm of the house. Californians, and Angelinos, in particular, are notorious for not really comprehending what gives New England its deep charm. I learned this firsthand the one time I got to go to California. Bill, in a very rare moment for him because it meant actually spending money, decided we needed to take the kids to Disneyland on vacation. So without telling me, he booked plane tickets and secured a hotel in Anaheim. He was so excited when he surprised me with the trip that I didn't have the heart to tell him that there was a Disney World in Florida which would have been much closer and cheaper than going all the way to California. That's Bill, his heart is in the right place, but his brain takes a while to catch up.

The reality was that I was actually excited to go to California, I had already been to Florida a few times but never California. Growing up on the East Coast in the 70s, California was the Mecca of the Western world. Every movie and television show portrayed California as the hippest place, the rest of the country was in a 1950s time warp in comparison. Every new thing happened there, from the latest rock and roll trend, to electronic gadget, to social craze. For about forty years California generated most of what was cool in America. So the thought of going to check out this crazy place was very exciting.

Once I got there, what I found elicited the typical reaction. With such a build-up of anticipation, once someone from New England makes their way there, it is usually a bit of a disappointment. The roads are not paved in gold. The beaches are no nicer than the beaches in Rhode Island, and the water is so cold you can't really swim in it. But after so much build up and so many sacrifices made to get there, no one ever really wants to admit to their disappointment, so they come back home extolling the virtues of the Great California, while deep down wondering what all the hype was about.

On one of our side trips that Bill likes to take when he visits a new place, we took a trip from Anaheim to the nearest beach, which is Newport Beach. On the way we drove through Balboa Island, a very cute island in the middle of the bay on the inland side of the strip of land that fronts the Pacific Ocean. We stopped for lunch at a little corner restaurant and when the waitress asked us where we were from and we responded New England, the waitress gave us what seemed like a practiced speech, "Oh then you must love Balboa Island, it was modeled after a New England fishing village. Everyone says it has the charm of New England."

Bill and I looked at each other and responded it was a very nice place and yes it was "just like" New England. After she left I commented to Bill that it must have been designed by someone who had never actually been to a fishing village in New England. We should know since we were born and raised in one and still lived in a house a few blocks from the fishing docks in Stonington Village. First of all they missed the most prominent aspect, the smell. There is a particular odor that permeates real fishing villages in New England, and that would be the smell of, yes you guessed it, fish. It's in the air and even a major rain storm cannot wash it out of the air for more than a few hours.

Secondly, New England villages have been around for hundreds of years, and many of the houses have been there just as long. When you look at a New England home built in the 1600s or 1700s, there is one major aspect that you can't help but notice, and it is what gives New England houses most of their charm. The houses are crooked. There are very few 90° angles. The sides of the houses are no longer perfectly straight, the windows are not exactly rectangle, they are more like trapezoids.

Usually there have been additions over the centuries as each successive generation of Americans decided that bigger houses were better. Many of these early additions occurred before zoning laws came into existence and they leave you wondering about the design skills of the architects at the time, and that is likely the point, there was usually no architect involved.

Take our house for instance; originally it had two rooms downstairs: a living room/kitchen and a keeping room that was also the master bedroom, and two bedrooms upstairs. At that time, the bathroom was an outhouse in the back yard. At one point in the 1880s they carted a small one room cottage down the street and tacked it onto the side of our house. And then when plumbing was brought inside around the turn of the century, they built another addition for a new kitchen and a bathroom.

While the rest of the country can brag about recycling, New Englanders were the first recyclers. When house engineers try to date old New England homes, sometimes it is difficult to do. That's because you can't just look at the age of the timbers used to construct a New England home and get an accurate date. Often New Englanders would reuse the timbers from older homes, so a house built in 1820 might be using 60 year old timbers from a house built in 1690 that was replaced after 70 years of use. It's the ultimate in recycling, but also the ultimate in hazard when rebuilding a New England home. One would think a house built in 1812 would have timbers no older than that, but our house had timbers that had hatchet marks on them, which means they likely pre-dated the water-driven sawmills that used rotating blades that cut timbers with straight cuts, which came into use in the 1700s.

This is why those of us who buy these old New England houses spend our twenties and thirties and most of our savings trying to make their interiors make sense for the world we live in today. With our house, we turned the one-room cottage and the kitchen addition, which together had been four small separate rooms, into one great room with a kitchen family room combination. We did our best but you can only do so much with old

New England homes unless you completely start from scratch and rebuild everything, but then you end up having a house that looks like it should be on Balboa Island. And that might be why Balboa Island would lead people to think it was a classic New England fishing village.

At the time, being confronted with a Disneyland recreation of the town I lived in, I started thinking about what really gives a New England town its charm and I realized something. It's not actually not the smell, and it's not the buildings, those are just outward signs of the state of mind of the people. It's not the cute clapboard New England style homes on narrow streets that gives New England its charm, it starts with the people. The same people who would live in a crooked house and not even think of trying to straighten it; who would live among the smell of fish twenty-four hours a day and not think anything of it; these are the same people who would wear the same overcoat for ten years straight even though at some point the dog might have bitten a tear in the sleeve; these are the same people who will literally drive a car into the ground despite the rust from the salt air and the salty roads, because it still gets them from point A to point B; and its these very same people that Californians will never be able to recreate. They can recreate the homes, the streets, even the chowder, but it takes real New Englanders to add the essential charm of a New England town.

So when I say Ellen was amazing at keeping the New England charm of the Sullivan-McCoy house, for an Angelino, she was really amazing. The Sullivan-McCoy house was one of the oldest houses on the Island. Like many older New England homes, it had small rooms and low ceilings. Few things were straight and the kitchen had never been updated. But she left it as is, except for one addition that I think has more to do with wealth than with being from Los Angeles. Ellen had floor-to-ceiling mirrors installed, almost everywhere, in the bathrooms, bedrooms, even in the hallways. I guess rich people like to admire themselves no matter where they are in their house.

One of the most interesting features of the Sullivan-McCoy property was not the main house, it was an out-building in the back yard about 100 feet from the main house. As kids we referred to it as the Backhouse and we would occasionally hang out in it with Betsy McCoy when we were kids. It was about 12' wide and 30' long and dividing into two rooms. It was originally built as a livestock shed for chickens and other assorted livestock, but had long ago been turned into a storage shed, a dumping ground really. It had old appliances, boxes, gardening things, you name it and it was thrown out into the Backhouse when it became obsolete.

Since Henry had come to Mystic on sabbatical to write a book, he decided to turn the Backhouse into his writing studio. He got Betsy McCoy's permission to clean out the backhouse, rented a 20 yard dumpster and did just that, cleaned it out. Once emptied, he added a wood stove for warmth, had the interior painted white, moved his nice leather chair and desk out there, took out one of his acoustic guitars, and made it into a really nice peaceful studio. The other room was turned into a sleeping area with a small bed and dresser.

It took Henry two to three weeks to get into the groove of writing, but he had been thinking about this for many years, so he had the story he wanted to write in his head for a very long time. Once in the groove, Henry got on a roll pretty quickly. Maybe it was the change of scenery, or the extra time on his hands from not having to teach, or maybe it was the privacy he had since Ellen was working all day and he had no students to teach or papers to grade.

Ellen was also getting into a groove at Mystic Manor. She had slowly taken charge from Dr. Jones who, as per their agreement and true to his word, moved out of his office four weeks after Ellen started. She was glad that he had stayed on for the transition but it was time for her to start making changes and some of those changes were not going to be to his liking.

One of the changes that Ellen had decided on was dealing with Patience and her classes. When she had told Henry their first night in Mystic that she was not going to allow a yoga instructor to harm her patients, she meant it. After her argument with Henry in the hallway when she caught him watching her class, her resolve only became more complete.

But Ellen was not going to be rash about it, she knew that Patience had been working at the Manor for many years, but she did not know what loyalties Patience had built up over that time. While Ellen was not really interested in whether the staff at Mystic Manor liked their new boss or not, she knew that she would be more in control of the facility if they did, people who work for you will be more apt to freely do your bidding if they like you. When she reined in Patience she was not going to make it worse upon herself by upsetting her staff if they were fully behind Patience and the work she was doing.

So Ellen watched and waited. She avoided being near the common room during the times when Patience held her classes. As Ellen held her one-on-one meetings with her staff over the first few weeks, during these get-to-know-each-other sessions Ellen would subtly bring up Patience and ask what the person thought of what Patience was doing. What she learned was quite interesting. It seemed everyone had an opinion they wanted to share.

Ellen learned from the nurses that Patience had been teaching Yoga at the Manor for many years. It started when one of her students outside the hospital introduced Patience to Dr. Jones at Mystic Manor when the woman ended up there after a minor stroke. She insisted on having Patience come to the Manor to continue their weekly sessions and Dr. Jones allowed it, and eventually curiosity set in with the other patients. Before too long, Patience was leading a class for a handful of patients twice every week.

To an outside observer it looked like Patience specialized in teaching Yoga to people who were in rough physical condition, but Patience knew exactly what she was doing. When James Dillinger was asked why he robbed banks, he famously replied "because that's where the money is." It was the same for Patience. She loved her work at the Manor because those are the folks with the biggest mobility issues, that's why they are there.

For Patience, her classes were all about increasing mobility and getting energy to flow to places where it did not previously seem to reach. She called it getting "unstuck". Healing is only enabled when the energy blocks that develop for a variety of reasons are removed. Teaching Yoga in a hospital that was dedicated to individuals with mobility issues was just like Dillinger robbing banks, it's where the wealth of the mobility problems are. For Patience it was a dream come true.

For the most part everyone liked Patience, and in some cases a few people simply adored her. The reasons the alpha females in high school despised her, which was because she got more than her share of attention and admiration without even trying, did not bother older adults, they don't get jealous in that way. But there were a few nurses who expressed similar concerns to Ellen's about Patience's classes and her lack of formal training. And it was those few that Ellen smoked out over the first few weeks that she was going to enlist in her plot to get rid of Patience Passion.

Six weeks after Ellen began her job ay Mystic Manor she received a call from Violetta Andropov. After six months of inpatient therapy at Mystic Manor after her stroke the year before Ellen arrived, it was clear that Violetta had not been making any more progress in regaining the use of her arm so it was determined that she would return to her home in Mystic for further rehabilitation.

Despite leaving the hospital months before, Violetta still talked to the friends that she met at Mystic Manor and occasionally would return to visit as it was less than a mile from her home. Violetta had learned from her friends that Ellen had taken over for Dr. Jones and would be introducing some new advanced rehabilitation techniques. Despite her poor prognosis, Violetta was determined to regain the use of her left arm so she could get back to her professional career. She had called Ellen to request that Ellen stop by her home for a visit to talk to her about some of her new therapy ideas and whether they might help her regain her movement and career.

Home visits were not something that Ellen had planning on as part of her position, but Violetta was a rather famous person, and ran in some of the same wealthy circles that Ellen did. She knew that if she could help Violetta resume her career, it would be a story that would make the New York Times and other National newspapers, let alone the medical trade journals. So Ellen agreed to stop by the next day to talk to Violetta and assess her prognosis personally.

The next day arrived and Ellen drove off to her appointment at Violetta's house and as she was driving up the long driveway she passed Patience's car coming out of the driveway. At first this surprised her, but then she remembered that Patience taught Yoga to a number of people in their homes, and Violetta certainly could have been one.

As Ellen approached the door, Violetta, who had seen her coming up the driveway, was there to meet her. Violetta spoke first in her very thick Russian accent, "it is so nice to meet you Ellen Chandler. You know I have had the pleasure of meeting your mother and father, and your brother, in Los Angeles," she said as she gestured for her to come into the parlor sitting area. Despite Violetta's thick Russian accent, Ellen was able to discern when they spoke on the phone the day before that Violetta's speech was slightly impaired, likely also a result of the stroke. But as she watched Violetta walk, Ellen noticed that Violetta's gait was very impaired, her left leg clumsily went through each cycle of the walking motion, and the reason Ellen was there, Violetta's left arm, Ellen saw that it hung down and swung in the typical way for a stroke victim.

They sat down in Violetta's parlor and her nurses aide was dispatched to get some coffee. Ellen replied, "yes my parents told me all about those fancy parties in Los Angeles back in the 1980's. Those were crazy times I hear. Of course I was off in college and med school so 1980's partying was not really on my agenda."

"As it should be for a young woman trying to establish herself." Violetta snuck in. "Although I seem to remember your brother had a healthy appetite for those times."

"I think he had a healthy appetite for the young ladies," Ellen joked.

"And the older ones too," Violetta said as she winked.

"Oh Violetta that is too much information for our first meeting," and they both laughed. "As you can imagine I am so happy to meet you. My parents have spoken about your friendship over the years. But something tells me this is not just a social call. What can I do for you?"

"Ellen, you are being coy, you know exactly why I wanted you to come here. You know exactly what I want, correction, what I will get."

"Violetta you have some rather severe damage to your left side. Watching you walk right before this I can see the impact on your leg and arm. Nerve damage like that does not just go away with exercise, or Yoga." Those last two words were said with disdain and were clearly referencing the fact that she had seen Patience leaving as she pulled in.

"Don't detract from Yoga Dr. Chandler; it has helped me tremendously in getting back the sensation in my affected extremities. And as to Patience, she is a complete dear, and has helped me more than any of those pompous doctors over at the Manor. She is a national treasure," from her comment, it was clear that Violetta was fond of Patience and Ellen was not about to pick a fight on that topic.

"Me knock Yoga? I am from Los Angeles, we made Yoga popular," Ellen said with a chuckle in her voice. "Actually, I was the one who brought Yoga instructors into Cedar Sinai to help with movement and stretching. The older doctors thought I was crazy, but slowly and surely they came around. I just insisted that the Yoga instructors had formal training in a certain type of Yoga and weren't just making it up," Ellen said as another subtle knock against Patience.

"Violetta I am going to examine you, is that okay?" Ellen asked and stood up and approached Violetta. She stood about two feet in front of her, leaned forward and grabbed both of Violetta's hands in hers. She pulled them forward toward her so they were nearly straight out and horizontal to the floor. "I am going to let go of your hands and I want you to hold them straight for three seconds and then slowly bring your arms down to their sides." When Ellen let go of her hands, Violetta's right arm stayed up but her left arm almost immediately dropped down, and Violetta grimaced as if she was in pain.

Ellen took out a paper clip from her pocket, an old doctor trick for probing the skin for numbness. "I am going to lightly poke you with this paper clip, I want to see if you are numb anywhere. Please let me know if you can feel the paper clip. Ellen poked different places of her right arm and Violetta immediately complained of the sharp pokes on her skin, "are you trying to paralyze my other arm too, Ellen Chandler?" Ellen moved to Violetta's left arm and using the same pressure of poking began on Violetta's upper arm, working her way down the arm. Some of the nerve traces in her arm were sensitive, some were not. It was clear that there was damage to certain neural pathways that worked their way down Violetta's arm, but others seemed to be fine.

This confirmed Ellen's original thought, Violetta's prognosis was not very good. After almost a year, any further recovery would be minimal.

But Ellen also knew that Violetta was determined to regain her strength in her arm and that was a positive so she decided that continued therapy would not hurt for now, even though the prognosis was not good for a recovery.

Turning professional in her demeanor, "Violetta, I am going to suggest a home physical therapy regimen for you. I think we should send a physical therapist to your house every day for one hour therapy sessions and then I will drop by myself once a week to check in and see how you are progressing. Does that work for you?"

Eagerly looking for any sign of positive news, Violetta asked "Does this mean you think there is some hope for this aging prodigy?"

"To be honest Violetta, I am not sure, improvements this long after a stroke are not usually that profound, but we have developed some new techniques to re-stimulate nerves, so there certainly is a possibility or I would not even try. I'd like to start the program on Monday, and then I will come visit on Fridays. "

"Okay Doctor Chandler, I was hoping for some more encouragement about my prospects, but I'm not naïve, I know the chances of a full recovery are slight. So Monday it is. Who can I expect to show up at my door?"

"I am not sure yet, I'll talk to the physical therapy staff and look at their schedules, is there anyone in particular that you have worked with that you like?"

"Besides Patience you mean?"

"Yes Violetta, besides Patience, she is not a licensed physical therapist. But that reminds me, I'll need to know what she is doing with you. The physical therapy program I plan on using will push you pretty hard and shouldn't be combined with any other exercise or stretching program that puts any exertion on your nervous system."

"You'll just have to come and see what my sweet Patience does with me, you might learn something," Violetta said with an attempt at a wink, knowing that was going to get a rise out of Ellen.

"I've seen it all Violetta but you never know, maybe she's onto something. She certainly has developed quite a following."

"She's one of the most spiritually gifted people I know, and I have been around the world numerous times and met many people who claim to be spiritually gifted, a few popes included."

"Yes you have, yes you have Violetta. And with that I must bid you adieu, Violetta. Time for me to get back to the hospital and make my rounds."

"Of course Doctor, let me walk you to the door," Violetta said as she took Ellen by the arm and headed back to the door Ellen had entered. "As to other therapists I worked with at the Manor, I remember Bridgette very fondly, she and I seemed to work well together. Maybe she can come work with me here"

"Well good, that's a start, let me talk to the staff and see about Bridgette." Ellen said as they arrived at the door and said their polite goodbyes.

As Ellen walked back to her car and drove back to Mystic Manor, she was thinking about Violetta's comment about Patience being the most spiritually gifted person she knew. Coming from most people, Ellen would have simply ignored it, but not coming from Violetta Andropov. Her stature in the music world took her all around the world and during those travels Violetta had most likely met some of the most prominent thinkers in the world, including religious scholars from the East and the West. She met at least one Pope and a whole host of Bishops, and maybe even the Dalai Llama and Desmond Tutu.

There was something to Patience Passion that Ellen was more and more intrigued by, even a little challenged by, and she was going to get to the bottom of it.

CHAPTER 8

Charles Mason Sr.

Meanwhile Henry was true to his promise to Charles Sr to come visit once per week. Of course he always made sure the visits fell on a Tuesday or Thursday to ensure that Patience would be there so they could resume their talks down at the pond.

On the second visit, as Charles Sr had suggested during their first visit, they talked all about Henry's career, his position at UCLA, what got him excited professionally, and what books he was teaching. Eventually they came to the topic of the book that Henry was trying to write.

"So tell me your idea for this book that you writing, Henry." Charles Sr asked.

"Well Sir, respectfully, I have not told anyone about it, not Charles Jr, nor even Ellen." Henry responded trying not to appear to be difficult.

Charles Sr. interrupted Henry, "Henry if you are worried about me stealing your idea and writing my own book, while it may appear I have too much time on my hands here, I can assure you that is not the case. There will be no books from Charles Mason Sr. coming anytime soon."

"It's actually not that Sir, it has to do with the fact that I, admittedly, have a bit of an irrational fear. I have been suffering from writers block for a long time and it has taken me some effort to start writing this book. I am using any and all motivation I can muster to see it through to the end and get it written and published. One of my main motivations is to convince myself that the plot is such a great story, that it absolutely needs to be shared with the world, and the only way that can happen is if I publish the book. So my irrational fear is if I start telling people about the plot now, I won't need to finish it anymore because the story will be out there without ever having to publish it."

"Hogwash, Henry," Charles Sr., saw right through Henry's silly excuse.

"Well it may be hogwash, but it is my hogwash, and I told you it was an irrational fear, but I am sticking to it until something better, or more accurate, or useful, comes along for me to use to get this damn thing to the publishers," Henry said with a smirk.

"Okay Henry. I am not an artist, but I have known quite a few, your mother was a superb artist, God rest her soul. I have always wondered what motivated artists to do what they do. I think it starts with the fact that they are willing to expose their souls. In some medium it doesn't even take that much artistic talent, most modern artists I would consider talentless in the traditional artistic sense. So the talent is in being able to communicate with the audience, beyond being willing to expose oneself, what all great artists share is an ability to expose themselves to others in a way that gives the receiver the sense of being understood. Art has to reach the audience on the spiritual or sensual level, the eyes and ears are just the medium that translates the message to the psyche where emotional reactions originate." Charles Sr. was getting uncharacteristically spiritual.

"Mr. Mason, all those years of having Lois Passion growing your vegetables might be affecting you, I have never heard you mention the topic of spirituality outside of Sunday morning at St. Marks." Henry said somewhat sarcastically.

"As you age Henry, and get closer to death's door, your spirituality starts to come home to roost. It's what all of us old fogies think about as we contemplate our imminent demise," Charles Sr. responded with a bit of sarcasm of his own. "And on the topic of Lois Passion, she has taught this old codger quite a bit about the world we live in. I have her to thank for much more than just vegetables, beautiful gardens, and fresh flowers every week," as Charles Sr. pointed to the vases of flowers all over his suite.

"Lois comes to visit you every week also?" Henry inquired.

"Yes Henry, Lois has been an extraordinary friend to me over the years, and especially since Emma passed on." Charles Sr. responded, then realizing he might have let on a little too much, quickly tried to change the subject. "You know Patience teaches Yoga here every week, and gives me a private class. I'm a modern man Henry. Who would ever have thought that

Charles Mason would be taking Yoga." And Charles Sr. laughed, not remembering that they had discussed this on the first visit.

"Well Sir I would love to someday hear the story of how it came to be that Lois Passion ended up living on the Mason estate, knowing Lois, I am sure it is one heck of a story." Henry was risking being a little too forward with Mr. Mason.

"Well Henry, it may be an exciting story, but I am afraid that's a story you will have to get out of Lois, not me. All I can say is that my dear Emma and Lois became friends and shortly afterwards Emma announced that Lois would be moving into the gardener's cottage and would be tending to our gardens. And once Emma Mason had her mind set to something, it was beyond me to change it. So one day there she was, and our lives were changed forever. For the better I might add. And then came Patience." At the mention of Patience, Charles Sr. faded off into a memory, and began to smile.

After a few minutes of silence Henry decided it was time to end today's get together. "Well Sir, you have managed to keep me once again longer than I had planned. Same time next week I assume? What will our topic be next week?"

"I'll let you choose, Henry." Charles Sr. responded.

"Yes Sir I will be sure to come back with a good one." And with that Henry excused himself with just enough time to make it to the end of Patience's Yoga class.

Henry headed down the stairs and into the main wing of the building and walked into the main hallway where Patience's class was being held just as Patience's class was ending. As Henry entered the room he saw Patience in the corner of the room and walked over to her and whispered so no one else could hear, "can you meet at the duck pond again?"

"Sure Henry, give me about fifteen minutes." Patience whispered back.

Henry immediately turned around and headed out of the room and down the hallway to go outside. Patience followed a few minutes later. Once again Henry was at the pond sitting on the same bench by the time Patience made it down to the pond. Once again, Henry got up to watch Patience float down the path. Henry remembered that Patience used to take dance lessons when they were teenagers and as she approached that was what he started with.

"You walk like a dancer, like you are floating on air, every move so natural yet so practiced. Did you continue taking dancing lessons after I left?"

"Yes I did, and that's an interesting and long story, I hope you have more time today than last week," Patience smiled that cute but devilish smile and she chided Henry's rushed exit after their first meeting the week before.

"Well not really. But let's see how far we get. I have twenty years of your life to catch up with, and I have a feeling that's going to take months."

"Yes Henry it could take years with ten minute get togethers under the watchful eye of Ellen Chandler. We are going to have to figure out somewhere to meet that allows us more time than ten minutes if you are going to get through my life story."

"You are right, let me think about some place that won't raise suspicions if someone happens to see us talking. Ellen is pretty jealous and unforgiving, so we'll need to be careful."

"I am not sure I like that answer Henry. I don't want to sneak around like a criminal just to talk to an old friend. You really need to tell Ellen that we are going to get together to meet, to catch up. You should tell her where and when, so there is no suspicion that this is some type of illicit meeting behind her back."

"You are right. I am putting you in an awkward position. I'll tell her tonight. We have nothing to hide." Henry said this half knowing that Ellen was never going to allow Henry to meet with Patience in any public way, so deep down he knew these meetings, if they were going to happen, would have to continue to be held secretly.

"Thank you. To continue with the lifestyles of the odd and infamous," Patience continued "after you went to college I kind of stopped going to school."

"What do you mean you kind of stopped going to school?" Henry was confused.

"I mean I kind of stopped going to school. I stopped going to classes. I had no interest in what they were teaching. I had done a bunch of research on what interested me and none of it was taught at Stonington High School. So I found out that I could be home schooled by Lois."

"Doesn't the State have some set of minimum requirements to get a high school diploma, like English and Math?" Henry seemed even more confused.

"Yes, but home schooling is perfectly legal. So Lois taught the basics to get me through, but allowed me to spend the majority of my time excelling in what I was really interested in. And that was dance."

"Lois found Madame Cheville, who was formerly trained in France to teach me to dance. Madame Cheville was totally on board with the non-traditional education concept, she thought English and Math were completely unnecessary skills in the real world. To her, the free expression of modern dance was the only essential skill to be taught to kids. I became her protégé. She taught me everything she knew."

"And you learned to float like a butterfly."

"And any other insect or bird you might request," Patience responded with a smile. "Guess this one." With that Patience started to dance like she just left the set of Swan Lake.

"That's easy, Swan Lake." Henry responded.

"You are good, Mr. Moore. But that was a softball. Anyway, I continued on with Madame Cheville for five to six years. At one point I really thought I was going to have a career in modern dance."

"Well I guess Yoga is pretty close." Henry said, trying to relate to a subject he knew nearly nothing about.

"Well, smarty pants, yes actually it is. The first person to start teaching Yoga in the area, and that was over twenty years ago when Yoga was still a novelty, was a woman named Heather Graham."

"Any relation to the actress Heather Graham?" Henry asked still trying to find something in this topic he could relate to.

"No I don't think so, but I see how your mind works." Patience responded with a bit of sarcasm. "Relate the topic to a pretty girl you know, or at least saw on TV. Very enlightened of you Mr. Moore." Patience said with a big smile.

"Okay, guilty as charged. So continue with your story."

"So I started learning Yoga because of how it strengthens the body with the hopes of improving my dancing. After a few years of overlap I found I enjoyed the Yoga more than the dancing, and slowly my dancing faded to a few times per week, then a few times per month. Instead I found myself going to Yoga classes every day, and..."

"Let me guess, you became the teachers protégé." Henry chimed in.

"Well, yes. I know you are making fun of me, but it's true, I was Heather's most dedicated student. It wasn't that difficult, I was going there every day. After a few months she asked me to start filling in for her as the teacher of a class here and there, and then she asked me to lead my own classes, and it kind of built over time. I became too busy with Yoga to dance every day, so I eventually stopped dancing. One day Heather announced that she was moving to California with her husband, and that she would be expecting me to take over her Yoga studio so the students could continue on."

"So what happened to the studio?" Henry asked.

Patience started with a sigh, "I learned a lot about myself, what I am good at, what I am not good at, and one thing I realized is that running a Yoga studio is a real business. It means you have to get serious about it and treat it like a business. I realized that being forced to look at something I was passionate about, to have to look at it as a business, it just took the passion right out of it, it reduced it to a job. It meant finding other instructors, and dealing with their issues, their not showing up on time or at all, having to negotiate class rates, payments to the other instructors, all the money part of it to me was just something I didn't want to think of. So after a few months I realized I was miserable and I handed it to one of the other instructors who was more interested in running a business than I was."

Henry, trying to follow, asked, "So you just walked away?"

"Well sort of. I went back to being an instructor and let Angela take over the studio. It's not that glamorous of a business Henry. People don't pay a lot for Yoga lessons, and you have the constant worry of paying the rent and heat whether anyone shows up or not, the constant marketing to get new customers. The worst was feeling obligated to keep up with the new Yoga styles that people see on TV or read about in diet magazines."

"I can imagine," Henry finally had something to share on the topic. "My friend Jeff dragged me to my first Yoga class a few years ago in LA. When he was telling me about it he mentioned something about it being hot Yoga which meant absolutely nothing to me, so I paid no attention. When I walked into the studio with my new Yoga mat, the previous class had just ended, and the room must have been something like 90°. I just figured the body heat from the previous class made it real hot. So as we were getting prepared for our class, I asked the instructor if we could open a window or turn on the AC. She just laughed. Then I noticed she started turning on all these portable ceramic heaters in the room, and I looked at Jeff and asked him what the hell were they doing making it even hotter when it was already almost unbearably hot. He looked at me and said, "I told you it was hot Yoga." I think I said something like "What the hell is hot Yoga?" a bit too loud and everyone in the studio started laughing. Jeff said, "Dude, it's Yoga and its hot. It's not a complicated concept. The heat relaxes your muscles so you can stretch more." I remember looking at him and feeling so uncomfortable already from the heat, and saying that I would meet him outside afterwards, I got up, grabbed my mat, walked out and went for a walk down the 3rd street promenade instead. And now you know the full extent of my experience with Yoga."

"That's a really funny story, and that's exactly what I mean. Yoga has been around for a few thousand years, it has been perfected over centuries, it's somewhat comical to think within a decade or two in the Western world it has already been turned into the next weight loss fad. So, even in your admitted limited understanding, you do understand where I was coming from."

Henry, though understanding he was being made fun of a bit, agreed, "Yes even with my limited understanding, I do get it."

"Sorry, I don't mean to make fun of you. But this is my life and I believe in Yoga as it was discovered and should be taught. Yoga is an ancient spiritual process that is one aspect of the path toward enlightenment. It is a spiritual cleansing process. I was not interested in teaching hot Yoga, or Baptiste Yoga, or any other fad that will be gone faster than it arrived. So I gave the studio to Angela, told her I would continue to teach my traditional Yoga, and that was the end of my life as a Yoga Studio owner. You know me Henry, I have never been good at conformity. I need to do things my way, the way I think it should be done."

"I wouldn't expect it any other way, Patience." Henry said looking at his watch.

"Is it time for you to run off again?" Patience asked as she noticed Henry looking at his watch.

"Yes it is, time to step back into the real world."

With that Henry and Patience gave each other a hug said their goodbyes and Henry walked back up the path to the hospital.

Just like that, Ellen, Henry and Patience established weekly routines. Ellen got more and more comfortable in her new job taking charge of more aspects of the hospital therapy programs and remembered to visit Violetta every Friday to check on her progress. Henry would work in his new backhouse studio writing his book during the week, and on Tuesday would visit Charles Sr. for their chat, and then meet Patience for their weekly rendezvous down at the duck pond.

Ellen and Henry's relationship was uncharacteristically civil for the weeks throughout the summer and into the early fall. They each settled into their routines, did not see each other during the day, would have dinner together at night at the Sullivan McCoy house, and would go over their respective days over dinner.

While Ellen and Henry slept in the same bed every night, they were one of those married couples that had given up on the thought of having frequent sex. For Ellen, sex had always been more about power and control than love and pleasure. For Henry, that made sex with Ellen just another opportunity to be manipulated and criticized.

Something else was in play also and I have always wondered if some professor of psychology has ever done a study to prove a theory I have had about wealthy folks and procreation. It seems that with each successive generation in wealthy families, the drive to have children, the essence of the sex drive, seems to dissipate somewhat. Over a few generations after the first wealth was created, almost all wealthy families simply die out due to the last generation not producing heirs.

This idea first hit me when I went to visit my Godmother Lillian in Florida when I was a teenager. I loved my Godmother, she was originally from Mexico, and had met my parents on a cruise that my parents went on before I was born, and my mother was so enamored with Lillian that when I arrived a few years later, she asked Lillian to be my Godmother. I can see why my mother loved her so much, she was funny, and crazy and was quite well off by American standards at the time.

Upon my arrival for my visit with Lillian, I got to meet her new husband Luis, who was a very nice and unassuming man. It was revealed that despite also being Mexican, Luis had actually been born in the United States, but had lived in Mexico nearly his entire life. When I asked him to share the story as to how he ended up moving to Mexico as a boy, I was stunned at the story he told.

He had been born in San Francisco and his maternal grandmother was the last surviving member of the famous Sutter family to be born a Sutter. This was the same Sutter family that Sutter Street in San Francisco was named after, the family that built Sutter's Fort, one of the first western settlements in the central valley of California, which eventually became the city of Sacramento, and of course built Sutter's Mill, the famous location where gold was first discovered in California and where the Gold Rush of 1849 officially began.

John Sutter Sr, made his fortune not in gold, but by gaining a monopoly on the sale of the mining equipment to the 300,000 optimists that came to California during the Gold Rush. Part of Sutter's wealth went to purchase a large portion of land in central Mexico on the western coast, which eventually became Acapulco.

Sutter's son, John Jr. was born with poor health and was sent to live in Acapulco on the Sutter estate to convalesce. While there he married a Mexican woman, had a few children, and was appointed US Consul to Mexico by President US Grant.

While John Jr. remained in Acapulco most of his life, a few of his children made their way back to San Francisco to enjoy the spoils of the family's wealth in what was becoming one of the great cities in America. Luis was a descendent of one of John Jr.'s children. Luis' grandmother, the last person to be born with the Sutter name, married and had one child, a daughter, who married a young dashing man. When the depression hit America, the young couple decided to try their luck in Mexico and settled in Mexico City and took Luis, their only child with them. Luis never had any children of his own.

This is what struck me as so odd. People from all over the world have come to America for the promise of great wealth. A very few have been lucky to achieve that dream and amass a fortune that should last for generation after generation. You would think the stature and stamina of a fabulous wealthy family would endure for generation after generation.

My first thought when I heard Luis' story was to think it was ironic that someone from Mexico was a hell of a lot more American than I was. But what struck me as very odd, was that a family as prominent as the Sutters of California could somehow have their lineage die out in one man named Luis from Mexico City. Luis eventually passed away childless, and when he did, so did the last descendent of the famous and once fabulously wealthy Sutter family of California.

In thinking about it, that seems to be the fate of many of America's great and storied wealthy families. Great lineages ended when the last heir dies childless as an only child, often in obscurity.

This seems to likely be the fate of the Chandlers of California. Neither Ellen nor her brother have any children. We know it's too late for Ellen, and her brother is a drunk who is more interested in booze and chasing the next hottest movie star than generating heirs.

It might be as simple as selfishness in not wanting the burden of raising children impinging on the freedoms that their wealth has allowed them to enjoy, but I think it is more subtle and instinctual than that. I think that the drive to procreate comes from an innate survival instinct. In centuries past, having children provided the likelihood of being cared for in old age. Having children meant more workers for the family farm and more ways to generate an income for the family. But having inherited a family fortune guarantees both those results without having to procreate. So the instinct to procreate slowly fades away in the genes of each successive generation until the lineage stops, ironically usually about the same time that the family money runs out.

So with Ellen and Henry, I suppose that's what was going on in their sex life. Ellen's sexual instinct as procreation had been bred out of her as the offspring of a wealthy family. She could very much do without it, but saw the opportunity to use sex as a way to control and manipulate Henry.

While Henry certainly had a strong sex drive, he had enough self-respect to not open himself up to the manipulation that always resulted. He was not interested in enduring the weirdness inherent in having sex with Ellen. She would be merciless in her complaints about Henry's sexual prowess, such as not lasting long enough to bring her to orgasm. But this was a rouse, Ellen didn't have orgasms, nor did she really care to. It was just a way to reinforce the negative dynamic in the relationship.

This was the dynamic that Henry and Ellen brought to Connecticut. Their sex life was non-existent, Ellen didn't care, and Henry told himself he didn't care either. But deep down that was not the case for Henry. Deep down he did care, deep down he wanted to have a normal sex life and he needed to prove that whatever issues he had, it was due to the situation he was in. He thought that, he felt it, but he could not prove it without actually starting a sexual relationship with another woman, an action that had the potential to end his life as he knew it, his marriage, his career, his reputation and his financial situation.

But it was more than that, Henry was interested in more than just what sex would be like if he was in a loving relationship, Henry wanted to know what true love itself felt like. We all desperately want to experience what it is like to wake up next to someone, look over, and fall in love all over again, every morning. Henry was no different, he wanted to know what it was like to ache every morning when he left the house to go to work. He wanted to do what his father had done with his mother, which was to call her every day at lunch to tell her how much he loved her.

Privately Henry Moore had spent an inordinate amount of his time over the past twenty years wondering what that would be like. He wondered what he would be like if he was in a normal loving relationship. When living in that headspace, you develop a healthy imagination, an imagination that can conceive of an entire relationship, the days, the nights, the eating, sleeping, all of it, an imaginary world conceived as an escape from the tortuous relationship you are currently in.

Every woman you meet you wonder "could this be the one? Could this be my soul mate?" You start with all the girls you dated in school, and you go through them one by one, you ask yourself "why didn't I get serious with her? Look at her now, she's so happy, her husband is so happy, that could have been me."

Then you expand to those you didn't date but could have. You ask yourself "why didn't I ask her out? She was obviously such a nice person, what was I thinking?" Then you expand to those that you have met since being stuck in a crappy marriage. Women at work, new friends, each and every women gets the once over and begs the question "is this the one?" But it doesn't even stop there. Next it moves to complete strangers, "that woman across the aisle on the train, the way she holds her newspaper, that's exactly how I hold mine! We could be perfect for each other." Of course that thinking is a type of insanity, fantasy taken to an unhealthy level. But it shows how desperate some people can be when they find themselves in a relationship with a complete lack of the bond of love and trust that is essential to existence.

But after the fantasy comes the guilt. You eventually realize that you spend more time thinking about not being in the relationship than being in it. You realize that these thoughts of other women are actually quite negative; they are contrary to the Christian belief system. And a lifetime of negativity cannot be healthy physically or spiritually. At times Henry even thought he would end up going to hell for having harbored for so many years such negative un-Christian thoughts as leaving his wife for another woman. But then he would convince himself that any loving God would not pass judgment on someone for exiting a spiritually unhealthy relationship and entering one that was based on absolute love, compassion and understanding.

Over the years, as Henry's mind wandered and meandered through this thought process, and he analyzed what was probably hundreds of women for compatibility, eventually it always came back to one thought: Patience. It always came back to the one person that always made Henry's heart just sink. Just thinking about Patience made Henry feel like he was home. He knew that he belonged with Patience, she was his soul mate, they didn't need to even talk, they could look into each other's eyes and have an entire conversation.

This was why Henry knew that the weekly meetings with Patience were incredibly ill-advised. Week after week, as Henry and Patience met and got to know each other all over again, he was slowly and intractably falling deeply in love with her.

As the fall progressed and the New England weather did what it will do, which is to get colder and colder, Henry realized that he would need to move their weekly rendezvous to a warmer place. He thought about the places where they could meet, but there was no place on the grounds of the hospital where he could be alone with Patience where there were not hospital staff walking around, staff that reported to the one person who could not find out what Henry was up to.

And then one day it dawned on Henry, and he realized how stupid he was for not thinking about it right away, the tunnels in the basement of the hospital. He and Charles Jr used to play in them and had explored every nook and cranny of them. He knew exactly a place in the tunnels where they could go where no one would know or see. So after one of his Duck Pond rendezvous with Patience, Henry went back to the hospital and went down to the basement. It took a few tries and wrong turns to remember exactly how to get there, some because it had been thirty years, and some because over the years they had added doorways and hallways that did not exist back then.

He finally made his way around the basement to the tunnel entrance in the east wing of the hospital. Of course, the door was locked. Henry sat for a few minutes disappointed and then he had a thought, it was a crazy thought, but he would have to at least try it. Charles Jr and he had always hidden a key to this door in a crevice that they had created by chiseling out enough mortar between two bricks. He reached over to the bricks and saw that the bricks and crevice had been painted over where the key used to hide. At some point they had painted the entire basement, floors and walls, including painting over the hiding place. At first Henry was disappointed, but he decided to explore a little more. He took out his car keys and started to tap the paint where the crevice was with one of the keys, and realized that the paint was flexing when he pushed on it. There was obviously a hollow behind the paint. He used the key to scrape away the paint, and he turned on his key light to look inside the crevice. And there it was. The key. Henry sat down against the wall and laughed. After a few minutes of contemplation, he got back up and pried the key to the basement door out of the crevice with his car key, and it fell into his hand.

He took a deep breath before taking the next step. He was actually a little nervous. These tunnels were fun to play in but they were scary. Really scary. A great horror movie plot could be written using the tunnels, either as the antagonist themselves, like the hotel in the Shining, or as the hiding place for the evil that lurks.

He slid the key into the keyhole and with a little bit of wiggling back and forth, managed to get the key all the way into the keyhole and started to turn the key and to Henry's surprise the lock turned. He slowly opened the door. One can only imagine the musky smell that comes out of a dark locked basement that has not seen the light of day or any airflow for what was likely twenty years. It was dank to say the least.

He reached in to the left where the light switch always was, and groped for the switch in the dark, found it, and flipped the switch not expecting anything to happen. Thank God for General Electric. A light came on. Not just one light, but the entire tunnel lit up all the way to the end. Only one of the seven or eight bulbs that lit up the tunnel didn't come on. He laughed again. He thought to himself "how is it possible that the light bulbs in my house can't seem to last for two to three months, but these are still working after twenty years?"

His eyes slowly got used to the scene in front of him. While he was told in his first visit to the hospital since returning, that some of the tunnels had been used for storage, for the most part this tunnel was completely empty. There were a few empty grey metal shelving units that had once held stocks of canned goods for the months of living during the eventual nuclear war, and a few old metal chairs. But other than that this tunnel was pretty much the way that he remembered it the last time he was in it.

The question was, while this was fun to explore and reminisce on times with Charles Jr., was this really a place that he and Patience could meet secretly, and be comfortable to sit and talk for a half hour or more?

Henry would have to contemplate that idea. It's not like he could order a couch to be delivered to the basement of Mystic Manor, someone would notice that. But it was possible he could sneak a couple of card table chairs downstairs from a common room and no one would question why he was entering the stairwell with two chairs, he could be going upstairs with them as easily as downstairs.

So Henry decided that's what he would do. He would look for an opportunity to grab two card table chairs from the common room and bring them down to the basement at some point before next Tuesday's rendezvous. At some point he would have to broach this with Patience. It was certainly not as pretty as the Duck Pond, but it was at least thirty degrees warmer.

Meanwhile, as the fall progressed, Ellen's weekly trips to observe Violetta's progress were reinforcing what she first thought: Violetta was not making any progress whatsoever, nor was she going to. Her left arm was simply never again going to be able to play the bass notes of a piano Mozart concerto. At the end of September, Ellen decided to deliver Violetta the bad news. Further therapy was a waste of time and resources.

Ellen showed up at her normal time, noon on Friday. Violetta always had her maid make a nice lunch of little finger sandwiches and tea for Ellen and her to eat while the talked each week. After sitting down and putting some sugar in her tea, Ellen started, "Violetta, remember when we started this I told you not to get your hopes up."

Violetta looked up at Ellen and interrupted her. "Dr. Chandler, do not say another word. You are going to tell me that I have made no progress; that my chances of recovery are terrible, and I should give up this silly dream of playing piano again. Yes I see it in your eyes. You are giving me the look that I am correct. This is no surprise to me. You see, I knew what you were going to tell me today before you even showed up. But let me make this very clear Dr. Chandler, I don't want to hear it, I don't want to hear your news, so please keep your breath," Violetta's thick Russian accent was coming through stronger and stronger as she got more emotional and animated, mixing her metaphors.

"This dream I have is more than about playing piano, it is about my life style. I had a lifestyle Ellen Chandler, I traveled the world. I have friends who live on every continent. That was my lifestyle since I was in my early twenties. I am older but I am not old enough to be put out to pasture like some old mare. I still have a few good races in me."

"So take Bridgette back, don't send her here anymore. And please don't speak unless you are telling me that there is hope. Hope. Hope is the one thing that keeps me human. Without hope we become mindless creatures, acting on impulse like a tiger in the Siberian desert. Hope is the only thing I have to live for Ellen Chandler, and my hope is my dream of playing again. So I would prefer to live with my hope intact. My dream is my future. Let me have my dream, let me have my future. Please, please, let me keep my hope." And with that Violetta did something she does not do very often, she broke down in tears.

Ellen sat quiet for a while and realized that she did not need to say anything more. Violetta was well aware of her situation, and Ellen did not need to reinforce that, she knew everything there was to know already.

Ellen finally spoke, "Violetta, I am sorry. If anyone deserves a miracle, it is you. Would you mind if I continued to come by once a month on Friday at the same time? I have begun to enjoy having our tea and sandwiches, they have become a habit for me that I look forward to all week."

"Of course my dear, you are always welcome in my home. But we will talk about other things than my health. Can you see to that?"

"Yes Violetta, we will talk about anything you want except your health."

With that Ellen announced that she needed to get back to the hospital. She let herself out the side door and when she got back to the hospital sent an email to Bridgette that she would no longer need to go to Violetta's house for therapy.

The following Tuesday Henry met Patience before her class to talk to her about the change in plans, he described the basement and the rendezvous spot, but he could tell she was uncomfortable about it. "Okay, I know you well enough to know when there is something wrong," Henry spoke with a tinge of uneasiness.

"It's more than just this new meeting place Henry, this whole thing is just getting too weird. You are married, your wife works here, what are we doing? Don't get me wrong, I love reconnecting with you, but this whole secret meeting thing is starting to feel a bit underhanded. My work, everything I do is about healing people, about getting people closer to truth, it's what I teach my students every day. But we are not being honest, it goes against everything I stand for Henry. We're just two old friends talking, reconnecting. There is something innocent in that. I just have to insist that you tell Ellen we are meeting."

Henry knew immediately that Patience was right and he realized that he was leading this absolutely pure soul down a path that could jeopardize everything for her. His heart sank. "Oh my God, Patience, you're right. I have led you into some place you don't deserve, everything I love about you, your purity, the purity of your thought, I am taking you to a place that is going away from that. I am so sorry. You have to understand something, I have never stopped loving you."

"I have never stopped loving you either Henry," Patience whispered, "but there is the love of old friends and of two souls that are deeply connected in the world, and then there is the love that two married people have that includes a whole bunch of other things like trust and commitment. For better or worse you made a decision those many years ago, and it's not as easy as you might think to undo that. I love you Henry Moore, I have always loved you, and I always will, but we owe it to each other not to mess up such a beautiful thing with silly thoughts about scenarios that are not possible or likely, and worse are so hurtful and against everything I believe in and I think you believe in too." With that, one of Patience's students shuffled into the room and Henry and Patience knew the conversation would end right there.

Henry excused himself with a smile, saying "thanks for the info Patience, some day I will sit in on one of these classes," and walked out of the room. He was devastated at the obvious truth and deeply angry with himself. He knew Patience was absolutely right, as she always was when it came to understanding truth and decency. He had all of a sudden become very concerned with potential damage he had done to their relationship and what Patience thought of him for pushing headlong into a deepening relationship that of course had no place in going there with his current situation. He had come to face to face with the reality that had been looming for many years, the situation that he had entertained as fantasy for so many years and it hit him like a ton of bricks. He found a couch in a common area around the corner and sat down. He was numb.

Today Henry had met with Patience before his meeting with Charles Sr., so after a few minutes of sitting on the couch, he got up and slowly made his way up to Charles' suite as he had every Tuesday for the last few weeks. As Henry and Charles talked through many things over the last few weeks in their get-togethers, they started to run out of things to talk about, and their visits started to center around an ongoing game of Gin Rummy.

As Henry approached Charles suite, he was still consumed with thoughts of Patience, their relationship, where it was going, how he might have jeopardized it, along with any future together. He thought of Ellen and how he had to finally admit that he had been living a lie for the past many years. His time with Ellen was always filled with fear and anxiety, but he had made that his new normal, he had made his alternative reality his actual reality. But his time with Patience was tearing the cover off of that rouse. The normalcy and peace he felt in her presence was forcing him to come back to the real reality, and to put the screwed up relationship with Ellen back into its proper place, which was completely screwed up.

These thoughts were swirling around Henry's head as he knocked on Charles door expecting one of his aides to open it. As the door opened, Henry turned ashen white. Ellen opened the door. "Hey there H," which was a nickname that Ellen had given to Henry early on in their relationship at Harvard and she still used when she was in a good mood. "Wow you look like you've seen a ghost. You okay?"

"Hey sweetie, what a pleasant surprise, yeah I'm fine. You surprised me, I was expecting an old man to open the door."

"I heard that," Charles Sr. said from behind the door.

"Sorry sir," Henry responded to Charles Sr. through the door, which was still only partially opened.

"Well I'd probably be in shock if I opened a door expecting to see a beautiful young lady and instead got me, I'm not the looker I used to be."

Charles Sr. joked.

"Nonsense Charles, you are still quite a looker, if you were just a few years younger, you never know," Ellen joked with Charles in return and they all enjoyed a short laugh.

Henry asked, "Ellen, you want me to deal you in to a rousing game of Gin Rummy? But I have to warn you, Charles is kicking my butt."

"No that's quite alright, I wouldn't want to interrupt this little thing you two have going. I've got a few patients to check in on, but Henry, I am free in a little bit, I need you to stop by my office when you are done here." Ellen put too big of an emphasis on the word "my". Henry's mind immediately started wandering. What does she mean by "my"? Does she mean "as opposed to someone else's"? She's obviously referring to someone else's office. Does she mean Charles? or Patience? Does she know? Henry played it cool, and took the stance that she must be talking about Charles Sr. and responded, "yeah I guess I have been coming to see Charles for a while now and have not stopped by to see you for a few weeks, give me 40-45 minutes to see if I can finally win a game of Rummy from this card shark. See you in a few sweetie."

And with that Ellen excused herself leaving Henry and Charles in the living room together. Henry sat down in his usually spot and grabbed the deck of cards. "Okay sir, this time you better bring your A game." Henry had quickly recovered from the shock of seeing Ellen right when he was thoroughly consumed with thoughts of Patience and what to do with his future. But after a few minutes, a melancholy started to creep in. Henry was deep in thought and somewhat distracted from his game with Charles Sr. and after a few more minutes, Charles Sr. began to notice.

"Your mind elsewhere Henry?" Charles Sr. asked.

"Well I guess it is sir. Every week that goes by that I live in this new sabbatical lifestyle it makes me think more about my future and what I really want to be doing. I am really enjoying writing. I am really really enjoying not grading papers and dealing with students who are there to simply fulfill a requirement and not because they are that interested in what I actually have to say or teach them. God knows I am not doing it for the money. Thank God the Chandler thing allows me to continue." Henry continued as he performed a set of air quotes when he said the words "the

Chandler thing".

"Well yes, having wealth makes the choices of one's career a bit simpler, with a few more options." Charles responded. "I would guess you are not worried about putting food on the table."

"No sir we are not. At least that's one problem we have not faced."

"And what problems are you facing?" Charles asked taking the cue from Henry's comment and his emphasis on the word "one".

"Well sir, I'm not sure you want to hear all that. I think it would come across as the whining of an extremely lucky yet ungrateful man."

"Henry, marrying into a wealthy family is not as easy or as glamorous as it sounds. My father told me when I was young, long before he had made his fortune, "Son, if you marry someone for their money, you'll spend the rest of your life earning it."

Henry laughed, "Your father was a very wise man. And earn it I do, every day. Honestly, there is a realization that creeps up on you, that you are not really in control of any aspect of your life. "

"Well is anybody really in control of all aspects of their life?" Charles Sr. asked.

"I am not sure sir, I would hope someone has figured that out by now. But for me I am not sure I am in charge of any aspects of my life. I married into an enigma, it takes hold of you, entices you, seduces you, offers you a lifestyle most dream of. I voluntarily signed up for it when I married Ellen, I know that, but despite your father's wise counsel, no one ever really tells you what it's actually going to be like. You get lulled into complacency and you wake up one day and you are miserable and you don't know why. You feel silly because you have every material thing at your disposal so you don't feel you are entitled to complain. One by one you simply reshape yourself so you fit into the mold that the family demands of you.

"That's the realization. You are expected to act the part, look the part, and be grateful for all of it, but in the end you know you are not really a full time member of the cast in this play. You are a stand-in. You never really get the feeling of commitment because you know you can get the boot any day. At best you get a pat on the back, at worst a letter from the family lawyer reminding you of all the things you agreed to in your pre-nup. I guess I hoped that she would choose me over the family but in hindsight that was a bit ridiculous to think."

There was a moment of silence as Henry and Charles Sr. digested what Henry had just said. "I am sorry, was that too much information sir?"

"Nonsense Henry, I hope you can be honest with me, and I don't think you are ungrateful at all, sounds like you are experiencing what I would think most in your shoes experience. But you have to make a decision young man. This is not going to make this any easier on you, but I can tell you that the dilemma does not ease with time, it actually gets worse, as your options fade with age.

Charles continued, "I was accused recently by someone, I can't remember who, maybe it was you, maybe it was Charlie, anyway, someone, but I was accused of purposely bringing Ellen here so I could get you back to Mystic. Now to be honest, I would be lying if I said that was not some part of my motivation in convincing Ellen to come here and take this job. Your father was my best friend, and for better or worse, I do feel some weight of making sure your life is something he would want for you. Charlie had told me enough about your life over the years for me to know what you were going through. I could not help you while you were out there, I can help you here. You are back in my world where I can feel some sense of ability to watch and help you Henry."

Another silence pervaded the room. Charles continued changing his tone to a more upbeat one. "So have you seen Patience since being back in Mystic?"

If he only knew. "I have actually yes. Our Tuesday get-togethers coincide with Patience's Yoga class downstairs so I do get to see her almost every week. We have had some time to catch up and talk about what we've been doing over the past twenty years."

"That's wonderful. My Patience has turned out to be quite a lady, hasn't she?"

"Yes sir, she is still one of the most amazing people I know." Henry responded but Charles Sr. use of the word "my" before Patience caught Henry by surprise. He thought about commenting on it, but thought better of it. As Patience was raised on the Mason family estate without a father and Charles Sr. has known her his whole life, Henry felt it was possible that he feels the same way about Patience as he does about Henry, sort of like a father figure in absence of one being there. He might refer to Henry the same way, as 'my' Henry. That gave Henry some comfort, for him as well as for Patience.

Henry spoke next, "Speaking of which, I think I will go see Patience now, we always try and get together after her class for a few minutes to catch up."

"Henry, I don't want to be your conscious, but I think you told Ellen earlier you would stop by to see her after our visit" Charles Sr. reminded Henry.

"Sir you are absolutely right, I did, better not keep the good doctor waiting. Thank you for your kind words today sir, it is always nice to know that you are thinking of me and my welfare, someone has to, right?"

"Right you are son. We'll continue our Gin Rummy game next week."

And with that Henry headed down to Ellen's office. As he made his way he wondered why Ellen was so cheery when he saw her earlier. She hasn't called him "H" in a very long time. He got to her office and the door was open but Ellen was not there. He thought about leaving and going to catch Patience before she left, but he thought better of it. So he sat down in one of the old leather chairs that Dr. Jones had left behind and that Ellen kept in her office in the transition. He looked at the book collection and recognized some from Ellen's old office in Los Angeles. After about three minutes Henry could hear Ellen walking down the hallway, her gait was very distinctive and after twenty years of marriage he could tell her walk from others. She had that Chandler walk in the way her feet landed on the tiled hallway, it showed determination, confidence, and that sense of "listen to me, hear me walk". Ellen walked in and said, "Great, I was hoping you would hang out."

"Of course sweetie, I know you are always on time." Henry responded and Ellen closed the door and locked it. Henry showed a look of puzzlement on his face by that.

"Don't worry H, I just wanted some private time with you."

"Okay honey, I always look forward to private time with you. What do you want to talk about? " Henry asked.

"Actually I don't want to talk. I've been sitting in this office for a few months now and looking at that leather couch and there is one thing that keeps coming into my mind when I see it. I've been thinking about this for a while. Would you make love to me on it? And I mean right now?"

Henry was stunned. "Really? Ellen? If you want to have sex, we do sleep together every night, we could wait until we get home tonight."

"I know that H. But we've done that. I've been thinking about this for a while, I want you to fuck me on that couch right now. I have cleared the next hour, I want you to get naked, and strip my clothes off and have your way with me. Can you do that for me H? Still got it in you?"

Henry was speechless and didn't know what to think. "I don't know what to say? It's been quite a long time since we have actually made love sweetie, and I don't have any protection."

"Taken care of, I just came from the bathroom where I put my diaphragm in. It's a wonder it's still in one piece, but it looked fine. Any other excuses Mr. Harvard man? Can you figure this one out or do I have to give you instructions?"

"No I think I can remember how to do this." Ellen sat up on her desk and spread her legs. Henry paused for a second still completely confused and not prepared for this at all, but decided he needed to play along. What choice did he have? He walked over to Ellen on her desk and she pulled him into her and gave him a kiss, quite a passionate one. He started to unbutton Ellen's blouse. She smiled. He lifted her shirt over her head and she was down to her bra. He looked up and Ellen responded by grabbing Henry's turtleneck and bringing it over his head exposing his bare chest. She then stood up, unbuttoned her pants and they dropped to the floor. Henry, realizing the next move was his, removed her panties, and she sat back down on the desk. Ellen then removed her bra so she was now completely naked still sitting on her desk. Henry, despite still feeling unsure of what was going on, seeing Ellen naked on her desk was starting to get aroused. He kicked off his loafers and Ellen unbuttoned his pants and they dropped to the floor and then she removed his boxers and let them fall to floor. He was now down to just his socks.

Henry came back in between Ellen's spread legs and grabbed her buttocks bringing her toward him. By this time Henry was completely aroused and their privates touched. Ellen slid forward so she was barely on the desk and grabbed Henry's penis in her hand and slid it into her. Henry thought back to the last time they had been intimate. He had definitely not been inside Ellen since they had moved to Mystic. And he thought back to LA and realized they had not had sex since last Christmas eve. He picked her up and she wrapped her legs around his waist, making sure he did not fall out, and Henry carried Ellen over to the leather couch and laid her down without falling out of her. He was on top of her and they started passionately having sex on the couch that Ellen wanted to have sex on.

It had been a long time for Henry since he had had sex and from previous long dry spells that had happened frequently enough, he knew he was not going to last very long. So he pulled out of Ellen when he felt he was getting too close to orgasm and slid down her belly so his mouth was below her belly button. He started using his tongue to get Ellen more aroused. After a few minutes of this, it seemed from Ellen's moans that she was getting close to an orgasm, so Henry slid back up and put himself back in to Ellen, much more easily this time since they were both pretty wet with excitement. After another minute Henry thought he was going to explode and Ellen started moaning like she was about to have an orgasm and Henry finally let himself go, and they both screamed a passionate moan as they both climaxed at the same time. Henry continued to thrust into Ellen for another minute or so as she screamed "don't stop, don't stop" in between her moans.

Finally they stopped and just laid there with Henry still on top of Ellen. After another minute Henry rolled over onto the floor and gave out a big moan. He was full of emotion. He was dumbfounded, he was ecstatic as any man is who has sex for the first time in months, he was out of breath. Ellen just laughed. It started as a giggle, but turned into a full laugh. Henry joined in and they both laughed real hard in between gasps for breath.

And then there was a knock on the door. Henry jumped up and mouthed "Oh Shit!"

Ellen grinned and responded "that must be my 11:00," and then more loudly speaking in the direction of the door, "I'll be right there, please give me a minute."

When the voice from the other side of the door spoke again, Henry blanched and turned white for the second time that day. It was Patience. Ellen spoke to Henry "Jeez preppy, you look as white as a ghost for the second time today, you need to stop being so transparent."

Henry was in a state of shock. He was still assessing what had just occurred and therefore was somewhat distracted while Ellen was quickly putting her clothes back on. He was actually dumbfounded and thinking very hard. Why would Ellen ask him to have sex in her office when she knew she had an appointment with someone at the same time? Why would she invite Patience to her office, someone who she rarely spoke to? And then Henry had the epiphany. He felt like a fool. This had not been a romantic morning fling with her husband because she wanted to get laid on her couch. This was a set up. This was another one of Ellen's carefully calculated events. It was another manipulation and a sick one at that. Henry went from surprise to deep rage in a heartbeat. His face went from blanched to flushed just as quickly. And his heart sunk. Then Henry realized what was about to happen. Ellen was mostly fully dressed, but still somewhat disheveled, and heading for the door to open it. He was still in his boxers and socks when he realized what was about to happen, he had to get his clothes back on before she opened the door, but it was too late. He was still in his boxers and socks when Ellen opened the door to Patience.

Patience peered into the room and quickly assessed the scene. She saw Ellen, dressed but clearly still a little disheveled, and she saw Henry half dressed, no shoes, no shirt, pants around his ankles with a panicked look on his face.

Henry was heartbroken. He was speechless. Ellen had a huge grin on her face as she stood there watching Patience stare at Henry half dressed. She was completely basking in the awkwardness and painfulness of this situation for both Henry and Patience.

But Patience, who had understanding down to the core of her being was of course not shocked at all by this scene, and at that moment Henry once again realized why she was so special. Patience smiled and she said the most perfect thing, "Well I hope I interrupted something fun. It's good to know that someone is still getting laid around here. Should I come back or have you two reached your," and she paused for a few seconds pretending to try and find the right word, "goal?"

Ellen responded first as Henry was still in a state of shock, "well I don't know about preppy over there, looks like he still has some dressing to do, but I am ready to talk. Can you manage the rest by yourself Henry?"

"Yes Henry do you need some help with your shirt and shoes?" Patience joined in on the friendly ribbing.

With that, Henry finally gained his composure and responded, "No ladies, I am perfectly able to get dressed, thank you, please don't let me interfere with this pre-arranged get together. I wish I had known I was on the clock."

Patience responded, "Well hurry up then, your 10:30 was over a few minutes ago and now you are cutting into my time."

"Okay okay I know when I am being ganged up on." And with that Henry finished getting his clothes back on and started heading out the door.

"See you tonight dear?" Ellen asked as he was about to head out the door.

"Of course dear, maybe we can finish this later?" Henry asked sarcastically and prophetically. But deep down there was another emotion that Henry was feeling. He was absolutely outraged and furious, deep down he knew he had been set up, lied to and completely taken for a ride.

Ellen continued the friendly but sexually charged banter that all three were engaged in, "I'm not sure Henry, you kind of wore me out."

Henry, who at that moment vowed that was the last time he would ever have sex with Ellen Chandler again, responded with a smile on his face, almost too prophetically and deep down referring to more than the obvious, "As you did me, as you did me." And Henry left the room and headed down the hallway and out to his car.

When he got to his car, the rage started. He pounded his fist on the steering wheel so hard he made the horn sound and realized he had to get out of there before he caused a scene, so he started the car and drove out the driveway. He needed to talk to someone, but who? He grabbed his cell phone and dialed Charlie, but there was no answer and he did not leave a message.

He needed to go somewhere to decompress and he thought about where he could go. "I need to take a long walk" he thought to himself, so he headed for the place that he and Patience always went as kids when they wanted to get away from everyone and think: Lantern Hill.

Lantern Hill was about ten miles inland and was the highest point in the Mystic area. At 600 feet it did not qualify as a mountain, it was aptly named a hill. It got its name because it was where colonialists during the wars with Britain would warn the area residents of British troop movements.

During the War of 1812, when a fleet of British naval ships were spotted in Block Island Sound, a few colonialists hiked to the top of Lantern Hill and set a large bonfire which was already agreed would be the signal that the British were coming.

While these colonialists did not get the same billing as their more famous brother to the north, Paul Revere, they were just as successful. When the British tried to take Stonington by sea using their cannons to level the town, the Stonington Village residents successfully kept them far away from the shore with their own cannons. They managed to get a couple of direct hits on the British naval force which successfully encouraged the British to try some other less fortified port. Those same cannons are now proudly displayed in Cannon Square in the middle of Stonington Village as a testament to those brave ancestors.

Lantern Hill is basically a gigantic block of quartz that protrudes quite steeply out of the woods. It was left behind when the melting ice of the last Ice Age washed away the surrounding softer terrain. Despite being only 600 feet in elevation, from the top one can see south as far as Long Island, east as far as Block Island, and north for dozens of miles. The Indians in the area claim that Lantern Hill is sacred ground because the local Indian tribe would hold their council meetings at the top.

While the Pequot Indians maintained their small reservation on land a mile or so from the bottom of Lantern Hill, which is where they built their now famous casino Foxwoods, Lantern Hill itself had too much strategic value to the early settlers to be included in that reservation, and now it basically served as a sightseeing spot for descendants of both the settlers and the Indians.

My dad used to take my brother and I up to the top of Lantern Hill at least once a year. Besides the benefits of the view, it was a pretty strenuous climb to get to the top, and when we were driving our mother crazy, dad would get the "look" from mom, and that meant we were going somewhere to run it off. Lantern Hill was one of those inevitable destinations.

As teenagers, it was also a great place for a party. It was remote enough that loud music was not going to bother anyone, and even if the locals could hear it, it was a difficult enough climb that the local police were not going to harass us.

Henry and Charlie and many others of our friends would meet up at the bottom, some of the boys would be tagged with carrying the beer, the girls would carry the blankets, and someone would lead the way up to the top, using a flashlight at night.

The very top of Lantern Hill is a large flat rocky area. From there one can see the entire area. It was where the Indians claim their Tribal Councils were held, there is even a natural alter conveniently carved into the rock, which is known as Council Rock, so I can imagine that it was a very inspiring place to hold tribal meetings. It also happened to be a great place for a teenage keg party. The only downside was that looking to the east, the flat area ended with a 100 foot cliff straight down. Luckily no one ever managed to get too drunk that they fell off, though there were certainly some close calls.

Council Rock is also where Henry and Patience would go by themselves from time to time to get away. It was silent, it was peaceful, the view was great, and it had a very spiritual sense to it. We all knew they would go there when they were teenagers to get away and we would joke with them about what they would do up there, but Patience always said they just went to sit and stare at the horizon.

Henry instinctively knew this was where he needed to go right then. What he did not know was as he was heading out the driveway of Mystic Manor, Patience and Ellen both saw him leaving from Ellen's window which overlooks the driveway.

As for Patience, she knew exactly what had happened a few minutes before. She knew Ellen had sprung some type of trap, and she could feel very strongly that Henry, despite his humor as he was leaving, was deeply upset about it. When she saw Henry take a right turn out of the driveway, which is the opposite way of going home for him, she also instinctively knew exactly where Henry was going, it's where he always went when he was upset, and she watched as he took a right out of the driveway which led north instead of south back into town. She decided at that moment that after she finished up with Ellen, she would need to head up to Lantern Hill also to try and calm Henry down.

Ellen on the other hand had thought her little trick had worked. She had been suspicious of Henry's motives from the first time she saw him staring at Patience the very first week. She also suspected that Henry's get-togethers on Tuesdays with Charles Sr. had more to do with being able to conveniently run into Patience, then talking to Charles Sr. While she couldn't control Henry's feelings for Patience, she knew how women operated, and she thought that her little trick would make it clear to Patience that whatever Henry might have told her, he was still Ellen's toy to play with, and she was in control.

She knew Henry was meeting with Charles Sr., and she purposely went there and acted friendly and flirtatious toward Henry to get him into her office. What Henry did not know was that right after leaving Charles Sr. suite, Ellen had gone to find Patience and asked her to meet in her office right after her Yoga lesson, knowing that Patience would walk in on her sexual encounter with Henry.

There was another reason Ellen asked Patience to her office, and this was the beginning of Ellen's next plan, to get Patience removed from her hospital. After Henry left Ellen's office, and after some smalltalk between Ellen and Patience about what had happened right before Patience appeared, Ellen started. "Patience, as you know I have been introducing some new physical therapy techniques that I helped develop at Cedar Sinai to improve patient mobility. In order for the program to work, the patients have to follow a rigorous and precise protocol, do you understand?"

Patience knew where this was going and she was way too secure and confident in herself to feel slighted by Ellen's attempt at talking down to her. So instead of giving Ellen the pleasure of additional conversation where she could be talked down to, she did not respond, she just smiled and nodded when appropriate.

"So here's the deal, I know you have been here for a very long time, and I know the patients find very real value in what you do with them, and Lord knows you are such a sweet and kind person, so I'd like to figure out how the two of us can work together to incorporate you into my program. Honestly, I have to make sure you are complementing what we are doing, not working against us. I have said before, I am a big believer in Yoga, and we incorporated it into the program out West, but we made sure all the Yoga instructors were certified and trained properly in the method we use so they were working with us. Are you still with me?"

Patience continued to smile and nodded again.

"So because I know how much you mean to the hospital, I am going to offer to have you trained in the method. Now it may require some travel to Los Angeles because that's where the certified instructors are, but it should not be too long. I will agree to pay for the training itself, but you will have to pay for your travel."

There was a long silence.

Patience finally spoke. "Ellen that is an amazing and generous offer, I can see why Henry and Charles Sr., and everyone for that matter, speak so highly of you. We have never really talked about me, so I'll give you a quick introduction. Over the past fifteen years I have been trained and certified in four or five different Yoga methods. From that education, I have taken bits and pieces of each and worked to combine and refine them, and in the process I have created my own method and like you, I also have had tremendous success with it, especially with the elderly." Patience was curious how far Ellen was going to take this. Was she going to fire her from Mystic Manor if she refused? She decided to push back a little bit. "So I appreciate the offer, I really do, it is so kind, but I am not sure I am interested in taking my practice in another direction right now. And there's another problem," Patience beamed a big smile, "I don't like to fly."

There was another long silence. Ellen frowned and then after a minute or so her frown turned into a smile. At first she was taken aback at Patience's obvious hard stance wondering if Patience realized this could mean the end of her teaching in Mystic Manor. But it quickly dawned on Ellen that since her real goal was to get Patience out of her hospital,

Patience just handed her the gift she was looking for. She smiled because she realized this might be much easier than she thought. But Ellen was not ready to lower the boom on Patience yet. She had not completely thought through all the repercussions of Patience leaving so quickly after Ellen took over. No matter how Ellen communicated it, it might appear that Ellen forced her out on purpose and she was still not completely sure of all the relationships and loyalties that Patience had developed there over the years.

Ellen's biggest question was Patience's relationship with the Mason family, and especially with Charles Sr. Ellen knew that Patience grew up on the Mason family estate, so she suspected there was some type of bond between Charles Sr. and Patience and Lois. She had thought about this for quite a while. She wondered how deep those bonds go. If she got rid of Patience, would Charles Sr. have an opinion?

Patience could tell that the wheels were turning in Ellen's head. She knew that Ellen was going to try and get rid of her, and she knew that was likely inevitable. There is an old saying "never wrestle with a pig, you both get dirty, but the pig loves it." Patience had no intention of wrestling with Ellen over her staying at Mystic Manor. It was clear that Ellen was a brilliant, entitled and potentially vindictive person, who was not interested in playing fairly, she played to win and always got what she wanted, one way or another.

The scene that had just played out a few minutes ago confirmed in Patience's mind the extent that Ellen was willing to go to fight this battle, she was willing to lie to, and use, her own husband to get what she wanted. In reality, Ellen, the brilliant Harvard-trained physician, the star of the Chandler family, who prided herself in being so complex, in reality was no match for Patience Passion. To Patience, the game Ellen initiated that morning was so obvious and simple that it was not going to be a wrestling match at all. Patience was not going to be playing any type of game or involved in any tete-a-tete with Ellen, but for the sake of Henry, who she loved dearly, she decided at that moment she was going to engage with her, not wrestle, but manage Ellen through this. But she would have two simple rules. First and foremost, Henry does not get hurt. Second, as a spiritual healer, Patience had no choice but to ensure that everyone was going to end up healed, everyone was going to end up spiritually in a better place from the experience, even Ellen, especially Ellen, who was the one in need of healing more than anyone. Patience knew that would be difficult, Ellen's spiritual consciousness was deeply buried.

Before I can go further with this story, it is time to go a little deeper into the depth of Patience's spiritual understanding and capabilities. This may sound somewhat cheesy for those who don't believe in this stuff, but simply stated, Patience Passion was enlightened.   With Lois as a mother it was certainly possible, but in her late twenties Patience went through a spiritual experience that freed her from the weight of the material world and she reached enlightenment. As I have said before, Patience was always spiritually gifted, even as a child, but her evolution from gifted to fully enlightened was completed before she reached thirty.

The concept of enlightenment, an Eastern concept, is difficult for most Westerners to understand. I still don't really understand it all myself, but in trying to tell this story, I have studied it enough to understand it intellectually.

That's partly what Buddhist teachings say, that to be truly enlightened requires a complete intellectual understanding of what it means to be enlightened.   But reading books and intellectually understanding enlightenment does not make you enlightened.   You actually have to undertake the journey to reach an enlightened state. It takes understanding and work.

A common and simple analogy used to explain enlightenment is someone trying to get to a particular destination, let's say Asheville, North Carolina. It takes two things to reach "Asheville". First you need directions to "Asheville", and second you need to actually put one foot in front of the other and start and then complete the journey to "Asheville".

You can read the directions, study the map and become the world's foremost expert on how to get to Asheville, but unless you actually start and complete the journey, you cannot say you have been there. On the other hand, you can decide to head out to "Asheville", but without knowing which direction you are going, what roads to take, etc, you will likely never reach it. Sure you may stumble across it one day by dumb luck after years of wandering, but that is a much longer and likely unsuccessful journey.

Great people have lived who have directed numerous people to enlightenment without ever having taken the journey themselves. There is great spiritual benefit to the world in having experts on how to reach enlightenment because not everyone has to get there, nor will everyone who wants to, actually finish the journey.

Patience actually reached enlightenment and she got there relatively young in comparison to most. The intellectual understanding of enlightenment is something she was schooled in from birth, Lois saw to that. It was just inherent in the way that Lois lived her life. Her Eastern philosophical tendencies, the conversations at dinner, and the books that lined her ample bookshelves all ensured that Patience was well prepared to take that journey, and she likely started it as a toddler.

Some say that when we are conceived, we start out enlightened, it is the natural state and the core of our essence, and it is only the influences of the material world and the dynamics and interactions with others that quickly and consistently cloud and mask that natural state. In that, the journey to reach enlightenment is really a peeling away of all the layers of suffering, and all the negatives from life that cloud or completely hides that natural state, such as anger, greed and contempt. In that, Patience was lucky because with Lois as her mother, Patience's natural enlightened state at conception never became that clouded, so the number of layers she had to peel away to return there was considerably less than most.

In being enlightened, one becomes almost completely aware of the motivation and appearance of the behavior of others. It was with this insight that Patience knew exactly what Ellen was up to. It was with this same insight that she knew what Henry was going through, not just his insecurities about his life, his career and his marriage, but his feeling toward Patience. She knew that Henry was deeply in love with her.

While Ellen was not enlightened, Ellen was a woman and her intuition told her that Henry had feelings for Patience and this was something she needed to keep an eye on. Patience knew Ellen was concerned about Henry's feelings toward Patience, she knew what Ellen was capable of, so Patience was very concerned about what Ellen was capable of doing to her or Henry in response, it deeply worried Patience.

Ellen decided she was not ready to lower the boom on Patience yet. She was too worried about Charles Sr.'s reaction, so she was going to have to postpone that conversation until she was ready. Ellen finally broke the long silence. "Well. I can't ask you to take the bus to Los Angeles, and I certainly can't have one of the instructors come east just to train you. So I am going to need some time to think about how we solve this little dilemma." Ellen broke into a smile, "Patience we are two very different people."

Patience smiled back, "In many ways we are Ellen, I'd even go so far to say that we are very different in almost every way, but we share one thing in common, we both care deeply for Henry Moore." Patience was being a bit sarcastic in that, Patience knew she cared for Henry, but knew that Ellen's feelings for Henry were mixed at best.

Ellen continued, "Yes we do Patience. And we both live in a very small town, and it appears that we are now hanging out in the same circle of friends, so whether we like it or not, the two of us are going to have to learn how to get along. I want that very much."

In a very strange way, while it would be so easy to pass that last remark off as another lie told as part of the dance that these two ladies were doing, Patience knew that Ellen actually meant that last comment. Somewhere deep down, Ellen actually wished that she and Patience could come to an understanding on how to peacefully coexist in this little town of Mystic Connecticut. While Ellen was very disrespectful of Patience's career, there was something about Patience's capabilities that was undeniable. Ellen had met spiritually gifted people over her lifetime, and it was becoming clear that Patience was no ordinary person.

Patience of course worked every moment and thread of her being toward being in harmony with every living creature she came in contact with, and to that end, Ellen Chandler was not going to be an exception. Patience knew that Ellen was a very complicated person, with a very complicated mix of emotions and obligations ingrained into her soul. But she could feel the unbridled rage that lurked very close underneath the surface of Ellen, and despite Ellen being in almost complete control of herself, that rage could come out, and when it did come out, the damage that Ellen Chandler was capable of wreaking on the world could be remarkable destructive. Patience knew that the one way that Ellen could lose control of herself and let that rage out of the bottle in an uncontrolled way, was if Patience consciously got the better of her in this game they were playing, conscious to Ellen that is. And the worst would be if she got the better of Ellen in any public way. To embarrass a Chandler in public would bring out the worst, not just the worst in Ellen, but the entire Chandler dynasty would come out in force to protect their own, especially their star prodigy.

So in that way Patience deeply hoped that Ellen and she could come to an understanding of how to coexist. The consequences of failure were too extreme and Henry would most likely be the biggest loser.

The scariest thing for Patience was the knowledge that the only way she could permanently ensure that Ellen would not wage this war, was to fix Ellen. That meant that Patience was going to have to clean up Ellen's soul, she would have to undue forty-two years of built up rage, contempt and entitlement, and do that for someone who would fight that process all along the way in an epic and enduring battle of wills.

So in reality Patience knew that healing Ellen was not going to be an easy feat. Patience knew that would be impossible without acquiescence from Ellen. But how could she get Ellen to acquiesce to being healed when she was convinced that she was on top of the world, and had no inkling of the healing that she actually needed?

Ellen was so comfortable in her current state of dominance that she was never going to get into a better place without some absolutely monumental event that absolutely required her to do so. An event so monumental, so life changing for Ellen, that she would have no choice but to acquiesce to Patience and let herself be healed.

And as she stood in Ellen Chandler's office, Patience Passion had a vision, it was the vision of what was going to happen over the next nine months. She could see it play out in her mind like a movie. It was going to be extremely painful for everyone involved, but it was the only way to save both Henry, who she cared for more than anyone else in the world, and Ellen, who she needed to heal in order to save Henry.

But it was going to be most painful for Patience. To do what she was going to have to do would require her to risk everything she had worked for, to place her faith in the thought that the end result would justify the means of getting there. But until Ellen was in a better place, it meant that there was no hope for Henry, no hope for a better life, no hope for true happiness for him.

But no one was going to be able to heal Ellen other than Patience. Patience's only hope was that she herself would survive.

CHAPTER 9

Lantern Hill

Normally Patience pulled out of the Mystic Manor parking lot and turned left to go back into town, but after the scene in Ellen's office she knew she had to go find Henry and she instinctively knew where he was headed, so this time she turned right out of the driveway of the Manor.

Lantern Hill was about a fifteen minute drive north of Mystic Manor, and by the time Patience had left Ellen's office, Henry, who had quickly left Mystic Manor after his encounter with Ellen, had already arrived there, parked his car in the lot at the base of the trail, and after sitting in his car for about ten minutes to collect his thoughts, got out of his car and started heading up the well-marked path to Council Rock at the top, which was about a twenty minute climb.

Patience arrived fifteen minutes later and saw that Henry's car was the only one in the trail parking lot. She smiled when she pulled up to see Henry's car there. When you are psychic, despite having your psychic powers proven time and time again, it is still somewhat surprising when you are right, and Patience was right about where Henry had gone. She immediately got out of her car, grabbed a blanket from the back of her car and started up the trail to follow Henry. She figured she was about fifteen minutes behind but she didn't want Henry to be up there too long by himself so she started walking very quickly.

Twenty years of doing Yoga puts one in great physical shape, so Patience could do the quick climb to the top of Lantern Hill and not really break a sweat. Henry on the other hand was not nearly in that shape, so he walked much more slowly, resting every few minutes.

The timing of their collective starts from the parking lot, and their different paces meant that despite Henry's fifteen minute head start, both Henry and Patience arrived at Council Rock at the same time. Just as Henry reached the summit he heard someone coming up 100' feet behind him, and when he turned around to see that it was Patience, he sat down and put his head in his hands.

Patience caught up to Henry and sat down beside him. Neither said a word for a few minutes. They both just stared off into the horizon looking south out toward the Atlantic Ocean. Nothing needed to be said, as always Henry and Patience knew exactly what the other was thinking. Patience, who always had a smile on her face was of course smiling, and after a few minutes that smile began to move over to Henry's face.

By that time they were both looking at each other, smiling and were sharing a deep, deep love through their mutual glances. The urge that Henry had at that moment to reach out and hug Patience was stronger than it had ever been before. He wanted to not just hug her, he wanted to be completely enveloped, he wanted to completely disappear inside her.

Despite being in love for over thirty years, Henry and Patience had never had a sexual encounter. Their mutual love was way too pure, too lofty for that. Not to say that either had never thought about it nor even talked about it at length a few times. And the last thing that Patience needed was to start a physical relationship with Henry Moore at that time, with his current relationship still in place, and all the negative dynamics that would start and complications that would ensue.

But a few minutes ago Patience had had a vision of how the next nine months was going to play out, and in that vision, a sexual encounter was exactly how it was going to start. Despite what Patience had said just that morning when she told Henry she was uncomfortable sneaking around, what had happened in Ellen's office, and the vision that Patience had afterwards, changed everything for her. She realized that the potential pain and backlash she had been worried about was nothing in comparison to the pain and anguish that Ellen would continue to wreak in Henry for the rest of his life if she did nothing. She knew that despite some very near term painful and tense moments, the pain would eventually heal, whereas if she did nothing, it never would.

So Patience laid the blanket she had brought up to Council Rock down on the leafy area they were sitting in. It was a weekday, so while on weekends the number of people at the top of Lantern Hill at any one time could be in the dozens, on a weekday morning it was rare that anyone ventured up the mountain.

So Patience laid out the blanket on the leaves and she gave Henry the look that he had been wishing for his entire life, the look that said "now". Henry knew exactly what that look was, he had been waiting for it for his entire life, and a warmth came over him that he had not felt since his mother held him.

For most of Henry's life he had been like a sea captain in the 1880s that left from Mystic on a journey around the world, not knowing what to expect, but knowing that many dangers would be encountered along the way. And because of the unknowns ahead, for the entire journey there was the inescapable feeling of dread, an instinctual emotion embedded deep into the DNA similar to the fight or flight complex. And when the sea captain finally makes his way home after months or years at sea, traveling those last few miles into Fishers Island Sound and then turning up the Mystic River, only then does that dread finally go away, and the feeling of comfort and warmth takes over, that's what it's like to finally come home.

Henry felt like that right now. He felt like he was finally coming home. For the past twenty years he had been on a voyage to foreign parts of the world, both physically and emotionally, and he at that moment realized he had been in a state of panic the entire time. It started when he lost his parents, his idyllic world was shattered, his childhood ended in an instant. He entered a state of panic, and every decision he made after that was based on fear.

Henry went through an amazing transition of self-realization at that moment. He knew what the Buddhist books said about not being driven by want and aversion, and he instantly realized he had spent the last twenty years making decisions based not just on aversion, but on absolute panic.

The Gita that he kept with him since college told that all suffering comes from living life through want and aversion. Those are simply the most mild levels of those emotions. At the extreme of want is greed. If want is a one on a ten point scale, greed is a ten on the scale. Similarly, at the extreme of aversion is fear, panic and terror. If aversion is a one on the scale, then fear, panic and terror are probably 8, 9, and 10 respectively.

And what leads to the most suffering is to act with greed that is fueled by terror. And that's exactly what Henry had been doing. His decision to marry Ellen was exactly that. His feeling of panic of being alone in the world after his parents were killed stirred up an extreme feeling of fear, which led to want, almost approaching greed in knowing that Ellen's wealth could solve his financial problems.

Despite knowing and understanding all this, Henry stepped right onto the path that was inevitably going to lead him through years of suffering and to where he was right now, in extreme pain and suffering. And he knew at that moment that he needed to get off that path. This is the path that Lois was talking about and he knew it.

So without another word being spoken, Henry and Patience did what in thirty years of being in love they had not done, they slowly and lovingly removed each other's clothes and made love. Not just love, they made passionate love. Not just passionate love, they turned thirty years of deep spiritual love into a physical melding to match the spiritual melding that they had shared for decades. With tears flowing down both of their faces, this was more than an act of making love, it was spiritual redemption. It was spiritual cleansing. It was two beings opening up their hearts and spirits to become one. On an unseasonably warm morning in late September, two souls who had probably been linked for eternity, became one.

With smiles on their faces, intense love in their eyes, and nothing but absolute adoration for each other, Henry and Patience made love at the top of Lantern Hill for what seemed like an eternity.

Someone who knew Patience over the past twenty years would think what Patience did that morning was completely out of character. While being a free-spirit as a young teenager, Patience stopped playing around with boys by the time she was sixteen, right about the time that most girls were just getting interested. And over the past twenty years not a single man held any interest for Patience. She had moved onto a different passion, one of spirituality, one of teaching a spiritual cleanliness, using yoga and her psychic skills to clear people of their pain and suffering.

On the surface, what Henry and Patience did that morning would seem to be a complete violation of everything spiritual, an act of treachery, an act of gross lust, not an act of compassion or love. But to understand what happened that morning, one has to step back and look at their entire lifetime, not just what had happened up until that point in time, but also what was going to happen over the next forty years. From the vantage point of that moment as a single moment in an entire lifetime, the act of making love by Henry and Patience on that morning made all the sense in the world. It was exactly what the universe had called for at that moment, and exactly what all involved, Henry, Patience and yes even Ellen, needed to move this story to a place where everything would finally be not just good, but perfect.

After another ten minutes had gone by after their love making, Patience finally spoke the first words that had been uttered by either of them since either had left Mystic Manor. "Henry I want to continue our get-togethers on Tuesday's after my class, but I want to do it at my house on the Island, can you do that for me?"

"Of course, but won't Lois be there and think that is rather odd?" Henry responded, somewhat puzzled that Patience would even propose such as thing. "Would she be okay with that?"

"Yes Henry, my mother knows as much as anyone about us, the path we are on, that we have been on our entire lives. And anyway, she has plenty of things she can do in town on a Tuesday morning, that's actually when she typically does her shopping."

"I would like that very much. That sure beats the basement of the Mystic Manor." Henry said as he gave out a laugh.

"Yes it does, I can't even believe you thought that was a possibility." Patience responded with a laugh.

"Touché, yet another thing I won't live down too easily. Just add it to the quickly growing list." Henry responded half sarcastically. "Patience, I feel like I have taken you by the hand and I am starting to lead you down a very dark path, a path that could lead you to a horrible outcome. Your gift to this world is your positive spirit, your clients all admire you for the uplifting and positive spirituality that you bring to their lives. If you get caught up in some messy affair, that could lead to a lot of heartache in your life and your career. If my returning to Mystic causes you to be harmed in any way, I will never forgive myself."

"Henry, I am not a young teenager anymore, I am a forty year old woman, you don't have to protect me anymore, I know exactly what I am doing. You are not leading me down some dark path, if anything I have been leading you down a path, a path that I can see where it is leading to, and what I see is a path that has a bright shiny light at the end of it.

"But I want to warn you, this path we are headed down is going to get very dark at times, there are times when you will wonder what you were thinking, there are times when you will cry with pain and anguish and wish you could undo it all. But I will tell you now that just when you think you cannot take any more heartache, and you think you may have lost everything, when the world and the future appear to be absolute darkness, that is exactly the moment when the light comes on.

"So no matter what, promise me you will not lose hope, or lose your resolve, no matter how difficult this becomes, because that is how you could hurt me. Henry I will be exposed, but as long as you stick by me, in the end everything will be perfect, just how you would want it to be. Everyone will be healed and happy."

Henry looked at Patience with awe, he wanted to say something profound, but something Patience said reminded him of a song he knew by heart because he used to sing it to Patience all the time when they were teenagers, and though he wished he could think of something as profound as what Patience had just said, instead he found himself singing words to a David Crosby song he had not sung or even thought about in over twenty years, "and you know, the darkest hour, is always just before the dawn."

Patience smiled and then started to laugh, and then they both started to sing the rest of that song, quietly at first, but before they reached the end they had both stood up, stark naked and were singing at the top of their lungs: "and it appears to be a long, appears to be a long, appears to be a long time, such a long long long long time before the dawn."

And then they continued with the rest of the song: "Speak out, you've got to speak out against the madness, you've got to speak your mind if you dare, but if you want to get yourself elected, you had better cut your hair."

Henry started playing air guitar, "And it appears to be a long, appears to be a long, appears to be a long time, such a long long long long time before the dawn."

As they sang the chorus one last time they began dancing. Maybe it was the fact that they were at Council Rock where many an Indian dance is thought to have taken place, maybe they were just drunk with giddiness at finally consummating a relationship that had been so intimate for over thirty years, whatever the reason, Patience and Henry were dancing around naked, singing at the top of their lungs, at the top of the tallest point in New London County, in the middle of the day, right at the peak of the fall leaf season in Southern Connecticut. It could not be a more perfect start to a new era in the relationship of Henry Moore and Patience Passion.

When they finished the song, Henry and Patience laughed, held each other one more time and both said simultaneously, "let's get dressed." They quickly threw their clothes on and walked over to the edge of the south facing cliff and sat down to admire the view of the entire Mystic River Valley in front of them. A hawk come circling by, and then another, and then another, before long Henry and Patience had counted nine hawks circling around the peak of Lantern Hill in the thermals created by the southwesterly breeze that comes up the Valley and are driven upwards as they hit Lantern Hill.

Then Henry turned to the west and saw another bird off in the distance, at first it looked like a hawk but as it got closer he saw its bald reddish head, and as it got closer he realized it was a turkey vulture and Henry said, "look it's a turkey vulture coming at us." It was flying right at them about 100 feet away when it suddenly veered left toward a tall pine tree growing about fifty feet down the cliff and to their right. As it landed on an upper branch of the pine tree which was right about eye level for Henry and Patience, they realized the turkey vulture was not alone, there were ten or eleven other vultures roosting in that tree.

The sight of the vultures sent shivers down Henry's spine and he shook noticeably. Patience saw the look in Henry's eyes and it reminded them both of what Patience had said a few minutes before about dark days ahead, and they nodded in unison.

After a minute or so of eerie silence, Patience said "Probably time to head back to town."

Henry responded, "Yes it is. I hope that the only vultures we encounter are the ones that roost in trees, but something tells me we are not going to be that lucky."

"Yes Henry, I think you can count on that, and much more sinister ones than the kind that roost in trees."

With that, they both got up and made a hasty retreat down Lantern Hill to the parking lot where they had left their cars. The parking lot was still empty except for a black Chevy Suburban with tinted windows that was not there when they arrived.

Henry said, "that's odd, I didn't see anybody else up there. They must have taken the other trail to the top," pointing to the Suburban.

Patience did not respond, but thought to herself, "I think we just found our vulture."

CHAPTER 10

Violetta Andropov

When Ellen decided that Violetta's physical therapy would stop because she was showing no signs of improvement, Violetta was incredibly discouraged, but she was still determined to try and do something to get movement back in her arm. She was a strong and tenacious Russian woman, and was never going to give up.

While Ellen's physical therapy technique had not worked for Violetta and the sessions were terminated, Violetta had not stopped with Patience and her private yoga class twice per week at her home. When the physical therapy sessions had ended, Violetta and Patience talked about it, they talked about how disappointed Violetta was, they talked about what the physical therapist was doing with Violetta, and after a few of these discussions, Patience made a decision that maybe the time was right to do something more for Violetta.

While Violetta had an intense inner drive to regain her movement, Patience knew that sometimes that can work against someone in a recovery from major physical trauma, if the intensiveness is focused and stuck in a negative pattern. Patience suspected that Violetta's resoluteness was based in anger, and this might be blocking her own improvement by blocking the natural energy flows that she needed to heal her injuries. Up to that point in time, Patience thought that Violetta's strong-willed nature was more stubborn than resolute, and therefore Patience thought that she could never get Violetta to let go of things she needed to let go of, to find her inner strength and inner peace required to let her body heal itself by tapping into a spiritual energy source that had the power to heal anything.

Patience's level of understanding and knowledge about the power of the spiritual psyche to heal one's physical body was as advanced as anyone's, but in almost every case her students would not have any capability of understanding what Patience was doing and how it was working.

Patience's normal yoga classes looked and felt like no others. It was not an exercise class, her students rarely broke into a sweat. Each hour long class started with ten minutes of a guided meditation, much longer than normal yoga classes.

For any healing to take place, Patience first needed her students to change their normal thought patterns. She needed to lead them through a change in their subconscious understanding of the pathways that lead from their spirituality to their physicality. Since they would never consciously and intellectually understand those pathways, and it was not really necessary for them to do so, Patience never tried to explain to her students what she was doing and why. She simply used subtle techniques to trick her students into healing themselves, without them knowing intellectually exactly what she was doing to them, for them, and how it was they were experiencing healing. They simply knew that Patience somehow made them progressively get better.

Up to that point Patience's work with Violetta was basic energy work, she was trying to remove energy blocks in Violetta's body in the hopes that Violetta's body might heal itself. But she knew there was more that she could do for Violetta, but she could only do so if Violetta would be a willing participant, and that meant changing dozens of years of thought patterns. Unfortunately, the very thought patterns she needed to change were likely the same thought patterns that gave her the drive to conquer the professional music world and drove her success.

But Violetta's latest level of despair changed Patience's mind. She now suspected that finally Violetta's state of mind might be at a point that she would try anything, even agree to let go of a lifetime's worth of drive and ambition that, while leading her to great success and fame, was now stopping her own recovery.

The vision that Patience had in Ellen's office the day before included an important part for Violetta, and Patience decided to use the next Wednesday session to talk to Violetta about a new plan she had envisioned for her.

All the way from her house and up the driveway to Violetta's house, Patience worked on the speech she was going to give Violetta. She parked her car and walked to the side entrance where she always entered, and as Violetta greeted her at the door as she had always done, Violetta could tell that something was different in Patience's demeanor. She grabbed Patience's arm as she always does as she walks someone from the door to the parlor, and they started that same walk as they had done dozens of times.

"Patience, my darling, I can tell you have something on your mind, don't you dare tell me that you are about to give up on me also," Violetta said in her heavy Russian accent.

"Violetta, you know I would never do that. But I do have something I want to talk to you about. I have an idea on a new path that I want to take with our work together, a path I think that might give you want you want."

Violetta stopped walking, she turned and faced Patience and stared into Patience's eyes for over a minute and then spoke in clear and slow words, "Please do not give me false hope." Violetta stared into her eyes for another minute, obviously trying to read what Patience was thinking. "My precious Patience, I know you are a healer, I feel there is a healing capability that lies within you that no one understands, perhaps even you. I have worked with you all these months because I have always believed that I could benefit from that deep well of healing you have in your soul. But all along I have felt like you have been holding something back, and while I suspect that was more my fault that yours, I have not been able to tell exactly if that was the reason. I know you would never hold something like that back without good reason, and I have always trusted you would open that well of healing to me in your own time.

"So I want you to know that below this stone façade of mine, carefully cultivated over many years, is a deeply sensitive and deeply terrified little child. I am willing to do what you ask, to do anything, give up anything, sacrifice everything. So if you have come here today to tell me that it is time for us to enter a new stage of partnership and love together, then I want to tell you that I am ready, and this is the time. Patience, I trust you like I trust no other person I have ever met, I give you my life."

Patience was a little taken aback. She had practiced the speech she was going to give Violetta over and over again, and Violetta had just recited that speech to her, almost verbatim. There was not much that Patience could say, Violetta got it, she got it without even Patience having to say a word. So she said the only thing needed to be said, "Okay then let's get started."

That day Patience started a new healing program with Violetta Andropov that was going to change them both, and the world around them, forever. Patience knew she had the ability to heal Violetta, but because it would take such a radical change in thinking for the patient, she knew it would only work with someone who was ready to give up everything, every old thought pattern, and she now knew that Violetta, more than anyone she had ever met, was ready.

Patience changed her schedule around to meet with Violetta every morning, Monday through Friday. They started at eight in the morning on Tuesday and Thursday so Patience could continue her class at Mystic Manor, and at nine in the morning on Monday, Wednesday, and Friday.

For the first three weeks all they did was deep meditation. Patience knew that Violetta's healing would only be possible by teaching her the spirituality it would require to open up the spiritual to physical connections. This was not going to be easy for a Russian woman who grew up at foot of the altar of the Russian Orthodox Church.

To understand Russian Orthodoxy is to not only understand the centrality and idolatry of Christ within their belief system, which is consistent with most of the Christian religions, but it is to understand the role that suffering plays in the Russian Orthodox Church, that is absolutely essential for salvation.

This should not surprise anyone, the Russian people have suffered more than most over the centuries. All one has to do is read any one of dozens of novels by the leading classic Russian novelists to see a central theme: suffering. Suffering is the antagonist in all classic Russian novels, with plots that usually revolve around a cast of characters who are all in a perpetual fight with or flight from their suffering, sometimes together, sometimes in competition.

The first thing that Patience was going to have to teach Violetta was that emotional and mental suffering is not only unnecessary, suffering does not really need to exist at all. Like all emotions, suffering is created in our minds as a way to explain the feelings we experience after either a loss of some kind, or an anticipation of loss. It is created because we develop misplaced expectations to set ourselves up for the feeling of loss, misery, heartache, and all the emotions and feelings that are associated with suffering.

The fundamental belief of most Christian religions, and especially with Russian Orthodoxy, is that Christ's entire existence was to relieve us of our suffering. So when you tell a Russian Orthodox that their suffering does not actually exist, it undermines the main foundation of their belief system. And when you do that, you tend to not only lose the confidence in the person who you are delivering that message to, you can initiate quite a hostile and sometimes even violent reaction in the person toward the messenger.

A large part of the religious belief systems of the Judeo-Christian religions is the remembrance and retelling of the past. The Bible and Koran, the basis for these religions, is a recounting of the course of human history. And almost every Judeo-Christian religious ceremony delves into our history to tell an allegory from that past and apply its lessons to right now.

That's a great way to teach if you believe in the theory that 'history will repeat itself if we forget the past," but it also tends to mean that we become infatuated with our past, and it becomes to define who we are today.

Experience a Passover Seder dinner with a Jewish family and you will experience a recreation of the original Passover, remembering the past is the predominant and overriding point of the Hebrew religion.

In general we look for the familiarities and the consistencies of the past to define who we are and to define our present lives to provide us comfort in a terrifying world. But that act only serves to carry past pain and anguish to the present and keep it there from moment to moment.

We set our children up for terror when we hammer into their

spongy brains at a young age all of the terrible things that have happened in the ancient past of mankind, hoping to protect them from events that are so unlikely it's not even possible to measure. I think we can agree that the chances of a plague taking all of our first born male children today is somewhat remote, but we still insist on placing kernels of terror in our children and then we walk around with these for our entire lives.

Eastern religions teach of living in the moment where suffering has no place. Every moment is new and becomes an opportunity to completely change the dynamic of our existence. The past holds no locks on, nor defines the present, we only allow it to and even ask it to in the hopes of preventing future suffering, when in the end that is exactly what becomes the main cause of our suffering.

Bridging the gap from how emotional suffering affects our physical beings is the key to understanding how Patience worked with her students. Life for a living being is a duality. We exist as spiritual beings experiencing the physical world through our physical bodies. Our bodies are in essence one giant sensory organ. We talk about the five senses, sight, smell, taste, hearing and touch, but the reality is that the entire body works in consort to detect and respond to physical stimuli, and to store memories of each stimuli as a learning pattern for when future stimuli happen.

Think how our immune systems work. Linus Pauling discovered the cure for polio by realizing that our bodies have sensory memories, and the radical discovery by Pauling was to create a polio vaccine that contains the polio virus, albeit a form of the virus that has been neutralized. The body then stores a memory of that polio virus experience and is able to detect and overcome the next polio stimuli before it can harm us.

But what most do not realize is that our bodies do that at every moment. And because we live in a world where there is a constant barrage of inputs, stimuli, and interactions with other humans, animals, and plants, and all of these interactions give us stimuli that is stored by the body. The problem with this system of stored memory of stimuli is that the storage of those stimuli is done in our physical bodies and the shear amount of stored stimuli eventually overwhelms our physical bodies, and is what makes us sick. So in essence, most sickness and disease happens because of the cumulative weight and gravity of the negative stimuli we have stored in our own bodies, a vast majority of that stored negative stimuli is utterly useless to us. Beyond being useless, these stored memories actually harm us. These stored memories take what was an emotional reaction to a physical stimuli, and turn it into a physical phenomenon, a physical reaction. The body's arsenal of physical reactions to emotional stimuli varies from a loss of blood flow, to a clogging of some other seminal vessel, to retention of fluid, to any number of possible reactions. Whatever the body's myriad reactions to stored stimuli, they all have one result, they stop the body's natural energy flow.

Patience's physical work with her patients is about energy flow. Patience's specific practice is to rid her students of these stored negative memories through a number of physical and spiritual cleansing processes. By ridding the body of these stored negative experiences, the body's natural energy flow resumes.

Once the burden of these negative memories has been lessened, and energy begins to flow again to areas that have been shut down, her students start to feel better. Patience then continues to teach her patients how to immediately rid themselves of stored stimuli and their bodies go through a change where negative stimuli are no longer stored, they dissipate instantly.

So Patience's first goal for Violetta was to help her rid herself of the negative stored experiences and energies that led to her stroke to begin with. Unlike traditional psychotherapy where the patient must rediscover past traumatic experiences to relive or re-experience the trauma in order to rid oneself of the negative energy and emotion associated with it, removing stored negative experiences in the form of cleansing that Patience practices with her patients does not require the person to relive or re-experience the trauma. Simply finding the associated physical pain or sensation that is associated with the storage of that negative stored experience and ridding oneself of the stored physical effect, dissipates all of the negative emotion and pain from that traumatic experience.

The storage of conscious experiences does not require an experience to be especially traumatic. Every interaction that we have as living beings, conscious and sub-conscious, is stored by the body in some fashion. The body makes it quite apparent where we have conveniently stored our negative experiences, they make themselves known through aches and pains and other sensations, or even lack of sensations such as numbness.

Individuals who have mastered the technique of cleansing their bodies of stored stimuli become extremely adept at understanding the minutia of their bodies. They know when something is not right with their body and can pinpoint exactly where the trouble spot is, such as feeling the exact spot where a cold virus has embedded itself in their mucus membrane. Once found, they can use intense focus to concentrate the body's defenses on that exact spot, such as opening the blood vessels to that spot, bringing an extra dose of the body's natural healing properties.

In her practice, Patience teaches an ancient form of healing discovered by the Buddha himself and is still taught today. It is based around an ancient form of meditation that reacquaints her students with their bodies, allowing them to feel stimuli from head to toe that they may have not felt in years or decades. For instance, after a number of sessions with Patience, her students can feel the opening and closing of their sinus cavities, and the hairs on their big toes swaying in the breeze.

This was how Patience was going to heal Violetta. But this was going to take an incredible amount of work on Patience and Violetta's part. Violetta's injuries were not as simple as restoring blood flow to an area that was experiencing slight constriction of blood flow, Violetta's stroke and subsequent loss of blood flow to certain extremities most likely killed thousands of nerve and muscle cells needed for full movement. Patience was going to have trick Violetta's body to regenerate cells to replace those that were lost.

It would take weeks to get Violetta into the emotional and spiritual place where she could even begin to get to the physical healing that would be needed. It meant first teaching Violetta how to unlearn decades of thought patterns, teaching her how not to react with the typical human emotions such as anger, rage, jealousy, helplessness, replacing those emotions with the Godly emotions of compassion, love and understanding.

It meant getting her to understand the concept of living in the moment and not in the past which is nothing more than stored memories, or the future that has yet to take place and we have no control over.

Once Patience had Violetta in the emotional and spiritual place where she needed to be, only then could Patience begin to get Violetta to start the physical healing process that she was going to need to do on herself, and that too would take weeks if not months.

But despite the amount of work that this was going to take from both Patience and Violetta, Patience knew exactly what she was doing, and she already knew what the outcome was going to be. The vision that she had of how the next few months were going to play out, the same vision that led her to have her encounter with Henry which she knew would start the ball rolling on that vision, also gave her the insight into how the work with Violetta was going to proceed. She could not tell exactly the timing, that would be up to all the actors in the story that was going to play out over the next few months, but she knew how the sequence of events would play out, and she knew how this would end for Violetta.

During the first few weeks Patience worked with Violetta on her meditation, concentration, and focus. She taught Violetta how to focus her concentration on a single point of her body, starting with her breath as it flowed through her nostrils. When sitting perfectly still, the air passing through the nostrils is the only sensation that is readily apparent to most everyone.

Over the first few days that is all they worked on, the breath and the sensation of the breath through her nostrils. After the first two days, Violetta became frustrated with this and as they began their third day, she broke her silence with a question that she answered before she even finished the question, the answer becoming obvious as she got further into her question. "Patience, darling this is becoming monotonous, can you explain to me what feeling my nose hairs has to do with regaining the feelings in my arm? Don't answer that. You are going to tell me that recovering the ability I lost decades ago to feel the slightest vibrations in a nose hair will train me to look for the slightest vibrations in my paralyzed arm, and this is going to retrain the nerves in my arm to my brain to sense vibrations."

"You're a quick study," Patience replied. "We have one more day of this focus on your breath, tomorrow we will move your focus onto another area of your body."

"Thank heavens, I'm not sure I could last another day with my nose hairs."

The reality was that Violetta's quick understanding that morning was only part of the answer, and it was the easiest concept to understand of what Patience was actually doing to Violetta. But as said before, there is no requirement for Patience's students to completely understand what they are going through to regain their health and movement, the body will heal itself by the physical aspects of the therapy by itself, an intellectual understanding to go along with the therapy is simply a nice-to-have.

On the fourth day of the intense therapy, Patience gave Violetta her next set of instructions. She was to move her focus to the crown at the very top of her head and starting with a square inch of skin on her scalp, to make a mental note of the sensations she felt, whatever they might be. After five or ten seconds of observation on that square inch of scalp, she was to move to an adjacent square inch of her scalp and focus on that for five to ten seconds. In this manner, Patience and Violetta spent the entire hour, the entire day's therapy session focusing on and discussing the sensations that Violetta was experiencing in her scalp.

She made it clear to Violetta that tickling and vibrations were not the only sensations she was to look for, any absence of sensation was equally important, for instance complete numbness of an area of her scalp was a form of sensation. At the end of the fourth day they took some time to discuss the day's work.

"Violetta, what do you think you accomplished today?" Patience asked.

"I am slowly getting reacquainted with my body. I have felt sensations from areas of my head that I have not felt in years. Quite frankly if I had felt a sensation, I would have tried hard to ignore it and then been angry about it if I could not get it to go away. In hindsight, how absurd a notion, we spend so much of our focus and attention on thought, training our minds to think, think, think, we have completely forgotten to pay attention to our bodies, at least until it is screaming so loud that we can't ignore it. And then we take a pill. We take pain pills to dull the pain instaed of understanding the root of the pain and trying to fix it," Violetta trailed off for a few moments and Patience let the silence in the air linger as long as it needed to.

"That's what I did Patience, I ignored my body and what it was trying to tell me for my entire life. I likely caused my own stroke by not paying attention to what my body was trying to tell me, it was warning me for years, trying to get my attention, but in my zeal to be the best concert pianist in the world, I told it to shut up, to stop complaining, to get with the program and perform at all cost, and I took pills to dull my pain." Violetta trailed off again, this time for even a longer period of time. Again Patience remained silent.

Tears welled in Violetta's eyes and Patience knew that a breakthrough had been made in that day's session. She gave Violetta a hug and saw herself out, leaving Violetta to her own thoughts, knowing she would return tomorrow to a new level of understanding and commitment to the program.

In this manner, over the next few weeks, Patience led Violetta through her entire body, first rediscovering every square inch of the surface of her body, and then working inwards to her muscles, organs, and bones.

Eventually they got to the limbs on her paralyzed side, since that was where the damage was. When she got to the affected limbs Patience modified the therapy a bit. Instead of just looking for sensation, she instructed Violetta to imagine the blood system in her affected limbs, and once she identified a sensation, she was instructed to focus on opening the capillaries that were feeding blood to the area of sensation or numbness.

She next had Violetta move to the nerves that ran from her neck down her limbs. This was going to be the most important part of the therapy for Violetta and Patience, for it was the nerves that ran down her paralyzed limbs that needed to be regenerated in order for her to be able to regain her abilities. The regeneration of nerve cells is not something that the current medical community sees as likely, so this is where Patience was going to have to reach far down into the depths of her healing capabilities to overcome. She had success with other patients who were stroke victims at Mystic Manor, but only to regain enough mobility to get by. But Violetta was not looking to regain normal mobility. The ability to play Chopin and Mozart at the concert level is another skill all together, a skill that requires the finest of fine motor skills, the most detailed connection between the brain and the muscles, signals all carried by nerve pathways that for Violetta were horribly damaged.

Patience was going to have to teach Violetta how to go inward so deeply in her focus that she would be able to isolate and form individual neural pathways that would bypass the damaged neural pathways from the stroke. To do this Patience was going to have to go way back in time, back billions of years to the start of life on this planet. Life has existed on Earth for about four billion years, and for the first three billion all that existed were single cell organisms. After that three billion years of single cell organisms surviving on their own, they started to clump together, mostly for survival. These first clumps were just that, clumps of identical cells that provided protection for each other. But as the great economist Adam Smith wrote, "the division of labor is the key to efficiency", these clumps of cells began to work in consort with each other, they formed a grand bargain. Cells on the innermost part of the clump no longer needed to worry about sensing the outside world, the cells on the outer rim of the clump were doing that, leaving the inner most cells to take on other responsibilities for the clump. As time progressed, despite having a full set of DNA that would allow them to form into any type of cell in the clump, slowly the cells began to specialize into unique types of cells. Over the next few hundred million years, as evolution progressed, those clumps of cell began to take on forms that we now recognize as distinct organisms. The early sea-based species led to land-based species which led to reptiles and then to mammals in the last few million years. But all that evolution did not change a singular fact, all living organisms are still basically clumps of individual, unique specialized cells, working in consort to form a unique multi-cell organism. Each cell in our bodies is a living entity onto itself, while it has ceded its ability to survive outside the clump since it has ceded its ability to generate and source the essentials for life such as oxygen and fluids, each cell still has a unique awareness, and a will to survive.

And while individual cells can sense they exist as part of a greater organism, these individual cells, in their fight to survive, do not always realize that their individual survival might mean the death of the greater organism as a whole. In the same way that ant colonies act as a greater organism, and individual ants will sacrifice themselves for the greater survival of the colony, some of our individual cells will sacrifice themselves for the greater survival of the organism, but that is not the case for all cells in our bodies, some fight so hard for individual survival that they end up damaging the rest of the organism.

The work that Patience had done with Violetta up to that point was to get her to know the sensations of small areas of her body, the next step was to get her to focus on individual cells. Patience would use her understanding of biological evolution and how our bodies were formed billions of years ago and still exist to this day, to bring Violetta's focus from the micro sensation level, which she had already mastered, right down to the microscopic cellular level. And the key to regaining her motion was not just to sense what was going on at that cellular level, but to begin directing it, to consciously take charge of each individual cell, to purposely coordinate the rebuilding of her neural pathways, in some cases directing the generation of new neural cells, in some cases prodding individual cells that had gone dormant in a form of self-preservation to wake up again and start functioning normally.

It was in this way that Patience would regenerate the neural pathways that Violetta needed to regain her motion and control, and it was in this way that she did. Over the next few months, through deeper and deeper meditation, Patience guided Violetta's concentration and focus to the point where she could sense and was keenly aware of every cell in her affected limbs, and she began her reconstruction project.

But it was not just a physical process that Patience had to teach Violetta, while we exist as biological organisms, and it was Violetta's biological organism that was not working properly, at the heart we are spiritual entities that are experiencing this physical world through these biological bodies. And it is our spiritual energy that gives us life. Without our spiritual energy, we would be no different than rocks and other inanimate objects. Our bodies and molecules would be subject to the laws of entropy as are all inanimate objects, constantly devolving. But living entities do not devolve while they are still living, they evolve, they go against the basic laws of nature and entropy, and it is our spiritual energy that drives that evolution. Once we die, once our bodies can no longer sustain the process of evolution, we become simple inanimate objects and devolve to ashes. In between ashes to ashes our spiritual being drives the evolution of our bodies.

Our individual organisms are driven by a spiritual energy that gives every individual cell the sense of community, the sense of a greater good. In this way we have unique states of consciousness, and it is the spiritual state of consciousness that Violetta was going to re-establish, develop and manage to direct the reconstruction of her body.

As Violetta was learning to sense and control individual cells in her body, she was also developing an understanding of the nature of spiritual consciousness, and it was this spiritual consciousness that over the next few months guided Violetta's physical rehabilitation.

CHAPTER 11

The Beginning

For most people that are in a marriage that is extremely painful and manipulative, there comes a specific moment when something snaps. Up until that moment, despite the suffering of trying to maintain a relationship not meant to be, suffering that may go on for years, there is a desperate and increasingly futile commitment to try and make the marriage work. It might come from family pressure, a deep desire not to break a promise made, nostalgia, or it could be fear, fear of the unknown, fear of God's wrath for breaking a solemn vow, fear of financial collapse. It could be many or all of these.

This happens despite the fact that as time passes, the personal costs of staying in a failed marriage begin to far outweigh the costs of getting out, when staying in the relationship becomes more harmful to one's personal psyche and well-being than ending it. But eventually that moment happens, the moment when you suddenly realize that you are done, completely, thoroughly, without question, utterly, done. And when that moment happens, it can happen in an instant. Something snaps. It might be something simple as a hurtful sentence uttered, or could be a big event, like being lured into a false sexual encounter. The snap of that moment is not just a slight change of heart, it can incite a fundamental change of one's core beliefs, and the moral compass that had made certain acts unthinkable disappears, making them possible.

In that state of mind, the guilt that would normally pervade someone for thinking about or actually doing hurtful acts disappears. And when we take an action where there is not a shred of doubt in our mind as to whether it is the right action or not, however it might be perceived by others when judged against societal morals, and whatever the immediate consequences, the guilt disappears.

Henry's moment was caused by an act so bitter and cynical that it betrayed him to his core. The snap was so loud in Henry's head that it changed his moral compass. When Henry realized that Ellen had lured he and Patience into a well-orchestrated meeting in her office, all to insert her dominance over both of them, it was Henry's moment, he snapped.

Years of feeling guilty for his repressed negative emotions for Ellen, his guilt for his feelings of anger, and sometimes even hatred, disappeared in an instant. But Henry was good at his core, so as Henry's guilt vanished in an instant it was not replaced with the normal emotion of rage, it was replaced with something much worse to a marriage, indifference. In an instant, and at his deepest emotional and spiritual level, Henry simply no longer cared.

It was with this feeling of indifference toward Ellen that Henry found himself at the top of Lantern Hill right after the office betrayal. And when he turned and found Patience standing there at the top of Lantern Hill, there was not a shred of doubt in Henry's mind. No doubt, no guilt. He knew exactly what he wanted. He never felt more sure of something in his entire life.

And when he got home after that fateful day, the entire essence of Henry's being changed. Whereas before Henry would feel guilt over his secret get-togethers with Patience at the Mystic Manor pond, despite nothing happening that would technically break his marital vows, from that day on there was no guilt. From that moment he began to plan for the rest of his life, and for the first time in years, Henry was optimistic for his future.

By the time he got home from Lantern Hill, he had his plan. He moved a few more of his belongings to the Back House so he could stay there day and night. For meals he would go out to eat. The only time he would enter the main house was to shower, and he would do that when Ellen was at work.

And that's exactly what he did. After a few days of this, Ellen asked Henry why he was spending so much time in the Back House and not sleeping in the main house. Henry simply told her that after years of having writers block, he was finally on an amazingly productive creative streak with his book and he did not want to interrupt that. He was writing many pages every day and told her that he would move back in once the book was written or his creative streak ended. But for now he was elated over the fact that he was writing profusely. Ellen bought it. She knew that Henry had been suffering from a writer's block for the last few years, and she was happy that he was writing again.

Henry was absolutely pleasant to Ellen in their increasingly brief encounters. He was not overtly angry at Ellen, in a strange way he was ecstatic with her for the gift she had given him. In her attempt to rein Henry in, she had accomplished the exact opposite, she had completely freed him. In her attempt to control him, she had lost all control. In a relationship, the one who cares less has all the power, and now Henry no longer cared.

As planned, Henry and Patience's Tuesday rendezvous began to occur at Patience's house. But to the outside world nothing had changed. Henry still came to the Manor each Tuesday for his get together with Charles Sr. Patience continued to teach her class there, as she had done for over a decade.

When he left the Manor, he would go home. If the weather was nice, he would park his car in his driveway and then he would head out for a walk. While his Tuesday walks would alternate down certain roads, they always led to the Mason family compound. Once there, Henry would head down the service road that led to the Great Salt Marsh and to Lois and Patience's cottage. There were no other houses on the service road to the Great Salt Marsh, it ended in a cul-de-sac with a small public parking lot and a bench for those who wanted to park and sit and gaze at the Ospreys and other birds that were abundant in the marsh.

If the weather was not nice enough to walk, Henry would drive to the small parking lot and park his car. In either case, either on foot or in his car, he would wait in the parking lot until he saw Patience's car appear and park in front of her cottage, which was within line of sight to the parking lot. At that point Henry would look around for other people that might be curious as to why Henry was visiting the Great Salt Marsh every Tuesday. But there was never anyone there to see. It was secluded from all other houses and Tuesday mornings had most people in their homes or off island doing something other than hanging around to gaze at birds in the Great Salt Marsh.

For the first rendezvous planned at Patience's cottage, Henry could see Lois' car in her driveway and that Patience had not arrived. He decided to pay Lois a visit since he had not seen her since his encounter in the Mason statue garden a few months ago on his first night back in Mystic. He knocked on the door, and heard the enchanting yet aristocratic voice of Lois say, "Come on in Henry."

He was puzzled as to how she knew it was him, but he had learned years ago not to ask questions like that of Lois. She always seemed to know everything just slightly before everyone else. "Come have a seat my dear boy, let me get you that tea that I promised you all those months ago when I saw you in the statue garden. You can sit here and wait for Patience to come home, she should be here shortly."

He got the distinct feeling that Lois knew exactly why Henry was there, and that while deep down she was understanding of the eventuality of this, she was not going to speak of it, condone or deride what Patience and Henry were about to embark on.

She made some tea for Henry from the kettle that was always simmering on the stove, placed his cup in front of him and sat down at the table across from him. And then she asked Henry the oddest question, "Do you ever wonder who Patience's father is Henry?"

That was classic Lois. Hit you right between the eyes. Of course he wondered, everyone did, it was the most asked question on Masons Island, from adults and kids, for years. "Well Lois, it's not really any of my business. But since you ask, I have always wondered, hasn't every one? I have asked Patience and she has always said that she does not know."

"I know that the rumors have been that I don't know who her father is, that I was sleeping around back in the sixties, free love and all that nonsense, and I couldn't tell which of my lovers was the father, and I never cared to find out. Do you believe that Henry?"

"Well Lois, you're right, that's what the common Island lore has always been. And I guess in absence of another better story, I always just went with that one."

"Well that's a load of cow dung Henry. I know full well who Patience's father is. It was not planned, that part is true, but he and I were in love. But he was married, and I loved him too much to see his life destroyed with a sordid affair. So when Patience was born, I let the ugly rumors from the ugly people persist to protect him and to protect her."

Henry was a little uncomfortable where this was going. He was about to have a sexual liaison with Patience, and was quite sure that Lois knew that, and yet she was trying to tell him something with her questions. He all of a sudden had a horrendous thought, was it his father? Was that what she was trying to tell him? That Patience's father might be his father? The consequences of that were so distressing that he had to ask Lois. "You are not telling me what I think you are telling me are you? Was my father...."

Lois let out a huge laugh. "Henry, you poor boy. No, your father loved your mother, and she loved him, and I loved them both, especially your mother. You can put that thought right out of your head. Not that your father was not an attractive man, and I always loved that he called me "beautiful" when he would see me, it made me feel so special, even though I knew full well it was how he greeted most women, but no Henry, Patience is not your sister."

"Thank God!" Henry said with too much emotion, as he thought of the recent event on Lantern Hill.

"No Henry, I am not going to tell you who her father is, that is not the point of this, the point is to tell you that Patience's gifts are not shrouded in some fanciful mystery, it was not immaculate conception, her gifts are rooted in the deepest foundation of love and understanding by both her parents. Even though she does not know who her father is, she benefited by both our love."

"Is he still alive?" Henry asked.

Before Lois could answer that question, Patience walked in the door, and the conversation ended as abruptly as it had started. Leaving Henry with more new questions than answers.

"Hello dear, how was your morning?" Lois asked Patience.

"It was wonderful mother, Violetta has made some wonderful

progress, she is starting to understand the spiritual connections that she needs to make in order to heal herself."

"That's so good to hear. The world will be a more beautiful place when Violetta Andropov can make music again."

"Do you really think that Violetta will play piano again?" Henry asked in amazement. He had heard Ellen talk about Violetta's injuries and dim prognosis, and until that moment did not know that Patience was making any progress with her.

"We'll see Henry. It's all up to her, not me. I can only guide her, she has to walk that path. But from what I can tell, she has a deep desire to resume her career, so I bet she gets to where she needs to be."

"Okay kids, I am off to do my weekly shopping. I'll leave you two to talk." Lois was half way through the door but then paused and looked back, "It is so nice to see you two together again. The love you share is as special today as it was when you were little." And with that Lois left, got in her car and drove up the driveway.

After a few moments, Henry and Patience's eyes met, they smiled at each other as they contemplated Lois' last words before she left. Patience got up and poured herself some tea and as she did this she looked out the window and then sat back down.

"Patience, why the change of heart? Before that fateful encounter in Ellen's office, you had told me you were very concerned about us meeting secretly like this. Why is it okay now? I want to make sure I understand what we are doing here."

"Well, to be honest Henry, that encounter in Ellen's office really scared me. Let's admit what she did. That was a set up. For you and for me. It made me realize what she is capable of."

"Well wouldn't that mean we should be more careful, not less?" Henry was asking the obvious.

"Of course we need to be very careful with what we are doing here, but I had a vision that day Henry. I can't describe it, but the vision has a happy ending for you and Ellen. What I want to do now is to continue to get to know the Henry I lost track of. It is important for that happy ending for me to know who you have become since we lost track of each other all those years ago."

Patience continued, "so to be clear, I'm not looking for these get-togethers to be sexual in nature, we still have a lot of catching up to do. Who is this Henry Moore?" In reality, what she could not tell Henry, was that she already knew exactly who Henry was, but because Ellen had showed her hand of what she was capable of, Patience needed to keep Henry close as this played out. The next few months were going to get bumpy and she needed to make sure that Henry was not going to lose it along the way. So getting together weekly was Patience's way of keeping Henry close and monitoring his emotional state as this played out.

And this is how the next several Tuesdays were scripted for Henry and Patience. Every Tuesday for the next few weeks leading up to Christmas, it was pretty much the same routine. Henry and Patience would attend to their appointments at the Manor and then head back to Masons Island in separate cars. Henry would either park at his house and walk, or drive to the Great Salt Marsh. Only two times there was someone in the parking lot when he arrived, and after the obligatory "hellos", Henry always volunteered why he was there, it was an easy excuse to say that the marsh gave him the peace and inspiration he needed to clear his mind for writing his book. He would bring his laptop with him, and sit on the bench and write, or at least appear to be writing.

Henry would walk to the parking lot, sit for a little while, and then walk to the cottage and either visit with Lois and wait for Patience to get home, or wait for Patience to arrive if Lois was not there. If Lois was there, she would head out for her errands. They always ended it with a walk.

The fourth weekly meeting brought about a change in their routine. After pouring herself some tea, Patience began looking out the kitchen window. Henry noticed, she looked like she was looking for something.

"Looking for someone?" Henry asked.

"Ha. No, just looking at the trees, they are so beautiful this time of year." Patience told a white lie to Henry that day. She was looking for something, she had been looking for that thing since they started getting together at her house, and that day she finally found what she was looking for.

Patience put her tea down and went into her bedroom. This was the same bedroom that she had had for forty years, the same room that

Henry had spent hours in talking with Patience and Charles Jr. and other friends. In an odd way, Patience's bedroom was a second home to Henry. But there was one thing he had never done here. He had never taken off his clothes. His feeling in this room had always been about being Patience's best friend, her protector, almost the brother she never had.

Henry sat at the kitchen table for a few minutes and when Patience did not return, he got up and went into her bedroom to see what was up. He found Patience in bed under the covers. They looked at each other and smiled.

Henry was puzzled, he thought that sex was not part of these get-togethers. "Is there something I need to know?"

"Only if you forgot how to take off your clothes," she responded.

Henry, still slightly puzzled, smiled and slipped off his shoes and then the rest of his clothes and slid naked under the covers next to Patience. It was a strange feeling, comfort and discomfort at the same time. He was nervous, this was a big step. Lantern Hill was spur of the moment, a moment in passion, this seemed more planned. Patience could sense his uneasiness.

"It's okay Henry. I want this. Make love to me Henry. Please do this for me and you. And remember, wherever this goes, I will always love you."

"I love you too Patience. I always have. You are my soul mate. It's so depressing to think of how two people can be so right for each other yet have so much keeping them away from each other. It's like the universe is always finding a way to conspire against us."

"The universe does not work that way Henry. It gives us exactly what we need, exactly when we need it. And right now I need you to make love to me."

Henry had no idea what was about to happen, nor how this was going to end, all he knew was that he needed regular contact with Patience, emotionally, physically, and most importantly, spiritually. Patience of course knew exactly what was happening at that moment, how this was going to end and how it was going to play out to get to that end.

After they were done making love, Henry suggested that they take a walk down to the marsh. Patience agreed and they got dressed and headed out the door, Henry noticed off in the distance that there was another car in the parking lot of the Great Salt Marsh besides Henry's. It was a red small late model car, one that he did not recognize to be anyone from Masons Island. But that was not unusual since off-Islanders would come to the Great Salt March also. As they walked closer, they did not see anyone nearby, so he assumed the person must be out for a walk. They walked down to the marsh and sat on the bench and looked out onto the beauty of the marsh. They did not talk for quite some time, they simply bathed in the adoration they both had for each other.

After about 30 minutes of sitting in silence and looking at the beauty of the marsh, Henry told Patience that he needed to get back home and Patience agreed that it was time for her to get on with her day also. They gave each other a hug and Henry got in his car and drove home. Patience walked back to her house and a tear came to her eye. The vultures had come home to roost.

CHAPTER 12

Evil Lurks

Ellen Chandler was not only a brilliant woman, she was used to getting her way in every encounter she had with another person, especially a rival. She had learned at the feet of the masters on how to win, Chandlers always won encounters with rivals. So while she was very pleased with herself for arranging the sexual encounter with Henry in her office and arranging having Patience walk in right in the middle, she was not going to rest on her laurels and assume that was all it would take to drive a wedge between the two of them.

So Ellen did what all wealthy people do when they suspect their spouse has feelings for another person, she hired a private investigator. Hiring a private investigator is not something most average folk have to worry about, nor would they have the slightest clue how to go about finding one if they needed to. But wealthy families are security conscious by necessity, and most have a security company on speed dial.

In this case, Ellen put a call into her family's security company in Los Angeles who made a referral to someone in New York. Within weeks of moving to Mystic, Ellen had met with Bobby Burnside, a twenty year retired veteran of the New York Police department, and hired him to start snooping around on Henry and Patience.

As with most well-financed law enforcement, Bobby drove a black Suburban with tinted windows. While that might be ubiquitous in Washington DC or New York City, in Mystic black Suburbans with tinted windows get noticed. And notice him Patience did. She first noticed the car at Lantern Hill the day of her first encounter with Henry. She knew what the car was doing there and who was in it, because she knew how the next few months were going to play out, but she was not going to let Henry know what she knew. She was simply going to allow this to play out because she also knew how it was going to end.

Bobby was smart enough to know that repeated sightings of his black Suburban might give him away in a small town like Mystic, so after following Patience to Lantern Hill that one day and realizing that his car might be suspicious if it was seen again, he started renting cars from the local Enterprise rental agency, a new one every week. One week it was a red Ford Escape. It was this car that Bobby used to follow Henry to the Great Salt Marsh one Tuesday. Once he had parked, he followed a hiking trail that led along the edge of the marsh for a few hundred yards, and once out of sight of the cottage, he doubled back through the woods toward the cottage, finding a protected perch where he could keep an eye on the cottage and the comings and goings. From this perch his high zoom camera could get a rather detailed close-up photo though the windows of the cottage, luckily for Bobby, right into Patience's bedroom window.

Suffice it to say that after a few weeks of following Henry to Patience's on Tuesday mornings, Bobby got what he needed to earn his fee, and Ellen got what she needed to carry out the final act in her plan to rid herself of Patience Passion for good.

CHAPTER 13

A Christmas Party to Remember

One evening a few weeks before Christmas, Ellen came out to the Back House, where Henry was holed up writing his book, to tell Henry that she was planning the traditional annual Christmas Party at Mystic Manor, which was normally just for the staff and patients, and she thought it would be a great idea to invite Henry's friends as well. She wanted his advice on who to invite. Henry, who had learned to always be suspicious of Ellen when she sprang ideas like this on him, told her he needed to think about it, but his initial thought would be to invite the standard group, basically the same group that had come to their welcome surprise party in the spring.

Ellen asked Henry to get the list and the addresses together so she could send out invitations, and over the next few days, despite his suspicions, he gathered them together. While it was not unusual for the Mason family, including Charles Jr and Amy, to get invited to the annual Mystic Manor Christmas party since the Masons were the founders of the hospital, it was unusual for Bill and I to get an invitation, so when one came in the mail, while I was not quite dumbfounded, I was intrigued. I was intrigued enough to call Henry and ask what was up. I had not spoken to Henry in a few weeks so a call was due anyway.

After a few rings on his cell phone, Henry answered. "Is this Ernest Hemingway?" I started.

"Ha! Hey there beautiful," a term of endearment that Henry had picked up from his father when addressing ladies. "Its so good to hear your voice. I've been holed up in the Back House writing away for the past few weeks, I have not seen a soul, nor have I been out other than to go on walks around the island to clear my head."

"Excuses excuses. You have to eat, and you could have come by the Duck for at least one lunch over the last few weeks, you know we have to survive until the next summer tourist season." I liked giving Henry shit, it was how we blue collar types stayed on the same level as the intellectuals, we mocked their aloofness, and for some reason they liked it, maybe it gave them the veneer of feeling humble and it kept us on the same level in conversation, something we could both talk about and feel comfortable with the subject.

"Well that's true. Let's do that, I'll make it over there tomorrow for lunch, I promise."

"I am going to hold you to that. Hey H," I used the nickname that me and a few of Henry's closest friends used, "H" instead of Henry, "what's up with the invitation I just got in the mail? Bill and I got invited to the Christmas party at the Mystic Manor? I know they have them there every year, but we've never made the A list before."

"It was actually Ellen's idea, and despite my curiosity as to why, it seems like a fun idea. They have to throw the annual party anyway, why not invite another dozen or so of Charles and Amy's friends. Ellen has not really been reaching out to my friends since we arrived so I think this might be her way of doing so."

"Well I have to be honest H, Ellen has popped into the Duck a few times over the last few weeks for lunch." I responded, not knowing whether I was breaking some new news to Henry or not.

Henry was initially speechless, "She's what? Now I am really suspicious. That is so unlike her. First of all she hates shellfish."

"Um, well, we do have other things to eat here, maybe she happens to like our food? Did you think of that? I love it when a Harvard man puts his foot in his mouth." I was of course joking, which Henry was prepared for.

"Well if anyone's food could get Ellen out of the office it would be yours." Henry tried to save himself. "What did she want to talk about?"

"Nice save, Einstein. We would sit and talk for a few minutes, she's been especially nice and friendly. What do we talk about? I don't know, she seems interested in your childhood, but that seems pretty normal as she is your wife, and I am surprised by how little she seems to know about it. Were you purposely keeping us all a secret? She did spend a lot of time one day asking about Patience's parents, she seemed really intrigued by that. I was surprised because I'm not sure why she would care, but she really wanted to know all the dirt on that topic."

"What did you tell her?" Henry queried.

"I gave her the standard story that we have all told a hundred times, that no one knows who Patience's father is. It was the sixties, Lois was all about free love, and she got pregnant, but didn't know who the father was and she never ventured to find out. She pressed on who the possibilities were, and I told her I had no idea, that it was discussed a hundred times as we growing up and none of us could ever come up with the answer and at some point we simply got bored with the topic. She asked about other men of our father's age, I laughed at that one. I couldn't even imagine my father having an affair with Lois. I told her that while some families have come to Mystic and stayed, there have been a number of people that have come and gone over the years. It was probably someone who has been long gone from the Mystic scene. Maybe even someone she met at Woodstock or one of the music festivals that Lois talks about going to."

"Did she seem satisfied with that answer?" Henry persisted.

"Yes, actually she seemed relieved once I mentioned the Woodstock possibility. And then she stopped asking about it and we moved onto a different topic. Why, should I have said something else?"

"No you told the truth as we know it. I just wonder why she is so curious."

"Honestly I think Ellen is genuinely curious about Patience because of the work she does at the Manor. She mentioned that the patients love Patience and tell her that they think Patience makes them feel better, more so than the physical therapists there. So I'll guess she is trying to learn more about her. Come on Henry, Patience has been an enigma to everyone for her entire life. Everyone wants to know more about her. Why should Ellen be any different?"

"Well that's certainly true. I guess she's struggling to figure Patience out. I wish her luck. I am one of her closest friends and I still can't." Henry responded.

"Ain't that the truth. No one ever has. Well we plan on coming to your fancy soiree. Its going to take a little effort to get Bill into his suit jacket. We're going to have to dust off the cobwebs and he'll have to lose a few pounds, or twenty, more like. I have not seen that man in a suit since our youngest's first holy communion, and that was eight years ago. And you know he has put on a few pounds since then."

"I can't wait to see that. Bill DeCastro in a suit. That will make the entire evening worth while."

"Okay champ. I gotta go serve this order. I'll see you tomorrow right? For lunch? You promised and you're not backing out on me."

"You got it sweetie, I'll see you tomorrow." With that Henry hang up.

Henry thought more about Ellen's secret lunch trips to the Duck. What was she up to? Ellen does not engage in casual conversation, there is a specific point to every one she has. She either tries to influence someone or something to a premeditated outcome, which is always going to be in her favor, or she searches for information so she can then try to influence someone or something.

It was obvious that Ellen was not a fan of Patience, she made that clear the very first day they were in Mystic. And Henry also knew that Ellen was not one to change her mind, quite the opposite, she would go to then ends of the earth to prove herself right, long after she discovered that she may be wrong. So Ellen's questioning of me about Patience were of grave concern to Henry.

Wondering about Patience's father is not unusual, everyone does, including Henry. But when combined with the conversation Henry recently had with Lois about the same topic, Henry's desire to know the truth about Patience's father was elevated to a higher curiosity. He needed to make sure he knew more than Ellen about this, because having Ellen possess a piece of information that Henry did not was a dangerous thing, a dangerous opportunity for Ellen to manipulate someone or some outcome, and usually at a moment when Henry, or whoever the intended target was, would least suspect, and be most vulnerable.

Henry had no idea how vulnerable he actually had become.

As Christmas approached, the planning for the Christmas party was in full swing. Invitations had been sent, a caterer had been hired, and the Manor was all decked out in Christmas swag.

Most importantly, the swing band had been hired. That is another aspect of notoriety about the Mystic area that needs to be mentioned. Besides the famous seafaring history, its famous art subculture after the Depression, and besides the more recent and slightly odd fame with pizza, Mystic was also known for its bluesy swing bands. One band in particular, Roomful of Blues, garnered a lot of fame in the 1970s, winning a few Grammy awards. Once Roomful put the Mystic area on the music map, it started to attract other musicians to the area. Being on tour with and befriending the more famous blues musicians that toured the world, the members of Roomful would encourage these bands to stop and play in the Mystic area. The Fabulous Thunderbirds and the Vaughn brothers would often make a tour stop in the area, a treat for small towns that would otherwise be passed right over for these national music acts. It was only a matter of time before members of well-known bands began to make the Mystic area their home.

For the amateur musicians in Mystic it was a double edged sword. The number of professional musicians making their home in the area influenced many of the locals to pick up an instrument and try to play. But due to the professional musicians that lived in the area, the level of musical ability that one would see in the local bars was much higher than normal. While this encouraged amateurs to get better, it also was slightly discouraging at the same time. Bill was an example of this. He was a professional fisherman, which meant in the winter months he had a lot of extra time on his hands, time he spent in the basement trying to pretend he was Jimi Hendrix or Stevie Ray Vaughn. But he was never going to be, he just was not talented enough, like most of his friends he jammed with a few times a month.

With the expectation of good music much higher than normal in Mystic, when you are having a party with a band, it better be a good band, or the music critique will start before the band has finished its first set. For this year's party it was discovered that some of the original members of Roomful would be in town, and someone suggested that Ellen try and get them to play. A few calls were made, favors called in and before she knew it, both Greg Piccolo and Al Copley, two of the original members of Roomful of Blues had agreed to play at the Christmas party, quite a treat for all of us who had grown up listening to these guys play.

The week of the party, Henry and Patience were having one of their Tuesday get-togethers. Patience had received an invitation to the party but was very reluctant to go. Patience announced, "so Henry, I got one of the invitations to the queen's ball," in a somewhat mocking tone of voice, referring to Ellen as the queen. "You know how much I hate parties like that, so I emailed Ellen that I was going to miss the party. And to my surprise, Ellen called me."

"Really!" Henry responded quite in shock. After all the vitriol from Ellen about Patience, Henry thought that Ellen would be happy that Patience would not show up. "What did she say?"

"Well she basically told me that she really wanted me to come, and more importantly, that the patients really wanted me to come. She told me that she had recently begun to understand how important I was to Mystic Manor,"

"Does that seem odd to you?" Henry asked.

"Yes Henry, it seemed really odd at the time and still does. I may not understand everything but reading people's feelings is what I do best, and Ellen's feeling towards me are incredibly mixed. I mostly intrigue her, I guess I am an enigma to her."

"That's exactly what Cat said a few weeks ago." Henry said with a laugh.

"Were you guys talking about me? What else did she say about me?"

Henry immediately regretted mentioning his conversation with Cat, Patience was only going to know more than he would want to reveal. "You know how much she adores you." Henry responded trying to not go too far down that path.

"You are not getting out of this with flattery. What did you guys talk about?"

"I don't even remember why she called, I think it has something to do with the party at the Manor, Bill's suit and tie or something. But while we were talking, she mentioned that Ellen had been stopping in to the Duck for lunch, which surprised me, and had at one point asked about you." Henry, still trying to avoid relaying most of the conversation he had had with me because the topic of Patience's father was something that Henry and Patience had rarely ever talked about.

"Did Cat happen to mention if Ellen had asked about my father?" As usual, Patience intuitively knew exactly what we had talked about and she went right to the heart of it.

Henry realized there was no holding back about the conversation he had with me about Ellen, she was too insightful so he was going to have to come clean. All the same, Henry was really getting nervous about this line of questioning. "Actually, yes she did."

"And what did Cat tell her?"

"She told her the same answer we have told for thirty years when someone asked that question. No one knows who your father is. It's a question that has been debated for years and no one knows, simple as that. I think she mentioned about the Woodstock possibility and that seemed to end the conversation."

Patience knew what Ellen was up to, but she was not going to reveal that much about Ellen's real motivation to Henry. Ellen was in a battle with Patience for Henry's allegiance. When challenged, Ellen Chandler was a vicious foe, and despite not really wanting to go down that road with Ellen, Patience was headed down it whether she liked it or not. Henry was in love with her, and as a woman, Patience knew that Ellen knew as much. That meant that no matter what Patience wanted, Henry was going to drag them both down that road because his feelings for Patience were real and they were uncompromising.

Patience knew that Ellen looked at it as if she was at war with Patience, and the first thing one does when they are war with someone is to gain the upper hand, and in this war, the upper hand was going to go to the person who had information the other did not have, information that could be used against them at the right moment. The topic of Patience's father was an unknown, and that deeply troubled Ellen and she was determined to get to the bottom of it.

"So what are you going to do?" Henry asked getting back to the subject of Patience and the party. "Are you going?"

"Yes."

"You caved that quickly to the queen?"

"Hah! No I didn't cave Henry, I did not do it for Ellen, I am going to go because I like my patients and I don't get to see them very often other than in my classes. And also I am interested in seeing where this little engagement thing I am having with your wife is going to go." The reality was that Patience knew exactly where this was going to go, but she could not tell Henry what she knew because if he knew what was in store for him and her, he would never agree to allow it to play out that way.

Finally Saturday night arrived and everyone spent the day getting ready for the Christmas party. All of Henry's local friends had been invited, Charles Jr and Amy, Bill and I, the others that were at his welcome home party back in the spring, and even Charles Sr was invited, though he had declined due to his health.

As Patience was getting ready at home, Lois, who had not been invited, came into her room. "Honey, you know you don't have to do this. You can change your mind."

"Why would I do that mother? I am perfectly at peace with tonight." Patience replied.

Lois took a more serious tone with Patience, something she had not done in a very long time. "Don't underestimate me dear child, I am wiser and have more insight than even you do, I am your mother, and you know full well what is going to happen tonight. So I say again, you can change your mind."

"No mother, I cannot change my mind. What is going to happen tonight is going to happen whether I am there or not. Henry and I are both better off if we face it together. I am not going to abandon him to deal with this by himself, he will completely and utterly fall to pieces. And that puts the eventual outcome in question. So once again, I really do not have a choice."

"You can go to Ellen directly, talk with her directly, you do not have to let it play out this way. The unknowns and risks are simply too great." Lois was clearly concerned for Patience's future.

"Mother you are right, you are as insightful as I am, so you know as much as I know about where this is going to end up, and you know there is only one path that this has to take. And that means I have to go to this party."

Lois was silent. As her mother, Lois hated what she suspected Patience was going to go through. Due to Patience and her mysterious birth, Lois had lived a lifetime of sideways glances, and under-the-breath comments. It deeply impacted her life, her friends, her ability to work, everything. She knew how painful that could be, and she was loathe to think that Patience was about to experience that for herself.

"Mother, I love you more than anything. You are trying to protect me, you always have. You will never abandon me, and that is all I need to know to have the courage to do this. I know what I am doing, eyes wide open." After a minute pause where they both simply stared at each other, Patience continued, "So help me get this dress on so I can get on with this."

Ellen had planned that the first part of the evening would be mostly for staff members and patients in the main cafeteria with the band. At around 9 pm, Charles Jr, Henry and their friends would move up to Ellen's office where Ellen had a slide show that she had put together that she wanted to show everyone, made up of some old pictures she had found of Henry and others in photo albums.

By 6:00 pm the food was ready, the band was ready and the guests started arriving on time. Patients who could walk by themselves made their way down to the cafeteria. Staff members wheeled the others who were in wheelchairs. Other staff members who were not on duty that night came in their party best and everyone was excited, this was a much more elaborate party than in previous years at the Manor.

At a party where a swing band is playing, dancing will quickly follow. And within minutes the crowd was dancing away to the music. The staff and patients who were mobile started the dancing, and very quickly patients in wheel chairs began to do the same.

For the first hour or so Henry purposely avoided dancing with anyone. But after a little while Ellen came up to him and asked him to dance with her. Of all the things that Ellen and Henry were amazingly bad at as a married couple, dancing was not one of those. Henry had learned to swing dance as a teenager listening to Roomful of Blues play at the local bars, and of course Ellen had studied dance along with all the other social manner classes she was forced to attend as a Chandler. So while they could barely hold a conversation without stepping all over each other, they could dance like few others. That was most likely because Ellen, who took the dominant position in everything they did together, leaving Henry trying and failing to assert himself whenever he could, did not do that when dancing. Ellen was classically trained that when dancing she was to let the man lead. And she did. Dancing was the one thing they could do as a couple where Henry did not have to awkwardly fight for dominance in the endeavor, when dancing with Ellen, Henry was uncharacteristically allowed to be the dominant person, and he was good at it.

But despite that, Henry was not in a dancing mood and did not want to dance with anyone, let alone with Ellen, so he put her off. After a few minutes Patience came up to Henry, the first time they had talked all night, and asked him to please dance with his wife. Henry didn't quite know how to respond to her request but he figured Patience had a point, so Henry went up to Ellen and told her he was ready to dance.

When Henry and Ellen started dancing, all heads turned. Henry swung Ellen around him like his arms were rubber, a twist and a twirl, from left to right, arms outstretched, the other's fingers sliding down their arms until right before they were about to lose touch, when their fingertips would curl and grab hold of each other and swing each other back into their arms again for another twist and a twirl. This was repeated over and over again, Henry sometimes twirling Ellen to his left, sometimes to his right. And every minute or so they would do the "blender," the penultimate swing dance move, where Henry would reach his right hand behind his back and grab Ellen's hand and twirl her around so she was facing away from him, twirl her back to his right and then left and end with a tango-like move where their arms slid down each other's until their hands clasped where they would start all over again.

The party continued over the next hour. Henry was miserable. He was extremely uncomfortable being in a room with both Ellen and Patience and found it almost unbearable. He was absolutely head over heels in love with Patience and therefore loved everything about her. He was mesmerized at the grace in her walk. He had not seen her in a ball gown since his senior prom in high school and she was as stunning as any actress walking down the red carpet at the Oscars.

He watched her dance with other men, including Bill, and he was mesmerized by the fluidity in her dancing even more than her walking. Dancing is mostly back and forth motions, either side to side or front to back. At some point one's motion stops moving in one direction and returns to its position by going in the opposite direction. When Patience danced there was no back and forth, no jerky stops and starts, Henry stared at her as she danced for a few minutes trying to understand what she did that was so different than others and it finally came to him, she moved in figure eights, but not her whole body at once, her head, upper body, arms, hips and legs all moved independently of each other, each doing figure eights that were at times parallel, at times perpendicular, and at times on a different axis to the figure eight above or below it. It was beautiful to watch, and he could have watched her all night but Henry had to look away or it would be too obvious he was staring.

At around 7:00 pm, during the band's break in between their two sets, Ellen went up to the microphone to make a quick and perfunctory thank you speech. "Hello everyone, I cannot thank you enough for coming tonight. A few people have asked why the elaborate party this year, and here is my answer. As you all know all too well, since I arrived at the Manor a few months ago I have been making some changes here. We have modified our therapy regimens, and brought in some additional resources and that has required some work on your part. To the patients, it has required some new therapies, and I appreciate how much you have all been willing to give them a chance to work. To the staff, you have all had to learn a different approach to rehabilitation, and that has required some time commitments on your part, and I wanted you all to know how much I appreciate your confidence in me and the changes I have made. Along the way we have lost a few of our therapists, but we gained some new ones also. So what better way to celebrate all the hard work by everyone than to have a party?" With that a huge applause went up in the air.

"So tonight I want you to all enjoy yourselves, have a fun time, eat the great food, and I hope to see some great dancing out on the dance floor to the great music by Al and Greg."

Seeing Ellen and Patience stand side by side, knowing how much Ellen despised Patience, not knowing why she was being so gracious, and seeing how gracious Patience was being in return, Henry wanted to end the entire charade right there, it was all he could do not to go up to the microphone and announce to the entire world that he was in love with Patience and that his marriage to Ellen was a hoax. He wanted to tell everyone that he had been secretly having an affair with Patience for the past few weeks and that the Mystic community could finally relax, the great love affair between Henry Moore and Patience Passion that had been in the making for 40 years was finally consummated. All was now right with the world.

Maybe he should have, it would have put Henry on the offensive and would have caught Ellen off guard. But he could not do that to Patience. Henry was terrified of harming Patience and if it became public that Patience was having an affair with a married man, it could ruin her life, her career, everything. So as so often was the case, he stuffed his feelings, his passion, his desires, he gritted his teeth, clenched his fists and Henry acquiesced to the reality of the life that he had made for himself.

At 9:00 the band announced that they would play one last song, and everyone went to the dance floor for one last song. Ellen and Henry clasped hands, Bill and I did the same. One of the older male patients in Patience's class who had recently recovered to the point where he could walk asked her to dance and she was very moved. For the next 8 minutes or so we all danced to a slow love song that finally came to an end.

Ellen returned to the microphone and announced to the crowd that the party was concluding and asked if the staff could escort the patients who needed assistance back to their rooms. At 9:30 or so after a number of thank-yous and goodbyes, Ellen asked our group of about 16 friends and some of the staff members to move to her office, because she had a surprise for everyone. As we slowly moved down the main hallway, continuing goodbyes to those lingering there, we all talked about what a fun evening it was, and everyone remarked at how well Ellen and Henry danced. Henry and Bill started to reminisce about sneaking into bars when they were young to swing dance and how they would try to pick up older girls in their twenties by asking them to dance.

We finally got to Ellen's office and all went in. It was a very large office and could easily fit more than twenty people comfortably. There were a few couches to sit on, and a table with chairs to sit around. A bar had been set up on the credenza, there was food on the table, and a large wide screen TV on a small desk against a wall. The conversation continued with Henry, Bill and the other guys regaling their teenage conquests about dancing and picking up girls in bars. I reminded Bill that he and I had been dating since high school, so despite his delusions about picking up girls in bars, he better admit that there was no picking up going on if he wanted to sleep at home tonight.

Bill obliged, "Yes dear, you know I am completely full of hot air. I can without a doubt say that, despite trying, since we first started dating, I have never picked up another girl in a bar."

Bill was too drunk to realize what he had just said. "Oh my God, you are such an ass. Despite trying? Why were you trying to pick up other girls while we were dating?"

"Fuckin' a, Cat, why you getting so upset? We were teenage boys, we all tried to pick up the older chicks back then. It was like, a challenge, you know?" Bill was trying to defend himself, but everything he said he dug himself in deeper.

"The only thing that was challenged was you, you dumb ass." I let him have it. Everyone stopped talking and stared at me, not knowing whether to laugh or not, I didn't want to change the happy festive mood of the party at that point so I broke into a big smile, started laughing, and tried to say something to lighten the mood, "That's my husband, the high school lady killer," and laughed some more.

At that everyone else started laughing too. Charles Jr., trying to defuse the situation spoke up, "and as you can see it ended well for the lady killer, he wooed the best chick in the bunch and somehow convinced her to marry him."

"Thanks, now I'm looking like the dumb ass," I joked. Everyone laughed again.

That kind of banter between Bill and I and our friends had been going on for twenty years. Everyone knew that Bill was more brawn than brains and because of that his mouth got him into trouble all the time. Everyone knew I was incredibly smart but was as tough as I was smart. I was not a push over and was going to let him and anyone else have it if they deserved it. Bill just deserved it a little more than others.

But despite that difference, Bill and I were actually perfect for each other, we complemented each other and deep down we really loved each other. While many want to get out of Mystic as soon as they can, move onto bigger pastures once out of high school or college, I could not imagine living anywhere else, and I could not imagine being married to anyone else.

Nor could I imagine being married to someone who was not from the Mystic area, someone who I had not known for their entire life. There is a feeling you get when you are in a relationship with someone that you have known for their entire life. Everyone has their warts that they try to hide, but warts are on the surface and eventually they are visible for all to see for those who simply look hard enough. But everyone also has skeletons in their closet, and those are the things that people can successfully hide. Except when you have known someone for their entire life. There are no skeletons in the closet when you have known someone since they were born, and have known their family just as long. We may not talk about each other's skeletons, and new friends may not know about them, but when you grow up with a group of friends for your entire life, there are no secrets, and there is comfort in that.

There is also comfort in the fact that we were more than just friends, this group of friends that I had known since I can remember, like Henry and Charles Jr and Amy, we were closer than siblings. We all knew that if any of us found ourselves in a bad situation, or needed anything, each of us would fly around the world, risk our lives and spare no expense to help the others. There was no value that could be placed on the friendships we had, it meant more than money and our lives.

While we all understood what Henry did when he moved away and never looked back, it had happened numerous times as people we grew up left because they needed more challenges than they could get in the Mystic area, but we all knew that he couldn't stay away forever. That bond of childhood friendship was too strong for this group of friends. It was the comfort it brought. That comfort of having no skeletons to hide, no lies, no exaggerations, no distrust. The comfort to know that at any time or any moment that one would be taken care of with no expectation of anything in return. It was a stronger pull than any other force in nature. Gravity itself could not keep us from each other over the long term.

The thought of moving to Los Angeles and marrying into a family that I hardly knew was terrifying to me. Especially one that had so much to protect. It was clear that Henry was in trouble when he was in college. Having lost his family right at the moment a young man needs his foundation to build his life upon, one would think at the top of the list would be to stay where people would take care of you. But he needed something else at that moment. He needed to prove himself, as all young men need to do at that age. But at the same time he was terrified of failure. So he needed to prove himself, but he needed to do it away from his friends in case he failed. That way they would not be around to watch him fail and that way it would cause them less grief.

He loved his friends more than anything. He had weighed his odds and he had bet against himself, he had bet against his success. In moving to Los Angeles he had dealt his friends out of the hand so they would not lose either. And by doing that, Henry had thought that he had also walked away from all that comfort of friendship that I experience every day in Mystic. He had placed himself in a shark tank. He woke up every morning, got dressed and dove in, hoping to be in one piece at the end of the day when it was time to climb out again. While he thought that would toughen him up, it didn't, it simply wore him out. So Henry was simply not prepared for what was about to happen. He had lost his strength, his will, and his compass. But he had not lost his friends. Whether he knew it or not, we would never abandon him, he was part of the gang, and we would go to any extreme to rescue him. If only he understood that.

Ellen spoke up. "Hey everyone, I have a surprise for you. Since I have been in Mystic I have heard story after story about the last forty or so years of you all growing up together. But it appears that no one has ever documented this. So over the last few weeks I have been collecting photographs from a variety of places, thanks to some of you have helped me with that. I have put together a slide show." With that everyone formed a circle around the wide screen TV on the credenza, and Ellen hit play on the DVD.

We were all smiles, everyone but Patience, who stayed at the back of the room behind everyone. If anyone had turned around to notice, they would have noticed tears in her eyes that slowly became tears running down her face.

The slide show was ordered by date starting out with photos when we were very young. There were photos of Charles Jr and Henry as young boys, our prom photos of Bill and I and the rest of us in silly looking outfits. Everyone laughed and cheered at every new photo. At the sight of Bill in his orange colored prom tuxedo with ruffly shirt, everyone almost peed themselves and fell on the floor with laughter.

"Go ahead and laugh, but I was the dance king that night, admit it, admit it!" Bill yelled.

"More like a dancing fool, with an emphasis on the fool." I yelled back.

The photos moved to shots on the water, the boys racing their sailboats off the dock of the Masons Island Yacht Club, the boys on the Mason's schooner the Pequot, of Bill in his orange lobster bib-alls on his first small fishing boat, no bigger than a small runabout. Everyone cheered or had some funny comment on each photo.

Next were photos of us as we got into our 20's. Weddings, children, the first day of when I took ownership of the Duck. We were all enjoying ourselves. Then came photos of Henry in Los Angeles. Ellen announced "I know most of you didn't get to see Henry while he was on the West Coast, so I wanted to share some photos I have of us over the past twenty years." More photos of weddings, and other events in Henry's life.

Ellen once again spoke up,"and I know Henry and Patience have been friends a long time, and I was able to get some photos of that friendship." Everyone was surprised at Ellen's announcement and cheered. Not the least was Henry who was pretty sure there were very few photos of Henry and Patience ever taken.

Bill spoke up, "you must have paid a pretty penny to get photos of those two."

"Yes I did, yes I did." Ellen responded prophetically.

Patience leaned up against the back wall prepared for what was next.

The first few photos were of Henry and Patience as kids, and looked like they were taken on the Mason estate. And then it happened. The next photo was of Henry and Patience, as adults, and they were in bed together, covers on but clearly naked.

At first no one knew what to say, everyone first thought it was a joke, staged, and someone laughed a nervous laughter. That photo was quickly followed by another one. It was from the same angle, and looked like it had to be taken by someone looking through a window into Patience's bedroom.

Henry, who was across the room from the television and Ellen all of a sudden realized what was happening and yelled out, "For Christ's sake Ellen, what the hell are you doing?"

The tone of Ellen's voice, which had been so friendly all night immediately changed into a one of distraught. "Actually Henry, the question is what the hell are you doing. What the hell have you been doing. Why Henry, why? You had everything. And you just threw it away for that, that..." and her voice trailed off. As Ellen said that her gaze moved over to Patience who was still in the back of the room. As she did that, everyone's eyes moved over to Patience who had her back up against one of the book cases and was crying. In their shock from the last few seconds, most did not notice that she had not just started crying, only a few of us noticed that she had been crying for quite awhile because the tears had already stained her face.

I was in emotional overload. It was one of the most shocking changes in emotion that any of us had ever experienced. We were all happy and laughing and then all of a sudden the entire mood of the room was ripped away and replaced with horror, as if someone had just been shot to death in front of our eyes. For one of the few times in my life I had nothing to say. Everyone just stood there in silence alternating looking at Henry, Ellen and Patience.

Henry was in shock. He looked at Patience and the reality of what had just happened sank in. Tears started flowing down his face also. For the second time in his life, he had completely abandoned the most precious person in his life. The first time when he left Mystic married Ellen and never called Patience to explain any of it. But this would be worse. Patience had just been publicly shamed, and it was his fault.

He knew Ellen had it out for Patience since they arrived, but he had falsely thought that she had moved on and was no longer that interested in Patience as a rival, just Patience as an enigma. It all of a sudden hit him like a ton of bricks that he had clearly been wrong. Ellen had not moved on, he remembered her words the first night they arrived in Mystic, the venom in her voice about Patience when she said that she would put Patience in her place.

In her brilliance, Ellen had figured out a way not just to embarrass Patience, but to humiliate her, and to do so in front of the two groups of people that Patience counted on, her friends and the staff of Mystic Manor. And to do so in a way that would destroy Patience's entire life. Ellen knew that people's impression of Patience would instantly go from one of healer to one of destroyer. The aura of goodness and peacefulness that always surrounded Patience would be replaced with an aura of doubt and scorn.

Ellen knew that adultery is almost universally accepted as an unforgivable act. Societal norms in almost every society on earth place the utmost importance on the family unit. The belief is that without which, the earth would be a perpetual state of Sodom and Gomorrah. Scripture does not allow for exceptions and excuses to adultery. There is no excuse for it with religions and societies who have built their rules on maintaining peace and harmony. And just like in the Scarlet Letter, while the married one who cheats may be shamed, an unmarried person who breaks up a marriage in an adulterous affair is completely and utterly scorned, especially if it is a woman. Hester Prin wore the scarlet letter, not the man who she slept with.

Henry knew Ellen well enough to know that she planned everything she did down to the finest detail, there was never anything left to chance. She played life like a game of chess with every possible move planned out well in advance. It had been less than a minute since the first picture came on that television, and everyone was still in a state of shock, and Henry needed to react immediately, he needed to say something, but he also knew that every comment or reaction had already been anticipated by

Ellen, and she already had her next moves well planned out. He contemplated every move and his heart sunk, all of a sudden he realized he had been checkmated, he realized there was nothing he could say to undo the damage that had just been done.

To yell at Ellen would be yelling at the broken-hearted wife. To be sympathetic to Patience would just confirm his adulterous feelings toward her. He didn't need to ask Ellen why, he knew why. The only thing he could ask was why here and why now?

Another photograph of Henry and Patience, covered by sheets but clearly naked in bed came on the screen and Henry had had enough, he walked over to the television it was playing on and shut the power off. As he did that he realized he needed to break the silence, so after turning off the television he turned and asked Ellen the one question that would provide the least damaging response. "Why, in this way, Ellen? Why here, why now, and why with these people? Why cause this scene? My friends do not deserve this, to be involved in this mess in this way."

"Why Henry? You want to know why? Because I wanted everyone else to know my pain. I wanted everyone who supports that woman, and surrounds her with such warmth and love, to know that she is a fraud. She is not a healer, she is a destroyer, she destroys things. I knew no one would listen any other way. I needed to expose the hypocrisy. I needed this hospital to know exactly why she cannot work here anymore. And I needed to do it in a way that would shock everyone out of the delusion that Patience Passion is some kind of wonderful human being. Look at her. Take a good look at the person who slept with my husband."

It was Patience's turn. She had known for a few weeks that this was going to happen, she felt the energy that surrounded Henry and her and all their friends. She also knew that sleeping with Henry would be potentially devastating to them both and to her career, especially at the hospital. But there was something else she knew that had kept her from stepping off the train she was now on.

And finally Patience spoke. But true to form, despite what just happened, despite all the emotions that she could have revealed, despite everyone looking at her with shock, she spoke in the most calm and gentle manner, with no anger or malice or embarrassment. She was not going to apologize or acknowledge Ellen's manipulative attempt for symphony. "We look for truth, we feel and we protect those we love. Its human nature. You have to ask yourself Ellen, what truth are you looking for? What do you feel, and what or who are you protecting?" And with that Patience walked across the room and headed out the door.

Henry was being torn in two. When all eyes turned to Patience a sudden feeling of desolation and intense sadness had come over him. Of course he always knew it was possible that his affair with Patience could become public but he dreaded the possibilities and consequences of that happening. As he had thought about it, he had promised himself that he would sacrifice himself and his life before Patience would suffer. He was most worried about what it would do to her, her career but mostly her reputation. She was beloved by people in the area, how would they react?

As Patience walked out of the room Henry was torn. He could follow after her but he knew that would just confirm what everyone suspected, and it would give Ellen time with those in the room to get the sympathy she wanted. If he stayed he would have to endure the continued intense awkwardness. He was starting to get contemptuous stares from some in the room that he did not know so well, like the hospital staff.

He made a quick decision to stay in the room to try and manage the scene. "I am so sorry. I am so sorry to all of you. I had no idea that was going to happen." Glancing at Ellen he continued, "I am so sorry that my wife decided to involve you in all of this. It should have been handled a different way. I am so sorry. I won't make excuses, obviously you all saw the photographs. Patience and I have a long and complicated history," Henry paused for a second, "and that history just got more complicated."

There was a long silence. Henry and Ellen had given their speeches. Someone needed to break the ice and end this scene. In our circle of friends that was either left to me or to Charles Jr.. If the moment needed levity and humor, it was my cue to speak up, if the moment needed something touching or heartfelt, everyone looked to Charles, and he could tell people were expecting him to end this incredibly awkward moment.

Charles spoke, "Okay everyone, I think it's time we left these two alone, they have a lot to talk about, and we should give them some space to do that." Turning to Henry he said, "if you need a place to stay, your room is available." Charles was referring to the same room that Henry slept in the very first night he had returned to Mystic when he and Ellen had gotten into their first fight over Patience.

At that we all headed out of the room and down the hallway. There was dead silence. No one uttered a word other than simple goodbyes until they were in their cars in the parking lot. Bill and I got into our Toyota, I got in the driver's seat as I do whenever we drive home from a party assuming that Bill has had too much to drink. Bill got into the passenger's seat. We closed the doors at the same time and turned to each other and gave each other the look that says "Holy Shit!"

Bill started. When he is excited his New England accent shines through, which usually means using an f-bomb in every sentence and he did not disappoint. "Oh my fuckin' God, can you believe what just fuckin' happened? That fuckin' bitch. Why would she fuckin' do that?"

I responded, "Honey if you want to talk about this here, can you lose a few of the f-bombs?"

"Yea okay, I'm sorry."

"Thank you. Its pretty clear why she did it. She hates Patience and wanted her thoroughly ridiculed in the most public way possible." And then it dawned on me, I had a few conversations with Ellen over the past few weeks about Patience during my lunches with Ellen. I had been completely fooled into thinking that Ellen's intentions were okay. "Oh my God! Oh my fuckin' God!" Now it was my turn to start swearing.

"Cat, what the hell?" said Bill who had just been scolded by me for dropping f-bombs.

"I can't believe she used me that way. I thought she was really interested in Patience so I helped her understand who Patience was. I hope to God I didn't somehow just cause that. Patience didn't even want to go to the fucking dance."

"Cat!" Bill responded once again.

"I'm sorry Bill, but I'm in a friggin' panic. Ellen and I have been having lunch at the Duck for the last few weeks and she has been asking a lot about Patience. She said she wanted to get to know her better. Now I have to rack my brain to figure out exactly what I told her. Did I give her any info that could have caused that?"

"Honey, Ellen has had it out for Patience since she first arrived here. I doubt you did anything to cause that scene. I mean, you might have helped it along some, but..."

"Thanks!" I was really upset and the last thing I needed was my husband's misplaced humor. "I need to think. Can you drive?"

Bill immediately answered, "Of course I can drive."

"I mean are you too drunk to drive, how many drinks did you have?" I asked.

"I'm fine sweetie. I'm fine. "With that we got out of the car and switched seats and Bill drove us home in silence as I thought about the entire evening.

Adultery. It's a nasty sounding word. With thousands of cultures on this planet, there are few societal norms that are common among them all and adultery is one, probably the most common one of them all. Even murder is accepted in many cultures, often for avenging adultery. Which means that in many societies, adultery sits at the top of the list of heinous crimes, above murder, on par with rape and child molestation.

The marital vow is sacred. The vow we make when we marry someone is to persist in that relationship forever, until the end, "what God has put together, let no man put asunder," no matter how bad it gets, "for better or worse." For centuries the Catholic Church would not even recognize divorce.

So though I was not surprised at what they did, as a good Catholic I was still supposed to be disappointed. But I was not. Nor was I angry, in a way I was relieved. It was an indication that Henry might be finally getting some love that he so thoroughly deserved. So there must be a loophole in the law somewhere, there must be something that, if not justifying, at least excuses it, otherwise what Henry and Patience did would just feel so wrong. As I thought about it on the ride home and then half that night, the more I thought about it, the less it seemed so wrong, and the more it seemed so right.

CHAPTER 14

The Aftermath

Over the next few days the phones in Mystic Connecticut were ringing off the hooks. Within a few hours the entire town had heard about what had happened at the Mystic Manor Christmas party. People were basically divided into three camps. The traditionalists, which included my fellow Catholics, thought that what Henry and Patience did was horrendous, and ironically were mostly unforgiving. The laissez-fairs, which included people who knew the story of Henry and Patience, were mostly forgiving. The longtime salty New Englanders, true to form, thought it was none of their business, and refused to talk about it.

Henry did not go back to Charles & Amy's house that night, he stayed out in the backhouse where he had been sleeping most nights anyway, and continued to stay there for the next three nights as he tried to figure out how to go on with the rest of his life. There was no contact with Ellen for those three days. On the fourth day at about 9:00 am in the morning, there was a knock on the door. When he opened the door he was stunned to find Ellen's father and her brother Billy standing in front of him.

Henry and his father-in-law had a comfortable but distant relationship. Henry was his daughter's first husband. For a father from Los Angeles this means that at the wedding he is handing his daughter off to a groom he assumes is not going to stick around too long. Henry had often heard his mother-in-law say to her friends whose daughters were having their first wedding, "he's nice for a first husband." He chuckled when he heard that, it was so LA, where everything is most admired for its temporary convenience. He wondered whether the oft-repeated saying was the chicken or the egg. Did the "he's nice for a first husband" attitude cause first marriages in LA to fail because no one, including the bride and groom, really expected them to last? As soon as trouble came along, it was splitsville? Or did they not last for some other reason and the saying simply reflected the reality?

Another thing about the state of marriage in LA is that everyone assumes that everyone is having affairs. It is not a horrendous act like it is in more traditional parts of the country like New England. In LA having an affair is not the scandal, in LA the scandal is about who you had the affair with. It's not the what, its the who. And once an affair happens, the shock is quickly replaced with dollar signs, what kind of financial leverage does it bring you when your spouse has an affair. Wives are often happy when their first husband has an affair, as a first husband, the marriage was going to end anyway, and this gives the wife the uncomplicated reason she needs to end it, and the leverage she needs to get something out of it while she's at it.

So after twenty years Richard Chandler was not at all surprised about the affair, he was much more surprised that it took twenty years to happen. Likewise he was not surprised his daughter's marriage was in trouble. But he had a family reputation to uphold, and the Chandler family was always going to come out on top with their reputation in tact. So leading up to the public outing of Henry and Patience, which Richard Chandler knew was going to happen a few weeks in advance, the Chandler family already had the plan on what to do with Henry and what to do to him.

In LA there is only one way to rid oneself of a sordid past, a long stint in rehab. It's like a hangover tonic, it amazingly wipes the slate clean so one can live for a new day. Since Henry's sin was not drugs or alcohol, the Betty Ford clinic was not going to do it. The only rehab that would be sufficient for Henry's crime would be one for sexual deviancy. Sure enough, as the Chandler's were planning out the entire process of outing Henry, a call was made to the Carver Clinic in Rochester, New York, a well-known rehab for sexual deviancy, and a bed was reserved for a 12 week period, which would be sufficiently long period of time for the penance to occur.

The only real question that Richard Chandler had was how to guarantee that Henry would go along with this plan without a fight. But Richard Chandler was not that worried, his leverage over Henry was years in the making. Henry's net-worth and career were in Richard Chandler's well-manicured hands. So the pitch would be simple, "go to rehab and walk away with the ability to continue to work at a prestigious college" or "refuse to go to rehab and walk away with hundreds of thousands of dollars in legal bills from a long and contentious divorce and a future job at a community college." Staying married to Ellen was a possibility, but that would be solely up to Ellen, and he would only know that answer when she was ready to make that decision. Given the prospects it was quite clear to Richard Chandler which way Henry would go.

So here he was on Henry's doorstep about to execute a plan that he had been working on for a few weeks while Henry had absolutely no idea why Mr. Chandler was standing at his door. It was not going to be a fair fight, just like it had never been a fair fight during his twenty year marriage to the Chandlers.

"Mr. Chandler, what a surprise," Henry finally uttered after a few moments of shock.

"Good morning Henry. I know you are surprised to see me here, but obviously Ellen has had quite the traumatic week and I thought it would be a good time as any to come visit her and support her through this crisis. May we come in?"

"Of course, of course sir. How are you Billy?" Henry said as the two Chandler's walked through his door into the tiny but cozy backhouse.

"Interesting place you have here Henry," Mr. Chandler said after he got inside.

Billy spoke next, speaking before thinking which was typical of Billy Chandler, "I love it. Looks like a great bachelor pad."

"Well let's hope I'm not about to become one," Henry said only half jokingly, "is that why you are here, have you come all this way to tell me that I am about to reclaim my bachelorhood?"

"Good boy Henry, I'm glad you've kept your sense of humor. You know I don't beat around the bush so let me get right to the point. As you can imagine Henry, you have caused quite a stir and a bit of an awkward scene for Ellen and my family. We can't be having a son-in-law of the Chandler's off gallivanting around having himself photographed naked in bed with strange women. It is unseemly."

"Yes, it is sir. I am truly sorry for the situation I have put you and Ellen in," Henry replied. He was serious. Despite his negative feelings for Ellen, he did understand the position he had put the family in.

"But of course you are my son-in-law, and you have managed to remain an integral member of my family for over twenty years, and I have come to look at you like a son, so I want to help you through this as much as I want to help Ellen through this. It seems son that you have a bit of a problem," Mr. Chandler was quickly getting to the heart of the matter.

"What problem is that sir?"

"Well its nothing to be ashamed of, it is quite common among us men. Billy has had a similar problem most his life, maybe much worse than you I would guess."

"Thanks dad, yes I like the ladies but I'm not married am I, so I don't really see that as much as a problem as it is a virtue."

"Billy, my son, sleeping with four or five woman at a time is not something I would consider virtuous." Turning his attention back to Henry, Mr. Chandler continued. "So here's what we are going to do Henry. I have arranged for you to go off for a little while to the Carver House in Rochester. It is a very nice facility, completely anonymous and private. No one will know you are there. They have a very good reputation for healing those with sexual deviancy issues."

Henry was dumbfounded. It took him a few seconds to compose himself. "You want me to go to rehab for my sexual deviancy issues? Sir I don't have sexual deviancy issues."

"Well from where I sit it appears that you do, and I would think the public perception right now says that you do also. But let me make this clear before that Harvard head of yours has come up with a number of reasons as to why you will fight this. I am not asking you if you want to go to rehab. I am telling you that you are going to rehab. And you are going today. You have one hour to pack enough clothes for twelve weeks." Richard Chandler was getting more stern, and like Charles Mason Sr, when he wanted to be stern, Richard Chandler could be very stern.

Henry was almost speechless. "Sir, I am not going off in one hour for twelve weeks of rehab. I have a life here."

"Henry, lets look at the facts here. One, at UCLA you hold the Chandler Chair of English Studies. I singlehandedly decide who sits in that chair. What's more, since I have given millions to UCLA, I carry quite a bit of weight on their employment decisions in general. Two, you are on a sabbatical from your job and are writing a book. Good, you can write a book in Rochester as easily as you can write it here. So let's just say that a twelve week detour to Rochester New York is not going to derail your career aspirations. Three, you just thoroughly pissed off your wife who doesn't want to see you right now. What a perfect time to take a break and get away. Four, you are living less than a mile from the woman you had an affair with and who, as I have learned, you have likely been madly in love with for years. The risk of this affair reoccurring is quite likely as long as you are sitting on this island. Five, you have no parents or children that need you. So from what I can tell Henry, there is not a reason in the world why you can't go to Rochester for twelve weeks, is there now son?" While it may sound like Mr. Chandler had that speech planned out word for word in advance, he didn't really, nor did he have to. It was clear to everyone what the facts were, he just had to lay them out for Henry.

Mr. Chandler continued. "I know this is quite a shock Henry, so I'll give you two hours instead of one. I have hired a private limo to take you up there, he's waiting outside. He can wait a little longer. Once again Henry, I am not asking you if you want to go.'

Henry looked his father-in-law in the eyes and Mr. Chandler stared right back. They stayed that way for thirty seconds or so, and Henry saw that the old man was gravely serious. He knew that he had few options. He knew what Mr. Chandler could do to him if he lost his support. He would be without a job and few prospects for one comparable to the one he was in now. He would be completely broke. He likely had no support system in his personal life. He had walked away from his personal support system in Mystic years before, and was not sure he had completely regained their confidence since coming back. Whatever confidence he had regained, he likely had completely blown three days ago. The one person who would support him unconditionally was Patience, and after the public shaming she received, she could not afford to be seen with him.

It became all too real for Henry that he had no support system in place. He was back where he was when he was twenty years old, even worse. As Mr. Chandler had said, Henry saw the facts and they looked grim. So he looked up at Mr. Chandler and said, "Okay sir, let's go. I'll pack a bag and my laptop, and as you said, I can write my book up there as easily as I can here."

Billy, who had been mostly silent spoke up, "You'll like it Henry, I've been there, although not for twelve weeks, but it's a nice place. Can't say that it helped me with my issues since I've relapsed about a hundred times since, but it's peaceful and you get to hide from the world for a while."

"Thanks Billy, if you survived it I guess I can too." Henry chided Billy, who once again missed the cutting remark.

Within thirty minutes, Henry was packed and ready to go. He got into the limo and six hours later he was in Rochester New York where he would be for the next twelve weeks, completely oblivious and out of the way to interfere with the rest of the plan that the Chandler's had set in motion. There was one more person's life and reputation they had to ruin.

The day after the Christmas party at the Manor, Patience received a phone call from the human resources assistant at Mystic Manor, a phone call that she was expecting, though she was not sure who was going to make the call. "Patience? This is Angela at the Manor."

"Hey there Angela. How are you? So you have been given the job of sacking me?" Patience said with complete empathy in her voice.

"I am so sorry Patience. You know how much I love you and how much everyone here does too. But yes, I am the lucky one who got the task of calling you. So here it goes, Dr. Chandler has decided to hire a new instructor for your class." She paused for a few seconds to let that sink in. "And this is the hardest part for me Patience, and you know I would never come up with this, but I have to tell you that Dr. Chandler thinks it would be better if you did not come for visits either. Oh, man let me just come out with it, I know this may hurt Patience, but basically they don't want you to have contact with any of the patients here in any way, either in person, or over the phone." Angela paused again. "Once again I am so sorry. What's hardest for me is that means I won't be seeing you for a while. I know this will pass over honey, it's just an awkward time, with what happened the other night and all. Obviously you are free to do what you want off the hospital property. But I'd be careful, it's probably not a secret that Dr. Chandler is holding somewhat of a grudge."

"It's my fault Angela. I gave her all the reason in the world to do this." Patience said with some humor in her voice. "Angela don't worry about me, I'll be fine. It's my students that I am concerned about."

"Well, we'll all keep an eye on them If things take a turn for the worse, I am sure Ellen will change her mind, I mean how long can she hold a grudge anyway?"

"Well I don't know her that well, but my gut tells me it will take a monumental event to get me back at the Manor anytime while Ellen Chandler is still there." Patience was once again speaking prophetically, though of course Angela had no idea of what was she was referring to. "Well thanks for calling Angela, sorry it had to be you, but I love you too. And maybe we'll see each other around town."

"Sure thing Patience. I'll be mailing your last paycheck in the mail, you should get it in a few days. See you soon." And with that Angela hung up.

Patience sat down at her dining room table. She had poured herself a cup of tea right before Angela called, and she slowly sipped it as she thought about the next few months, how they were going to play out, and all the things she needed to do to make sure the outcome she had foreseen would become a reality.

CHAPTER 15

Losing Patience

Ellen was extremely proud of herself. In private she beamed from ear to ear. In public, she acted as the aggrieved wife. She had gotten everything she wanted.

Patience was out of her way at the Manor. Olga, the replacement Yoga instructor that Ellen had been interviewing for a few weeks to take over Patience's class started on the following Tuesday. She would be able to finally prove that Patience had no positive effect on her patients, that their care would vastly improve with the techniques that Ellen had perfected.

Henry would never have the nerve to see Patience again. He would never risk it. The consequences would be too grave for him and especially Patience. She knew he would never leave Ellen, it would ruin him financially. She felt slightly sorry for him.

But mostly she was happy because she was back in control. She had come to Southern New England, a new place where she knew few people, where her LA connections did not help her much. The New England culture was foreign to her. It was one thing to go to Harvard, a University filled with people from all over the world, and because of that, it carried an international culture, with no one culture dominating beyond the upper middle class social values they all shared. It was something else to live in a small New England town with small New England town culture, a culture that is mostly opposite the culture she knew growing up in LA. Like Caesar, Ellen could proclaim Vini Vidi Vici. She had come, she saw, she conquered.

But despite her brilliance, Ellen was missing a very important piece of the puzzle. In her arrogance she had never stopped in to watch one of Patience's classes. She never looked at what Patience was actually doing with the patients. Like Julius Caesar, Ellen was about to get a lesson in proclaiming Vini, Vidi, Vici too soon.

After Olga took over Patience's class, things slowly began to deteriorate. With each class it seemed one or two patients were not returning. What had been two classes of about twenty each on Patience's last day was slowly dwindling, and within a month was down to about fifteen. After her tenth class Olga reported this to Ellen, her patients were slowly disappearing. Ellen was puzzled by this. Attending this class was part of the rehab routine for those patients that were mobile enough to do Yoga. This type of rehab could be done one on one as most physical rehab is done, but doing it in a group session makes it more fun for the patients, real physical rehab made to look like a Jazzercise class.

The next day, Ellen went to talk to some of the patients and the nurses responsible for them. She wanted to know why the class was dwindling. She basically got the same response from everyone who had stopped coming, they no longer felt like the class was helping them. Ellen had nothing but contempt for that answer. It was clear to her that what they missed was Patience and her warm presence, but Ellen was adamant that they were projecting their warm feelings toward Patience into the misconception that Patience was actually healing them. Ellen had nothing but contempt for Patience and her work from the beginning, she only allowed her to continue her classes because she thought she would do no harm. The thought that Patience was helping or actually healing the patients was a ridiculous thought for Ellen.

After a few more classes and a few more drop-outs, Ellen began to realize that replacing Patience with Olga was not the right way to handle the situation. The patients had become used to the class as more than a simple yoga class. Word spread from patient to patient that Patience's yoga class was really helpful as patients would cycle through the hospital for rehabilitative periods that typically lasted from a few weeks to many months. And that word of mouth reputation had persisted for years. It became clear to Ellen that what Patience had created was unique and could never be taken over by anyone else other than Patience. The patients would never allow it as long as Patience was still being talked about as some type of miracle worker. It was clear she was going to have to end the classes all together, at least until the word of mouth from one patient to another would stop, and then start them over again with a new method and motivation. So after another few weeks Ellen stopped the class all together.

When Ellen took over for Dr. Jones, she initiated a weekly meeting each Monday morning with the head nurses and the doctors in which they would go over patient progress. Each major case would be discussed and the team would offer professional suggestions on treatment. One of the administrative tools she introduced was a twenty point scoring system that ranked each patient's condition each week. As their condition improved they were assigned a number closer to twenty. This meant it was easier for her to assess overall patient improvement across the hospital. The patients could be grouped numerous ways and trends could be identified. For instance, patients could be grouped by injury type, age, severity of injury, length of stay, doctor, nurse team, floor, etc. At each weekly meeting a report was presented that showed overall patient improvement in all the categories according to the twenty point system.

Of course Ellen's goal for the hospital was to slowly increase the speed at which patients were rehabilitated and moved up the twenty point system. A few weeks after Patience was asked to leave the hospital, the weekly progress report that was delivered each Monday began to show that certain groups of patients were beginning to trend downward. It is not unusual for the overall group scores to vary slightly as new patients are brought to the hospital and start their rehabilitation, so at first, while it was noticed, it was assumed it was a temporary variation. But after a few weeks it was clear that things were not improving for some patients, quite the opposite, the condition of certain patients was getting noticeably worse.

Ellen knew there was a negative trend in the numbers, and her analytical mind was convinced that the answer was in how the data was grouped. All she had to do was find the right grouping of patients to uncover the answer. Was it the patients of one particular doctor? Or nursing team? Was it the sicker patients, which would indicate the initial rehab processes needed review? Was it the healthier ones, which means the end-of-stay process needed to be reviewed? Was it patients from one building, which could indicate they had a sick building syndrome? The answer was in the data, if she could only find it.

In a Monday meeting a few weeks after she had ended Olga's class, as they were sharing reports of their patient floors, Beverly, one of the head floor nurses, brought up an interesting observation to the team. She reported that the patients were starting to notice and comment on the fact that the condition of the patients was not improving in the way they had been a few months before. They were starting to talk among each other and had convinced themselves that it was due to Patience's absence at the hospital. Another head floor nurse reported the same thing, and then another.

Of course Ellen met this news with utter contempt. "I am not going to even entertain the notion that Patience's absence has anything to do with the decrease in the scoring results. That's simply absurd. My God, what will it take to get that woman out of my hospital? She's been gone for weeks and they still talk of her like she's a miracle worker. She's more like a lingering virus, once infected it takes a long time to get it out of the system. I do have to give her credit though, she certainly has these people wrapped around her finger."

All of the staff knew of Ellen's contempt for Patience. The public outing of Patience's affair with Henry gave Ellen the public cover to talk of Patience disdainfully in public in a way that she could not have before the affair was exposed. This tacit permission was given to Ellen as a wife who had been cheated on by another woman, of course it is okay to talk scornfully of the other woman. Due to the fact that Ellen and Patience worked in the same hospital, this extended into Ellen's professional life and she was given the same tacit permission to do so in a professional setting also, as long as the disdain was kept professional.

The staff at Mystic Manor was already intimidated by Ellen. She was brilliant, a foremost expert in her field, and while not always intentionally so, she was extremely intimidating. In a professional setting, the intimidation came through her confidence and arrogance, not through meanness. Due to the public knowledge of Ellen's feelings for Patience, the nurses were a bit intimidated about discussing the subject of Patience with Ellen. So despite many of the nurses thinking that there might be something to what the patients were thinking about Patience's absence being associated with the decline of the hospital health scores, no one was going to bring that up if they valued their job at Mystic Manor.

So while that unspoken feeling of many in the room lingered in the air after they had moved on from the topic after Ellen changed the subject, no one was going to raise it again. But Ellen was adamant about proving them all wrong. So after that Monday meeting she went back to her office and started crunching the scorecard numbers. She added a couple of fields of data to the scoring spreadsheet that would identify those patients who had been in Patience's class with a start date. She then cross-referenced the patients' health scores with the roster of Patience's students. She was determined to show the hard facts to the staff and to the other patients that there was nothing to the rumor that Patience Passion's absence from her hospital was having any negative effects. Once she had all the data downloaded, she built a report to show the results, and kicked off the report generator. It would take about thirty seconds for the report to generate.

When the report finished processing, Ellen sent it to the printer, twenty copies, so she could hand a hard copy of the report to the staff to show there was nothing to this rumor. She walked across her office and pulled the report off the printer and looked at the results for the first time. Ellen's blood ran cold. The report showed that every one of Patience's students scores had declined. It was not even close. In some cases the numbers showed drastic decline. Ellen went back to her computer to check that she had the numbers correct. She checked the download, the inputs, and the cross-references. She checked them again. There was no mistake. For the first time in her professional career, Ellen Chandler began to doubt herself. But the doubt only lasted a minute. It quickly went from doubt to curiosity.

Ellen talked softly to herself, "What were you doing Miss Passion? What were you doing to these people? There is something there, something, what the hell is it?"

Ellen did not want to go to her staff with this info, but she wanted to know more, so she decided to go straight to the patients who had been in Patience's class to get their thoughts on what was going on in Patience's class. She started with Mary Clark, an elderly patient who had been at the Manor for almost two years due to a debilitating stroke that left her incapable of returning home. She had also been in Patience's class the longest of anyone at the Manor.

She caught Mary right before dinner was to be served in her semi-private room. As she walked in, Mary, who was quite lucid despite the stroke and her advancing years was also quite a character. "Hi Doc, what do I owe this great pleasure? Come to spring me loose?"

"I wish Mrs. Clark, but not quite yet, you'll be here a little longer I'm afraid."

"Don't BS me there young lady, I'm not going home and I know it. But that's okay with me, I get a nice bed, free meals, and handsome young doctors to flirt with. Though I haven't yet convinced any of them to go on a date yet."

"As pretty as you are? What's wrong with young men these days?" Ellen played along with Mary.

"Hell if I know." Mary responded. With that, Ellen asked the nurse to step outside saying that she wanted to talk to Mary alone.

Once the nurse was gone and the room was empty except for Mary's roommate, Ellen asked her the question. "Mrs Clark, I want to talk about the class you used to take with Patience."

"Oh that poor dear. I am so sorry how that ended for everyone. Are you and your husband working everything out?" Mary asked.

"Mrs Clark I wanted to talk about her class, maybe we can leave the personal stuff out of this discussion?" Ellen responded.

"Of course my dear, I guess that's all still too fresh to talk about. So sorry to see her go, but I understand, you had to do what you did. Certainly can't have the woman who slept with your husband hanging out with you every day, can you?" Mary took full advantage of the freedom of expression that advancing years gives people.

"No, Mary, that would be somewhat awkward wouldn't it?" Ellen responded, somewhat annoyed at the way Mary was taking the conversation. Trying to get the conversation back on track, Ellen continued, "Mary what I want to know is, what is it about Patience's class that made you feel like you were getting better?"

"Well Doc, it wasn't that I simply felt like I was getting better, I was getting better."

"What do you mean? Describe that to me in a little more detail if you could."

"I'll try, but I am not sure I actually can. What I can describe is what she did for me. I have my theory on why it was making me better, but who knows. All I know is I was feeling better. Patience helped me think about my body in ways that I had not even thought about since I was a teenager. Remember when you were a teenager? It should be easier for you than me since it wasn't that long ago for you. I remember as my body was growing and changing I spent much more time getting to know the new body parts that were being formed. If you were like me, as my breasts began to grow I was amazed at the change, and if I could concentrate hard enough I could feel what was going on inside. At that age, our minds are focused on growth and new healthy changes, which are positive exciting thoughts. As we get older our thoughts turn to focusing on the decay of our bodies as they change for the worse. We think about our skin as it ages and loses its suppleness, we start taking drugs to try and dull the pains we get."

Mary continued, "Patience would start each class having us visualize our bodies, we would start at the top of our heads and scan down our body from one place to the next, rediscovering parts of the body that I had not really thought about in years or decades. We take our bodies for granted you know. When was the last time you really focused your attention on each small part of your body? Your toe hairs, when was the last time you felt them waving in the breeze? How about your left hip joint? Or your earlobes? Your body is just the sum of its parts, and everything has to work properly. We just assume it will all work properly, but we hardly ever give it a thought. We only really think about the parts of our bodies that give us pleasure, if you know what I mean." Mary winked and paused for a second.

"As I began to focus on body parts I hadn't thought of in years, I began to feel the sensations in those areas, and at my age there was mostly pain. But an amazing thing would happen, when I would sit quietly and think about my left hip joint, first I would feel the pain, but slowly the pain would go away. Patience would have us run our hands over the areas we were focusing on a few times, like we were brushing lint off a towel, and then wring our hands out. And slowly, one body part at a time, I felt better. And not just physically mind you, I was feeling better emotionally. I felt like

I felt when I was forty." Mary paused again.

"Patience has a way of seeing into you, she could tell what you needed. She would walk around and tell me to do one thing and the gal next to me to do another. It was a group class, but everyone in there got a slightly different experience. So I can't really explain what was happening, but I can tell you my pains went away, and I started getting movement back in these old muscles and bones."

Ellen had heard what she needed to. "Well thank you Mary, that is a fascinating story. I am glad she made you feel better. And we'll see what we can do to get you back on track."

"Well that would mean bringing her back. And that would require you to learn some humility and forgiveness." Once again, Mary took advantage of her age and laid it out on the table for Ellen, who was taken aback by Mary's last remark.

"I'm doing the best I can Mary. But the best I can do right now is to see what we can do to emulate Patience's style. I am sure there are others who have that magic touch. Thank you so much for talking to me Mary. " And with that Ellen got up and walked out.

The talk with Mary did not sit well with Ellen. Ellen was a Western trained physician, and that meant she was trained in the Scientific Method. What Mary was describing in Patience's style was a typical Eastern medicine style, which pre-dates the Scientific Method by many hundreds of years. Even acknowledging the claims of the healing effects of the Eastern medicine was grounds for being ostracized by the mainstream medical community, of which Ellen was at the top of the pecking order. She was all-in on the concepts of Western medicine, she firmly believed it was far superior to Eastern medicine, which she put in the same league as witch doctors and faith healers.

Despite that, over the next few weeks, the health scores of the patients in the hospital continued to slowly trend downward. What's worse, it was no longer limited to just Patience's students, it was spreading to others, and the head nurses began to get worried. Beverly, one of the leading head nurses decided to ask for a meeting with Ellen to discuss the obvious findings, and to get her to consider bringing Patience back to the hospital. The meeting was scheduled for the next day, a Wednesday at 3:00

pm. Word started to spread among the hospital staff about the meeting.

The following day, at 3:00, Ellen was behind her desk in her office when the five head nurses came to the door. She invited them in and came out from behind her desk and she sat around the conference table with her back to the office door, and the five head nurses around the table, and the conversation began. Beverly, knowing she was risking her relationship with Ellen, took the lead.

"Ellen, I think its time we admitted that whatever Patience was doing here in the hospital was having a positive effect. I know we can't exactly explain it, but some things are just not explainable. Some things are just mysteries, but that does not mean they don't have efficacy. Now I know you have your issues with Patience, we were all at the Christmas party, we all know what happened. But the facts are facts. We have all gone over the data and nothing else can explain the degradation in the numbers since she left."

Ellen sat back and thought about the situation and weighed her options. Her staff was losing confidence in her, and there was no way she was going to allow that to happen. She had three choices, bring Patience back, continue to undermine Patience's reputation by attacking her work, or undermine her reputation by attacking her because of her affair with Henry. On the first, there was no way Ellen was going to admit defeat and bring her back. That would be admitting defeat and Chandlers do not do that. While she wanted desperately to attack Patience's work, it was getting harder and harder to defend her position that Patience had only a neutral effect on patients after the last few weeks of regression. So she had no choice but to choose the latter. She was in a hospital that was dominated by women, they would be sympathetic to her situation. It was still her best option.

"Ladies, I really do appreciate your coming here today. I understand how you feel. We are all a bit disappointed by the degradation in the health scores, and while we have not yet figured out what is causing it, I am sure we will shortly. As for Patience, you have to give me some leeway on this. She had an affair with my husband. It was immoral. I cannot and will not have people with questionable character in my hospital." As those last few words trailed from Ellen's mouth, she noticed that all of the nurses had turned their gaze from Ellen and were instead staring at the door to her office. She turned around to see what they were looking at, and saw an imposing figure in the doorway of her office, someone who she had never thought she would see in that particular place. Charles Mason Sr. was standing in the door to her office holding onto a walker, and he was alone.

"Charles, oh my gosh, to what do we owe this honor? I have been at the hospital for months and I have never seen you come this far in one of your daily walks." Ellen spoke as she started to get up to walk over to Charles Sr.

"Sit Ellen, sit. That won't be necessary." Charles quickly motioned for her to stay in her seat. "I won't stay very long. Would you mind if I came in? I didn't mean to disturb your meeting."

"By all means Charles." Ellen replied.

"Ellen, in this setting maybe it would be best if you referred to me as Mr. Mason."

Ellen was surprised at the tone in Charles Sr.'s voice. He was usually a very formal man, but was never stern in how he had spoken to her up to now.

"Ellen I apologize, I could not help but to overhear the last part of the conversation you all were just having as I was standing in the doorway. As you know I have known Henry and Patience since they were born. In many ways they are as much my children as Charles Jr and his brothers." Charles Sr. paused for a few moments, seeming to be a bit flustered. "Excuse me. What I wanted to say was this. Ellen, affairs... well they come in all types. While society wants to label them all bad, and even worse, label those who partake in them as all bad, I don't necessarily hold to that opinion. See..." Charles Sr trailed off again,

He wanted to say something but was obviously having a difficult time saying it. He started again, but this time his tone had gone much softer, much more introspective and he started by asking the other ladies in the room if he could have a private moment with Ellen. "Ladies, I must apologize, I have something I need to talk to Ellen about, and I think it best that I do that in private. I'll only be a few minutes. Would you mind terribly stepping outside?"

The nurses all in unison of course all agreed to leave the room.

Once they were all gone and the door was closed, Charles Sr. continued, but he started the conversation by talking to himself, "Oh hell, Charles, she's gone, she can't be hurt." And then looked up at Ellen, and continued, "Ellen I once had an affair." He paused once again for a few moments almost as if to catch his breath. "And I would not consider myself to be devoid of moral character. Sometimes affairs simply happen because two people, well they simply love each other. Plain and simple. They are not trying to hurt, or to destroy, anything. Having watched Henry and Patience grow up together, I know what they have between them is a deep, deep love. I am not excusing what they did, I am an old-fashioned man, but sometimes in a marriage you have to trust and understand. Emma, God rest her beautiful soul, trusted and understood me. We never spoke of my affair, but I knew that she knew. She loved me deeply and I loved her deeply, and she knew that. I believe she looked deep inside herself and knew it was all going to be okay." Charles Sr paused.

He continued, but this time his tone changed back to be a bit more stern. "See before judging anyone Ellen, it is best to look deep deep inside oneself. I do not approve of your Christmas Party. Yes I know all about it, I know everything that happens in my hospital, and yes this is my hospital, my father and I founded it, and while I have asked you to run it for me, don't ever think that it is yours. I know everything that goes on here, I knew about this meeting, it's how I knew to be here right now. You are a very hard working and successful person Ellen Chandler, you expect and demand success, it's the curse of coming from the families we came from. See I understand you, it is why I asked you to come work here. I like successful people, I have been around them all of my life. But make no mistake about it, while I respect you professionally, Henry and Patience are like my family, you are not. Henry and Patience have my love. You and I have a professional business relationship, one that I hope will be very fruitful over the next few years.

"What Henry and Patience have between them, what they have always had between them, is based on a very deep love, one that goes much deeper than this affair that you would like to make so much of. What they did, while I do not approve, I can only imagine was an act based out of love. What you did at the Christmas party was not a loving act, it was cruel

198

and humiliating act. And for that I do not approve."

Charles was not finished. "It was calculated. I expect you to take calculated actions in business as you bring your magic to this hospital. You suspected something was going on between them, congratulations, we have all suspected that for forty years. Unlike the rest of us, you had them followed, photographed, and publicly shamed. That was highly unfortunate. But as family, I will expect going forward that the motivation behind your relationship with these two young people will <u>not</u> be calculated. There will be only one agenda and that is to heal. You are a doctor. You have taken a Hypocratic oath to heal. So heal this. Make it better. For the sake of Henry, for Patience, and for your own sake. There will be no more destruction of my loved ones here at my hospital as long as I can do anything about it."

Charles Sr continued but once again took a softer tone, "now, after what happened, I do understand that having Patience walking around the hospital would be awkward, but when you fired her, I lost access to her also, and I too am losing ground on my rehabilitation. I was walking without a walker two months ago and I am now back to having to use it. So I am going to bring her back to the hospital on Tuesdays and Thursdays for my personal rehabilitation. You may not like that but please understand that I do not need your permission. Once the other patients here see Patience walking the hallways, they will assume she is back to teaching here. As such, I would find an arrangement that you can live with." Charles Sr paused once again. He sighed a very deep sigh. "And with that I will bid you farewell. That was a long winded speech and I am tired. Oh, and one last thing, as you can imagine, my admission of an infidelity could hurt some of my family members, so I would ask that you treat that information with the utmost of discretion until I have told them myself."

Ellen was speechless. She clearly understood that there was nothing she could say. She looked up to and respected Charles Sr as much as her own father. She knew that while she was the Chief Physician of the Hospital, Charles Sr was the founder and Chairman-for-life. He outranked her, permanently. There was nothing she could say at that particular moment. All she could think of saying at that moment were words that Ellen Chandler had not uttered in a very long time. "Yes sir. I understand."

With that, Charles walked to the door, opened it, and seeing that the nurses were still standing outside the door to Ellen's office, said," could one of you ladies be so kind as to escort me back to my room?"

Ellen jumped in, "Maureen could you escort Mr. Mason back to his suite? I think our meeting is over for now, we can resume this another time."

As Maureen turned to escort Charles Sr back to his suite, all the others that had been in the meeting walked back into Ellen's office, gathered their things and left Ellen's office in silence.

After they had all left, leaving Ellen by herself in her office, she quickly started contemplating what Charles Sr had said. She replayed everything he said over and over again. Her brilliant analytical mind was looking for the meaning in between the lines. Why did he feel the need to come to her office, what was so important? Was it simply to tell her that he was going to ask Patience to return to the hospital? Was it to remind her of how much Henry was like a son to him, and therefore to treat him kindly, despite his actions?

Of all that Charles Sr had just said, Ellen was stunned at his admission to an affair. Knowing Charles Sr as she did, as proud as he was, as respected as he was, that was a huge admission to make. But she also knew that even in his advancing years, his mind was sharp, and he knew exactly what he was doing. Ellen couldn't really disagree with what Charles Sr. had said, she knew she was calculating, she also knew that Charles Sr was a master chess player, he had proved it time and time again his entire life.

CHAPTER 16

Violetta's Reprise

Despite being fired from the hospital, Patience kept on with all of her other classes and students outside of the hospital, including her sessions with Violetta.   Over the few weeks leading up to the Christmas party, Violetta was making good progress toward regaining the feeling in her left side. The blood flow that Patience was able to reestablish in Violetta's injured limbs was having the expected effect. Neural pathways that had been diminished in the time after her stroke were being reawakened and slowly but surely Violetta was getting not just her feeling back in her limbs but her ability to control her motion as well.

In the weeks after the Christmas party, Patience took the time she would have spent at the hospital and just stayed with Violetta for the extra two hours. She was working Violetta rather hard, but Violetta was a very determined woman. The work that Patience had done to get Violetta to feel her body, identify the areas of her body that needed to be restored, open up the blood flow to each and every cell, and to understand how to open her blood vessels at will to specific areas of her body, were like revelations to Violetta. At every new understanding she would revel in her new found ability to understand and control her body.

A professional piano player's entire livelihood and expertise is based on their ability to control their body. Sitting at the piano with a musical score and converting the notes written on a staff into the sounds that thunder from a grand piano is one of the most extreme examples of human body control. Like muscles in athletes, the neural pathways to the limbs and the fingers in professional musicians get exercised with every practice and become major highways of movement. Even more, the neural pathways and muscles develop their own memory. Like the proverbial chicken with its head cut off that can still run around the backyard, the brain is not the only organ that has memory and controls movement.

Over fifty years of playing the piano almost daily, Violetta had developed extreme control over her limbs and fingers as she raced up and down a keyboard. But she had never really attempted to understand or delve into the science behind that control. She just took it for granted. Patience had taught her an entirely new way to look at and understand her limbs. Now she could feel the blood flow through her limbs, and beyond the normal understanding that her limbs were made up of individual muscles and cells, she could actually feel each muscle, she could envision the blood vessels that fed each muscle and each cell in her arms and fingers. In the grueling process of relearning how to control and reuse her limbs she also developed a better understanding of her body and how to control it than she ever had.

In the weeks leading up to Christmas, while she first had regained the feeling in her arms and fingers and then had begun to regain the ability to move her arm and fingers, she still did not have the strength in her muscles to hold her arm up and play the piano for any more than seconds at a time. If she was going to regain her ability to play, she would need to regain not just the feeling and ability to control, but also the stamina and strength to hold her left arm up for an hour, and that was going to take some time.

Over the twenty years that Patience had taught Yoga, the main understanding she developed was how the muscle structure in the body was connected, from the top of the head, down the neck, into the back and shoulders. From the torso through the hips and into the legs and feet, the web of our hundreds of muscles were all interconnected and it was a finely tuned choreographic dance to get us to move something as simple as our pinky.

When someone has a stroke and loses the ability to move the muscles in the arm, it is not only the arm muscles that are affected. Any muscle that is interconnected in movement with those muscles also becomes affected. In Violetta's case, the muscles that are needed to lift the arm included the scalene muscles in the front part of the neck, and those had become very weak in the eighteen months since her stroke.

So once Violetta began to regain some of the movement in her arm, Patience started working with her to strengthen all the muscles groups that would be required to lift, hold and control the movement in her arm. Over the few weeks after the Christmas party, Violetta slowly but surely began to regain the movement in her left arm and fingers and to hold her arm up for longer periods of time, long enough to play an entire piece by Mozart.

While she lost many things with the stroke, after fifty years of playing Mozart and other classics, Violetta had not lost the learned memory of how to play the classical pieces that she was world famous for playing. So once she began to regain the ability to lift her arm and play, the only thing she did not have to relearn was how to play the songs that were burned into her memory decades ago, they were still there, and once she began to play, they came and they came quickly.

Another typical aspect of the character of a professional concert pianist, the one that most likely drives them to be at the top of their game, is the character trait of being an absolute and unforgiving perfectionist. They are incredibly hard on themselves, every piece must be played to absolute perfection, note for note, rest for rest, fortissimo from pianissimo. Patience was very worried that Violetta would get discouraged at the extreme degradation in her ability to play and would give up before she had regained her ability, but that was not the case. Instead of disillusionment in the ability gap between being at the top of her game right before her stroke and where she was at present, she found hope in every slight improvement. And that hope gave her the courage to keep up with the exercises that Patience had taught her to do, even though they were physically and mentally exhausting.

After Patience had finished working with Violetta each day, Violetta would continue working, most likely for hours, and the improvement she was making each week was truly extraordinary. By February she was playing with both arms for a few minutes at a time, and by March she was playing entire concertos.

On the last Thursday of March, Patience came to Violetta's home for her regular session, and entered as normal, driving up the driveway, parking her car and being greeted at the door by Violetta. On this day Violetta was clearly very excited.

"Patience, my precious, please come in, I have something I want to discuss with you." As always, Violetta would hold Patience's arm and they would walk hand in hand to the living room where they had been doing their work, where the grand piano also happened to be situated. "Please sit on the couch for a moment, I want to talk to you." Patience sat down as instructed by Violetta. "I think I am ready." Violetta continued.

"Ready for what?" Patience had a feeling that she knew what Violetta was about to say, but she had not expected this so soon.

"Patience, when I begged you to work with me last summer, I had only one goal, that was to regain my ability to play. And you have worked a miracle. I know it is a miracle, because I was told by Dr. Chandler that it would take a miracle to regain my ability to play, and I have, and that makes you a miracle worker."

"Oh Violetta, that's so sweet of you to say but I am not a miracle worker. You are the only miracle worker in this room. You did all the work, not me, I was just the guide on this path, you had to walk it."

"Oh my dear Patience, I know I will never get you to admit anything of the sort. But here is what I want to tell you, even though I know you won't listen. I have been around the world. I have met some of the greatest people on earth, people who have entered a special place. I want to tell you that you have entered a place that is reserved for very few. You see worlds that others don't, you see paths that others cannot. Each morning you awake in a different realm of this world than the rest of us, a realm where everything in interconnected and every interaction makes sense. Most of us exist in the world that we see and hear around us. You exist in the world that you feel, where many more possibilities exist."

"What's exhilarating is that you have given me a glimpse into the world that you exist in, and in that comprehension my eyes have been opened to the possibilities. For the last fifty years I have woken up every morning with the motivation of desire or fear. I have woken up with the desire to be the best concert pianist in the world, and I have woken up with fear that if I do not, I will have nothing."

After sitting quiet and just listening, Patience responded to this, "Want and fear Violetta. It's how most of the world exists every day Violetta. You have not been alone."

Violetta continued, "it's the curse of mankind. We have evolved from beasts that know nothing but immediate survival. In God's grace he gave us the gift of understanding and the gift of hope, and what have we done with those, Patience? What have we done with God's gifts? We have used the intelligence that God gave us to understand and create, and we have used those gifts to become more brutal than the beasts we evolved from. But there are those who understand, those who silently work to change those around them by giving them the gift of insight into that other world. And you are one of those, Patience, you are one of them, maybe the greatest of them all."

"Oh Violetta, that is so sweet of you to say." Patience paused for a second. "All I have done for these past few months is to give you a glimpse into the other world that we exist in, the spiritual world that has been around for eternity. Because it has existed for eternity, it is the perfect place. It's a world of peace and compassion and understanding.

"We humans have become so overwhelmed by our detailed cognition of the material world that we have lost sight of the spiritual world, it exists and we exist in it, but we do not know it. We get glimpses of the spiritual world when something happens that we cannot explain, but we have been conditioned to use science to explain everything around us, and if it can't be explained and proven through the scientific method, we simply deny its existence.

"Too many people say that the spiritual world does not exist because science cannot prove that it does. Well there was a time when mankind could not detect radio waves, but that does not mean they did not exist. Radio waves in our atmosphere did not come into being when someone invented the radio, they were always there, we finally discovered a way to scientifically detect them. But that's how discovery goes. Someone theorizes that something exists, not because they directly see it or detect it, but because they can see or detect its influence on something that they can see or detect. They say 'something else must exist because I can see it influencing this that I can see.' They then go about to discover a way to detect the thing that can't be seen. But that only becomes the moment they can detect it, not the moment it was created.

"In that way hundreds of natural phenomenon have been discovered by man, from radio waves to radiation. But what happens when we can see something, and even measure it, but still can't explain it? Gravity is like that. Gravity is something we all can easily see its effects on everything around us, we can measure it on something as simple as a bathroom scale, but despite seeing it and measuring it, none of the greatest minds in science can explain exactly what gravity is. But we don't deny its existence.

"In that way some still want to deny spirituality, the divine, they say it can't be seen nor measured, therefore it doesn't exist. But one way to understand the existence and eternalness and persistence of the spiritual world is to imagine what is left when we start peeling away the layers of our cognition. If mankind were to be wiped from existence, and all the knowledge that we have accumulated lost to history, including our religions and our notion of God, would all of those discoveries no longer exist? Would God no longer exist? Of course not, everything we have discovered and yet to discover already exists, discovery is only the documentation of things that exist. And when we lose the documentation, the things still exist, they have just been lost to our body of knowledge.

"When all living creatures on Earth are wiped from existence, and all the stored learnings that are passed from generation to generation in our DNA, the instincts that drive the survival of the animal kingdom, when that is all lost, and when this universe and everything in it finally ends, the planets and billions of stars all disappear in one galactic calamity, then what? Does everything cease to exist? No, there is one thing that remains, the eternal spiritual world. And when the next universe takes shape, and billions of years later some future sentient beings are created, they will also be driven by the eternalness of the spiritual world. The compassion and understanding of everything will not have disappeared in those eons, they were always there only to be rediscovered.

"It has been that way forever. Universes have come and gone and one thing has remained. We have simply rediscovered what has always existed. But we have a long way to go in our discovery. Humans are still too much driven by their instinctual consciousness, it drives our survival instincts, which make us behave like animals. So when you said we behave like animals, you are right, but that's not how it has to be, that's simply the results of people not seeing and understanding their eternal selves, they are completely overwhelmed by their instinctual consciousness, so much so that they cannot see their spiritual consciousness. I see spirituality every moment of every day, I see it, and I feel it. I feel the love from you right now Violetta, I can feel the love grow in your heart every day we are together.

"See that's what I do Violetta. Everyone thinks I am a simple yoga teacher, but there is so much more to it than that. I awaken people to their spiritual consciousness. Those who awaken to that understanding change the world Violetta. From the Buddha, to Jesus, to Gandhi, to thousands of others who have been enlightened to the truth of our spiritual existence have changed our world, some in large ways like those I just mentioned, but most in small ways, with the community around them."

Violetta, who had been listening to Patience, responded, "Patience, if I ever get back to traveling the world, I will take you with me my dear, the world needs your message to be heard."

"Well I would look forward to traveling with you Violetta, I'll be your guru." Patience said and started to laugh, and Violetta laughed with her.

"That's what's been missing from my world all this time, a guru!" Violetta said as she laughed even harder.

Patience laughed and responded, "I promise that if you get back to traveling the world and you want me to come, I will. I love Mystic, but I would love to see more than this small town." With that Patience drifted off into so many thoughts. She thought about how she has been in Mystic her whole life, traveling around from time to time, but always coming home. She thought of Lois, and the focus and clarity that Lois gives her in her life. She thought of Henry, and how after twenty years he came back home. She wondered if she could simply walk away from all that, from all the people in town that have been with her for years, of all the people she has helped get better at the Manor over the many years. While she has stayed, so many people have come through Mystic that she has gotten to know and to influence. She wondered what her destiny was. Was it to have her influence grow bigger from the small town of Mystic? Or was it to be a filter for this small town, to filter out the pain and suffering of those she came into contact with through teaching them a greater depth of understanding of the world.

Violetta and Patience both drifted off into deep thoughts and sat in calm and peace for many minutes.

Patience finally broke the silence. "Thank you Violetta, we talk a lot about what I give to you, but we never talk about what you have given to me. You have given me the greatest gifts of all, your love, your deep friendship and your trust, and for that I am forever grateful."

"Thank you my precious, those are things I have been reserving all these long years for someone. I thought it might be a husband, but alas, that is not in the cards for this old lady, so I guess you get it all." And Violetta and Patience squealed with laughter once again.

After laughing, Violetta continued. "So my dear, this is what I have wanted to tell you all this time. Are you ready? I am ready to start preparing for my piano recital." Violetta paused a few moments and Patience, sensing Violetta had more to say, waited to let her continue. "I have been practicing my pieces after you leave, and I think that in 60 days I will be ready to play again. What do you think?"

"Violetta, there are a few things I have learned about you over these past many months. One, never doubt that you mean what you say. Two, never stand in your way. Three, you understand yourself better than anyone. And four, you always get what you want. So if that's what you want, lets do it!"

"So where do you want to have this concert?" Patience asked.

"I have been thinking about that. I could contact my friends at Carnegie Hall, I have played there dozens of times, but I have come to look at this part of Connecticut as my home, and I think I want to honor that. Do you know much about the Garde Theater in New London?"

"Yes I do. I have seen many concerts there over the years. It's a lovely old theater, with lots of history and beautiful architecture. The acoustics are actually quite good also. I think that would be a lovely gesture. They would be honored to do that for you, you being a world famous concert pianist and all." Patience said that last sentence with some sarcasm in her voice.

"Do I still qualify?" Violetta responded and laughed.

Patience continued, "Of course you do. I happen to know the right person to talk to at the Garde, we went to high school together, I'd be glad to call her for you."

"Would you do that for me dear?"

"I'd be honored to help you plan for this. Okay now that that is out of the way, we have some work to do. I need to whoop you into shape and I have only 60 days to do it. Let's get back to work. We still need to increase your strength so you can play an hour long concert, so I've got some exercises that I want you to work on." With that Patience set to work to get Violetta ready for her concert.

When she got home that afternoon, Patience called her friend, Jenny Brown, who was the program director at the Garde. "Jen, its Patience".

"Patience? The Patience? The one and only Patience Passion? The best Yoga instructor in, in, well anywhere?" Jen responded as she answered her phone. "I am so sorry I have not been to yoga lately, you know how life gets busy."

It was funny how whenever Patience talked to one of her former students they always first apologized for not coming to yoga as often as they should and always promised to come the next week, though few ever did. Life gets busy, and yoga seems to be one thing that people can get back to later, after everything else in their life is perfect.

Patience jumped in, "Sweetie, I didn't call to hassle you about coming to yoga. You'll be back when you come back. Thank heavens I have plenty of other yoga students who keep my classes full."

Jenny responded, "Okay now I really feel guilty. And I feel terrible. I have this pain in my back that goes right up to the top of my head. It causes such headaches. I never seem to have it when I come to class. I am such an idiot."

"Well I am not sure idiot is the right word. Masochist more like." Patience let Jenny ramble on a bit about all the other aches and pains she was experiencing and talk about how they all go away when she is doing her regular yoga.

"So what did you want to talk about? Any new men in your life?" Jenny asked.

"That's a bit of a sore subject that we should probably avoid for now, well maybe forever." Patience responded thinking of the Henry affair.

"Well now that you said that, I need to know everything. Spill girl."

"Sweetie, its a bit raw right now, so let's put that on the agenda for next year. But I did call for a reason."

"Hell you're no fun. You're holding out on me, but okay, sounds like you need more time with that. What's up?"

"Do you remember Violetta Andropov? The concert pianist who lives in Mystic?"

"Of course. How's she doing, that poor dear. I heard she had a stroke and her concert playing was over. Such a shame."

"Well actually she's taken a turn for the better. She's been in rehab for the past few months and she has mostly recovered. So this is why I am calling. She and I were talking the other day and she would like to have a comeback concert."

"Are you shitting me? Tell me she wants to have it at the Garde." Jenny was getting excited.

"That's what I called to tell you. She wants to have it at the Garde. In 60 days."

There was a brief moment of silence on the phone before Jenny finally spoke up, "Oh my effing God. She is world famous. She plays Carnegie Hall, for Christ's sake. Violetta Andropov at the Garde? In 60 days? Crap, crap, crap. Let me pull out the calendar. 60 days, 60 days, let's see, that would be two months from now."

"Still good at math aren't you?" Patience had to interject.

"Wow. Patience Passion being sarcastic, that's good, that's good, have you finally come back down to earth where the rest of us mere mortals exist, with our sarcasm and suffering?"

"Very funny, you set yourself up for that one sweetie."

"Touché, touché. Let's see, that's sometime in May, well holy shit, yes we have one weekend in May where the theater is dark. Saturday night, May 15th, would that work? Oh my God you don't know how much we need an event like this. She would fill this place right up. She'd get people from New York and Boston to come, and they got bucks. We could charge $40, maybe even $50 bucks. It's been hard lately. This theater is expensive to maintain. You can only make so much from the local school plays. Occasionally we'll have a more famous person come through, like a Jesse Colin Young, or Jeff Beck or something, but they don't even sell this place out. We hold 1,500 people you know."

Patience smiled as she remembered how much fun it was talking to Jenny. She loved to talk and could go on for minutes by herself. She could feel the excitement coming from Jenny. "Well, we'll need your help putting this together on such short notice. I have no idea how to put a concert together. I hadn't even thought about what to charge."

Jenny responded, "well you're talking to a professional here. You may be the world's greatest yoga instructor, but putting concerts on is what I do for a living. We'll make this happen babe."

Patience started thinking about all the things she hadn't thought about, like what to charge. "I really don't think she needs the money, maybe we should do a fund raiser? I'll talk to Violetta about it. Can you talk to the powers that be over there and lock that date in for us while I talk to Violetta?"

"You got it boss. I'll do that right now. Can we talk later today? If we are going to do this we got a bunch of planning to do." Jenny started thinking of all she would have to do to fill the Garde up with customers.

"Sure thing Jen. I'll call you later today." With that Patience and Jenny hung up. Patience took a deep breath and realized that there was a lot to do, but she also knew this was the next step in the process of healing that would play out over the next few months that everyone needed to go through.

After her conversation with Jenny, Patience realized she had some questions to ask Violetta, so she picked up her cell phone and called her home.

"Hello, this is Violetta Andropov."

"Violetta, this is Patience."

"Hello my dear, were you able to talk to your friend?"

"Yes I was, good news, they happen to have a Saturday open in

May and she thinks we can have the concert hall that night. She is checking with her boss."

"Well everything is coming together nicely isn't it. I must have that good Karma I have heard so much about."

"Yes Violetta, thinking of the life you have lived, I can confidently say that if anyone has had good Karma over the years, it's been you. Violetta, my friend Jenny had some questions that I had not thought of to ask you. First of all, we will have to rent the Garde Theatre for the night to have the event there, and Jenny wanted to know what you wanted to charge those who want to attend."

"Charge? I don't want to charge. Patience, this is a celebration with my friends. That won't do. That simply won't do. But I do understand that they need to be paid for their services, that is only fair. Did she mention how much it would be to rent the Theatre for the night?"

"No she didn't, but she did mention the idea of holding the event as a fund raiser for a good cause, and then people can pay whatever they can afford to attend. And from the proceeds, we could pay a portion of the donations to the Garde, and the rest to some other worthy cause of your choosing."

"I like the way your Jenny thinks. Some other worthy cause. Well I would have to say that I always try to support the Arts Center here in town. If I had to choose, I would choose them."

"Okay Violetta now we are getting somewhere. Now we have to work on the guest list. Have you been thinking about who you want to invite?"

"Well that's a silly question, everyone Patience, everyone."

"What do you mean by everyone?" Patience was confused.

"What does everyone mean? It's an English word Patience, you should know it. Unlike me, English is your mother tongue? Everyone means everyone. I will run an announcement in the papers here and in New York and Boston, and expect everyone to come. It's no Carnegie Hall, but that Garde Theater can hold many many people, so let's fill it up. And since it is now a fund raiser for the Arts Center, then lets fill it up even more." Violetta was being funny, but she meant every word.

There was a few moments of silence on the phone before Patience was able to respond to this latest news. "Okay Violetta, we will work to fill up the Garde. But announcements cost money Violetta, how much are you prepared to spend on this party?"

"Consider my budget to be unlimited. I am getting old, and what better way to spend my money than on a big party with friends."

"Okay Violetta, its your money. I'll work with Jenny to create an announcement that we can place in the newspapers. Any other crazy ideas that you want me to work on?"

"I hear sarcasm in your voice Patience. There are no crazy ideas when you have been given your life back. Now you go to work and make this event as big as you can. I am ready to show the world that I am back." And with that Violetta hung up the phone.

Patience smiled to herself at the spirit of this lady as she put her phone down. She thought how far Violetta had come in such a short amount of time. She smiled at the warmth she felt in her heart that she was able to help Violetta regain her movement. And she even allowed herself to feel a little comeuppance that she could when the so-called experts couldn't.

Patience next called Jenny back. "Jen, its Patience."

"Oh, good news. You have that date if you want it. Did you talk to Violetta?"

"Yes, I just got off the phone with her. At first she reacted very negatively to the idea of charging an admission fee. But when I suggested it be a fund raiser and we let people donate whatever they could afford, she warmed up and she mentioned the Mystic Arts Center as the place where she would want to donate the money she raises. She did want to know how much the Garde is going to need to open for the night. Of course I have no idea what to tell her."

"Yea, I figured that's what she would say. Well, the good news there is that since most of the people that help at fundraiser events are volunteers, we only need to pay the bartenders if alcohol is served. It costs us about $2000 to run a fundraiser. So she only needs to get 100 people to come and donate $20 to cover the expenses for the Garde for the night. But Patience, I can't imagine she won't get at least 500 people to come, so the event should more than cover our expenses and have plenty left over for the Arts Center."

"Okay, that sounds great. Now Violetta mentioned wanting to place an announcement in the local papers and also in New York and Boston. What do you think about that?"

"We always place announcements in the local papers, hardly ever in the New York or Boston papers, they're too far away for people to come here, but you know, since she has a following in those cities, and this is the only concert she will be doing, people may come for the night. If we decide to do that, I can arrange for that also since we do have contacts there. And let's not forget that we will send out an email to our regular mailing list, this would be a special email. I can see it saying something like 'Announcing world-famous concert pianist Violetta Andropov, in her only concert appearance of the year.'"

Jen's response was exactly what Patience wanted to hear. "I was hoping you were going to say all that, I have no idea how to put on a concert, it's just so overwhelming all that you have to do."

"Well honey, as I said earlier today, this is what I do for a living, so I got this covered."

"Okay, I'll call Violetta back and give her the good news. Oh one more thing, I think she's going to want to invite some of her friends from Mystic Manor, and many of them are older and use walkers and canes, is that okay? I mean I know you don't care, but will they be able to get to their seats easily?"

"Yes honey, we have a side door where they can come in right near the handicapped seating, and they'll all be right up in the first row to watch her. That will be so cute."

"I know, I know," Patience trailed off as she thought about how much she missed the people at the Manor since she stopped teaching there. "Okay Jen, thank you so much. I'll call you in a few days, but call me if you need anything from me."

The plan was set in motion. The next day Jenny and Patience started working on the announcements together. Patience thought about what the reactions would be once people read that Violetta had been rehabilitated and was going to hold a concert. Almost immediately her thoughts went to Ellen. What would she think? What would her reaction be? Would she be incredulous? Angry? Would she suspect that Patience was involved, or would her arrogance not allow her to go there?

CHAPTER 17

Henry's Penance

Henry's first few weeks at the Carver House in Rochester were a mixture of rest, peace and humiliation. The Carver House is a rehab hospital that specializes in sexual addictions and other sexually-related psychological problems, similar to the Betty Ford Clinic for drug and alcohol addictions. As one can imagine, the type of people that are so out of control that they require treatment in an in-patient setting are mostly a mixed lot of dysfunction and deviancy. Fortunately for Henry, the extreme deviants that had been convicted of a sexually-related crime were not allowed because Carver did not have the security needed to keep watch over them. Mostly it was people whose addiction was so out of control and had caused such havoc that it had become some other person's problem as well, and a stint at the hospital was negotiated with the other party to avoid some type of civil suit.

There were those there who had a combination of sexual and drug or alcohol addictions, but they could only be at Carver once their drug and alcohol issues had already been successfully treated. There were a surprising number of college-aged young men who were required to do a stint at Carver after an accusation of sexual misconduct on campus. From their athletic build and demeanor, Henry guessed that these were likely athletes that their University wanted back on some sports team but had to cleanse the student's actions in order to reinstate them as students and cover the University's political hides for the sake of the athletic boosters.

Fortunately for Henry, there were a few married spouses who had been caught in extramarital affairs and who had been given the ultimatum: attend rehab or get divorced with an extramarital affair hanging over their heads during their divorce trial. Due to the similarity of circumstance, it was those that Henry became friendly with.

An interesting observation to Henry is that very few of the husbands in this group had any obvious sexual addiction, at least as far as Henry could tell, these were normal husbands caught having a pretty normal affair, and they were remorseful enough to want to keep their marriage and family in tact to agree to humiliate themselves by going to Carver.

On the other hand, Henry came to quickly learn that some of the women in this group of cheating spouses were complete and obviously incurable nymphomaniacs. Over the course of the three months that Henry was there, he had to decline numerous offers to have sex from these women. There were notes subtly passed to him in the hallway, a few winks with suggestive lip-licking, and even one grope of his genitalia while sitting on a bench outside during a break.

Despite the obvious interest and opportunity, Henry managed to refrain. He was not a sex addict, he had gone for months at a time during his marriage without having sex, and in all the years he had been married to Ellen, despite the advances of many women, Henry had stayed faithful. His affair with Patience was not about sexual deviancy, it was about something very simple, love. Henry had a deep lifelong and pervasive adoration of Patience.

In fact, if anything in Henry's life could be considered sexually deviant, it was in his marriage. For Ellen, sex was about control and manipulation, which outside of marriage would be considered deviant sexual behavior. But in today's modern society, where everyone has become a pop psychologist and wants to issue an opinion on everyone else's day to day behavior, when it comes to sex within a marriage, as long as no one gets sent to the hospital, every sick manipulation and motivation seems to be within bounds and no one wants to get involved.

All too often, a young newlywed bride seeking help from her parents after what should be considered sexual abuse early in the marriage by her new husband, will be told that it is her wifely duty to give it up to the young asshole. When Lorena Bobbit famously cut off the penis of her husband after a few years of sexual abuse early in the marriage, an obvious call for help from a wife in extreme distress, her father seemed to defend Mr. Bobbit, and many in society questioned her betrayal of her husband.

But as it was, the nuances of how Ellen's deviancy contributed to the sad state of Henry's marital sex life were nuances that no one seemed to really care about, even the professional staff at Carver. It was clear that the doctors and counselors were not going to give much latitude in the theory that the real cause of one's sexual affair was the spouse who was safely at home. The easy assumption was that the spouse who was in the hospital was the one with the problem, that's why they were there, or it would be the other way around.

Henry learned this very quickly after trying to describe his sexual history early on in his stay. He was quickly chastised by his social worker for not looking at how his behavior had contributed to his being at Carver. Henry realized that this was a no-win battle. He wanted to get released from Carver as soon as he could, and playing along was the best way to do that.

At the same time, Henry was not a completely innocent party, and he was willing to admit that and look deeply into it. He had had an extramarital affair with another women and had lied to his spouse about it. And while social norms in modern society have become extremely liberalized, there are a few actions that continue to be universally considered inexcusable. An extramarital affair is one. There are very few justifications available for having one, even in today's modern liberated society.

He tried to steer his therapy to address the reasons why he would allow himself to give in to his sexual desires to enter an extramarital affair. But every time he looked deeply into it, he always came back to the same conclusion. Ellen's extreme manipulation and control had left him devoid of any true love and closeness. True love requires opening oneself up in a very vulnerable way, it requires replacing fear with trust, a trust that overpowers ones fears.

But Ellen was incapable of allowing herself to be vulnerable. Opening oneself up to vulnerability is an act of humility. It is a trusting act. It is a giving act. "I give myself to you. I trust you with my vulnerability. I put myself in your hands." Ellen did not have the required ingredients. No glint of humility had ever graced her soul. As to trust, she trusted in one thing. She trusted that no one would ever betray her, not out of love or loyalty, but out of fear and retribution. She cultivated that in every interaction she had with others; with her mannerisms, her confidence, and her constant yet subtle reminders that above all else, she was to be feared.

To Henry, psychoanalyzing his extramarital affair required an extreme amount of nuance and deflection. During his affair, and early in his stay at Carver, he justified it with rage, which he deflected back onto Ellen and her issues. He told himself that she was this, and she was that, and this caused something else, which led to that, which placed Henry in a position of having no choice but to gain the affection that he lacked for so many years through an affair. But slowly over the weeks that Henry was at Carver, with the absence of any day-to-day interaction with Ellen, which allowed him to let his guard down, as he delved deeper and deeper into his psyche that allowed him to have an affair, the rage faded and he was left without the foundation upon which his justifications had been mounted. He was left with only himself and his actions.

Without the rage, Henry was left with digging into how his actions over the past few months and the past few years had contributed to his predicament. And as his justifications melted away, he slowly was left with the realization that he had no one to blame but himself. He had numerous choices. He could have realized he was hopelessly in love with Patience and simply left Ellen before he had the affair, that's what society expects, even demands. His reasons in his early twenties for not wanting to engage Patience in a relationship, mostly due to his insecurities about his future and ability to provide for her, were no longer valid. He had a career, he could make money. Despite the fact that a divorce would wipe him out financially, he could find a job and make an income, and he knew that Patience could care less about money.

But he didn't do any of that, and he had to come to terms with the fact that his affair was simply due to his own weaknesses, which were classic causes of suffering. He had been operating out of want, a desire to maintain a lifestyle he had become accustomed to. And he had been operating out of fear, fear of loss of that lifestyle. When want is derived from fear, those are a difficult combination of negative motivations to overcome and change. And that led to inaction in his own life and meant that he had spent most his life being a passenger in someone else's car. Ellen was clearly in the driver seat of their marriage, and he made the choice to go along for the ride. He had spent most of his adult life simply being along for the ride. And as all those realizations sunk in, Henry got very depressed.

Ellen was right. She was strong, he was weak. She was a hard driving successful person at the top in her medical field, he was an English professor at a prestigious University, but he had to admit, he was a mediocre one at best. She commanded respect from those in her presence, at best he would elicit a smile as people quickly moved on. She had powerful friends in high places, he had acquaintances, but no real friends.

The more Henry let go of the pretense of his life, the more Henry got depressed. After eight weeks at Carver, Henry was not doing well. His life had been turned upside down and it was settling into an even worse place. The book that he thought he could write while he was there had not progressed much at all. He had sunk low and he was sinking even lower.

The only thoughts that Henry could muster that brought any joy to his life for the last few weeks at Carver was the thought of Patience. She had become his beacon. He needed hope. Hope is the last thing that goes before someone decides to end their own life, and Patience was Henry's hope, the last thing that tethered Henry from slipping from depression into despair. When one has lost everything and hope is all that remains, and it is a hope of a new life with new priorities, it is that hope that reminds you that what was lost must not have been that important anyway.

So oddly, it was that same love that he had for Patience and that was reciprocated for him that was also slowly changing his feelings for Ellen. His rage for Ellen had slowly dissipated and was replaced with sadness. He realized that while he was adrift in life, and from all external appearances in a mid-life crisis, and depressed about his situation, he knew he was deeply loved by someone, a love that very few shared. And in that he might just be the luckiest man alive.

He began to see that Ellen was the one who was in a tragic situation. Without some major life change, change that is usually only

220

brought about by some catastrophic event that shakes you to your core, Ellen was going to continue on without every really experiencing true love. Without her ability to find humility, she would never allow herself to be an equal to her spouse. Without an ability to allow herself vulnerability, she would never open herself to trust. And the more Henry thought about that, the more his rage toward Ellen was replaced with sadness.

Ultimately Henry did find his remorse at Carver, as his time at Carver slowly wound down, and after his rage toward Ellen had greatly subsided, it was replaced with remorse, not remorse at having an affair with Patience, but remorse at the thought that his affair with Patience meant that Ellen, despite her ability to justify anything to her benefit, had to accept the fact that her husband was able to find a deep connection with another woman, and that understanding has to wound anyone's soul, however hardened it may be.

Henry was discharged from Carver on time at the end of his three month scheduled stay. Over the course of the three months at Carver, he had not made any progress on his sexual addiction, mostly because he had none, and even the best hospital can't cure a disease that a patient doesn't have, they can just trick themselves into believing they have, and Henry dutifully played along with them to satisfy them that he was "cured". He had however, made tremendous progress on many other aspects of his confidence and self-image issues over his last few weeks there. Having lived in a household for over twenty years with someone who manipulates their surroundings to keep a firm grasp on control, Henry realized that he was suffering from something akin to Post Traumatic Stress Disorder. The constant little slights and put downs of Henry by Ellen were most effective for her when Henry least expected them to occur, and after a while he learned to be on guard at all times, twenty four hours a day, 365 days a year. It was like being in a battle and not knowing when the next shell is going to rain down on you. In war, you hope to deal with it with the attitude that you simply don't care, versus living in constant anxiety and fear, but that was not possible in a relationship with Ellen, fear and anxiety was the goal and she worked it until that's what she got. But over the course of his stay at Carver, Henry had figured this all out. At the very end of his stay at Carver, after he had found his remorse, and he had forgiven himself and

Ellen, his depression slowly lifted, and what remained was a calm that he had not felt in many years.

But there was one thing the hospital could not cure, Henry was still madly in love with Patience. She was his soul mate, he had known it early in his life, he spent twenty years trying to forget it, but it was inevitably rekindled the moment he first laid eyes on her again. No amount of therapy and intervention was going to undo that. But he knew that when he got home, he was going to have to put those feelings in a box, lock it up tight and throw away the key. He had already risked ruining Patience's life and livelihood with the affair, and he loved her too much to do that all over again. So he resigned himself to the fact that when he got back to Mystic, he was going to move back in with Ellen, and would have to forget seeing Patience other than at social functions where there were plenty of others around. That made him extremely heart broken, but he had been selfish and he was not going to give into his selfishness again at Patience's expense. Instead he came to the understanding that the love he and Patience had for each other was eternal, and therefore would exist beyond the life he had to live for the next few decades with Ellen.

On the appointed day, Henry packed up the few clothes he had brought with him, his laptop, and a few other things, and a limo arrived to pick him up. Within seven hours Henry was back in Mystic, back at the Sullivan McCoy house, and back in his normal life, as normal as one can get. But something had changed in Henry. Not only had Henry found his remorse, not only had he found self-forgiveness, but Henry had found something else, a deep and resolute calmness. He was prepared for stepping back into the maelstrom of alternative reality he was required to live in with Ellen, where reality was what she demanded it to be, not what it was.

Henry arrived during the day, when Ellen was still at work. When she arrived home that night, Henry had not unpacked. He was sitting on the living room couch, not sure exactly what he should do. Was he going to go back to living in the backhouse? Was he going to be allowed to return to their bedroom? He did not want to be presumptuous. He had not talked to Ellen since the Christmas Party, there were no rules or guidance provided to him on what to do when returning home from a three month stay in a rehab hospital after having an affair exposed. So he simply waited for Ellen to come home and give him some direction as to what she was thinking, and he would have to be okay with anywhere she wanted to take it.

Around 6:30 Henry heard Ellen's car pull into the gravel driveway and he prepared himself for all the possibilities of which Ellen was going appear when she walked in the door. Would it be the nice Ellen? The nasty Ellen? The detached Ellen? The rageful Ellen? Henry had no clue what to expect, so he simply eliminated all expectation and was prepared for anything.

Ellen came in the front door and found Henry siting on the living room couch. "H. Wow. How long have you been home? Have you unpacked?" Ellen, was giving the nice Ellen signals, which was a relief because while not usually sincere, at least it was not immediately hostile. She put her keys and other things that she had carried into the house down on the credenza near the door and walked into the living room where Henry was sitting.

"I was not sure exactly where to unpack, so I figured I would wait until you got home so we could talk. Clearly we have a lot to talk about. And we have our whole lives ahead of us to figure out where I am going to sleep." Henry was trying to project his hope that the marriage could be repaired and they would continue on.

"Yes, of course. You probably have lots of questions for me." Ellen sat down on the loveseat across from Henry. "Well, I think we have both been through a lot." She placed the emphasis on the word both. "I can imagine that the last three months were not a picnic for you. I can't imagine how difficult it would be trying to rehab a sexual addiction that you don't have. When Richard Chandler makes up his mind, no one is going to change it. Well, it has been a long three months for me too H. And I am lonely, and if you are wondering where you should unpack, I want you in bed with me tonight. Did they leave any sexual drive in there, or did they beat it all out of you?" Ellen was trying to be funny and flirtatious.

Henry decided to play along. "Well, to be honest Ellen, I am not sure, I've not had the opportunity to test drive it for quite some time." Henry had resolved himself to be open-minded, to be ready for most anything, from knives being thrown, to divorce papers, to the cold shoulder. He realized the one thing he had not actually prepared himself that well for was a nice Ellen. Though in hindsight, that was just as plausible as any other outcome.

Ellen, stood up. "Well it's going to take a long time to figure this all out, but first things first, I am starving, are you hungry? What did they feed you up there? Mystery meat and canned string beans? I can imagine the institutional food was awful." Ellen was trying to warm up to Henry being home. "Would you mind if we went out to dinner? I am not in the mood to cook." Ellen asked.

"Sure, why not. You're right, institutional food is horrendous. I could use a good meal. Want to go to the Duck? I could stand to see some old friends."

"Henry, I don't think I'm ready for that. I've spent the last three months running between work and home, and have not really put myself in a situation where I would run into anyone that I didn't have to. I've been having the groceries delivered and when I eat out, it's usually in New London or someplace where I am less likely to see familiar faces. The Christmas Party..." Ellen was struggling for a word, "incident? Is that what we will call it? Was not particularly well received with your friends. I even got a tongue lashing from Charles Sr. How did he word it? 'It was not a loving act, it was a calculating act.' So I am dealing with my own issues on my motivations and why I handled the whole thing the way I did."

Henry could not believe what he was hearing. Ellen was being really nice, he even heard a bit of humility in her voice. "Well I guess that makes two of us. I've had a lot of free time over the past three months, they don't pack your day full of activities up there, they purposely give you plenty of time to rethink your actions, which for most of the people there, were pretty outrageous to land them there to begin with. Ellen, it's going to take me a lifetime to know for sure where my head was at last fall, so if you are looking for some fast answers, I don't have any either. All I can say is that I am sorry." Henry was still basking in his new-found remorsefulness.

"Thanks H. I never thought I would say this, but I am too. The way I handled that was pretty gruesome. When Chandlers feel wronged, I guess our first instinct is to bring out the heavy artillery. Deploying the

Powell doctrine in domestic matters may not be the best approach."

"Yeah, I think Colin Powell probably expected the concept of decisive and overwhelming force to be strictly in the battlefield, and not be applied to a marriage. Hey, I want you to know, I understand what the immediate future holds here. My goal for the next few months is to finish my book. I was not able to get much writing done in the first few weeks at Carver, but over the last two to three, it's been pouring out of me. It was like I had to come to an understanding of my own psyche, I had to get really grounded to be able to reach inward enough to create the scenarios in my head that I need to tell this story. And, well, let's just say I was not particularly grounded last fall. I was living in a fantasy, and you can't create a fantasy when you are living in one yourself."

"I appreciate that H. I hope I don't have to say this, but I hope you understand that any contact with Patience for the foreseeable future is not really possible."

"Yeah, I got that one figured out. That's actually one of the few things they did tell me at Carver about what life after rehab was gonna be like. Avoid the situations that created the scenario and atmosphere that led to the problem to begin with. Clearly my complicated, long-running, and uh, codependent, if that's the right word, well anyway, my relationship with Patience was the situation, and if I know her at all, she will be doing her best not to create any more drama in town. So if I am to avoid her, did her job at the Manor survive the ordeal?"

"Um, in a word, no. It was just too awkward, for everyone. But to my surprise, she seems to have Charles Sr. completely wrapped around her pinky. He walked to my office one day, which is amazing in itself since he had not been out of his suite for months, to tell me that he felt like he was regressing in his rehab from his stroke, and he asked me, well, to be more accurate, he ordered me to call Patience to have her return so she could work with him."

"Wow, the old man is determined, that's for sure." Henry thought of memories of Charles Sr as they were growing up.

"Oh, that reminds me, there is one bit of gossip." Ellen remembered Charles Sr.'s confession of having an affair.

"Ellen Chandler spreading gossip?" Henry was being funny, but it was a serious question, Ellen was not one to spread gossip.

"Well this is something that may actually affect you. When Charles came to my office to tell me to rehire Patience, he admitted to something. He told me that he had once had an affair."

Henry was dumbfounded. "What? Charles Mason Sr.? The most self-controlled human being on the planet? Had an affair? Whoa! That's a bombshell. Why would he admit that now, and why to you?"

"He said it had happened a very long time ago. And now that Emma was gone, she couldn't be hurt by the admission anymore. I think he was trying to tell me to be easy on you, that it happened to him, so it can happen to the best of people. It was so unlike him. He was so soft, I am not used to that side of Charles Mason. He was so, philosophical, he kept fading off into thought as he was struggling on how to say what he wanted to say."

"I'll guess that news has been spread all over town by now?" Henry was still shocked by the news.

"Actually no. He advised me in a very strongly worded and pointed manner, to not say a word about it to anyone."

"Well I guess that's not so amazing. Break Charles Mason's confidence and you are probably looking for another job in another state, or country for that matter."

"Well it obviously did have an impact. You're the first person I have told."

Henry was really struck by Ellen's sudden deference to Charles Sr. This is a woman who for as long as he could remember, cowered to no one, and who was, for the first time that Henry can remember, seemed really rattled by Charles Sr. Henry wondered if there was something else that Charles had told to Ellen that she was not fessing up to. Had he threatened her job, in the same way that Ellen threatened Patience's? Charles, while a powerful person, his power came from a steady confidence, not from manipulation, Henry could easily see him not taking kindly to Ellen's tactics in the Christmas party debacle, since it led to such upheaval, Henry being sent off for months, and Patience's being fired. And Henry had a thought, for the very first time since the party. Was it possible that was Ellen's entire motivation? Would she really go to all that trouble, hold a party, invite all the town, all to out her husband's affair with someone who worked for her, just because she wanted to fire them? Henry needed to think.

"Ellen, would you mind if I took a rain check on going out to dinner? On second thought, I'm pretty tired from the long drive, and I have to unpack. I think I'll just grab something from the kitchen and chill out. Getting back in a car to go all the way to New London doesn't sound that appealing after all the time I spent in the car today."

"No, that's fine. I'm pretty tired too. There are some frozen pizzas in the freezer. I'll throw one in the oven."

"Has anyone been in the back-house since I left?" Henry was curious about the condition of the back-house after a long and cold New England winter.

"Yep, I've been going out there every few days to check it out, you know, make sure everything was fine, make sure the heat was coming on and no critters were getting in."

"I think I'll go on out and have a look. I've got another few months of writing to do to finish the story, and as I said, I've been pretty prolific lately, so I want to get right to it in the morning."

"Okay, I'll call you when the pizza is ready. Pretty crazy about Charles, no?"

"You can say that again." After what Henry and Ellen had just been through, talking about someone else's affair was a conversation that was loaded with landmines, and Henry didn't want to stir Ellen up since she seemed to be in a forgiving mood. So Henry got up and headed through the living room patio doors to the back yard and walked the 150 feet out to the back-house. When he got inside, everything seemed to be just the way he had left it. The heat was on, and nothing seemed out of place. He had left in somewhat of a hurry, but from what he could remember, everything was right where he had left it. He sat down in his reclining chair. The whole story about being tired was a bit of a ruse, he really needed to think. He had a million thoughts running around his head. He had thought for months about how he was going to feel when he first saw Ellen after the cruel way she handled outing the affair. First he had forgiven himself for the affair, and then had found forgiveness of Ellen, but three months was not enough time to rebuild the trust that had been lost, though in reality, the trust between Ellen and Henry had been lost years ago. He thought he was completely prepared for whatever Ellen he would meet, but he realized he had spent all his thoughts and energy preparing for the controlling or nasty Ellen, he was not at all prepared for the pleasant Ellen. Was it an act? Was she trying to lure him into lowering his guard? Henry needed to process that scenario.

Charles' admission to an affair was as troubling as it was shocking. Since it was a secret that had been kept for years, maybe even decades, of all the people that he had not admitted that to over the years, why would he mention it now? And to Ellen of all people? Was Henry supposed to believe Ellen? Was Charles trying to give her advice about affairs in the hopes that she would be less difficult on Henry when he returned? That was certainly plausible. Henry knew that Charles cared for him greatly, and he was humbled that Charles would go out on such a limb for him. Henry wanted to believe that.

But it could also have been about Patience. If Charles felt that Patience was helping him get better, it was just as plausible that he was trying to get Ellen to lighten up so she would let Patience back in the building. Although in reality, he didn't need her permission for that, it was his hospital, he could do whatever he wanted.

As Henry sat in his recliner his thoughts turned to Patience. At Carver, they had successfully convinced Henry that even thinking about the object of your affair needs to be off the table. So for the most part Henry had learned to suppress his thoughts about a life with Patience by the time he had returned to Mystic. He filed that thought in the fantasy folder along with his other life fantasies, like cruising the Caribbean or being a best-selling author, things that one can dream fancifully about, but are just that, fantasies, they will never come true. He still could not see how he could end his marriage to Ellen, his life as he knew it would be over. So while it was also mostly a fantasy that Ellen would magically start treating Henry as an equal in their marriage, he needed to put the thought of a pleasant future with one of these women in the fantasy folder. It was a classic fear and hope dilemma, and when fear and hope are in conflict, fear usually wins. Fear is real, you can feel it in your stomach and in your bones, it's what rules our reptilian brains. You feel hope in your surroundings, it's where you want to be, not where you are. When pitted against each other, hope is no match for fear, so the hope becomes the fantasy and the fear becomes the reality.

So Henry had filed a life with Patience away in the fantasy folder. Sort of. One of the very possible outcomes of Henry's return from Carver was divorce papers. He somewhat expected to receive them almost every day he was at Carver House. At first he was convinced of it, but as each day went by without a sheriff coming to the door to serve him papers, the thought slowly faded. So at first, he spent a lot of time imagining what his life would be like if Ellen divorced him. He of course assumed that if that happened, he would immediately enter into a relationship with Patience, they would get married and live happily ever after. But with each passing day with no sheriff serving him, and with Carver therapy sessions devoted to getting him to sever the ties to the person he had an affair with, the thought of a life with Patience slowly faded to the point where she became the fantasy, and resuming a life with Ellen became the reality.

But as he sat in his chair, the same chair he sat in for months over the fall where he fantasized about a life with Patience, those thoughts started creeping back into his head. He wondered how she had survived the last few months. Deep down he knew she would be okay, she was the most grounded person he knew. She never cared what others thought of her, why would she start now? Society embroiders the Scarlett letter on one's chest with the intent of shaming the bearer into punishment, but it takes fear and insecurity in the wearer for it to have its intentioned affect. Patience was enlightened, fear and insecurity were cast out a long time ago. And shame, well shame melts away with self-forgiveness very quickly. So in the end shame is really the outside looking in, masquerading as the inside looking out. Society needs shame to make things right in society, but the shamed can take it or leave it. And if Henry knew anything about Patience, it was that she had long ago lost her fear, her insecurity, and had much more inner-strength than required to deflect shame back onto those who tried to make it stick.

And this was Henry's dilemma. He was trying to make the best of his situation. He was trying to do the right thing, and while Ellen was willing to play along, and reengage in their relationship, he had to entertain that. But in the back of his mind, he also knew Patience was there. He knew that a life with her would be magical. He decided he would live in his reality, but keep the fantasy. His worst fear was that Patience would find someone else in the meantime. And that thought tormented him. It would mean that he would have to only live in his reality, and that was still a very scary place.

And that's how Henry existed from the time he returned home from Carver until the night of Violetta's concert, when everything changed.

CHAPTER 18

The Concert of a Lifetime

The advertisements of Violetta's concert hit the local newspapers and event calendars about a month before the event. In today's social media world, it was a matter of minutes before the news had traveled around the world. The ad that the Garde placed on their Facebook page was shared more than a thousand times by the end of the first day. The response was predictable. Violetta's home phone started ringing and didn't stop for a few days. She received calls from friends in Mystic and friends around the world.

After the first few calls she had her response memorized and could recite it verbatim. They were all quite similar to her call with Werner Reichert, an old German friend who called from Germany. "Thank you so much for your call Werner and your kind words. Yes I have recovered and it truly is a miracle. Yes I hear it is all over the Facebook. No I don't have it, Werner, (laughing) I don't even own a computing machine Werner. No. Traditional physical therapy did not work, traditional medicine failed me Werner. These days doctors know what they know and have no interest in exploring alternatives. But you know me, Werner, how long has it been, twenty years? I have not changed Werner. I am, what do they say here, a bull in a china shop. My horrible persistence paid me back and I found someone who had a new way, a new approach and miraculously it worked. No, I am not going to say who it is right now. I am going to wait until the night of my concert. I have become a modern woman in one way Werner, my concert is going to be a fundraiser. Yes a fundraiser. I am going to raise money for a charity Werner. So I am going to be a devil, I am going to hold onto that little secret about who helped me, and announce it at the concert as a way to get more people to come so we can raise more money. Will you come Werner? I hope so."

Violetta had a plan, but she did not tell Patience. Violetta was forever indebted to Patience for what she had done for her. Violetta knew Patience was extremely gifted and knew the world needed to know about her. So Violetta decided that immediately after playing her concert, she was going to bring her close friends up on stage and then announce that it was Patience that had healed her. She would ask Patience to come up on stage with her so she could thank her and tell the world how Patience had healed her. She knew this would be a shock to some, but besides being overjoyed at her recovery, she had also become a convert to alternative medicine. How could she not? Traditional medicine had mostly failed her, Patience had healed her. Violetta knew she had an opportunity to use her fame to spread that message and she intended to do so.

Ellen was sitting at her desk in her office when she got the first word about Violetta's concert by a phone call from a Harvard colleague of hers.

"Ellen, this is Robert Howes." Robert and Ellen had gone to Harvard Medical School together and had both gone into neuroscience and rehabilitation medicine. Robert was another very well respected doctor in their field and was still practicing in the Boston area. While good friends in college, he and Ellen only had had infrequent conversations over the past few years, and only saw each other occasionally at medical conferences they would both attend, but they were still good friends.

"Robert Howes? What's it been, two years? I think it's been since the AMA conference in Orlando where Jimmy Stein argued that we should be introducing reiki energy work into our rehabilitation practices."

"That's right, that was not well received, was it?" Robert replied.

"No that was a complete disaster. Didn't he have to leave Minnesota after that?" Ellen chuckled at her former colleague's demise.

"Yes, I think he did. I hear he's in Scottsdale now. I wish him well. Poor bastard." Robert continued the friendly rival bashing.

"So what do I owe this pleasure?" Ellen asked.

"You're being coy Ellen. I think congratulations are in order, aren't they?" Robert asked.

"If you're talking about my new job here in Mystic, you're almost a year late Robert. I've been here since last June. By the way, you never called to congratulate me did you?" Ellen chided Robert.

"No I didn't call, and I apologize for that. Ellen I am talking about the news about Violetta Andropov that came out a few minutes ago."

"What news? Poor woman. Sad really. We worked with her but her condition was too dire to rehabilitate her." Ellen was obviously not aware about the news yet.

"Well someone did. I assumed it was you since she was being rehabbed at the Mystic Manor." Robert was perplexed.

"What are you talking about Robert?" Ellen was flummoxed.

"Someone just shared an event on Facebook that Violetta is holding a concert in a few weeks, she will be playing some classical composer's music. I don't know, I'm not a classical music buff, you know me, Jimmy Buffet is more my style." Robert was getting off track which was frustrating a suddenly pale Ellen.

"What the fuck are you talking about Robert?" Ellen was now in shock.

"Let's see, it says that Violetta Andropov, the great concert pianist will be playing a series of Mozart conciertos, that's it, Mozart, Beethoven, it's all the same to me, at some place called the Garde Theatre in New London Connecticut on May 15th." Robert was reading from the ad on Facebook.

"That's impossible. Are you reading the ad wrong? Is she hosting other pianists? She can't play a Mozart concierto with one arm." Ellen was in disbelief. As Robert was talking Ellen had turned to her computer and opened up Facebook. As the words left her mouth she saw the ad and was stunned. The ad had been shared on her Facebook wall over a dozen times from colleagues. Some had even written messages like "Congrats!"

"Okay you obviously know nothing about this. I'll share the ad on your Facebook page." Robert said.

"Don't bother, I just opened Facebook and it's been shared over a dozen times on my wall. This is incredible. It's simply impossible. I spent three months with her last summer trying to get movement back in her arm, and Robert, it was nearly dead. People simply do not recover from that kind of damage."

"Well someone obviously figured it out, 'cause she's playing piano in a few weeks, and I'll guess it is not going to be one-armed Mozart. Though that would be interesting. One person playing the left hand part while she plays the right hand part. You know like how we used to play Heart & Soul as kids with two people?" Robert was being silly and it was pissing Ellen off.

"Fuck off Robert." Ellen was now seething, not at Robert but at the situation as she quickly turned this over in her head. She read the ad over and over again on her Facebook page. It could not be clearer. Violetta Andropov was playing a Mozart concert, she was not hosting one, she was playing one.

"Woah there. You seem way too upset by this. The poor woman has had a miraculous recovery. You should be happy for her." Robert and Ellen had told each other to fuck off numerous times over the years, so he didn't take it as an insult.

"Of course I am Robert, she's a lovely courageous woman, but I am, I am, stunned, dumbfounded." Ellen trailed off and thought about how she was going to respond to all the congratulations messages on her Facebook page. She clearly had nothing to do with Violetta's recovery, but even worse, she had tried and failed. It would be one thing if Violetta had recovered and Ellen had never tried to help her, she could say she could have done it too. But she had tried and failed. What's worse she had told Violetta to give up her dream, that there was no way to undo the damage done to her.

Robert continued, "Any thoughts on who it might be then?"

"Well it must have been someone we know, right? Rehab medicine is a small world." Ellen started looking at her Facebook messages, most of which were from her doctor friends who understood what ties Violetta and Ellen had together and made assumptions. "Well, I am looking at five or six Facebook messages from our colleagues, so clearly it was none of them. Do you think it was Peter? He's been doing some radical stuff lately and he refuses to talk about it with anyone. This would be classic Peter. Mr. Big Splash."

"Maybe it was Jimmie Stein?" Robert said half-jokingly. "That whole Reiki thing might just work."

"Christ almighty Robert, can you be more serious? This is a big fucking deal. I tried to treat her and couldn't. Someone else did, this is not good." Ellen was dead serious. The medical profession is extremely competitive, especially in the academic world, where massive egos clash like the Greek Gods. Where brilliant scientists compete for funding of their research because they know it will pay off for them professionally and personally. Ellen was right up there with the best in the field. Mystic Manor, despite being small, with private funding by Mason Industries was right up there with the best in the country in reputation. Lose your reputation and you lose everything. Colleagues start treating you like a pariah and making fun behind your back, just like Robert and Ellen were doing to Jimmie Stein not just a few minutes ago.

Robert was a good enough friend that she could talk openly with him. She knew he would not betray her by taking advantage of something told to him in confidence. He asked again, "Any thoughts, 'cause I can't come up with anyone. Let me make some calls to see if anyone is admitting to this."

"Okay thanks. And Robert, please keep it in confidence that I worked with her and couldn't make any progress, I don't need a controversy here." Ellen was worried.

"Of course sweetheart. I'll play dumb on that, but I'll let anyone who asks know that it wasn't you, at least to get your Facebook wall less cluttered." Robert was a serial wise cracker.

"Hah, thanks. You're always the comedian." Ellen was lightening up a little bit. "Let me know what you find out Robert."

"You'll be the second to know." And with that Robert hung up the phone.

Ellen expected there to be another call like Robert's soon, so she put her phone on Do Not Disturb and sat back in her chair and processed the entire conversation with Robert and the news of Violetta's remarkable recovery. She racked her brain of all the folks she knew who could have pulled something like that off. Of course Patience never crossed her mind. Despite the mounting evidence of Patience's effectiveness with the patients at the Manor by their deterioration since Patience's absence, Ellen was still convinced that Patience was only effective by giving patients hope from her calm, good-natured and loving personality, but that there was nothing more to her healing capabilities than that, and fixing Violetta would have taken more than a pleasant personality. Despite having Patience followed all autumn by her private detective, and therefore knowing that Patience was going to see Violetta, she had simply always assumed it was for her yoga sessions that Ellen already knew about, and that was still her assumption. Ellen's state of mind simply could not even grasp that Patience could have been somehow involved.

Obviously Ellen wanted to be at Violetta's concert, and it was not that implausible for the concert to sell out quickly due to Violetta's fame around the world, so she immediately went to the Garde's Website and purchased two tickets, one for her and one for Henry, who after having returned from Carver House a few weeks before, had been living in a seemingly normal marriage with Ellen. She asked the Website to get her the best seats available and those happened to be two front-row seats in the left balcony. This was perfect, she would be able to look right down at the events and she and Henry would be very visible from the entire theater. Assuming Patience would be there, she wanted everyone to know that Henry was squarely back in a relationship with Ellen.

She thought some more about the situation and thought of a clever way to respond to the congratulatory Facebook posts and the few calls she received over the next few weeks without creating suspicion. Her message was that Violetta was an old friend of her parents, that she was ecstatic for Violetta and her recovery, but that Violetta had been discharged from Mystic Manor before Ellen started working there, and she had no idea who had been working with Violetta since. These were actually true facts, and she simply chose to leave out the fact that Ellen had been sending physical therapists to Violetta's home over the summer and had failed to reverse the damage from Violetta's stroke.

When announced, Violetta's miraculous recovery had made the daily news shows around the northeast, even making it onto a few news television stations in New York City and in Boston. True to form, one of New York's TV news stations even sent a camera crew up to Mystic to try and get an interview with Violetta. Violetta was not ready to speak to the public so she put them off, and instead the video crew once again took video of the front of Mystic Manor, the entry to Violetta's long winding driveway, and the Garde Theatre, film they would need for the story to run on the nightly news.

Just as Jenny Brown had thought, the concert was going to be a sell-out. Tickets were selling very fast as the Garde Theater was receiving calls from all over the world for tickets as some of Violetta's friends from Europe had decided this was a good opportunity to come to the US and see their dear friend. This was going to be a very big event.

Violetta sent word to the Mystic Manor that she wanted a handful of her friends that were still in residence at the Manor to come to the concert. Patience and Violetta had arranged with Jenny as they were planning the event that a block of twenty seats in the front row would be reserved for Violetta's friends who had mobility needs. They would be allowed to come in the side door and be seated immediately. Violetta personally called Charles Sr. to make sure he would come. Charles and his wife Emma had become dear friends with Violetta over the years that she lived in Mystic, and after much back and forth, Violetta, who would not take no for an answer, absolutely insisting that Charles Sr. be there, he finally relented and agreed to come. It was arranged by Patience that Charles Jr and Amy would make sure he got there.

Over the next few weeks, Ellen and her colleagues in the medical profession were abuzz with speculation over who had performed a miracle, and somehow restored and rehabilitated a stroke victim to the point where they could perform at a classical concert. They were convinced it was one of them, but the miracle worker was not admitting to it, waiting for the big event to have their brilliance announced in front of the news cameras that were sure to be there filming the concert and the announcement that had been promised after the concert.

Violetta spent the last few weeks practicing her requisite three hours a day and spending four to five hours doing the meditating and other practices that Patience had taught her. Patience continued her regular daily visits to see Violetta, watching her piano skills improve greatly every day. Patience had been nervous that she and Violetta could not pull it off, but as the concert approached, Patience became more confident that Violetta was going to be just fine. She would not be the pianist she was in her thirties and forties, but no one is. No one else would be expecting Violetta to be either. Everyone was simply happy to see her play the piano at all, let alone play a concert, and even if she struggled a bit during the concert, simply having Violetta up on a stage playing Mozart again was going to be a win for everyone.

Over the last few weeks leading up to the concert, Patience would tell Violetta that everyone's expectations would for her to be simply good, not great, and of course, the perfectionist that she was, Violetta would say that she would never expect to play any less than she could before the stroke. At least on the surface. Deep down, Violetta knew that she would never play as well as she once could but she allowed herself to be satisfied with whatever she would be able to do, deep down even she admitted that simply being on the stage was a lifetime accomplishment by itself.

The day of the event finally came. Violetta hired a limousine to take her, Patience and Lois to the concert. Ellen and Henry drove together. Charles Jr., Amy and Charles Sr. went together in Charles' BMW. The manor had a large wheel chair van to take patients to places they needed to go, such as other doctor's visits or occasional group outings, and the small group of Violetta's friends from the Manor were chauffeured to the Garde in the Manor's van, a few in wheel chairs, but most walking with canes or walkers.

Leading up to the night of the concert, all of us local girls were abuzz with phone calls establishing what we were going to wear. The last time we had all come together and gotten all dressed up was at the Manor's disastrous Christmas Party, which had put an impressive chill on formal social get-togethers for the last few months. We are gossipers like every other group of women, but what happened that night was so tragic for Henry and Patience that it was simply uncomfortable and sad to talk about. But it now had been many months since that night, and we were due for another nice dress up party so this one was very welcome.

I decided to wear my favorite royal blue cocktail dress and of course it took all I had to convince Bill to wear a jacket, let alone a tie. I finally won him over by telling him the thought of him in a jacket and tie turned me on, and he made me promise that we would have sex later that evening if he wore his jacket and tie, which I agreed to, just to get him out the door. Men are so predictable and easy to control.

Once we were ready at about six o'clock, Bill and I drove the twenty minute drive from Stonington to New London in Bill's Ford pickup. Once there, Bill dropped me off in front of the Garde while he went to park the car around the corner. Occasionally, very occasionally, Bill could be a gentleman, and ever since the Christmas Party, he had really become quite thoughtful. I am not sure what it was, maybe the heartache we witnessed that night made him realize the importance of our relationship, maybe Ellen put the fear of God in him what a scorned woman would do to a man. Either way, it felt nice to have Bill treat me like he loved me. Of course I knew he did, but loving someone and treating them like they are loved sometimes are two different things.

As I waited out front for Bill to come back, Charlie drove up, stopped his BMW in front of the Garde and Amy jumped out of the back seat to help Charles Sr out of the passenger front seat. Seeing how Charles Sr had aged since I last saw him was disturbing. Being Amy's best friend, I would get to see him at Mason family parties, but since Emma had passed away and Charles was living in Mystic Manor, I do not get the opportunity. He had been a very tall man, but now was quite reduced in stature, as is the usual case as people age. He needed his walker to walk and I went over to help Amy. Despite not seeing Charles Sr in a very long time he immediately recognized me and I was happy to see that he was as charming as ever.

"Cat DiCastro, how have you been, it has been too long. How's my favorite clam shack? Are you still the proprietor?" Charles Sr. spoke to me as he was rotating himself into the middle of his walker. "Damn these things, don't let anyone fool you into thinking that we age gracefully. There is nothing graceful about getting old."

"So good to see you Mr. Mason, yes I still own the Black Duck, everything is going fine. We have not changed a thing, so you'll still recognize it when you come to visit." I responded.

"I would look forward to that someday Ms. DiCastro. Amy, can you and Charles spring me from the Manor some day and take me into town. I would love to have a bowl of the best chowder in all of New

England. It must have been ten years." Charles Sr. was being affable as always.

"And don't let anyone tell you that you are not graceful sir, you are still the most graceful and most handsome man in the area." While most people were terrified of Charles Mason Sr., somehow I always had the ability to flirt with him and get away with it.

"Cat DiCastro you always know how to make a man feel special. I will be by to see you at the Black Duck soon. Prepare that chowder for me."

"It would be an honor sir."

As was planned, Amy and I helped Charles Sr. enter in the side door of the Garde and led him to his seat in front. I found my seat a few rows back and after a few minutes Bill and Charles Jr came walking down the aisle together after parking the cars. Slowly but surely everyone was arriving. Violetta's friends from the Manor were also led in the side door and seated in front. The ushers were very accommodating with those in front, knowing that most of those seats were friends of Violetta. While I was watching the crowd file in and take their seats, I was slightly distracted and it was only when I looked back up at the stage that I caught the sight of Ellen and Henry who had come in and taken their seats in the first row of the side balcony, looking right over the stage.

It was the first time I had seen Henry since the Christmas party. He actually looked better than what I would have thought. Since coming back to Mystic after his three months in Carver House, he had completely stayed out of the public eye. We all assumed that was the agreement he had struck with Ellen and the Chandlers, lay low, stay home, write his book, and don't get within half a mile of Patience. While that was expected, it was still sad. Though Henry and I had not spoken for twenty years, it was great to be able to talk to him on a regular basis again all during the autumn. So despite being away for so long, I had gotten used to talking to him, and now it was sad to go back to not talking again.

As I looked up at him in the balcony, I felt even sadder for him. I was convinced he had fallen back in love with Patience, it was likely he had never fallen out of love with her, yet there he was with Ellen. After the Christmas party, whatever good feelings I had developed for Ellen completely disappeared. The way she had humiliated two of my oldest friends in such a public way was unfathomable to me. It was so unnecessary. Sure Henry had an affair, and as a woman we automatically want to take the side of the scorned woman, we want to rally around and comfort her. But Ellen made it clear by the way she exposed the affair that she was not looking for female comfort, at least from anyone in Mystic. She played the hurt wife to her advantage, but no one thought she really was actually that hurt. She knew the affair was going on, she had pictures of it for weeks before she exposed it. It was clear that she didn't like Patience, she wanted her out of her life and her work, and I could not keep thinking that it was all a rouse, that she had used her husband, even worse, completely humiliated him, just to get to punish Patience.

As these thoughts were going through my mind, and I was staring up at Henry, our eyes met. From a distance and in the low lighting it was hard to communicate much, but we smiled and let the glance linger for a while. I tried my best to communicate my love and support through my eyes and facial expression and he responded by winking at me, which felt great. It let me know that he was doing okay. I turned my focus back to the stage, the last thing I wanted was to make eye contact with Ellen as she scanned the crowd of people in the lower seats.

As the seats slowly filled, it was clear that the theater was going to be at capacity. I saw so many people that I had not seen in a long time. From my seat in the side front, I could see Jenny Brown and Patience up on the stage on the opposite side behind the side stage curtains. On the stage there was nothing but a black Steinway grand piano, positioned sideways as I would guess is usually the case with piano concerts, not that Bill or I had really ever been to one. There were television camera crews from New York and Boston on both sides of the orchestra section about midway up, this event was being recorded, and was likely being streamed online for the world to see. A few minutes before 7:00 pm, Patience came down the aisle and took her seat in the second row next to Lois, right behind the Masons.

At 7:00 on the nose, the Garde's executive director James Hislop walked up onto the stage using the right-hand stairs that lead from the orchestra section to the stage, and walked up to the microphone that was placed in the center front of the stage and the audience quieted down.

"Ladies and gentleman, thank you for being here tonight at this extraordinary event for the Garde, for the local area, and for the world. It is not often that we actually sell out at the Garde, but tonight we have. And that is a testament to tonight's featured performer. For over forty years, Violetta Andropov has been a concert pianist on the world stage. She has played for kings, queens, prime ministers, presidents, and I hear even a few dictators." He paused for the laughter at his intended joke. "She has won most every award that a professional pianist can win.

"As you all know, two years ago Violetta suffered a stroke which left her left side paralyzed, and after forty years of entertaining millions, she was suddenly and tragically unable to do so, which was a terrible loss for the world, and obviously devastating for her. Due to a miraculous recovery, Violetta has recovered and tonight she is back on stage, a second coming out party in a way. We are so privileged that she chose to settle down in Mystic, in our little humble corner of the world, which has given us access to her music and her incredible generosity. I am especially honored that she chose to have this coming out party at the Garde.

"As a testament to her generosity, as I hope you know, a portion of the proceeds from this evening's concert will go the Garde, to help us fulfill our vision of keeping live music and theater alive in this area. The remainder will go to the Mystic Arts Center, our brethren a few miles away, which provides a place for visual artists to showcase their work. Violetta's lifelong commitment to the arts is still strong and we all thank her for that gift." Mr. Hislop paused and the audience gave a long round of applause. "Without further ado, I would like to introduce tonight's performer, Ms. Violetta Andropov." With that, Violetta walked out on stage in a long black gown and Mr. Hislop walked over to greet her, whispered something in her ear, gave her a hug and exited the stage, leaving Violetta alone on stage.

Violetta hesitated for a moment before walking to the piano bench and instead walked over to the microphone. "Good evening to all my friends. And you are all my friends tonight. I know it is not normal for a pianist to address the audience before a performance, but I am going to make an exception tonight. I hope you are not offended. As Mr. Hislop mentioned this is a coming out party for me. Two years ago I was stricken with a terrible tragedy, one that is the biggest fear of a concert pianist, more than death itself. For to not play the piano for me is, well I'll just say it, it is pure hell. I have fought for the last two years, fought for me, and fought for you. I had lost all hope. And then someone appeared in my life that once again gave me hope. They looked into my soul and gave me the path I needed to heal myself. They did not heal me, they taught me how to heal myself. I know that many of you are here tonight not only to hear this old woman play some Mozart, but to learn the identity of this miracle worker. I will introduce that person tonight, but not until after the concert, for now you must suffer a little more. So I thank you for coming tonight, and now I will play." With that, Violetta walked to the piano and sat down and started her hour long concert.

Up until that very moment, Patience had no idea that Violetta was going to make a public announcement to introduce the person who had healed her, her miracle worker. Although she never thought of herself in that way, she of course knew that Violetta was referring to her. Patience was not good with large crowds, and the thought of having to be publicly recognized was making Patience more nervous. As the concert progressed, she thought more and more about what a public introduction would be like to this crowd, especially with Ellen in the balcony to her right, a few feet away. What kind of reaction would she get? Did Violetta know about the Christmas party and the affair? Had she contemplated the potential mixed reaction from some of the people in the crowd?

Public perception of her after the party was not something that Patience thought often about. She had mostly stayed out of public view for the past few months, she had lost a few of her yoga students, she assumed due to the controversy, but most kept coming to her classes and treated her with the same respect and love they always had. But what would the reaction be tonight? Patience suspected that Ellen had no idea it was Patience who had healed Violetta, and therefore she was going to be in for quite a shock. How would she handle it? With so many people watching, Patience comforted herself that Ellen was sure not to make a scene. At worst, Patience hoped that she would simply get up and walk out of the theater in a silent protest. These thoughts raced through Patience's mind as the hour long concert progressed.

Ellen also was fixated on the topic of Violetta's healer instead of the actual performance. She scoured the audience for familiar faces, looking for someone from her field that was there that could be the person that Violetta was going to recognize. Robert and a few of her colleagues from Harvard came down from Boston for the concert, they were as curious as Ellen was to find out the identity of the miracle worker. Ellen suggested they also get seats in the balcony near her so they could be together. Throughout the concert she looked at every face she could see from her vantage point yet could not find anyone she recognized that could be the one. She looked at her colleagues in the balcony with her and wondered if one of them was the person, but they were simply hiding it from her. Why else would they have come?

I sat in the audience and watched this entire scene play out. From my seat on the left side of the theater, I could look over at Patience on the other side of the orchestra section, and at Ellen and Henry in the side balcony, which from my viewpoint was right above and slightly behind Patience. I could see Ellen in her raven hair and green strapless dress searching through the crowd. It was clear this entire scene was making Ellen very anxious. Ellen abhorred surprises, she liked to control every situation she was in, and she was in one at this moment that she had no control over. Someone was going to be recognized for doing something that she claimed as her expertise, but could not accomplish, and she could not for the life of her understand how that was possible. She still thought of herself as the best in her field.

I occasionally glanced over at Patience in her seat, she also seemed surprisingly anxious.

Violetta's performance was nearly flawless and when she finished her last concerto, she stopped and took a very deep breath. The audience of course immediately went to their feet with a very loud and long standing ovation. Violetta stood up, Mr. Hislop walked back on stage with a huge bouquet of red roses, and handed it to her and gave her another hug. They both walked to the microphone.

Mr. Hislop let the applause go on for another minute and then spoke. "Wonderful, wonderful. Wasn't that just wonderful?" Mr. Hislop asked the crowd. The applause only got louder and continued for another minute or so. Finally the applause stopped and the audience sat back in their seats.

"Violetta that was extraordinary. Thank you for that performance. I hope those piano notes that floated around this theater tonight continue to reverberate around the Garde theater for eternity. Now Violetta, you made a promise before you began that you would let the world know who the miracle worker was that, as you said, showed you the path to heal yourself."

Violetta took a deep breath. "Yes I did. But before I do that I would like my dear friends to come up on stage and surround me. Cynthia, Donna, Susan, Marjie, Charles, Miriam, all of my friends sitting in the front row, please come up on stage. I know you are all old like me, but there are stairs right there, please come. If we can have some of the ushers help these folks climb the stairs please." The people mentioned all looked at each other, they were as surprised as anyone about going up on stage, but they did as they were asked. A few ushers came from the shadows to help them up the stairs, as did a few other people sitting nearby. Charles Jr and Amy helped Charles Sr. up the stairs without his walker. It took a minute or two, but they all got up on stage and surrounded Violetta holding her bouquet of roses at the microphone. With the front row mostly emptied in front of Patience, she and Lois were now more visible to everyone, including Ellen and Henry in the balcony above and slightly behind her.

As Violetta began to speak, Ellen was feverishly looking at the audience below her, looking for any sign from someone to give her a hint.

"As I traveled the world with my career I had made friends from all around the world, many of them who I can still call as my friends. But when you travel as I did, friendships are difficult to maintain. When I moved to Mystic some years ago, this group of people that surrounds me right now took this weary traveler in and welcomed me into their circle. For that I am ever grateful. When I had my stroke, ironically I was lucky to live in Mystic near one of the best hospitals in the world for treating my ailment. I was lucky to be friends with Charles Mason, and he made sure I received the best care I could at his hospital. The same hospital that cared for him when he had his stroke by the way." With that Charles nodded in agreement.

"But for me, western medicine could only do so much. I was told after a period of time that there was nothing more than they could do for me. I had given up hope. But that loss of hope was unfounded. There was hope, hope found in someone who is the most gifted healer I have ever met, and I have met many people who claim to be gifted healers." Violetta and the audience laughed and she then continued. "This person took me under her wing."

Up until that time Ellen had no idea of the gender of the person, but Violetta's use of the word 'her' gave her the first clue, it was a woman. That puzzled her, there are not many women in her field. She looked over at her colleagues on the balcony and that eliminated Robert and a few others. She looked at Virginia Biggs, another colleague of hers who had come with the group, with a look of "is she talking about you?" Ginnie looked back at Ellen and pantomimed with a shrug of her shoulders the universal "Beat's me!"

Violetta continued. "She taught me to look inward, to understand that I am not just muscle and bones, but I am a being of energy, that I exist beyond this old quickly decaying body you see before you. If you could not tell from my accent, I am Russian." The audience again collectively laughed. "And like all Russians, I got my religious education from the Orthodox Church. I was taught the simple lessons of the commandments: love God, be kind to friends and strangers, trust your elders, don't steal or hurt, those things we all take for granted. But that education also taught me to be fearful of God, to be fearful of death, and yes even to be fearful of life. That education did not teach me how to look at myself, it did not tell me who I was, other than of course telling me that I was a sinner. Constantly a sinner. Like I didn't know that already." Another collective laugh from the audience.

"My miracle worker taught me that I am not just a bag of bones, she taught me that I am a spiritual being that exists for eternity. And as a spiritual being that will exist for eternity, I have power over this bag of bones, which will not be around for very much longer, twenty or thirty years if I am lucky." Another collective laugh from the audience.

"She taught me how this bag of bones actually is a collection of individual cells, billions of cells, each has a purpose, each has a perfect understanding of its purpose, and each needs to be continually nourished to carry out that purpose, nourished not just with oxygen, and blood, but with appreciation and understanding. When we store our life's pains and troubles in our flesh, we interrupt our harmony, our energy flow, and when we do that, terrible terrible things happen to our bodies. I got a stroke. I took advantage of my body, I did not eat properly, I was too busy, and too greedy for the 'Joie de vivre' that's French for 'live it up, baby'." Another audience laugh.

The more Violetta talked about her experience, Ellen was clearly understanding that what Violetta was describing was not traditional medicine. She had been introduced to something very alternative and something very Eastern in philosophy. At that moment a chill came over her body. A realization struck her that made her heart stop. Could Violetta be talking about Patience? The thought had never entered into her mind. There Patience was, sitting below Ellen, watching along with Ellen, and listening to Violetta use words that sounded like words that would have come right out of Patience's mouth. Energy, energy flow. Ellen was getting even more agitated. Her pulse started increasing.

From my vantage point, I could see both Ellen and Patience clearly, and I will try to describe as best I can what happened over the next few seconds, because what happened next changed the lives of so many people forever. It set in motion a course of events that people will talk about for decades. And it was all recorded on national television for all of the world to see.

Violetta continued. "I apologize, I am keeping you on the edge of your seats. Trust me, that is not my intention, I am trying to describe the transformation I went through, but I cannot, it is too complex, beyond me really, I had a guide and I only followed instructions. But I am stubborn woman you know. I know how to concentrate, how else do you play Mozart concertos like I do. So without further annoying you, let me introduce my miracle worker, and she is my healer, my guide, the most compassionate person I have ever met, Miss Patience Passion."

I, like everyone else in the theater, gasped at the mention of Patience's name, not because of the controversy of the last few months, but because everyone was expecting to hear the name of someone who was world famous. This was Violetta Andropov, a world famous musician, friend to Deepak Chopra and other world famous healers. We were all expecting to see someone famous walk out from behind the curtain. Television crews came from New York City to be the first to report on what famous person had pulled off yet another miracle of healing.

After the initial gasp, the audience murmured as they all started whispering to each other. I'll guess that half of the audience had no idea who Patience was, so those were asking each other who Patience Passion was. The other half of the audience was from the area, and most of those knew who Patience was, she was a fixture in the area for so many years that everyone had trickled through one of her classes at some point, or at least had a friend who had. The local half of the audience also murmured to their friends, likely either out of disbelief, or for those who loved Patience as much as I did, complete understanding.

I looked over at Patience, and it was clear she had no idea what to do. She must have known her name was going to be called from the beginning of the concert since Violetta announced that she was going to reveal her name. But she was completely unprepared. She didn't know whether to stand or stay sitting. Patience disliked public attention immensely. In all of the wonderful ways that she had helped her students over the years, with all of the recognition she would get in social settings as people would thank her for working with a parent or friend and nursing them back to health, Patience never asked for, nor received any public recognition, other than the personal thank you's and Christmas card notes of appreciation.

When Patience's name was announced by Violetta, I watched Ellen slowly stand up on her feet. Her normally alabaster skin on her face was turning red. She was clearly seething. For the very first time and the very last time, I was watching Ellen Chandler lose control of herself. As she slowly stood up out of her chair on the edge of the balcony, Ellen began to say something, quietly at first, but as she repeated it, she got louder and louder.

"She's not a healer, that woman is a fraud. That woman is a fraud." As she repeated herself, Ellen's voice was getting loud enough to be heard over the murmuring of the crowd and as the crowd began to get quiet, Ellen's voice became clearly audible to everyone in that part of the theater.

Henry, realizing what was happening, grabbed Ellen's arm to try and get her to sit down, and said something to her, and that act started a torrent of words that brought out every ounce of Ellen's rage toward both Henry and Patience.

Ellen directed her next sentence at Henry, "I will not sit down you coward. This is all your fault!" Ellen then turned to the audience and spoke as loud as she could muster. "That woman is not a healer, she is a destroyer. She is a fraud. She slept with my husband for heaven's sake. How can you possibly think she is a healer? This is utterly absurd."

Violetta was still standing at the microphone and heard every word that Ellen had just said and tried to stop her. "Ellen Chandler, please sit down. This is none of your business."

"None of my business? None of my business? That woman slept with my husband, she is not a healer, she is a destroyer."

With that the audience gasped again. I put both my hands over my mouth in complete shock at what was transpiring. Of course Bill could not control himself and muttered, "Oh man, this is getting good now." I gave him a death stare to warn him to not say another word.

Charles Sr., who was standing right next to Violetta on stage, was obviously in distress from what had just been said. He stepped up to the microphone stand and brought it to his mouth, "Dr. Chandler, you will show some decorum, I will not have you say such things in this forum."

Ellen, still standing and now leaning against the rail of the balcony, responded, "Charles, you have no right. You know exactly what she did. Why do you all protect her? Why do you pretend that what happened is okay? She slept with my husband and that makes her a whore."

With that Charles Sr responded, and he responded with the most stern voice that I had ever heard from him, slowly, emphasizing every word, "Dr. Chandler, you will stop right now. Patience Passion is nothing of the sort. She is a treasure. And I will not have you speak about a member of my family in those terms. I absolutely forbid it. Patience Passion is my daughter, and I absolutely forbid you to say another word."

A third gasp came across the audience, I looked at Bill and he looked at me, and we were both speechless. We both looked back at Ellen in the balcony, who was now leaning over the railing of the balcony pretty far, and there she paused for what appeared to be a minute, but was only probably a few seconds. I can only imagine what was going through her head at that moment. Her disdain of Patience started the first night she arrived in Mystic for the very first time. Disdain became contempt when she found out that Patience was working in her hospital. Contempt became hatred when it became clear that Henry had tremendous feelings for her.

But all that time, she felt she could get away with her animosity because of who she was in comparison to Patience. They were not equals in anyway whatsoever. Ellen was a Harvard doctor, she was a Chandler, she was wealthy beyond most, she had society on her side. She had based all of her animosity and contempt on the fact that Patience was a nobody, with no family, no money, no resources, and she had no known father. Ellen had thought she could crush her whenever she wanted. The sudden realization that Patience not only had a father, but that father was Charles Mason, someone whose wealth rivaled her own family's wealth changed everything for Ellen in an instant. Patience had money, she had resources, she had one of the most blue-blood pedigrees in America, Ellen's head began to spin as she realized that Patience was winning, and not just winning, she had won. She had won the heart of her husband. She had just won the hearts of the world on national television. And she was untouchable because she had won the heart of Charles Mason forty years ago when she was born from an affair that Charles had obviously had with Lois. She thought of Charles' admission to having an affair when he was in her office a few months before, but it never crossed her mind that Lois was the person, if she had, then she might have realized right then that Patience could be Charles' daughter.

Ellen realized in a matter of moments, that her entire world had just changed. A few seconds ago, Ellen was in control of everything that surrounded her: her job, her husband, her self-image, her social status, her friends, her entire life, and in a matter of seconds she now realized that she was in control of nothing, she had likely lost control of everything, and it was all due to Patience.

As Ellen contemplated all of that, her head began to spin. She was still leaning far over the balcony railing, and right in front of the entire audience of the Garde and on national television, Ellen Chandler slowly began to fall forward. Henry realized she was falling and tried to grab her but it was too late, she was too far over the railing for him to stop her. Her fall over the railing of the balcony seemed like slow motion. As the audience gasped, Ellen fell over the railing and to the floor about fifteen feet below her with a sickening thud. The entire audience gasped again, almost everyone screamed.

This time I yelled out, "Holy shit!" Bill was speechless.

There were immediate yells from the crowd to get an ambulance. Ellen had done a complete flip as she fell and landed somewhat right side up but went down very hard, hitting her head on the floor and lay motionless. Clearly she was gravely injured. What likely saved Ellen's life was the fact that there were half a dozen of the world's best neurologists in attendance that night, who all rushed to Ellen and immediately began to try to stabilize her.

In the madness and chaos of Ellen's fall and its immediate aftermath, no one happened to notice that Charles Sr had also collapsed on the stage. Amy was the first to look around and see him lying on his back and she yelled to Charles Jr., "Charlie, your father!" They both rushed over to Charles Sr, who was semi-conscious but having some sort of seizure.

Amy yelled louder and louder, "Oh my God. Somebody call an ambulance, somebody call an ambulance! We need an ambulance here now!"

The events of the last few minutes would have likely been too much for most anyone to handle, for Patience the roller coaster of emotion over the past hour was even worse. It had just been announced on national television that she was a miracle healer, which was immediately followed by being called a whore, and then the pronouncement from Charles Mason that he was her father, only to watch Ellen's fall from the balcony, landing not more than ten feet away with a sickening and bone-breaking impact, and then Charles Sr, the man who always treated her like a daughter, collapsed in seizures on the stage. She was in such shock that she hesitated for a moment. But with the sight of Charles collapsing on the floor, Patience forgot all of it and immediately ran to Charles Sr. When she got up on stage, it was clear he was in severe distress, but she was not sure if he was having another stroke, or had simply feinted with all of the emotion and commotion. She placed both hands on either side of his head to stabilize his head in case he had some type of spinal injury, and could tell from his temperature of his neck that he was going into shock.

The scene at the Garde over the next thirty minutes was complete and utter chaos. Ambulances had been called immediately after Ellen fell, and because the Garde is in the middle of New London, a rather large city with fire stations, police stations and ambulance centers all within one quarter mile of the theater, they all were on site within a few minutes. EMT stretchers were rushed into the theater and they went to work assessing, stabilizing, and loading Ellen and Charles onto the stretchers to get them to the hospital as quickly as possible. Both Ellen and Charles Sr. were rushed to New London Hospital, about three miles away, with doctors keeping them stabilized on the way, and were quickly in the care of the emergency room doctors.

After Charles and Ellen were rushed off to the hospital with Henry, Charles, Amy, Lois, and a few others following close behind, those of us who remained at the Garde were left nearly speechless. Bill, who always has something to say about everything, still could not utter any words beyond, "Oh my effing God!"

Those who had come from far away and had long trips back home dispersed quickly, the show was over, and there was nothing more to talk about. Those of us who were local and were friends of those involved, stayed behind. Patience stayed behind, going to the hospital seemed out of the question to her at this moment. I found her sitting on the steps to the stage with her head in her hands. I had no idea what to say to her, but I knew I had to say something.

"You okay kiddo?" Because Patience was two years younger than me, growing up, that was name I called her when we young.

"You haven't called me that in years." Patience said through the tears as she looked up.

"Yeah, well we haven't really talked in years, have we? That's my fault." I felt a tremendous sense of guilt come over me.

"Cat, no need, I love you and always have, and always will. You have always been one of the good ones. The time has never been right, that's all." Patience paused for a few seconds. "The time is right, right now,

I could really use a hug. Would you mind?"

"I would like nothing better, I could really use one too, and Bill, well, you know, that's not his specialty." I was trying to find some humor, and making fun of Bill always seemed like a sure bet. Sitting next to her, I opened my arms in a big hug, and Patience turned toward me and I wrapped my arms around her, her head falling on my shoulder, where she let out a few breathy sobs.

"That poor woman." Patience said. I was not quite sure who she was talking about. "So much rage, so little trust. I feel so sorry for her." That last sentence she said in between more sobs. That was classic Patience. Forget the obvious emotion and reaction, which for someone who had just been called a whore on national television, would probably have been angst and anger directed at the accuser, but not Patience, she was looking for the hurt, and she was already finding a way to heal it. Forgiveness was not something Patience had to take a deep breath, fight off the anger, and muster up, it was absolutely inherent in her soul in and in the graceful way she approached every interaction and thought.

"Yeah, she has some anger issues, doesn't she? But that thing she said, it had nothing to do with you Patience, that was all her. She thought she had you under control, and in a matter of seconds she realized that everything she thought was in control, had been completely turned on its head. Oh my God, Patience, Charles Mason is your father?"

"Cat, I had no idea. I don't even know here to begin to process that. I have so many mixed emotions. I love that man, I always have, and I have always looked up to him as a father, but he was not my father. My father was a CIA agent who came into town every few months for a secret rendezvous with Lois. He was a famous rock musician like Pete Townsend, that Lois met at Woodstock. He was an astronaut that had another family in Ohio. I had so many fantasies about who he was, or might have been."

"That's hilarious, I had those same fantasies also. My dad was not really my dad. I was the daughter of the President that my mom had a secret affair when they were young." I actually had that recurring fantasy when I was young.

"That's so funny Cat." Patience was starting to get control of her sobs.

I continued, "well it turns out the fantasy of the dashingly handsome, immensely rich, wonderful, caring man, was the winner." I tried to come up with more light humor.

"Well that was one of those fantasies, yes, but I never thought that Charles would be that immensely rich guy. It is such a shock. My mother and Charles had an affair? Oh my God, I feel so bad for Emma. Did she know? Was I the cause of any pain for that lovely woman who took such good care of Lois and I? What she must have gone through."

"If she did, it didn't seem to impact their relationship in any way, it's pretty obvious that Charles and Emma loved each other in a very big way. If she was half the saint we think she was, then forgiveness was all in a day's job." I thought of all the times that I saw Charles Sr and Emma walking holding hands like they were newlyweds.

"I guess you're right. The fact that she let us live on the estate all those years meant one of two things, either she had no idea, or she did and she is as much a saint as I have always thought she was. I so hope it's the latter."

At that point Bill came walking up and said something to us in such a kind way, it reminded of how nice and sweet he can be, "Hey there you two beautiful ladies, are we doing okay? We gonna make it?"

Patience looked up at Bill, "Yes Bill, I'll be all right. Cat's got her hooks in me here."

"Ayep, she'll do that." Bill responded. "Mother hen, she's right there, first with the hug when someone falls and scrapes their knee." He was trying and it was sweet.

"Quite a shocking evening though, so much to process. I am terrified for both Ellen and Charles, and Henry, and Charles' family." Patience sat up and cleared her eyes and her throat.

Bill continued, "Well I guess you're part of that family now, aren't you? Though really, I guess you always have been, whether you knew it or not."

"Yeah I guess I was, maybe that's why he kept us close by, he wanted us near so we could be part of the family, as much as we could. Wow, it's all so weird. As I talk and think of childhood memories, they will all take on new meaning and new perspective. I guess it's going to take me years to process all this. Do you think I should go to the hospital?" Patience still was feeling out her new role as a part of the Mason family, and what that meant.

I thought I better respond to Patience before Bill did, "Patience, I think they have enough people there. Charlie and Amy are there, Lois is there, she'll call you if there is any news, right?"

"Yes, I guess you're right. Well I guess there is nothing left to do here. I came with Violetta and Lois in a limo, and it looks like Violetta had them take her home, so I have no car and no ride home, would you guys mind bringing me back home?"

"Of course kiddo." I responded again with her nickname.

"I like it when you call me that, it brings back nice memories." Patience reminisced.

"Yeah, me too. Very nice memories. Do you remember swimming in secret beach?" I asked.

"Yep, I sure do." Patience responded somewhat sheepishly.

"Okay, I'm an idiot. Not good timing to bring that up. But for what it's worth, I loved that experience, and I would do it all over again, I mean, not now, not that there's anything wrong with that, but. Okay, shut up Cat. I'll quit while I am behind." I was blushing.

Bill broke in, very uncomfortable at where the conversation was going, "we ready to go ladies?"

"Yes sir." Both Patience and I responded simultaneously. Patience and I stood up and we proceeded through the front of the orchestra section to the side doors, which were still open after the EMTs exited that way with Ellen and Charles in stretchers. We wound our way through the few remaining people in the theater, a few saying good bye to us, and a few asking Patience if she was okay. She responded to those that asked, that she was okay but it had been a trying night and it was time to go home.

The three of us drove the twenty minutes back to Mystic in near silence, Bill drove onto Masons Island, and we dropped Patience off at her cottage and saw that she made it inside, and Bill and I drove the entire way home in near silence. The events of the evening were simply too overwhelming to say anything, we all needed time to process and think.

CHAPTER 19

Recovery

The good news is that everyone survived their injuries from the evening at the Garde.

Ellen had received devastating injuries to her head, neck and her left side where she fell, but she had not broken her neck or back. The fact that some of the nation's best neurologists were in attendance that night really saved Ellen's life and greatly improved her chances of a full recuperation. They immediately stabilized her and stayed with her throughout the night at the hospital as she was being treated by the ER doctors, who were happy to work side by side with doctor's that they usually only read about in trade journals.

Charles did not have another stroke, he was simply overcome by the emotion of the moment and his body reacted the way an eighty year old body reacts, which is to shut itself down to stop from over-exertion. Once at the hospital, he was stabilized and Henry and Amy stayed with him all night. Lois only stayed long enough to know that Charles was going to be alright and then took a taxi home, she knew that the revelation of her affair with Charles was going to have to be dealt with at some point, but now was not the time. Charles Jr. had more immediate and important things to deal with than have that conversation with her.

Charles Sr was transferred back to Mystic Manor after three days of observation at the hospital and he quickly regained his faculties. After a week or so, when he had his energy back, he broached the subject of his affair with Lois with Charles Jr. during one of Charles Jr.'s daily visits.

"Son, I feel compelled to address the situation that revealed itself the other night. I could ramble on for an hour on a stage in front of one thousand people on almost any topic, but when it comes to this subject, I am utterly speechless. I do not know how to even begin to apologize to you and your brothers. What's worse, you can forgive me, but what about my poor Emma. I never gave her the chance to forgive me. I loved her so much. I feel so ashamed. I have let her down so much." Tears welled up in Charles Sr's eyes.

Charles Jr. realized that this was going to be a very unique opportunity to have a conversation with his father that he had never really had before. Charles Mason Sr. was not the equal of many men, certainly not Charles Jr, but on this subject, at this particular moment, his father was lowered to the same level, and it allowed Charles Jr. to have his opinion, whatever it would be, without fear of intimidation. Charles Sr. needed to honestly know what his son thought of the whole subject, and needed to know what his son thought of him.

"Dad, please, of all things, do not worry about me, or my feelings toward you. I love you, I have always admired you more than anyone, and that has not changed, nor will it ever change. Everyone knows how much you and mother loved each other. You treated her with more respect than anyone, Presidents included. No matter what meeting you were in, if mother called, you would stop whatever you were doing, and take her call. I can only imagine how much pain you have been in over the years, keeping this secret from her. All I can say is that I watched the way you treated each other throughout my entire lifetime, the mutual love and respect.

"As to mother, she loved you more than life itself and she was the embodiment of forgiveness. Knowing the amazingly gracious woman that my mother was, I can tell you with no uncertainty that she would have instantly forgiven you of anything, including this affair."

Charles Jr. continued, "I have thought a lot about this over the past few days, and honestly dad, I think she must have known. Knowing who she was, the love she had for you and everything you did, I think she knew about it all, about Lois and Patience. Didn't you tell me once that it was her idea to have Lois move into the cottage after Patience was born? Lois was her best friend for the last forty years of her life, and she loved her, she showed her nothing but love, and I believe she did all that knowing full well who Patience's father was. She forgave both of you, instantly. And for Patience, I believe she wanted to have Patience nearby as much as you did, out of love for you, since she would have known that you would have loved any child of yours and would have wanted them nearby."

Charles Sr., who had been silently letting his son talk, responded, "I have never wanted to admit that to myself, but I have long felt that was the case. I have always believed that she knew, and the saint that she was had forgiven me before I could even begin to think I needed forgiveness. Let that be a lesson son, a lesson to us all, she bathed us every day in her embodiment of no other than God himself, in compassion and forgiveness and complete and unyielding love, to the day she died." With that Charles Sr. did what Charles Jr. had very rarely seen, he broke down in tears, in sobs.

Charles Jr. came closer to his father and held him the way that Charles Sr., had held him when we had cried as a young boy. His sobs continued for a minute or so.

"Well that was not very dignified of the old man, now was it." Charles Sr, was embarrassed at showing such emotion to his eldest son. "I am finding myself to be more and more emotional the closer I get to my ultimate demise."

"You're going to be around for a long time dad. And we'll make that release of emotion our little secret." Charles Jr, replied.

"More secrets are the last thing we need Charles. I think some brutal honestly is what is in store. Speaking of which, how is Ellen Chandler? Any prognosis on a recovery? I want her here when she is ready to leave the hospital and start her recovery. We are the best damn rehab hospital in the world, and I will see to it that she gets the best."

"It's too early to tell. She did not suffer any spinal injuries, amazingly, so her body is fully functional, it is her head injury that's the problem. It will take a few more weeks to understand the severity of her brain trauma and its effect on her ability to recover."

"Such messy business. I told her to find forgiveness for Henry and Patience in the hopes that she would find some peace with it all. Rage is a terrible thing son. It poisons the mind. Poisons the soul. She had to answer for what was probably a lifetime of rage. When Henry first moved back to Mystic, he and I would get together weekly, and we talked about his relationship with Ellen. He knew she could be a difficult person, and I felt sympathy for Henry, marrying into wealth is a difficult thing. I knew she was capable of immense pride, and pride, like all misplaced emotion, leads to rage. Let's hope she recovers enough to find her forgiveness. For Henry and Patience, but mostly for herself. She will never find peace until she does."

"Well if I know Ellen Chandler at all, that's going to be her life's most difficult accomplishment." Charles Jr responded.

"It is for all of us Charles. No matter how many times we read the Good Book, no matter how many lessons we hear in church, our biggest challenge is to realize the Godliness that's inside us all, right now. Find your love Charles, find your compassion and your love. It's in you, it's in all of us, and we won't be one with God until we find Him buried deep deep in ourselves, buried deeply under layers upon layers of fear, anger, greed and hatred." Charles Sr was speaking from deep within his heart.

"Well dad, one thing I know, is that we can't dig deep enough into ourselves, into those layers, and ultimately find God within us until we forgive ourselves. So please, forgive yourself, I do."

"Thank you son. I'll need to hear that a few more times, I fear." After a few moments of silence, Charles continued. "How are Patience and Henry doing?"

"Well, to be honest, I have not talked to either of them since the night of the accident. Henry has been parked at the hospital looking after Ellen. And Patience, she's been hiding out at the cottage I believe. Actually, I don't think Henry and Patience have spoken since the Christmas party. Henry was ushered away up to rehab in Rochester by Mr. Chandler and he stayed there for a few months. Since returning, he has played it pretty straight. We all know that he loves Patience more than anything, she's like a drug to him, the only way he cannot give in to the addiction is to quit cold turkey, which in this case means he simply has to keep her out of his sight."

"And how do you feel about Patience in light of the knowledge that she is your sister?"

"Well dad, it actually explains a few things. Remember those talks you gave us when we came of age? The one about wanting to explore our sexual urges, but Patience was off-limits? You hit that pretty hard dad. You told us we would be stricken from your will, no college funding. At the time we always wondered why, but obviously you could not let anything like that happen. And I thank heavens it never did, that would be incredibly awkward now."

"Yes son, I knew that was a bit harsh at the time, but the consequences would have been dreadful for everyone involved, so it needed to be done."

"Oddly enough, I have always thought of Patience as a sister. I have protected her like she was my younger sister since she was born. So it is not that much of a reach actually. But of course it will take some adjustment. I have always thought of my siblings as my family, and I'll need to adjust a bit on that. But you know how much I adore her, she is one of the most amazing people I know. She gives me hope that the rest of us might have some magic also."

"And Lois?" Charles Sr went a bit further.

"Wow, dad, I am not quite sure on that one. Lois has always been like my crazy cool aunt. But clearly this puts her in a new light for me. I'll have some of my own forgiveness to explore. I have to juxtapose my feelings for her against how she betrayed mom, who was her best friend."

"Well to make sure you have the whole story as you work this through, she was not your mother's best friend at the time, she was an acquaintance. It was only after Patience was born that your mother and Lois began the friendship that they had for the last forty years. And if you were right in what you said earlier, that Emma had forgiven Lois and I long ago, that means that your mother initiated that deep friendship knowing full well of our infidelity. So I would ask you to do the same. Lois worked off any debt she owed to your mother by being her valiant best friend until her death, she was by her side for weeks on end, every day near the end. She was the best friend your mother could ever have. Whether they ever discussed it or not, I do not know, but whether they reconciled it or not, in their own way, let's not debate that."

"Dad, please tell me if this is a question that I have no right to ask, but what was the extent of your affair with Lois?"

Charles Sr sat for a moment pondering that question, he himself had just said there should be no more secrets, so he decided he would answer the question posed. "It was very brief Charles, very brief. At the time your mother and I were having our own marital issues. I can be a difficult man son, and at the time I was still struggling to build Mason Industries. It's easy to look back on our lives and say the course of our lives was inevitable. The questions we all ask ourselves about where our lives are going to lead, well by then they have all been answered. But looking forward, all there is are the unanswered questions. So it is easy now to look back and say that what we were doing in starting a business was inevitable to lead to what it has led to, but that was not a forgone conclusion at the time. At the time I wondered if we were going to make it. I was insecure. I would say that spilled over into my personal life. Infidelity is about access Charles. Remove the access and the chance of infidelity declines greatly. And Lois and I were working together almost daily at that time to come up with some of the early herbal remedies that made Mason Industries successful. Access was great, we were having success after success, and I would say that that euphoria led to actions that were misplaced. But to answer your original question, it was very brief. It that a sufficient answer?"

"Yes thank you sir."

"I don't want you to be blind-sided by this information Charles, but I have always included Lois and Patience in my will. In her own way, Lois helped us build Mason Industries. In many ways it was her ideas and her expertise that allowed us to do it. But she always refused any official ownership of the company or any official role. She was a free spirit then and she still is. She had no use for money, she just wanted the opportunity to live her live the way she wanted, in that way, she is just like her daughter. But I have always thought that it would be a tremendous injustice to not recognize Lois' part in Mason Industries, so if my will ever gets a reading, and lets hope it is a long way off from now, I don't want you to be blind-sided by that. And Patience also. She is my only daughter and I will take care of her as such."

"I would not expect anything less dad. There is plenty to go around. My only concern is that their estate would be managed properly, as you said, they are free spirits who could care less about money."

"Yes son, that is taken care of in the trusts that have been set up. They will be taken care of by the same professionals that manage our wealth."

Charles Sr and his son continued on with their conversation for a few more minutes when Charles Sr decided he was tired and wanted to take a nap. They parted more close than they had ever been. Charles Sr had been terrified for years how his son might react to that news and he was tremendously relieved that Charles was as forgiving as he was, of both he and Lois. He was proud of his son, he was proud of his wife and the influence she had had on all their lives. On that day, Charles Mason Sr let go a little bit. He had opened a crack in the wall and he felt tremendously relieved.

Charles Jr left with a new outlook on his father and his life. He and his father had a conversation that was very open and deep. They had discussed tremendously personal things, things that they had never discussed before, at a level of conversation never before broached. There comes a moment in every one's lives where the parent child relationship changes. We spend our lives looking up at our parents in so many ways, we look for them to provide for us, to give us wisdom, to pave the way for us, and we never expect to have to provide for them, until one day we find ourselves in a position where we must. That can come at different points for everyone. Sometimes it is not until the frailties of old age require us to care for our parents in similar ways to how they cared for us as babies. For some that moment comes too early in life for those who have to care for parents who are bringing hardship into their lives through drugs, alcohol or crime at an early age. Too many teenagers find themselves in the role of parent to destructively alcoholic parents.

In that way Charles was incredibly lucky. Charles Sr's seemingly one indiscretion did not derail anyone's life. Lois and Patience enhanced the lives of the Mason family in so many ways. And now, as Charles Sr was starting to wind down his life, and right a past wrong, in an incredibly compassionate way he was leveling the parent child relationship with his son, allowing Charles Jr to grow and mature even more, and function at a level equal with his father. While a seemingly simple act, it was an incredibly selfless act. Letting go a bit at a time allowed his son to grow into his equal, and there was no one that Charles Sr wanted as an equal more than his beloved eldest son.

CHAPTER 20

Healing Wounds

As Charles Sr had demanded, Ellen was transferred to Mystic Manor as soon as she no longer needed acute care and her recovery had progressed to the point where she required rehabilitation. Her head injury was massively destructive, and it had jumbled her memories and ability to connect thoughts, but by the time she was moved to Mystic Manor she was beginning to regain her mental and cognitive faculties. Physically, she was still partially paralyzed on her left side. Fortunately, the staff at Mystic Manor were some of the best in the country and they knew exactly what to do. In the nine months that she led the hospital, Ellen had thoroughly trained the staff on her rehab protocols, and it was these such protocols that they started implementing on Ellen herself.

Henry had been by her side from the moment she was rushed to the hospital after her fall. Despite what they had been through over the past six months, when Henry returned from his rehab he had made a vow to stick it out with Ellen, and he had been true to that pledge. The accident had only reinforced what he had to do. He had checked out of his marriage over the past decade, and while most of that was due to Ellen's treatment of him in the marriage, he realized that for the first time in their marriage Ellen needed him. In a very strange and tragic way, Henry thought that this might be the opportunity for Henry and Ellen to finally have a relationship of equals. Ellen needed Henry, physically and emotionally and he was going to do his best to be there for her.

But Charles Jr was right. Whether Henry wanted to admit it or not, he was forever and hopelessly in love with Patience. For Henry, almost every thought of Ellen quickly morphed into a thought about Patience. While he did his best to be there for Ellen, he secretly worried that Ellen would be able to somehow read his thoughts and know that Patience was right there in his mind at all times.

Over the first few weeks, Ellen's recovery was noticeable and consistent. Her jumbled thoughts slowly stitched themselves back together into coherent memories. Her speech slowly recovered to the point where she could communicate more easily. Unfortunately her physical injuries were not healing as fast as her mental capacities. The physical therapy program that the hospital was employing had slowly gotten her to a certain point, but then the improvement stopped. She could move her limbs but her ability to control them was limited.

Over the next two months, with Ellen's mental awareness recovering quickly, Ellen began to take charge of her rehabilitation. She directed her therapists on what she needed to work on. And she was a remarkable patient. Rarely does a doctor who creates a cure for something get to benefit from that cure as a patient, and the rehabilitation programs that Ellen had helped develop in Los Angeles were cures of a sort. But they were rigorous programs and demanded difficult and often painful exercises for hours a day for weeks on end. But the most difficult part of the program was not the exercises, it was the mental stamina that was needed to persevere through the program. Every patient brought different levels of that stamina with them to rehab, some gave up quickly and resigned themselves to a life of disability. Others brought great amounts of stamina, and were able to continue with the program for week after week to get to a better place. Even with the therapy programs that Ellen had created, not all patients fully recovered, it was more often the case that a successful rehabilitation still meant that the patient's physical impairments were still severe and therefore left some type of permanent disability. These programs were meant to improve a patient as much as physically possible, and to set them up for a life of some type of normalcy, even if not completely healed like nothing had ever happened.

On one Sunday a few weeks into Ellen's rehabilitation, with Henry sitting in her room at Mystic Manor, Ellen said something to Henry that completely stunned him. In a slow and steady cadence, which is how Ellen spoke at that point in her recovery, she said, "Henry, I want you to ask Patience to come see me."

Henry was at a complete loss for words. He stammered to find something to say. "Ellen? Are you sure?"

"Don't worry H, I'm not going to stab her."

"Don't even joke about that." Henry was happy that Ellen still had a sense of humor, but he was really struggling to understand Ellen's motivation. "But I have to ask why."

"Don't worry, this has nothing to do with your affair, this is strictly professional." And in her slow cadence, Ellen went on to explain her request. "I'm not an idiot, H. I'm a rehab doctor, I know my progress has stalled. And while I would like to completely ignore what Patience did for Violetta, and pretend it was complete luck, I have to accept the fact that she may actually have something, some type of understanding that my formal medical training has not allowed me to see." Ellen continued in her slow but steady cadence. "I have not wanted to admit this to anyone, but for those few months that I had banned her from this place, the progress of the patients that went to see her went backwards. I tried my best to skew the facts, I looked for any other reason to explain it, but I couldn't. The stats we kept were pretty conclusive. And after what she did for Violetta, I would have to be an idiot to try and ignore the effect she has on those she works with. And while I could continue to be stubborn out of professional jealousy, this is my own life I am now playing with. I hate to admit, it, but I would like to see if she can do for me what she did for Violetta. As a doctor, I would never put a patient at risk with something I did not thoroughly understand, but as a patient, I am willing to try something, even if I don't quite understand it. I am willing to take that chance on myself."

"I don't know what to say Ellen. I have not spoken a word to her since the Christmas party, I have no idea where she stands with the whole thing."

"I know you haven't H, and I appreciate your discretion. But let's be honest, don't try and pretend that you have not thought about her, or haven't thought about calling her and checking in. You've been avoiding her to keep the peace. And while I really appreciate that H, I really do, let's not kid ourselves, you're completely in love with her, hell who isn't? It's clear that Charles Sr. loves her like a child, whoops, what am I talking about, she is his child, how silly of me. But here's your opportunity H to give her a call, your wife is asking you to call Patience, the chick that you have been in love with since high school, and schedule a time for her to come see me. And I promise not to mention the whole affair thing. I'm really not interested in reliving that ever again."

"Okay Ellen. I'll call her when I get home. And of course I have thought about her since the Christmas party, of course I care for her, she's one of my oldest friends. And you are also right in that I have not reached out to her out of respect for our marriage, and that usually means not calling the woman you got caught having an affair with. But I understand. If I was you I would want to explore every option to get better."

"Henry, not another word. Just call her please."

That night Henry did what he was asked. He thought about going to see Patience in person, but thought better of it. If anyone saw him at her house, the rumors would start flying that he was rekindling his affair with her while his wife was still in the hospital recovering. So he picked up the phone, and dialed the number he had memorized by heart twenty five years ago, 860-536-0539.

The phone rang a few times and Lois answered, "Hello. May peace be with you."

Henry took a deep breath, "Lois, it's Henry." There was a few moments of silence. Henry was all of a sudden terrified from a thought that had never crossed his mind, that Lois might actually be angry with him, so he decided he would speak again before Lois was able to say anything. "Um, Lois, I need to speak with Patience."

"Truer words have never been spoken Henry Moore. You needed to speak with her six months ago, but I guess now is as good a time as any." Lois took the phone away from her mouth, "Patience, it's Henry, and he says he needs to speak to you."

Henry could hear the rustling of the phone being passed from Lois to Patience. "Henry." Just one word. That's all it took. All Patience had to say was one word, his name, and Henry completely lost it. He didn't know it, but he had been holding back a great sadness for the past six months. The Christmas party ended with so much anger, contempt, shame and defensiveness that Henry never really got to look into his soul to understand the pain. With that one word, "Henry" the great dam of emotion broke. He could feel the emotion swelling up from the pit of his stomach into his chest, he could feel the warmth swelling in his head as the sadness was transformed into an emotion that he could use to expel it from his body. The tears came. "I have dreaded this moment for months. I don't know how to say how sorry I am."

"Henry, do you remember what I told you last fall? I told you that this was going to get really difficult. But I told you that you needed to stay strong. And it got difficult, much more difficult than even I anticipated. But is any of what has happened really that much of a surprise?"

Henry was silent for quite a while as he thought about what Patience had just said. He remembered her telling him about how he needed to stay strong, this made it worse, because he hadn't. He had been anything but strong. "Patience I did exactly what I promised I would never do. I ruined us, and I am afraid I ruined you in the process."

"Henry, don't be absurd. You didn't ruin me. I'm now world famous, remember? The miracle worker that healed Violetta Andropov?" Patience always had a way to make Henry feel better. "I've had television stations from Russia call me for interviews. Whatever happened over the past six months was what had to happen, that's why it did. Do you think any of this was a coincidence, or simple random acts? Life plays out the way it is supposed to. And what happened is exactly what was supposed to happen."

Henry was instantly reminded of the very first meaningful conversation he had with Patience, when he was ten and she was six, and she walked by as he and Charles Jr were fishing from the bridge over the ice pond. She told him that the fish he was catching from the ice pond had a right to a meaningful existence, and how he better put them back in the water unharmed or else he would have to carry their soul with him for the rest of his life as a consequence. He and Charles had laughed and told her that fish didn't have souls, but it was at that moment that Henry knew that Patience was a deep well, an old soul. He knew that at six she was already much wiser than he was and was deeply connected to something beyond what he could understand. It fascinated him, it scared him, and he knew at that very moment that this girl completely enthralled him.

He thought back to the first time he saw Patience after returning to Mystic last year, when she walked down the path at Mystic Manor to the pond where they met to get to know each other again. He was struck dumb by how beautiful she was, and he knew he was right when he was ten, he was enthralled by her.

"Obviously its been difficult for me Henry. Most people don't really want to understand, they see what they need to see to keep within their comfort zone, whether it's truthful or not. Mostly it's been difficult because of how my patients were impacted, especially at the Manor. But life is getting back to normal for them and me now that I am back teaching there. How is Ellen?"

"She's improved. But that's why I am calling. Patience, I am not sure how to ask this, it's going to be difficult, but..." Before Henry could finish, Patience spoke again.

"It's okay Henry, I know. Ellen wants me to come talk to her about helping her."

Henry was taken aback. "Yes, that's exactly it. Did someone else call you and ask you already? Someone from the hospital?"

"No Henry, you are the first to tell me that, but it's pretty obvious isn't it? I mean this whole thing is pretty damn obvious. The wheel of life is filled with irony. And what is more ironic than the doctor that is the most ardent critique of my work having to ask me for my help? That's a script even you could have written."

Henry laughed, "Ha. Very funny. Okay Einstein, or Nostradamus, or whatever I need to call you. She wants to talk to you and she promises not to talk about the affair, she said it's a professional visit."

Patience was not playing along. "Of course you know I am going to have to bring it up. The affair that is. I'm not going to be able to let that pink elephant sleep quietly."

Henry sighed. He thought about it for a moment. He realized that the dynamic that was going on between Patience and Ellen was beyond his ability to control. He could only watch as a bystander as it unfolded and then digest what had happened. These two woman, both in their own way, were light years ahead of him in the understanding of what they needed and where this was going. Henry sighed again, "Well I guess that's between the two of you. If you want to broach that topic, I am sure you know exactly what you are doing."

"Henry, I'm not trying to be difficult or start a problem. Ellen needs to heal in so many ways, physically, mentally, and emotionally. She's no different than any other person, that tough-as-nails front she has put on for her whole life is a shell that is hiding or protecting something. And while it may work for her professionally, it obviously is not working for her personally. And more importantly, she's not going to be able to heal physically unless she can first heal emotionally. I know this is going to sound like eastern spiritual mumbo-jumbo, but if she is going to overcome the injuries she has sustained, no amount of external intervention is going to do it, she is going to have to fix herself, and to do that she is going to have to rid herself of all her emotional blocks. Emotional blocks become physical blocks. To rid herself of her emotional blocks, she is going to first find her true self. How do you think I healed Violetta? It started with healing her on a deep emotional level and that opened up her body's energy flows so she was in a position to heal herself. Henry, if I am going to heal Ellen, I have to do the very same thing. That's how it works. And that means I have to dive into her psychological consciousness. The affair opened her up emotionally, the fall from the balcony caused injuries that have opened her up to vulnerability, and she knows it. The request to see me, is the first sign that Ellen is finally healing. And I don't mean just healing physically, but mentally, emotionally and most importantly, spiritually."

Henry understood, "As you have done for decades, you completely overwhelm me. Right when I think I have reached the depth of your understanding, you say something like that and I realize I'm not even close. You are a bottomless well. And it's clear you know exactly what you are doing, and I am only going to watch as this unfolds."

Henry wanted to ask Patience one more thing, but he wasn't sure it was really appropriate so he hesitated. Patience could hear the hesitation in his voice. "Ask the question Henry. At this point, what have we got left to hide?"

"Patience, um, you know I love you more than I have loved

anyone." Henry paused.

"Yes Henry. I knew it from the first time I met you, when I was like six or something. I knew that we were going to have a long and interesting life together."

"Okay, here it goes. Patience, where is this going? How is this going to end up right? How am I supposed to think I can stay in a relationship with Ellen when I love you as much as I do? She knows it. She told me that today. I feel like a weather-vane in a shifty wind, being blown one way and then the other, having no ability to control the direction I am pointing. I am just reacting to the strongest breeze of the moment, trying to make the world think I have purpose and direction when I have none. I am nothing other than the result of the culmination of forces beyond my control, being blown further and further through life in whatever direction the storms want to take me."

Patience laughed, "Doesn't that describe pretty much everyone? We are all just reacting to forces beyond our control. Some of us seem to be able to lift our heads up through the clouds and get a sense of where the storms might be coming from, and are better able to position ourselves before they hit, but those people are rare."

"Well you certainly seem to have your direction all figured out."

"Ha, nice one. Henry I may seem to have some power over where my life is going, but I don't. I am simply doing my best to follow my Noble Path, Henry. Everyone has one. Most are rarely ever on theirs. Most are off trenching through the thickets and brier patches of life hacking away trying to find their way back onto some sort of trail where the brush has already been cleared. There is a difference between walking someone else's path just because it has been cleared of the brush, and walking your own Noble Path. Walking your Nobel Path doesn't take a compass, it means looking inward and being your own compass. It doesn't mean using a map that someone else has drawn out of their experience, it means taking one step at a time, and the path will make itself apparent right in front of you, with each step."

"But how do you always seem to know how things are going to turn out? Have you ever played the Lottery? You should try that." Henry was perplexed at Patience's understanding of things.

"People who have the gift of premonition are operating on a spiritual level Henry. And unfortunately, lottery numbers are not drawn from the spiritual basket. They are of the physical world, and no one can predict physical occurrences with much accuracy. Heck, the weathermen are only right about half the time. But the spiritual world is relatively easy to predict. The spiritual world is based on some pretty simply rules, so understanding how things are going to turn out becomes rather simple. My premonition is nothing more than knowing the difference from right and wrong, and understanding how people are going to react when presented with those two options. We are all trying to get to a better place Henry, it is the sole reason that life exists, God looking back on himself. We are here to return to God, to return to a state of oneness, to return to a state of understanding and compassion, to return to a state of pure and unconditional love. We are conceived into purity, and from that moment on we are burdened with layer upon layer of opaqueness. Every decision one makes either takes them closer back to that place of purity or farther away. When we make decisions based on fear or anger and self-preservation, that takes us farther away from God. When we make decisions based on unconditional love and compassion and selflessness, we are getting closer to the core of our essence, which is to be one with the spiritual essence of our being, or to say it more simply, to be one with God."

Patience continued, "I was thinking about the parable of Adam and Eve the other day, and it struck me that this is exactly what it is saying. Before their fall from grace, Adam and Eve were spiritual beings, living an eternal existence in pure love, the real Garden of Eden. The serpent represents the physical world, a violent world where survival means that each creature exists on the flesh of others, a world filled with immense pain, fear, rage and death, which are all fueled by that need to survive. But also a world filled with desire, want, greed and selfishness. Adam and Eve lived in the spiritual world and only knew their spirituality, but with one bite of an apple, Eve tasted pleasure and wanted more, which lead to desire and then greed, and when confronted with this by God, she lied. Deceit is the opposite of Truth. And when God heard Eve lie to him, He knew he had lost her to the physical world, and it would take thousands of generations of human development and suffering to return to the understanding and knowledge of the spiritual world."

"You don't really believe that Adam and Eve existed do you?" Henry asked.

"No Henry, I said it was a parable. But humans communicated for thousands of years through parables, attempting to explain the world around them. And the story of Adam and Eve actually has deep meaning in how we as living beings should understand the world. This world will never be peaceful until all of us find our spiritual selves, and realize that the spiritual world is not a place we go when we die, we are in it now. And by finding your spiritual self, and learning to exist in the spiritual world now, premonition is not about being able to see into the future, premonition is about understanding that in the spiritual world, all is happening now. You don't see the future, you feel all moments that will ever be in the present moment."

"So to answer your question, the one about where this is going, it is going right where it is supposed to go. Follow your love Henry, be understanding, be compassionate in every decision, and your life will go exactly where it is supposed to. Henry, I know you need to know how you can live with Ellen when we are, well, so intertwined, but stop thinking into the future like that, it doesn't matter who you end up with Henry, as long as you end up there for the right reasons. If you end up with Ellen out of love and understanding, then that is where you will have belonged all along. If you and I end up together, then that is where our paths take us, but that can only happen if it happens out of love and understanding and compassion from you, me, and Ellen. So stop worrying about it, stop thinking about it, stop planning for something you simply cannot plan for. You have to feel your way through this Henry, moment by moment. Find your love Henry. Find your love in this moment. What is it telling you? We are all weather-vanes, and winds can come at us from different directions at the same time. What wind is the prevalent wind, which one is setting your direction? Is it the winds of the physical world, the winds of want and desire, fear and greed? Or is it the winds of the spiritual world, the winds of compassion and understanding?"

Patience continued, "You're a sailor Henry, think about it like that. Life is shifty, winds change at any time. You told me once that the sailor that wins the race is the one that most quickly reacts to the changes in the breeze. You can plot a course Henry, but feel the wind, feel what it is telling you, adjust your path constantly."

Patience paused to let Henry think about what she had just said, and then continued. "As for Ellen, I'll schedule some time to go see her in the next day or so. Henry, don't worry, this is all going to turn out fine, trust me on this."

"I have no choice now do I? I just hope that you and Ellen go through some healing process, that would be a good thing, whatever way this turns out, that has to be a good thing." Henry paused and started thinking about all the ways it could turn out.

Patience, noticing his mind wandering, spoke, "Your thinking about the future aren't you? You are wondering where this is all going."

Henry laughed at himself. "Of course I am, I can't help myself, I have some desperate need to know where this is going. I guess I have always had that need to know what the options are in the future, to have it all planned out, all the options that is, how I am going to react to this or that."

"Yes but think of all you are missing right here and now, in the world you are actually in, right now, the only world that actually exists. Most people spend their days writing their future story, day dreaming of how that plot ends up. And there's nothing wrong with day dreaming about the future as long as it doesn't take up so much time that they forget to think about their present. As I said, finding your spiritual self solves so many problems, and that takes work and thought, and that takes time. Most people are so wrapped up in what happened in the past, where anger and resentment play, or trying to predict the future, where want and desire direct us, that they have no time to explore their present, to find their love, to act out of that compassion they find. It is a complete other way to live ones life, and it is the way that Jesus and the Buddha taught us to live."

Henry thought about what Patience had said, and his inability to focus on the present, "Too bad that so few actually can, me included."

Patience recognized his frustration, the same frustration she had seen in so many of her students. "Well, keep trying Henry, it is a discipline that can take years to perfect. Okay Henry, I think we have finished today's lesson on living in the moment. Love you Henry."

"I love you too Patience, thanks for doing this." Henry hung up and sat back to think about what Patience had just said. He laughed at himself. All the things that Patience had said was nothing new to him. He had read dozens of books on being present, living in the moment, but reading about it and doing it are two completely different things. No matter how hard Henry tried, he could not stop thinking about how this was all going to play out. Patience helped him realize that if he got to a good place with Ellen, if that's where his life took him then that would be fine.

As promised, Patience called the Manor the next morning and made an appointment to go see Ellen after her next class.

Ellen was prepared. She had her raven hair washed and combed that morning. She had asked the nurses to sit her up so she could look at Patience eye to eye. When Patience walked into her room and their eyes met, Patience could sense that something was different with Ellen beyond her physical changes since the fall. Ellen normally greeted people with a quick glance and then looked away as if she had something more important to do then talk. She projected a sense that what she was thinking about was simply more important than the topic of conversation she was having with you, so while she would exchange pleasantries, that's as much emotion as most people got out of her. But the way that Ellen looked at Patience that morning was different. She looked right into Patience's eyes, and did not look away. While Patience mostly knew how this was eventually going to end up, she was not exactly sure how they were going to get there, so she was eager to understand which Ellen she was dealing with at that particular moment.

Patience spoke first, "Ellen, I can't thank you enough for asking me to come see you."

Ellen paused for a few moments before she responded, "Look at you. So beautiful. So full of life. Do you know why I asked you to come see me?"

"Yes Ellen, I do."

"Why?" Ellen was not going to make this easy.

"You are curious." Patience responded.

"Curious? Curious about what?" Ellen was playing a game of cat and mouse.

"Curious about me, of course." Patience was not going to assume the role of the mouse and allow Ellen to box her into a corner.

"In what way am I curious about you?" Ellen was going to try to gain control anyway.

"You are curious as to whether I actually have some special understanding, some capability to heal people. From the very beginning, once you heard who I was, and what I did, you discounted me. You were convinced I was over-selling myself. I am only a yoga instructor for heaven's sake. But over the course of the last year, you have seen outcomes of the people I work with. You saw it here at the Manor after you asked me not to return. You tried to find other reasons why the patients in my classes here began to deteriorate after I left, but you could find none. And then there was Violetta. Violetta was another story. It's impossible to fit that into your impression. And now you have a dilemma, and wow, what a dilemma Ellen. If you stick to the notion that I have no ability to help, then your own prognosis looks rather bleak. On the other hand, if I am going to actually help you, you will have to admit that maybe, just maybe, you were wrong about me, maybe I have some magical capability that can heal people. And that makes you very very curious."

"Well you certainly have this all figured out, don't you." Ellen was trying to stay in control of the conversation, but she knew that Patience was dead on.

Patience continued, "So, here's the deal. I am not going to ask you to admit anything to me, I don't need to know what you think about me, whether you have changed your mind or not. In the end this is not about me. And Ellen I want you to know, and I mean this from the bottom of my soul, I do care about you. I do want to see you healed. I want to see you healed in every way, in more ways than I think anyone understands how you need healing. And that is not for my benefit, I am not interested in healing the great Dr. Ellen Chandler for some egotistical reasons, to prove something. This is actually not even about you. I'll be honest, I am doing this for Henry. Henry needs you. He needs you in ways he does not understand. He needs you to be physically healthy, and he needs you to be spiritually healthy. The deepest way to reach the deepest understanding of our spiritual selves, for those who place God at the center of their spirituality, to understand God, is through the pure experience of unconditional love through a relationship of another human being. I want that for Henry, and you need to give that to him. So I am going to heal you Ellen. In more ways than you know. And I am going to do that so my dearest friend Henry Moore has a chance to feel and understand true unconditional love, spiritual love, some would call it God's love."

Ellen listened but did not speak. She took a few deep breaths and looked away. She continued to look away for quite a while. For all of Ellen's life, she had played the tough-as-nails female, never needing anyone, she chewed people up and spit them out. She was always in charge, from the moment she can remember when she was four or five years old, she was in charge. She knew what she wanted and she was not going to suffer very long with anyone who couldn't give it to her. For those who simply refused to give her what she wanted, she would always find a way to manipulate the circumstances to get it in the end, and Heaven help anyone that got in her way.

But at that moment, what Patience had just said to her, in the way that she had said it, pierced deeply through Ellen's steely psyche, and went very deep. This woman that stood before her was quite remarkable. Quite the opposite of what she had thought, Patience was not shallow at all, she was not a weak flower child, born to a hippie from the 60's, she was incredibly deep, and insightful, and without knowing Ellen very well at all, she knew Ellen better than anyone.

And at that moment, Ellen knew Patience was exactly right. She could continue to deny Patience's capabilities to heal her, but that would only lead to Ellen remaining in her present condition, maybe for life. If she had any hope of a recovery, she needed Patience to be not just good, she needed her not only to be very good, but she needed Patience to be the miracle worker that she had tried to deny her all along. Ellen took a deep breath and turned her head back to Patience, and in a very soft voice, whispered one simple word, "Okay."

Patience was touched. There were many ways that Ellen could have responded to what Patience had said, she could have argued, told her she was full of crap, tried to outwit her with technical mumbo jumbo she learned in med school, but she didn't do any of that. She responded in the exact and only way that she needed to, to show Patience that she was truly ready and prepared for the long road ahead. Patience's response to Ellen was similarly simple, yet also spoke volumes, "Okay."

They sat there looking at each other for a few more moments, absorbing the emotion of the moment. Patience could have felt many things at that particular moment, anyone else in her shoes would have, and most of which would have been negative. She could have felt victorious, she had a right to after the way that Ellen had tried to destroy Patience. She could have felt vindictive, after all, Ellen was extremely vulnerable at the moment. She could have felt pity for the sad state that Ellen was in. She could have felt anger for how Ellen had treated Henry most of their marriage. But she didn't feel any of that. Despite having the upper hand, Patience had only one feeling for Ellen, and that was compassion.

Compassion is not created by humans, it is not conjured up, manufactured, or derived. Compassion is granted to us by God, and only exists in the spiritual world, in the fact that the spiritual world is a state of pure compassion. Showing compassion for another living being is not showering someone with love, it is opening a channel to the spiritual world, allowing the love that is the spiritual world to shine directly into another living being. Patience knew that her ability to heal Ellen, to heal anyone for that matter, laid in her ability to tap into the spiritual world and create that channel, that path through her to the healing that is available when one gets a glimpse of absolute truth and understanding.

For Patience to heal Ellen, and to heal Henry, she was going to have to open that pathway to spirituality for Ellen, show Ellen what compassion really is, not logically or intellectually, but truly and deeply within her own soul, Ellen needed to absorb a healthy dose of compassion if her hardened heart was going to open up enough to let healing creep into her damaged body.

Patience had her eyes closed, she was focusing on walking on her Noble Path, dispelling all the negative emotions that wanted desperately to creep into her head and into her relationship with Ellen. Patience finally broke the silence, "Ellen, that's enough for today. I want you to know that I love you. I truly love you, and I will bring healing to you. I will be back in the morning, I'll work out the agenda with the nurses. I want you to look at me. Here is my first homework assignment," Patience said the next few words very slowly, "I want you to find your love."

Ellen did not respond, she nodded and smiled. That was all Ellen needed to say.

As Patience left Ellen's room she knew she had one more person to see at the Manor before she left. She had been avoiding it since the night at the Garde Theatre, but she knew that if she waited too long, it could cause tremendous doubt and pain in the other person. She headed up to the 3rd floor and knocked on the door. Annie, one of the nurses that Patience knew well opened the door and was both surprised and glad to see that it was Patience.

"He has been waiting for you," Annie spoke first.

"I know, and I have been waiting for the right moment. I guess now is as good as a time as any." Annie let Patience into the front entrance and announced "Mr. Mason, you have a visitor."

"A visitor? I am not expecting anyone. Doesn't anyone make an appointment anymore? Probably someone looking to get their kicks out of watching an old man age a few years in just a few moments?" Charles Sr. responded.

"Hasn't lost that sunny sense of humor I see." Patience whispered. Annie winked. "How is he Annie?"

"Physically he is fine. Strong-willed as ever as you can hear. But he has been melancholy lately, maybe you are exactly what he needs right now." Annie whispered back.

"What's all that whispering going on in there? Will the brave one show themselves? Did they lose their nerve to come visit the great and powerful Oz?"

"I better go in." Patience whispered again. She took the few steps into the living room and turned the corner to see Charles Sr. sitting in his favorite chair with a blanket over his legs. Their eyes met. The look on Charles Sr face immediately changed from the frown of a frustrated old man to a smile and his eyes changed from suspicious to deep immense caring eyes.

"Patience, my darling Patience. I was just thinking of you. You know there is no other person on this earth that I would rather see right now?" Charles Sr looked deeply into Patience's eyes. For the last forty years, Charles had worried what Patience's feelings for him would be if she found out that he was her father. Since it came out, he had thought long and hard about what she might be thinking. Would she be angry? Happy? Would she not care that much one way or another? He was trying to read the look in her eyes.

Patience could tell he was a bit apprehensive about not being sure what she was thinking and she did not want him to go on another second wondering. So she walked over to Charles Sr. and knelt down in front of his chair, and laid her head down on the blanket that Annie had lain over his lap and closed her eyes. Charles Sr instinctively placed his hand on her head and started caressing her hair. It was exactly what any father does when his daughter places her head in her father's lap.

"There there my darling. Everything is going to be okay." Charles Sr had never been a demonstrative father with his sons in the same way his father was not demonstrative with him. There was never much hugging between father and son in the Mason family. Emma was the hugger in the family when someone needed one. But despite missing out on over forty years of being able to show his fatherly instincts to his sole daughter, they showed themselves quickly and naturally.

"Patience, I am not sure quite what to say. It's quite amazing really. I have been thinking about what I would say to you for over forty years. I have practiced that speech countless times. But here I am, and here you are, and the time has come, and I am inexplicably and utterly speechless."

Patience wanted to comfort Charles Sr. "Then don't say anything Charles. There are no words needed, in the same way that no words can describe how thoroughly grateful I am to you. I have always thought that I owed you everything, my home, my childhood, but I never could figure out how to tell you that. But now I have come to learn that I owe you my life itself. It's amazing really. Countless times, starting when I was a toddler, I have thought about what my father was like, and I always wished that they would be just like you. I admire everything you have done sir. I have always admired the person you are. And not because of the trappings and the things, I have never cared for those things, but because of what's in your heart. And now I know. I feel completed. My only apology is that it took me so long to come here to see you since that terrible night."

"That was quite the evening, quite literally almost killed me." Charles said with the slightest grin. Not wanting to trivialize the evening and its tragic consequences for Ellen, he continued, "How is Ellen?" Charles Sr all of a sudden realized he had not heard about her for a few days. "How is she and what condition will she be left in? If she could only open that steely heart and analytical mind of hers and allow you to work your magic on her, the way you have been healing people here for years. That's the real tragedy."

"Well funny you should ask Charles. I just came from her room. That steely heart has opened a crack."

"Patience you really are a miracle worker. I'd have bet on you healing her body, but her soul? That's a suckers bet."

"Well, you might want to rethink that Charles, I think the ice queen is starting to melt."

"Well I guess she has no choice does she?" Charles understood what both Ellen and Patience had hinted at a few minutes before. Ellen had to believe in Patience's ability to heal for her own healing to progress.

Patience responded, "Well we always have choices, but they are not always good ones. But there is one clear choice that she has and it's the only good one she really has. We all need her to be healed, don't we Charles? You do, so she can continue on with her work here. Henry needs her to be the wife he always needed. And most importantly, Ellen needs to allow herself some tenderness and vulnerability into her heart."

"And what do you need Patience? What do you get out of this?" Charles asked.

"I'm not sure I need anything from this Charles, besides the obvious of course, I get to work at the Manor without worrying someone is out to sink me. Besides that, I am doing this for Henry. He is in desperate need of a deep caring love, a love he can trust, a love that is unconditional."

"You mean something like the love that you have for him?" Charles asked, knowing he was treading into some risky waters with his question.

Patience looked Charles in the eyes, she smiled and then she blushed and looked away.

"I am sorry, that was not a fair question." Charles continued. "A bit of a set up question I guess. But that secret has been out of the bag for decades. Even I know that you and Henry have a special friendship. I care for the two of you as much as my own children. Well, there I go, you are my child, I need to start a new narrative, now don't I?"

"That's okay sir, I understand, it's going to take a while for me to adjust to this new reality also. Like am I supposed to start calling you dad? Or do you prefer daddy?"

"Oh God no, definitely not daddy. Not very dignified is it? For me, my father was always 'sir'. But that was a very long time ago and a very different generation than we have today. Patience you call me whatever you want to call me, but Charles seems to have worked all these years, maybe we should stick with that."

"Okay, Charles it is... daddy." Patience was being playful with Charles Sr., a style of encounter they had never had before today.

"Very funny young lady."

Charles and Patience sat for quite a while without saying anything. They had many years of catching up to do, not about stories of their lives, they had been in each other's lives for decades and knew everything they were going to know. Instead they had many years of a father daughter bond to catch up on. They needed to simply be in each other's presence and let the father daughter dynamic take hold. It would take a while, but not as long as it normally would, because the love they had for each other had always been there.

After a few minutes, there was another knock on the door. Patience and Charles Sr. looked at each other with a puzzled look on their faces.

Charles asked Annie, who had been waiting in the other room while Charles and Patience were talking, to see who it was. Annie opened the door to find Charles Jr at the door.

Annie yelled back at Charles Sr. from the entry way, "well it looks like its family day today."

Charles Jr walked in and spoke, "Thanks Annie, how is the old man today?"

Charles Sr responded, "I heard that young man, just because I am an old man, that does not require you to advertise it. Come on in, I have a surprise for you."

Still in the entryway, Charles Jr responded, "Haven't we had enough surprises lately father?"

Turning to Patience, Charles Sr said with some sarcasm, "See that is exactly how not to talk to your father. Let that be a lesson to you my dear."

Charles Jr was not sure of what to make of his father's response, so he headed into the living room to find Patience and his father. "Patience. What a pleasant surprise." That phrase 'what a pleasant surprise' is usually one of those phrases that people utter that is exactly the opposite of what they are actually thinking, and Patience was not sure if that was the case here or not. She had not seen or talked to Charles Jr either since the night at the Garde, and while she could count on Charles Sr welcoming her into the family, it was still questionable as to how Charles' other children felt about all of a sudden learning they had a sister. Family dynamics can get tricky and in some cases quite nasty when new siblings are introduced into a family, especially near the end of a parent's life. Inheritances and the expectations they create can drive wedges between lifelong siblings let alone new ones.

Patience got up from her chair and walked up to Charles Jr and wrapped her arms around him. They had known each other their entire lives, Charles Jr had watched over and protected Patience as much as Henry had over the years, so the bond between them was incredibly strong, likely as strong as with any of Charles other siblings.

"Hey sis. I like that. Sis. It has a nice family ring to it." After a few seconds they released their embrace and looked at each other with big smiles and laughed. The laughs got louder until they were laughing really hard.

Charles Sr asked "What are you kids finding so humorous? Oh, well, what ever it is, I like it. More laughter is exactly what this family needs, and lots of it."

Patience looked at Charles Jr and asked "Charlie are you okay with this? Really? I mean are you really really okay with this?"

"Well, honestly, it was obviously quite a shock at first. But you were always part of the family and I have always treated you like my little sister, and not because that one over there coerced us into it." Charles Jr nodded in the direction Charles Sr as he said it with a smile on his face. "So the reality is, that it's not that much of a shock and I don't think it's going to require much adjusting at all."

Charles Sr spoke up, "I have to say, this has been a lot easier than I thought it might. All those fears I had for so many years, none of them have come true whatsoever. And why would they? You two young adults are really the most amazing individuals I have ever met. And to think you are my children. What are the odds of that?"

Patience responded, "I would say the odds were stacked in our favor, wouldn't you Charlie?"

"Yes I would sis, yes I would." Charles Jr answered.

Charles Sr, feeling a bit tired spoke up, "Now if you two don't mind, I have had enough excitement for one day and I think I need a nap. I am sure you two have some things to work out, so if you don't mind I will excuse myself. Why don't you two take a walk down to the duck pond, I hear it's a nice place to have a private conversation." As Charles Sr said those last words he looked at Patience and winked.

Patience blushed once again. She thought back to the first few meetings she had with Henry at the duck pond, and wondered if Charles Sr had been able to see them? "Do you have a view of the pond from here Charles?"

"Yes I do dear, it's one of the best things about this apartment, I often look out at it. It calms my nerves." Charles Sr responded. "But I promise I won't spy on you two, I'll be sound asleep before you even get there."

"Okay pops. I'll catch up with you later." Charles Jr responded, realizing that he never got to talk to his father about what he wanted to talk to him about.

"I'm sorry, Charlie, if there was something you came here to talk to me about, I'll have to take a rain check I suppose."

"No problem, nothing urgent. Patience, would you like to take a walk down to the pond?" Charles Jr asked.

"Sure Charlie. I have some time before my next class." Patience went over to Charles Sr and gave him a big hug, a hug that a daughter would give a beloved father, something she had never been able to do before in her entire life, and she whispered to him. "Thank you sir" as tears welled in her eyes.

"Now now dear, its okay. Everything is finally okay." Charles Sr patted her back with his stronger arm.

Patience let go of Charles Sr and she and Charles Jr headed out of the apartment and down the stairs to go outside toward the pond.

When they got to the bottom of the stairs and out the door to the walkway Patience turned to Charles Jr and asked him one more time, "Okay Charlie, without your father within earshot, tell me, honestly, are you okay with this?"

"Yes Patience, I swear, this is great. My concern is not for you or me, or for my dad for that matter, we'll figure it all out. That's the easy part. My concern is for Henry. He has had such a terrible time of it, his farce of a marriage, and now to make it worse, how is he ever going to get out now? He can't walk out with her an invalid, it would be unseemly."

"You mean more unseemly than having his affair with yours truly announced at a Christmas party like a PR event announcing the cure to cancer?" Patience was in a somewhat sarcastic mood.

"Yes, more unseemly than that." Charles Jr responded with as much sarcasm.

"Well first of all, I think you are getting ahead of yourself." Patience responded. "I am not sure that 'getting out' is what Henry needs to do."

"Wow, you're the last person I would expect to hear that from."

"Look Charlie, more than anything, Henry needs healing. And even more than that, Ellen needs healing. The best thing for Henry is for Ellen to get over her, her," Patience was struggling for the right word.

Charles butted in, "her complete absence of any people skills? Or love for something other than herself, her career and her family? Or a complete lack of the 'I give a fuck about someone else' gene?"

Patience was a bit taken back by Charles Jr's obvious dislike of Ellen. "That's a bit harsh, wouldn't you say?"

"No I wouldn't say. I have experienced the pain she has caused my best friend, I even got to listen to it first-hand. The very first night they arrived, when they were staying with Amy and I for those first few days, I got to listen to her verbally rip him apart, and rip you apart while she was at it, all because he came to your defense at the party we threw him."

"Well I can only imagine why he would have had to come to my defense, but Charlie, Ellen is who she is, she is a victim of her upbringing as much as you and I are. She did not have the benefit of a Charles Mason Sr, or an Emma Mason, or a Lois Passion for that matter. She was not raised in this town where people are relatively grounded. My God she grew up in LA, the most shallow place on the planet, it would be a shock if she were grounded. But Henry needs to experience unconditional love, and no better person to experience that than one's spouse, despite her 'I don't give a fuck about anyone else' attitude."

"Well then his chances are slim. I am not sure she is capable."

"Everyone's capable Charlie, even Ellen Chandler. And I think more so now than ever."

"Why now? I would think she would be more bitter than ever after that fall. She had her entire life taken away from her."

"You are looking at it the wrong way Charlie. Her bitchiness, or whatever you want to call it, was a consequence of her utter lack of feeling of vulnerability. She didn't need anyone and she tolerated no one. She had everything. Her health, looks, money, brains, career. What did she need from anyone? She looked at everyone for how much they were going to slow her down, because she was convinced that no one could move her along her meteoric trajectory faster than she could do it herself."

"But now everything is completely upended Charlie. For the first time, probably since she learned to walk, she finds herself vulnerable and actually in the need of some help. And to get help she has to learn to be needy. And that's why Henry needs to be there for her. You want Henry to be healed? We all do. Well for the first time, Henry can actually do something for her that she needs, and in that mutual need and care, they will find their love, the love that has eluded them for their entire marriage. See it's the perfect time for them."

"But what about your love for Henry? I mean the whole affair, didn't that mean something? Was that just about sex? I assumed you guys were going to finally confess your eternal love for each other and run off into the sunset. And I was so happy for both of you. What was all that about?" Charles was a bit baffled.

"I think you are selling true love short Charlie. Of course I love Henry. But because I love him more than I love myself, it's not about what I want, it's about what he needs."

"But how can you say that Ellen is going to be better for him than you would be? I mean for Christ sakes Patience, you are the most loving and understanding person known to man. Ellen couldn't show a selfless emotion if she had to. If, as you say, he needs love, then he needs your love."

"He has my love Charlie. What he needs is for Ellen to find hers. And she is the only person that can make that happen. With my help."

"With your help? What do you mean by that?"

"Ellen has asked me to work with her the way I worked with Violetta."

"And you said yes? Are you kidding me? After what she did to you? You are going to help this woman?" Charles was incredulous.

"Yes I am Charlie. It's what I do. I don't get to pick and choose. I have a gift Charlie, I didn't manufacture it. It was given to me. And because it was given to me, I share it, with everyone, regardless of the circumstance. And it's the best way to give Henry the happiness he needs. So for many reasons Charlie, yes, I am going to heal Ellen Chandler. Despite what she thought of me, or thinks of me. Despite of how she purposely humiliated me in front of the entire town, and Henry at the same time. Despite firing me from my job here. Despite all of it. I am going to heal her physically, and I am going to heal her spiritually, because I can."

Charlie was starting to realize that his understanding of the right thing to do was pretty lacking, he was also quickly realizing that Patience had this figured out pretty well. She had separated the personal feelings of hurt and was looking at this through the eyes of the healer that she was. He tried to say a few more things, but every time he started to say something he stopped before he got a word out of his mouth. They had reached the pond a few minutes ago and he just stared out into it looking at the ducks that were paddling around on the other side.

Patience continued, "It's called compassion Charlie. Some people read about it, some people get to understand what it is intellectually, but until you live it, until you practice it, you haven't really gotten very far down the path. And unfortunately I can't seem to see my way through life without living it."

"What is it with this Path thing. Your mother mentioned that to Henry and I that first night he came home. Walking your own path, or something to that effect."

"The Noble Path? It basically means that you are living a compassionate life at all times. We all stray off the path from time to time, we get led astray by our emotions, letting anger or greed or fear guide us, but when we do that we are off the path, and that's usually the most difficult way to get through life. The most heartache, tumult, pain in life comes when you are off your Path."

Charles responded half-jokingly, "Damnit, why can't you just let me be angry? It feels so good to be venomous. You release the emotion, you put it on the person who deserves it."

"If it were only that easy Charlie. You don't release the emotion to the other person, you have just reinforced the anger in yourself. Do that enough and you turn into Ellen Chandler. I take it back, it's not complicated. It's actually simple Charlie. Forgiveness. Remember those Sunday school lessons? God is Love. Love is compassion. Compassion is forgiveness. So what's that add up to? If you want to be one with God, practice forgiveness."

"I thought you were a Buddhist, what's all this talk of God?"

"I don't know what I am Charlie. At their base level, both Buddhism and Christianity are very similar. God is love, be one with God, and that sort of thing. I use the word God because I try to talk in a language that people might recognize. Christians don't own the concept of God, they only own their concept of God. Buddhists believe in Oneness and that Oneness is a state of Compassion, some call that Love, and if God is Love, then aren't they both just saying the same thing? However you get there, it's all the same thing. But it's all an intellectual exercise unless you practice it. So practice it. I will, on Ellen Chandler, you should try it."

"Well let's just say I am practicing compassion and forgiveness with myself on not quite yet being able to forgive her."

"Ha! Very funny. Well, since they say you can't truly forgive others until you forgive yourself, sounds like you are on the right path."

"Would that be my Noble Path?" Charlie was being funny.

"Wow, so witty today aren't we Mr. Mason? Yes actually, that would be your Nobel Path. Feel any different?"

"Let's see, I feel a slight buzzing in my eighth chakra." Charlie continued to crack jokes.

"Your eighth chakra eh? That would be a miracle." Patience was playing along.

"A miracle that Charles Mason Junior can feel his eighth chakra?"

"A miracle in that there is no such thing as the eighth chakra. There are only seven."

"Who's to say I didn't just discover the eighth chakra. It could be a friggin miracle, you naysayer. And it came to be written that on this spot, on this day, Charles Mason discovered the eighth chakra. They will be reading about this moment in hundreds of years." Charles was on a roll and Patience was giggling uncontrollably. It was just like when they were kids.

Patience caught her breath long enough to respond. "Well genius, where is this eighth chakra? They pretty much have the body covered with the first seven."

"It's a floater. That's it, I am a genius, I have discovered the floating chakra. It goes where ever it is needed." Patience started laughing even harder.

"How do you say floater in Sanskrit?" Charles kept on going with this.

Patience stopped laughing to think for a moment, "Well, let's see. Laghiman means lightness, so I think that would be the closest."

"Perfect. The Laghiman chakra, has a nice ring to it doesn't it?."

"You really are too much Mr. Mason."

"It's good to hear you laugh again Patience. I used to be able to make you laugh so hard you would pee. Glad to know I still have the touch."

"Do you remember that? That's so true. Well I managed to hold on this time, but to be honest, I came close." Patience admitted.

"Still got it! I still got it!" Henry pranced around like he had just scored a touchdown.

"Very nice, so humble. Oh my God what time is it? I'm going to be late for my 11:00 am class?" Patience all of a sudden realized she had lost track of time.

"Um let's see, it's 10:30 you are still good." Charles Jr responded.

Patience turned a bit more serious. "Charlie I have a somewhat serious question to ask you. You say you are all fine with me, and us, and how I came into the world. But honestly, Charlie, I am concerned about my mother. It's easy to say that I am innocent in all the sordid aspects of this whole thing, but clearly she is not so innocent. I know you loved your mom so much, and what a great lady she was, and that's what I am having the hardest time with in this whole mess. How does one sweep it all under the rug and still respect your mother, who was also an innocent bystander in all this. Do you think she knew Charlie? She was so kind to me. I want to know that all the love she showed to me was not based on a lie."

Charles Jr paused for a moment and peered out onto the pond as he answered Patience. "I've thought a lot about that question Patience, and I have even spoken to my dad about it. And honestly, I am convinced she knew. She had to have known. You want to talk about compassionate? Emma Mason owned compassion and forgiveness. And she loved my father, I'm sorry, our father," Charles corrected himself with a smile directed toward Patience and turned back toward the pond. "She loved him more than life itself. So yes I believe she knew and she forgave him, and she forgave Lois. It was her idea to have you move into the cottage, not my fathers. I believe she knew that you were my sister, and she knew how much dad was going to want to care for you as if you were her daughter. So she did the only thing she could do, which was to move you right onto the property so they could watch over you like their own." Charles turned back toward Patience to find tears streaming down her face. "Hold on their kiddo. What's the matter?"

"Charlie you don't know how good that makes me feel. It is overwhelming, really. I would be crushed to know that I was the cause of some rift in your family, especially between your parents. And to think of how this was handled with so much love and understanding, it's beautiful really. Your parents are special people, they don't make them like that anymore. But how are you with my mom? Knowing what you know now?"

"Honestly Patience, that's a harder one. I've got to be honest, there is some resentment there. But the reality is that my dad is as much to blame as Lois is, maybe more so. He was the handsome guy that every woman wanted. So if I am going to be angry at Lois, I've got to be at least just as angry with pops. And I am simply not angry. Lots of emotions running around but anger is not one of them. And let's face it, I have always had a crush on your mom. She is the coolest lady in the universe, since no one is quite sure where in the universe she came from. I can see why my dad was attracted to her. Hell, they worked together side by side in the early years, I am sure one thing led to another. So no, I'm good with Lois too. It's allllll good." Charles responded and drew out the word all.

Patience still had tears running down her face. She was relieved. She loved her mom and had been very concerned about how the Mason kids would treat her knowing what had happened. "I better head back up and clean my face up before my class, don't want to scare anyone with all these tears running down my face." Patience paused for a few moments. "Thank you Charlie. Thank you, thank you, thank you. I don't think I have ever been so touched by the generosity of you and your father, and mother for that matter. It's overwhelming really."

"It's okay sis. I feel closer to you now than I ever have. Let's head back up." Charles put his arm around Patience as they walked back up the path. They didn't notice that a few floors up, in an apartment overlooking the duck pond, sat an old man peering out of his window, with tears flowing down his face, a well of fearful emotion bursting that had been damned up for years.

CHAPTER 21

Melting Steel

Over the next few weeks, as promised, Patience worked with Ellen almost every day. She took Ellen through much of the same routine she had done with Violetta the year before. But relatively quickly it was clear that Ellen was not making much progress and therefore her recovery was going remarkably slower than Violetta's had progressed. As with Violetta, Patience needed Ellen to completely submit to the philosophy of what she was doing. But while Violetta had no vested interest in her preconceived beliefs around what made the body work, and therefore was quite willing to give up her preconceived notions and completely submit to Patience's version of how the body and brain interacted, Ellen's entire career, and life for that matter, was invested in her preconceived beliefs around how the body and the brain worked, things she had learned at Harvard from the best Western doctors in the world. Letting go of that belief system was not something Ellen was going to do quickly or simply. It was clear that in order for this to work, Ellen was going to have to have a major change in her ability to let go and listen to and learn from Patience.

Three weeks into their work together Patience realized it was not going to be successful without that change in Ellen's state of mind, so she decided on her next visit with Ellen that she was going to have to have a frank discussion. On the next Monday, she went to her appointment with

Ellen ready to have that conversation. "Good morning Ellen, how are we today?"

Ellen, feeling that something was different in Patience's normally positive demeanor, responded, "Uh oh, what's the message for today? I am a doctor, I know when someone is about to deliver bad news to their patient, I have had to do it too many times."

Patience smiled, "Ellen, I am going to be straight and honest with you. You are not progressing as fast as you should be. And before you go straight to the thought that you were wrong about my ability to heal you, I want to ask you something. Do you believe me? Of all the things I have told you over the last few weeks, the need to look deep inside of your body, all of it, do you believe me?"

"To be honest? I have doubts. Of course, anybody in my position would."

Patience paused and then continued, "When I am working with you and I try to take you into a deep meditative state, what are you thinking?"

"Well I am trying to follow you, I really am, but to be perfectly honest, I am also thinking that what you're telling me has no basis in science, and it's all been made up by people who don't know a thing about how the body actually works."

"Ellen, Violetta was not healed through dumb luck. She was healed because she utterly threw away whatever notions she had before we started working together, and her submission to what I was teaching her was absolute. If you can't do the same, this is not going to work. So Ellen, here's the deal, you need to make up your mind. I am willing to work with you, but you've got to help yourself by, and this may be harsh, but you need to get over yourself. You may be an expert in what you've been trained in, and what your friends in the scientific community know, but you are not an expert in what I know. You scientific types are experts in what you have proven, but that process does not make room to be an expert in what you don't know, in the unproven. But here's the reality, Ellen, here is your stark reality, settled science, the science you believe in, says you cannot be healed. The settled science says your injuries were too severe to be reversed. That's the reality you are operating in right now. That's the reality in your

293

scientific world, among your scientific friends. You have to be honest with yourself, is that what you actually believe? And let's be clear, it doesn't matter what you want to believe, it matters what you actually believe."

Ellen was silent.

Patience continued, "Maybe this will help, you need to stop thinking that what I am trying to teach you means that what you know is wrong. The knowledge that exists in the world today is not the totality of everything mankind will ever learn, it is only what mankind has learned, and documented, so far. But the totality of Truth contains more than all the knowledge that has been discovered so far, the totality of all Truth also contains all the knowledge that has yet to be discovered. The things that you and your science buddies will discover tomorrow, and what your children and their children will discover in the future. There is a vast body of knowledge that you are not aware of, but that does not mean that what you are aware of is wrong, it just means you haven't proven and documented it all yet. Nod if you are still with me."

Ellen finally spoke, "Patience I know there is more to be discovered, it is what has gotten me up every morning for the last twenty years, the ability to find the next advancement. So I completely understand that there is more to what's happening scientifically than I understand as of today. So it's not necessarily that I don't believe, but the scientific method is a method, so unless the method has proven it, it is always going to be in doubt. So it's the method to how you figured it all out that is in question. As far as I can tell, you did not follow a scientific method to discover what you know, so the claims you are making have no validity until they have been proven, and I mean scientifically."

"Ellen, do you realize how ridiculous that actually sounds?"

"I don't think that sounds ridiculous at all."

Patience was not going to give up on this, but she needed a way to get Ellen to let her in, so she used the same analogy she used with Violetta to help her understand. "Ellen, see the clock radio on your nightstand?"

Ellen looked over at it, "yes, I see it."

"The radio tunes into and converts the radio waves that are floating around the atmosphere into a sound from a speaker. How long have the radio waves existed?"

"Radio waves have always existed. We just learned how to manipulate them to our benefit about 100 years ago." Ellen answered that one easily.

"So in other words, it was only about 100 years ago that we could detect radio waves, or as you say, it was only about 100 years ago that science could prove that radio waves actually existed."

"Yes that's true, up until that point they were just a theory in some scientist's mind,"

"So if you and I were having this conversation 110 years ago, and I told you that I was going to treat your condition with a technique that depended on these invisible waves that I believed were floating around the universe, how would you have responded?"

"I guess, as a scientist, I would not have believed you. At that point, it hadn't been scientifically proved yet that radio waves even existed."

"So if I somehow convinced you to let me treat you with radio waves 110 years ago, before they had been proven to exist, and it was successful and you were healed, would that have made your healing any less real?"

"No that's absurd, if you treated a condition with radio waves, the treatment would have worked whether they had been proven to exist or not." Ellen stopped for a moment and thought about what Ellen had said earlier. "Okay what I said before sounds ridiculous."

"Can you possibly concede that I might have discovered a method to heal you that works, but that the scientific community has just simply not found a way to prove yet? It does not mean it does not work. It only means that you scientists have simply not caught up yet. But there is a major difference here. This method only works if you absolutely and utterly believe it's going to work. That's because I am not treating you, I am teaching you to treat yourself. So while most known medical treatments work whether the patient believes it's going to or not, that's not the way it works with what I do. You can't treat yourself without having the belief that it's actually going to work. So I am going to suggest a way that you can look at what I am trying to do with you in a way that this might work. Do not think of what I do as unproven, think of it more as merely not yet disproven. There is a huge difference. Violetta's recovery is some proof that it works, dozens of patients that you tracked at the Manor are proof that it works."

Ellen responded, "Well I have no explanation for what I saw happen at the Manor after you left, so I can find a way to think of it as plausible, or simply unproven, as you say."

"Well that's a start." For the first time, Patience thought that Ellen may finally be headed down the path that she needs to be. "This shit works, girl! You just gotta believe!"

Ellen laughed at Patience's attempt at humor. "Very funny. Well, you go girl!" Ellen tried to pump her first in the air, but she could not get her arm that high in the air since she was still not able to use her limbs in that way.

Noticing Ellen's inability to pump her fist in the air, Patience wanted to see where her limits were for everyday things. "Ellen, can you pick up that glass of water for me?" Ellen slowly reached over, and while she could barely keep her arm in the air without any weight in her hand, she managed to pick up the glass. But within a few seconds her hand started to shake and the water starting spilling out the sides. Patience reached out to steady her hand and helped Ellen place the glass back on the night stand. No one said anything, but it was clear to both of them that Ellen had a long road ahead to regain her normal strength.

The visits by Patience with Ellen over the next few weeks went similarly. Doubts would creep into Ellen's mind about what Patience was doing, Patience would remind her in different concrete ways about things that worked before they were proven scientifically, and Ellen would get back to doing the work that she needed to do.

Progress does not come evenly over the course of one's rehabilitation, in many cases it comes it fits and spurts separated by plateaus of little improvement. The noticeable improvements are met with great excitement, while the plateaus can bring such heartache as one wonders if the plateau is the extent of the progress one will make, only to be followed by another spurt of improvement. It can be an emotional roller coaster.

But Ellen had not yet had a spurt of improvement, and as such both Patience and Ellen needed Ellen to have one. She knew that seeing noticeable improvement would finally give Ellen the confidence in what

Patience was doing that she needed to believe without doubt. But the first spurt finally came and it came for Ellen a few weeks later. At first Ellen did not even notice it. Patience walked into Ellen's room on a Monday morning and found Ellen with a glass of water in her hand holding it up to her lips to drink. Since Ellen was not able to hold a glass of water just a few weeks before, Patience immediately realized that meant a significant breakthrough had occurred, but based on Ellen's lack of emotion around it, also realized that Ellen may not even realize the significant step she had just made. Four weeks previous, Ellen could not hold a glass of water without spilling it.

"Good morning. Thirsty?" Patience was trying to draw her attention to what she was doing.

"Yes, I guess I am." Ellen was still not realizing the breakthrough she was experiencing. For over forty years she had picked up thousands of glasses of water without giving it a second thought, and the brief few weeks since her accident where she could not accomplish that feat had seemed to have slipped her mind.

"Would you like me to help you put the glass back on the night stand?" Patience was still trying to get her to figure it out on her own.

"No, I can do that, thanks," Ellen responded as she reached over to put the glass back down. As she did that, all of sudden it dawned on Ellen what had just happened. She paused in thought looking at the glass for about ten seconds after putting it down, remembering how just a few weeks before she could not do that, looked up at Patience, who had a big smile on her face and was just waiting for Ellen to figure it out, and she smiled.

For the first time since they had met, Patience saw the steely Ellen melt a little bit. Tears came to Ellen's eyes as she looked at Patience, who was still beaming, and Ellen mouthed the words "Thank you."

There was nothing to be said by either at that moment, they just needed the understanding of that moment to linger for a few minutes. That event was the trigger that Patience had been waiting for, and the event that Ellen herself needed, whether she knew it or not beforehand, she did now.

Ellen said one more thing to Patience that morning, "Okay let's get to work."

From that moment on, the speed of Ellen's rehabilitation improved dramatically, almost as fast as Violetta's had in the weeks leading up to her concert. In a way, Ellen had an easier injury to recover from than Violetta. In Violetta's stroke, like with so many, her nerves had actually died from lack of oxygen, and Patience had to work with Violetta to go extremely deep into her consciousness to find new neural pathways. While Ellen's injuries were severe, no nerves had actually died as a result of her fall. Ellen had a brain injury that scrambled her memory of how to do things combined with extreme weakness in her extremities from trauma. Ellen merely had to wake her nerves up from the trauma to remember the motions they had done for years without any thought.

After a few more weeks, Ellen's rehab had progressed from picking things up, to getting herself into a wheel chair, to walking with a walker, to walking without a walker. As Ellen progressed through these stages, Patience arranged with the hospital to start traditional physical therapy, which was needed to strengthen the muscles that Patience was getting Ellen to wake up. Eastern and Western medicine working together in concert to get Ellen back to where she needed to be.

More importantly, as Patience had said to Henry, Charles Sr and Charles Jr, Ellen needed to be healed spiritually. And as Ellen healed physically, she also healed spiritually. A warmth appeared in her smile that had never been there. A sparkle appeared in her eyes that completely changed how Ellen approached her conversation with whoever she was speaking with. Instead of looking away and giving the impression she had something more important to do, Ellen began to engage at an emotional level with other people. For the first time in her life, Ellen was projecting compassion and warmth in her interactions with other people.

As Ellen healed emotionally and spiritually, her relationship with Henry was changing. As Patience had told Charles Sr, her main goal in healing Ellen was to give her back to Henry in a way that he could finally experience the loving relationship that he had needed for so many years. And that was happening. Ellen was finding her love, and her ability to project that love to others, and Henry was the main beneficiary of that transformation. As she found her love, she also found her empathy, and that led to her finding her compassion. And for the first time in her marriage, empathy entered into her relationship with Henry. She has always seen Henry for who he was, but for the first time she let that be okay. She no longer looked at him and saw all his failings, his weakness, his lack of drive, all the negatives that she had thought of every time she had thought of him. Empathy pushes aside critical judging of others, there is no room for both. And as empathy came into her feelings for Henry, the judgment disappeared, and that extended to her understanding and judgment of his surroundings. In her new eyes, Henry's father was no longer insignificant in comparison to her own father. Spiritual consciousness brings an entirely different viewpoint of the world. Instead of seeing people based on their place in the hierarchy of financial means and their span of control over others, you see people based on how deeply they are connected into a network of family and friends based on love, not power. For the first time she became jealous of Henry's family in comparison to her own. The love they shared was deep, the love that existed in her own family was buried too deeply to be felt. Henry's small town upbringing was no longer seen as cute and inadequate, she now understood how Henry's childhood friends cared for each other in a deep and lifelong way, friendships that she herself did not have with her childhood friends.

And with empathy and compassion, Ellen started genuinely caring about Henry, for his psyche and his future. Empathy is about finding God's love and reflecting it through to another to bring them closer to God. There is no room for selfishness in empathy. It is not about healing another person for personal gain, but healing another person to get them back on their Noble Path, and when they get back on their Noble Path, the healing becomes reciprocal. As Ellen found her love for Henry, her true unselfish love for Henry, she began to understand what Henry needed to truly find his happiness. With her newfound ability to be empathetic, she began to ask the unselfish questions about what would be better for him, what would really make Henry complete. After a few weeks of contemplating this thought, Ellen made a decision, and the morning came that would bring a new chapter in the lives of Ellen, Henry and Patience.

For all the weeks that Patience had been working with Ellen, Henry had ensured he was never visiting Ellen at the same time that Patience was with her. He knew that his deep feelings for Patience were still too out of control and it would be unfair to Ellen for her to have to witness any mixed emotions that still lingered if they were all in the same room together. And having a get-together with Patience outside the hospital remained completely out of the question. He had made a vow to stay away and he had maintained that vow for all that time, and it was still the case that the only time he had laid eyes on Patience since the fateful Christmas Party was watching her from the balcony the night of Violetta's concert. Henry always checked Ellen's schedule for the day and made sure that he visited Ellen after Patience had finished her work with Ellen and had gone home.

About 7:30 am that morning, before Patience arrived, Ellen picked up the phone on her night stand and called Henry. "H? It's Ellen."

Ellen had never called Henry from the hospital so he truly was surprised. "Hey. Good morning sunshine. To what do I owe this surprise?"

"H, can you come over to see me this morning?"

"Sure Ellen, that would be fine. Is everything okay?" Henry was puzzled at the request.

"Everything is perfectly fine H. Actually everything is almost perfect."

"Okay, let me finish my eggs and I'll head right over." Henry did not realize he was being set up for the second time by Ellen.

A few minutes after Ellen hung up, Patience arrived for her morning session with Ellen and they started with their normal routine of getting Ellen into a deep meditative state so she could work her way through her body as she had for the last few months. About forty five minutes later, just as Ellen was coming out of her meditation and the two of them were sitting together with their eyes closed, they heard footsteps in the doorway. Knowing who was coming, Ellen opened her eyes to see Henry approaching the door. Footsteps in the hallway was not unusual so Patience did not immediately react nor open her eyes, she was still in quiet contemplation. Henry walked into the room, to see both Ellen and Patience. Ellen was staring at Henry as he walked in the door and as his eyes looked up to see Ellen, he finally realized that Patience was in the room also.

Henry had not seen Patience's face that close up since the Christmas Party. He had seen her at Violetta's concert but only from afar and only from behind. But through all the aftermath of the party, the painful days following, the weeks away at rehab, Ellen's fall at the concert, the last few months of laying low at home, all that time, Patience had been on his mind almost constantly. He had been trying to separate from the emotions he felt about her, trying to find a new way to feel about her, a way that was not so threatening to his marriage, he was trying to place it all in a healthy space. But seeing her there, he was once again overcome, and it took his breath away. And Ellen, who was staring at Henry, noticed. She took in his reaction to seeing Patience.

Patience still had not opened her eyes, and was still expecting to see one of the nurses in the doorway as she opened her eyes. When she finally opened her eyes she saw Henry, and she took a deep breath of surprise. She stared at him and it took her breath away. And Ellen, who had changed her glance toward Patience, noticed. She took in Patience's reaction to seeing Henry. She watched carefully as Henry and Patience stared at each other, both slightly in shock, but trying not to show it.

Henry did not know what to say. He looked at Ellen, who he could only guess had arranged for this encounter, he was trying to read her thoughts. The last time she had arranged for a similar encounter, the realization of what she had done was so shocking and hurtful, that he all of a sudden became frightened that she might have done something like that again. But this was a completely different encounter. Ellen did not have that steely look in her eyes like she had just won some battle of wills. It was about as opposite as one could get. Her gaze kept going from Henry to Patience and back again. The smile that beamed on Ellen's face was not one of conqueror, not like the last time, it was loving acceptance, like a parent watching a child take their first steps: proud, loving, contented.

Not knowing that Ellen had arranged for this encounter, Patience spoke first, "Henry? Don't you usually come in the afternoon?" She looked at Ellen. "I'm sorry Ellen, I can leave if you two need to talk about something."

Henry was next to speak. "Actually Patience, Ellen called me this morning and asked me to come by about now."

"Ellen, is that true?" Patience was puzzled but she knew Ellen was up to something.

"Yes it is. I thought it was time for you two childhood friends to see each other again. And we all know you couldn't do that out there, in private." Ellen pointed out the window toward town. "People would have gotten the wrong impression. People love to get the wrong impression don't they? We all only see what we want to see, it's so hard to see the truth, we just are not ready for it most of the time, so we just see what we want to see so we can stay in the little stories we have created for ourselves." Ellen paused for a second. "Well here's a story for you. A long long time ago, two young kids, one male and one female, came to fall in love. And it was a love so deep that nothing could come between them, neither time, nor distance. And as they grew older and went their separate ways, that love never wavered."

Both Henry and Patience were carefully listening and watching Ellen as she continued. Both had learned that it was difficult to know which Ellen they were encountering, the nice Ellen or the nasty Ellen. Patience, being the more empathetic, more quickly understood where Ellen was that day. This was an Ellen that she had never seen before. This was neither nice Ellen nor nasty Ellen, this was a completely new Ellen, an Ellen at peace. Henry on the other hand was still trying to understand which Ellen he was in front of.

Ellen continued, "I have recently learned to put aside what I want to see, and to see what is actually there. That's a new skill for me, one I can thank Patience for. See H, as Patience has been healing my physical wounds, she has also been healing my spirit also. I have spent most my life existing in another world, an artificial world. One that I had to manipulate to be completely in charge of, to take what I wanted from it. And I did, boy did I take. But I am not interested in manipulating anyone anymore. I saw the truth this morning. Whether it was what I wanted to see or not doesn't matter anymore." She paused for a second and looked at Patience.

"Patience, you have not only put me on a path of physical healing, you have put me on a path to spiritual redemption, what you refer to as my Noble Path, for the first time in my life I'll have to admit. And as you have taught me, and Henry, you'll be happy to know I actually listened and learned, I have learned and deeply understand that I get no benefit by holding on to things that I have no business holding on to. I have lived a life of attainment by climbing higher and higher, but while I thought the ground behind and underneath me was a stable foundation, I now know it was shallow and was ready to crumble beneath me at any moment. But I just kept climbing, never caring to look back. But now I know, I need to set it all right, for my own happiness." Ellen stopped.

Patience knew exactly what Ellen was saying, but also knew that Henry did not. "Ellen, that is so wonderful. I am so glad that you have found yourself. But I think you and Henry need to talk, so I think I'm going to go take a walk out to the garden to take that all in." Patience walked out the door leaving Henry and Ellen alone in the room.

Henry still was not understanding what Ellen had really been referring to. He walked over to her and sat down in the chair next to her. The chair was by the window and from their positions, both Ellen and Henry could look down the two floors and out onto the garden and after a few minutes watched Patience exiting the building and walk into the garden and sit down on a bench near the fountain, in full view of Ellen's room.

"Ellen, I'm not sure what you are saying." Henry was still puzzled.

"Henry I care for you. For the first time in our marriage, I can tell you that I care you for all the right reasons. I have come to know you, who you really are. Patience has taught me something very important: true, pure love is completely unselfish. When you truly love someone, truly love someone, you truly want whatever is best for them. That's all that matters. See Henry, Patience healed more than my bones and muscles over the last few months, she healed me. I was broken and she healed me. But I came to realize that she didn't do it out of love for me, she did it out of love for you. When I first came to Mystic, and I caught a glimpse that first night how you felt about her, by the way someone who you had never mentioned to me throughout the twenty years we have been together, I was jealous. I didn't know it at the time, but I was suddenly presented with the fact that my husband could summon up a thorough and complete love in an instant that in twenty years I had not been able to elicit out of him. Of course my way of handling it the time was completely wrong, and for that I apologize."

Ellen paused for a moment. "I guess that's it, I apologize for all of it H, all of it. It was all done wrong. I did it wrong. I did us wrong. I have to live with that fact. I messed it up. My doing, my consequence."

"Ellen, nothing in marriage is ever one person's fault. I've been a horrible partner of late, I have to live with that."

"H, I set you up. It's the Chandler way, complete and utter dominance. And to think that we think we win with that strategy. Sure, we may get the money, but look at us H. Billy is a complete mess. My parents wouldn't know love if cupid unloaded his entire quiver directly into their hearts. I set you up H. I saw that you loved her and did the wrong thing. Charles Sr was so mad at me. I lost his respect with my Christmas Party stunt. He told me so. That was not good."

"H, when I asked you to have sex with me in my office, I set you up. But I set you up for all the wrong reasons. But she is good, H. She is really good. In return, she set me up. But she set me up not to hurt me, she set me up to heal me. After all I did to her, tried to do to her, she never wavered, her only goal was to heal me.

"She knew exactly what I needed, she knew that I would never see what I needed without my life completely and utterly imploding on itself. She started a train rolling, because she knew I would take to its horrible extreme, and would not stop until it was killing me. And I literally almost killed myself trying to outdo her. And in the strangest way, it is exactly what I needed. I have Patience to thank for all of it."

Henry finally realized that he was experiencing an Ellen that he had never seen before, an Ellen he had hoped to see years ago, but had given up hoping for. She had finally become the Ellen he needed. "Wow, that's quite an admission Ellen. What are we going to do now?"

"I'm not sure what we are going to do, but I know what you are going to do. Henry, go to her. You brought me to her, and she has completely healed me. Thank you, but now I need to return the favor because in order to truly love you, I have to let you go. Go to that sweet precious soul in that garden, and don't look back. I can't heal you Henry. I'll barely be able to keep myself in this beautiful place she has brought me to." Ellen looked away and continued, "Go to her Henry, and don't look back."

Henry looked at Ellen, with tears in both their eyes, he nodded. He lingered for a few minutes as he realized that this was likely a good-bye. Ironically, right when he had finally gotten the wife he had always wanted and needed, they both knew that Henry had to move on, to finish the story the way that it was written. As Lois had said many months beforehand, Henry needed to walk his own Path and this is where it started. This is where he got off of Ellen's Path, and onto his own. He got out of the chair, walked over to Ellen, gave her a hug and left the room.

CHAPTER 22

Epilogue

Over the next few months, Ellen regained most all of her physical abilities. She was gracious to let the medical community know that it was Patience who was responsible for her recovery, and she did not care what backlash that received. Having had experienced a major shift in her understanding of how the healing process can work, she made a decision not to resume her role as the Chief Physician of Mystic Manor. She felt a deep need to understand what Patience was doing, it was a remarkable new finding in medicine but Ellen needed to research it in her own way, and that meant in a scientific process, and running a hospital would get in the way of that research. So instead she decided to return to Harvard to join a research program into Eastern medical practices, and delve into the practices that Patience had intuitively discovered to ensure they could be documented and recreated by others. Ironically, after having tried her best to deny Patience's abilities, she become Patience's greatest supporters.

With the public attention that Patience received from Violetta's remarkable recovery, combined with Ellen's promotion of her techniques among the medical community, and the backing of Charles and the resources of Mason Industries, the techniques that Patience had discovered and mastered slowly worked their way into rehabilitation hospitals all over the world.

As to Henry and Patience, as one would guess, they did as Ellen had instructed. They consummated a lifetime's worth of adoration and became an official couple. At Ellen's insistence, the Chandlers were gracious in quickly ending Henry and Ellen's marriage, and in the process ensuring that Henry was able to continue his career in academia. Now permanently in New England, Henry decided to follow in his father's footsteps and secured a position as an English professor at Connecticut College. His father was still remembered by the older faculty members and they were glad to invite him into their ranks as a full professor.

While the events of the last year were tumultuous, this is New England. As I said at the beginning of this story, the same themes run through every generation, birth, romance, marriages, children, affairs, a reshuffling of a few relationships, and eventually death.

The reshuffling of relationships later in life can be controversial, and when a marriage ends with an affair, it certainly can create an environment of pain and hostility, not to mention the gossip and shame surrounding it from the rest of the community. But the reality is that no matter how relationships end, they often end messily. There is often some type of a mess created on the way out. Sometimes it's the mess that initiates the end of the relationship, like an affair, sometimes the mess happens after the decision has been made to end it, and it gets ugly on the way out as possessions, money, children and friends are fought over.

Henry's greatest fear was that the affair would ruin Patience. Her entire life and livelihood was invested in being spiritually pure, and being involved in an extra marital affair would make it impossible for her to continue her work. But in the end his fear was unfounded, for many reasons.

First and foremost, Patience had spent a lifetime building up goodwill in her community, there were too many people in town that she had helped over the years, they knew who she was deep down, she had proven that over many years.

It was widely known that the nature of Henry and Ellen's marriage was very strained to begin with. That meant that everyone knew that most likely it was not the affair that ended their marriage, in reality the affair started the ball rolling on ending a marriage that probably would have, and should have, ended anyway.

For the gossipers in town, Ellen's accident at the Garde, completely overshadowed the affair. It was a made-for-TV ending. If you

307

were prone to gossip, this was much more interesting to talk about than an affair, those happen every day. But people fainting and falling from balconies on national TV, that's a much more interesting conversation to share with other gossipers.

Unfortunately for the gossipers in town, the revelation that Patience was the child of Charles Mason and a result of his own affair many years ago, had a large impact on their ability and desire to keep the gossip going. With the Mason family at the pinnacle of society in town, none of them were going to risk perpetuating any gossip that might stir the pot that could end up with them at odds with the Mason family, so the affair simply faded from the chain of gossip.

But mostly, and this is the only reason that really matters, the affair become a non-issue for the most right reason of all, forgiveness. Ellen herself, the aggrieved party, forgave Patience. Despite everyone in this story coming out a little better, from Henry to Patience to Violetta to Bill and I, Ellen was the main beneficiary of the totality of the events of this story. Despite Ellen's last words at the Garde right before she fell, that Patience was a destroyer, the affair had not actually destroyed anything, in actuality the affair was the catalyst that solved everything. Ellen understood that better than anyone, and the rest of the community took her lead.

It is now generally understood that Lois was the one who planted the seed in Charles Mason to bring Ellen and Henry to Mystic. Both Lois and Patience knew from the beginning how this story was going to play out, they knew it could be painful along the way, but they also knew exactly how it would end.

They understood that Ellen would never change without some life changing event forcing her to do so. Normally psychics do not create events, they only have the understanding to know how events will play out given the circumstances. But when a psychic is involved in the story themselves, they get to insert certain events into the story and they then watch and play along as the story unfolds. So while at the beginning, Patience did not know that an affair was going to be required, it became apparent as events unfolded, that having an affair with Henry was going to be the catalyst that Ellen needed to take the next move that would lead to her own healing.

On the surface, this is a story of the test of wills between two women, Patience and Ellen, as they battled over the future of the man they both loved and over the future of Violetta and their conflicting Eastern and Western understandings of healing.

But the real story here, the one that is the foundation of those stories, is the story and understanding of The Noble Path. Life is not a destination, it is a journey, a path that we follow. There is the path that we are supposed to be on, and that is our Noble Path, and then there is the path that most of us are actually walking on, which is not our Noble Path.

Whether we remain on our Noble Path is based on the decisions we make at every moment of our lives. When we base our decisions on Godly attributes, which are described by the Buddha as the Noble Eightfold Path, and in the Bible in many Chapters and Verses, then we walk our Noble Path, which is clear and full of light. When we make decisions based on the negative attributes of fear, greed, anger, contempt, and selfishness, we walk off our Noble Path, right into the thickets and briars and darkness, and life becomes difficult and painful, and suffering ensues for everyone around us.

Patience knew that Ellen was off her Noble Path because she was living her life full of conceit and greed and yes even fear. But it was not Patience's responsibility to fix every person in the world who is off their Noble Path, even Christ cannot save everyone. We mere mortals only have the responsibility to try and help those who we know and care for. It was Henry that Patience cared for and was concerned for, and she knew that the only way to help Henry was to fix Ellen, and she could only do that in Mystic, and that is why Patience, with Lois' help, brought Ellen to Mystic.

In the end, the plan worked, the Noble Path guarantees that eventuality. Ellen was healed. Henry was brought out of the darkness that he had been walking in for so many years. The fact that Henry and Patience ended up together was not the end goal of the plan, the story would have ended perfectly even without that outcome, even if Henry had stayed with Ellen. But sometimes the Noble Path brings pleasant surprises that even the best psychic cannot foretell. And that was the surprise gift to Patience from the Noble Path, for her to end up in a loving relationship that she had not found up to that point. I know it may be corny, but yes, for Patience and Henry, the story had a fairy tale ending.

As a lapsed Catholic, the concept of the Noble Path and much of the spiritual message that made itself known in telling this story would have beyond my capabilities to describe, but through the events of this story, Patience and I have reconnected in a very deep way, and she has been generous in helping me understand enough of the Noble Path to put this story to paper.

Both she and Henry and others have been generous with their time in helping to fill in the events that I was not present for so I could tell the complete story. Henry's conversations with Charles Sr. were very private but he shared them with me in the hope that Charles' kindness and grace would be revealed. Henry was generous in openly discussing his encounters with Ellen in the hospital, at home and elsewhere. He was gracious in sharing the truth since while this story ended well for him, the path he chose took him down many wrong turns, often revealing a troubled and conflicted soul.

But most important, Henry trusted me with this story. He had always said I was a better writer than he in high school, and despite not going to college like Henry, instead working for twenty-something years at the Duck, it turns out those writing skills I had back then never really left me.

Someone asked me why I felt compelled to tell this story, and my answer has always been, I was not compelled to tell the story, the story was compelled to be told, I was just the person that the Noble Path nominated to be the scribe. I was a witness and a participant, and had a lifetime's worth of understanding of the people in this story, and I could write. The Noble Path knew exactly what it wanted, what it needed, and in the end, if you follow the Truth, the Noble Path always lays itself out right in front of your feet, all you have to do is have the courage to walk it.

As for Bill and I, I am not sure I would call our lives a fairy tale, but we are happy. We will likely continue to run the Duck until I hand the keys to the next person, but that'll be many years away if I can help it. Charles Sr., as promised, did eventually come by for one more bowl of his favorite clam chowder, Charlie and Amy sprang him loose from Mystic Manor one day and surprised me.

Having watched over the last year how difficult and complex people and their relationships can be, it is nice to know that Bill and I have a more simple relationship. He's kind of a dolt, but he loves me, and I love him, and we were simply meant to be together. Patience tells me that means we are both on our Noble Path too. When I look at my house and my life, it doesn't seem so noble, but who am I to argue, she is clearly on hers.

THE END

ABOUT THE AUTHOR

WS Parry was born and raised in Connecticut. While travelling around the world for his job in the software industry, Mr. Parry uses the downtime on long airplane rides to write fictional stories about New England, especially his hometown of Mystic Connecticut. When not travelling, he spends as much time as he can with his life-partner Priscilla Humphrey in Mystic.

www.ingramcontent.com/pod-product-compliance
Lightning Source LLC
Chambersburg PA
CBHW070222260626
47160CB00002B/656